MARCEL MALONE

LEW WATTS

Some of the author's poems in this book have been previously published.

Haiku, in order of appearance: *Tiny Words*, 2014, September 22, "summer solstice;" Modern *Haiku*, 2012, vol. 43.1, "5 star hotel;" *Modern Haiku*, 2013, vol. 44.1, "pawnshop;" *Frogpond*, 2013, vol. 36.3, "child lock;" *Frogpond*, 2015, vol. 38.1, "old Beatles tapes;" *Heron's Nest*, 2014, November, "evening calm;" *bottle rockets*, 2012, issue 26, "trying to recall;" *Modern Haiku,* 2013, vol. 44.2, "Thesaurus search;" *Modern Haiku*, 2010, vol. 41.2, "two dealers;" *Modern Haiku*, 2012, vol. 43.1, "first day;" *Modern Haiku*, 2015, vol. 46.1, "open casket;" *Modern Haiku*, 2014, vol. 45.3, "a patch of glass;" *Frogpond*, 2014, vol. 37.2, "sunlight through aspens;" *bottle rockets*, 2014, issue 31, "freezing lake;" *Modern Haiku*, 2011, vol.42.3, "birdsong dies;" *A Hundred Gourds*, 2015, vol. 4.2, "Yellowstone;" *A Hundred Gourds*, 2015, vol. 4.4, "after the flood." Haibun: *A Hundred Gourds*, 2015, vol.4.1, "This moment." Sonnet: *Autumn Sky Poetry Daily*, February 5th, 2015, "Mask."

ISBN 978-0-9973102-2-1
Printed in the United States of America

RED MOUNTAIN PRESS
Santa Fe, New Mexico
www.redmountainpress.us

For my father, Henry George Watts (? – 1978)

Two truths approach each other. One comes from within,
one comes from without—and where they meet you have the chance
to catch a look at yourself.

— from "Preludes," by Tomas Transtromer (1931-2015),
translation by May Swenson.

"Tell me what you're thinking...what's going through your mind, Marcel?"

He is curled up on the sole rug in the room, knees tucked into his chest, and arms wrapped around his head. We are ten minutes into our session, and he has lain like this for most of the time, ever since he tried to tell me about his latest disaster. Of course, I could just wait him out, wait for him to unwrap and turn to me with another inane example of the way he's treated, how it's not his fault, how he tries but that, time and again, the rebuffs come pounding in. And it's not as though I'm unable to empathize with this side of him. I do care in a professional way, which is why I am trying to be professional, with soft and soothing tones of inquiry—tell me in your own words, Marcel, take your time, we have forty minutes left.

From my notes, I know this is our ninth session. We have made little progress, although he now talks much less about his one-time girlfriend and how it felt the night she told him it was the end, how he has left the plates where they were the moment she fled. Their relationship had lasted longer than seemed possible. "She cycled in and out for several years," he once said.

What is Marcel like? Well, he's an underfed son of a steelworker, although he told me his mother was Italian and played the piano—but I get ahead of myself. He is ordinary, small and slight, and his skin is so pale that the veins on his forehead seem iridescent, like earthworms after rain. I would best describe him as unkempt. His most redeeming features are a head of dark curls, and a face that seems to be constantly asking itself questions.

"Do you want to talk more about this, Marcel?"

At times like this I make my mind as blank as I can, even though there are so many things to do this afternoon—patients, notes, a manicure, and then the rush to join Raymond for dinner. My office is intentionally warm, but not so warm that it would be a womb—more like a place of welcome, with two easy chairs set well away from my desk, a rug, and a single painting of sky. I am imagining it now and can feel myself...

"I do not want to talk about it any more than I have said, if that's all right with you. I know you want me to, but no."

That's a long sentence, Marcel. They are usually shorter, in that staccato way you speak to me.

How many therapists have waited for an adult fetus to wipe tears from its eyes before it sits up and blinks? This is what he does, eventually, and, as he leans back on his skinny arms, I can't help thinking how lucky he was to have met his girlfriend when he did. He once showed me her photograph, a two-inch square he keeps in his wallet—her hair was almost as long as my own, lighter in color, and her face was the shape of a tulip, with cheeks poised to smile. She must have looked especially beautiful as the evening wind caught her skirts the night she left.

"I'm sorry that the session was a waste. I couldn't stop myself from falling down."

And he picks up his folder—always the folder, pen clipped into the closed plastic envelope, as opaque its owner.

"You don't need to apologize, Marcel," I say in my sympathetic voice. "We're here to try to surface the way you feel and what's behind some of the patterns unfolding in your life. You clearly have strong feelings around rejection, and your recent experiences with dating are just one part of this. We need to better understand what's causing your reactions, but also the effect you have on others."

"I just feel that I'm wasting all your time," he whispers, moving towards the door.

Here are the notes I wrote as little as a few months ago—an age it seems, but this is how I saw him then, how he wanted to be seen, whether he knew it or not.

Marcel Malone:

Thirty years old, accountant, prone to strong periods of melancholy. Mother died when he was fifteen (cervical cancer), first generation Italian who met her husband-to-be in high school in Pittsburgh, the family hometown—passionate, pianist, occasional music teacher. Father (Irish stock) remarried shortly after to a woman Marcel believes was a longtime lover—she may have sharpened the tension between father and son, but this had simmered for some time. The father longed for an athletic son, with hands that, "could wrap right round a can of East End beer" (his quote). Instead, Marcel played with books, wasted a college degree by shunning engineering, and sunk into depression as he got older. No siblings.

Met his only girlfriend, Susan, while studying economics at George Washington University—she was diagnosed bipolar, and was in her depressive stage. She said she found his voice soothing, especially when he recited the sonnets he wrote for her. But when she was in her manic phase their relationship strained, and she would often distance herself for weeks or even months before returning. The night she finally left they had again failed to make love.

He rents an apartment in Adams Morgan on a rolling three-month renewal. Apart from a bed, a hard-backed chair, and a kitchen table that also serves as a desk, he tells me there is no furniture or clutter in the apartment. He keeps his clothes in two suitcases, and his only luxury is his precious hi-fi system—from one of the photographs he took for me, the speakers seem to be placed on stacks of books.

His passions appear to be Susan [oh dear], fly-fishing [he stopped just after his mother died], music, and writing poetry—he has been unsuccessful so far in getting any poems published. He also loves movies and one in particular: *A River Runs Through It*.

The nature of his anxiety: multiple, repeated rejections at all levels—father, ex-girlfriend, colleagues, occasional dates, poetry. Cannot tolerate being alone. Spends his evenings after work at the DC public library on G Street, hangs around the office coffee machine, and often lingers at the end of our sessions. Is unable to take ownership of problems—they're always the fault of others. No drugs, moderate alcohol consumption, has taken antidepressants but says they affect his work, washes hair daily, nails desperately need attention, pays on time.

That's all I knew of him really. Perhaps that's all there was, or all he wanted me to know. And what was the cause of his latest descent into the birth position? The night before he had arrived early for the weekly open-mic at *Busboys & Poets* on 14th and had seated himself at a vacant table for two. As the room filled, a young African American girl took the remaining seat and, seeing him writing, asked if he was going to read. He couldn't remember his reply, but she closed her book and left the room, supposedly to make a call, and never returned. It was a rejection—clearly— and the latest in a growing trend. I confess I hid a smile, unlike the smile I gave him when he told me of a lunch date with a colleague's sister. Halfway through the salad course her eyes had closed and she was lightly snoring.

But I am paid to listen with open eyes, bound by every word, captivated by the true self that emerges for me alone, for the shared secrets.

Secrets...he said he never took the lead, that Susan had always been the adventurous one. When she would return from her wanderings she was always willing to try some new form of foreplay. "I read it in a book," she'd say, but had she, had she? As with all my other patients, it was all I could do to just sit and listen.

She had not read it in a book, Marcel.

The afternoon had been the usual rush—all flush and flurry in that hurried swoon of tasks my days had become.

As Marcel left, Julie entered, in a smock that hid the weight, already whining in her rising west coast moan. We talked about her need for dependency, and I remember thinking that her voice was like the young interns from the Hill, the way they ended each sentence on a note of question. As she left, she asked me to help her manage her finances and open a bank account.

And then there was Julian—Jewish Julian with his secret closets—and small and painted Margaret who hated herself for hating herself. By the time I entered the small spa on 18th Street, I wanted it to be about me, but Vietnamese manicurists are incapable of listening. Once again, I had to endure Veronica's account of the latest scandal, and of the list of ingredients in the finger bath where my cuticles would soak until the skin turned white.

It is Thursday. I am at the entrance to a drinks reception at *The Willard* hotel, savoring minutes of quiet independence before I become an appendage. I have replaced my ankle boots and long green skirt with black pantaloons and matching one-inch-heels; these still match my white silk blouse that is overlain by one of red chiffon. Soon, my husband will escort me to a client's spouse before he discards me—so elegantly, my love—and moves to the next suspecting prey. I will take morsels from the passing plates, waiting for the question, "Are you Raymond's wife? How wonderful."

The room is filled with dark suits. The few female executives, also suited, wear Hermès scarves and there is not a neck to be seen. These denizens of K Street weave and mingle with targets that would much prefer to talk to each other, who dread that they will be caught, *in camera*, in conversation with a lobbyist.

There is the occasional beauty in a dress—always smiling, always discrete—with adoring eyes half-trained on a husband doing business. Here, for example, is Amanda Brock, wife of Cyril Brock. Cyril is founder and CEO of Brock & Associates, and past Assistant Secretary to the Secretary of Energy in the Reagan administration, a man who, ever since, has leveraged this to dizzying heights of influence and commissions earned through advising Commissions.

"Hello, Vera. Amazing how Cyril manages to get politicians to drop their work and join us, don't you think? And how are you doing, how is Raymond?"

Amanda has no interest in how *I* am doing, and she no doubt knows that Raymond has worked the last five weekends, including our twelfth anniversary. She knows this because she used to be Cyril's Executive Assistant, so many years ago that most people have forgotten the days his ex-wife appeared foaming and groaning at their offices. This was before Amanda's diamond clasps, and the Louis Vuitton purse in which she keeps a file on all that is seen and unseen, even the unseemly.

"I'm fine, Amanda, thank you—just arrived. What a lovely turnout indeed. You must be very pleased."

I have to admit I love watching the way a seasoned operator moves and stalks, and she is one.

"And Raymond, how *is* Raymond? Cyril tells me he's been working nonstop for such a long time. How *is* he?"

Meaning of course, how are *we*, how are we keeping our lives together? Her eyes seem intent on telling me that Raymond has needs, and I am the one to service those needs, that my purpose is keeping him succored, fit, and well. And what if I don't? Well, look at what happened to Cyril's ex-wife. As always, I decide to stroke rather than scratch.

"I'm so glad you asked. It's a comfort to know how much you and Cyril care—not just about Raymond, but everyone in the firm. He's fine and loving the project, just loving it."

"And the two of you?"

"Couldn't be happier. Makes the times we're together so…precious."

Just a word, two syllables—"Lovely"—and she is off, leaving me alone for seconds that are indeed precious. Lovely.

A drink tray approaches, and I wait until the largest white wine is facing me. The river-sounds of chatter rise and fall, and I wonder what secrets lie beneath the surface of these shallow conversations. How many here have torrid lives and seek their solace in private acts, or live with a veneer of contentment, burying pasts and feelings? Do the prim act out their whims in wayward ways? Do the brash bullies later cower beneath batons of self-doubt?

There is Christopher Evans, taller than his suit, forever bending forward giving the impression that he listens and cares, which he doesn't. Darren Carter has a different problem—he simply cannot find a place for his spare hand and cups his glass in both as though holding a chalice for a priest. How many priests have held you, dear Darren? Georgina Tuft is one who just stays put, rooted to her island in the river, sexless and staid tonight as always, except when she has captured some sweaty worker in her apartment. And then the diminutive Mrs. Iris Parker, picking at her nails in the shade of her husband, she who hosts perfect dinner parties in her perfect house, and who dreads the hours afterwards—all those trinkets, coasters, and candles slightly out of place. She and Raymond have a lot in common.

In this room there must be torrents of guilt and sorrow from hidden lives and buried pasts. There must be those who want to curl away alone, or slide into corners to watch and wait. You would not know it to observe them, but they know it, they all know. Eddies draw their doubts down deep, while ripples of laughter dance in the shallows and, now and then, cascade over waterfalls of anxious mirth.

"Ah, there you are! Lots of people!" This is my husband— Raymond, with his uniform of dark suit, pale blue shirt with a white collar, and broad-striped tie. "Let's go, there's someone I want you to meet," and, leading me by the elbow, he places and introduces me within a circle, then abandons me.

"So you're Raymond's wife," someone says, looking past my shoulder. And it is reassuring that the script is being followed.

"Who *was* that man, the one who took you aside as we were about to leave?"

We are home, drinking large nightcaps while making preparations before our literary half-hour in bed. I have an ankle seductively perched on the other knee while sliding off a shoe, and Raymond is carefully placing his cufflinks in their box, the clasps turned back at precisely ninety degrees to the squares of lapis.

"The best thing that happened tonight," he says. "That was Rob Williams of the EPA telling me they got the message. He's very influential, a key player in the emissions debate."

Raymond is a lobbyist. Raymond wasn't going to be a lobbyist, at least not when we met. In the early years of our marriage he still retained some semblance of a higher purpose, and I held on to that for several years, even when he withdrew his name from a secondment to Bosnia. I did protest. "We've *talked* about it," I remember saying. "I could apply for a local license to practice. It would be a fantastic experience"—a chance to escape, I could have added.

It was, of course, to no avail—his mind was made up; or rather, his mother's mind was made up. But it was several months later in a musty room filled with antiques that I felt the lid close, when I first heard the name of Brock & Associates and the pale endorsement in his father's words—"At least it's better than pushing rocks uphill in some failed state." Raymond had never discussed it with me.

That was when I knew I was an afterthought. It hurt— naturally—but who was I to think that I deserved more? There were even times when I considered I might have been wrong, that his chosen new career could reach the giddy heights of altruism. I know I was proud of some of his early projects— promoting a trade agreement, the advancement of worker standards in Asia—but there was always a lingering resentment, of what could have been. Perhaps this is why his secrecy is now almost welcome.

Tonight, at the mention of "emissions," I recall a rare conversation several months ago, with the sprinkling of words like "strategic plants" and, most oddly, "grandfathering." But I am too tired to ask further, and the bedside book is beckoning. Clothes folded away into a linen basket or, in my case, thrown to the corners of the closet, we nestle silently into our bed. Raymond's side is closest to the door, a mere eight steps to his bathroom. A bottle of hand sanitizer is always next to his bed, usually on top of a book he intends to read. My bedside table is stacked with novels, a foot manicure set, and a box of tissues rarely used for anything other than cleaning reading glasses.

As the clock moves to 10:30 pm, I receive a dry peck before he turns over to sleep.

I am unable to sleep. Waves of betrayal to Raymond have washed over me for most of the night. What I shared earlier, of my disappointment in him and my sense of hurt, should have never been allowed to surface. Here is what I should have said:

Raymond always looks after me and always has. He is usually forthcoming, and is a source of sanity and stability on days when I am caught up in the bizarreness of my work. There is rarely a thing out of place with Raymond. He is dependable and predictable, and he manages his days like ticked-off checklists. And when he feels passionate he is bold, and he never, ever falls asleep immediately afterwards.

He is tall with legs that reach above my waist, and he has a bald spot that he will not stop scratching. He showers and shaves daily, lies in when he can on weekends, plays golf (badly, despite the childhood coaching of his father), and doesn't force me to go to church with his parents when we visit them in Boston.

He has always been a good man at home. He loves cities and what he calls "the buzz of life," though he is never the one buzzing. He drinks single malt scotch to my Martinis—Highland Park or Springbank, on the edge of being peaty, just like his father.

We met almost sixteen years ago at an event organized for new students at Georgetown University. I had just escaped New Mexico, and I remember being bewildered by the wonder of Washington, DC. Raymond was halfway through a Masters in Public Policy and, compared to my fellow psychology students, was far more interesting in a worldly sort of way. He brought a sense of knowingness and never commented on the fact that I didn't drink. I used to love how he could drape his arm across my shoulder and down my side when we walked. I think that was what drew me to him, that with him I was safe.

I was originally convinced his name was Paul, even repeating the name after we were first introduced. But it was his nickname, "Pole." Some of his frat friends still call him this, but never at work. We started dating within a month of meeting. I used to joke with him that he only asked me out to impress his friends—I stopped when he stopped laughing. I had already turned down approaches from two of his classmates and was thought to be—to use his phrase—"a challenge," although, in truth, it was just my reaction to their come-ons. When one of his buddies, Simon, said Raymond "didn't have a hope in hell," I think that was enough for him. Raymond was polite, waited for the third date to kiss me, and we have lived together ever since he received his first small salary as a research assistant at Brookings.

He is a person of ambiguities, as though he were two people at the same time. At work he is refined, somewhat aloof, and always deferential to clients and to Cyril Brock, to whom he exudes loyalty. Outside of work, and particularly with his friends, he sometimes assumes a Boston accent and, over the years, has developed a liking for button-downs, chinos, and shoes with tassels. Unlike my Volkswagon Golf, his BMW is spotless inside and out—no stickers, nor even an indication of model type. The only objects visible are CDs—classical, of course, in case he should be forced to give a ride to a client. At home, when I am unable to stop him, he listens to vintage country-western music, the kind of songs where you know the tune and words ahead of time.

We have never really argued or, at least, never had—this is largely my doing, for Raymond is certainly not conflict averse. In the rare times I've allowed myself to study him professionally, I have seen through his macho persona to a child seeking the approval of a father incapable of giving love. I have marveled over his false confidence, at his constant need to put order into his life and into mine.

Overall, and this will never change, he is a mama's boy, as cosseted and smothered as any single child of

Protestant parents can be. But by a strange quirk it was something his mother said that gave Raymond the confidence, and permission, to propose to me, even though he knew his father disapproved. I had just started my doctoral program and we were once again visiting her in Boston when she said aloud, "How lovely, a doctor in the house!" I often wonder how many times her husband has reminded her of that small suggestion of approval.

Despite all this, we are as well matched as opposites can be. He loves to be touched, and I love touching him. Whenever we get away, whether to New York (in which he thrives) or to the Shenandoah Valley (which I adore), he is quickly able to relax and I can be in love with him again, just like the first time. He reads political history, while I devour mystery novels—we sometimes meet in the middle, at the opera. But I have to say that he is a book I would like to read faster. I would like to turn the page and find something that takes my breath away, that has a surprising turn and makes me ask questions of myself and of the world around me.

Yes, this is what I should have said.

The practice is on the north side of M Street, between 23rd and 24th. It has been in existence for almost twenty years. The two founders, Carolyn and John, took me under their wing when I graduated, offering me a part-time assistant role during my subsequent doctorate in clinical psychology at Georgetown. When I fully joined them, and had been able to show that I could bring in new patients (John still uses the term "clients," an impersonal word from someone who cares and thinks so deeply), they let me earn my way in, and I now own twenty percent of the company.

We are on the fifth floor. Two years ago, we replaced the ugly oak paneling and door with glass. When our patients exit the elevator, they now look past the engraved words *Gordon, Jones & Lewis* into a foyer with three armchairs, a table and a reception desk, behind which sits Sarah. We have the whole south side of the building, with a kitchen, two washrooms, and four offices—one is for guests, though only used for our weekly debriefs.

Carolyn's office is the largest and has a bay window. I'm sure its austere smell comes from her wall-to-wall carpet, but it could equally be from the wall of framed diplomas and photographs from her many conference speeches. John's office, by contrast, is warm and cluttered, with snapshots of tents, hiking trails, and golf courses. My office, the smallest, is simple but I hope inviting—a desk, two armchairs, a reproduction watercolor, and a red, black, and white "eye-dazzler" Navajo rug.

I remember, several years ago, Raymond asking if I enjoyed my work. I had several difficult patients at the time and it must have seemed obvious that I was under a lot of stress. But I surprised myself by telling him that I loved what I was doing, that I felt I was making a difference in people's lives—and in truth I believed it, at least at that moment. He gave me one of his rare but beautiful smiles and it made me feel proud, that he was proud of me, and that he cared enough to ask.

Most of my patients now are business professionals, seemingly normal people with normal lives who, in many respects, *are* normal, although they feel the need to talk. It is a terrible thing to say, but most bore me, bore me so much I would like to tell them to use their money to create a situation where even the most hardened therapist would say, "Well, that *is* a problem!" Even though I tire of hearing about their personal struggles, the repeated infidelities, that no one listens to their opinionated opinions, or that each month, in a rented room at a Day's Inn motel, they sit on the bed and can watch exactly what TV program they want, they are my patients, my clients.

But I am luckier than most because, occasionally, I have someone who has taken her last savings, and has signed up determined to deal with her issues honestly, with an agreed-on plan we stick to. And even a young woman like Julie, though she laments her weight between binges of chocolate cookies, has something deeply endearing about her. I have almost always received patients through referrals, and some of those who have recovered keep in touch and tell me how their lives are back on track.

It can be lonely feeling responsible for the future of a person. And for those who truly need this help, those precious few, there is a need to check that what you are doing is really for the best, sometimes against the first instinct. Which is why, most Fridays, Carolyn, John, and I sit together and go through our notes about our patients. We are open and candid, we laugh and shake our heads, and we always, always, use only our patients' first names.

John has finished sharing his notes on Paula who has become overly attached to her dog and now realizes he will die before her. By telling the story with such seriousness, he has heightened its absurdity—you would think that, as the sole psychiatrist in the practice, John would be staid. He is, instead, irreverent and very funny.

Carolyn had earlier shocked us with the news that Brian, someone who had appeared to be spoiled and obnoxious, had finally admitted he was unlikeable and then, in a rupture of emotion, had told of a childhood so appalling one wondered how his parents had kept their secrets from each other. It is now my turn.

Soon it will be time for our weekly cocktail at *Ozio's*, one of three places in DC where John can still smoke a cigar. But I see his name, and I start my story.

Marcel: another brush-off, curled up, inconsolable, surrounded by what appears to be multiple layers of rejections and disappointments. At our next session, I propose to confront him sternly—I will tell him he has to take responsibility, that it isn't always the fault of others. He and I will set a plan going forward that he will stick to. I will also suggest he starts a journal to review each week.

"Stop—let me ask you two things," Carolyn says. "You've been telling us about Marcel for some time, and things don't seem to be getting better. Do you think he's at risk?"

I confess this thought had been gnawing at me for some time, and I was indeed concerned that he could become suicidal. Marcel seemed able to cope when surrounded by others, but what if this were no longer enough, what if his melancholy cascaded into a maelstrom of depression?

"I think he could be, yes."

"And secondly, do you like him?" Carolyn asks.

We all knew this was not a casual question. To "like" someone in our world is to say that the person has, deep inside, something that is genuine and good. To not like someone implies a rather unpleasant person who, if he is able to deal with his issues, might be able to live an unpleasant life.

But I find myself unbalanced, and realize I have never asked myself this question. It is as though in my nine sessions with Marcel I had lost the ability to empathize at a very basic level. Or was it that? In an instant, a new thought flashes through me—perhaps it is *because* I empathize so much with Marcel that I have never needed to ask this question. Does Carolyn see this? In retrospect, I know she does, but she too suppresses any hint of emotion. Perhaps that's what happens to all of us. We suppress.

"Yes, I do," I find myself saying.

"Then if you think he's at risk, and if you like him, have you thought of doing something different, perhaps a bit radical? Of course, a therapist never knows what's safe, but what about trying Paradoxical Intervention, see if you can knock him out of a descending trend?"

This is something I have not considered; this would indeed be radical. Paradoxical Intervention is an approach opposite to what the patient would anticipate or want to do. It is a technique to desensitize the most sensitive things, challenging, and often slow to get results. I remember a tutor at Georgetown using the analogy of someone who is allergic to bee stings. Rather than living in fear, blaming one's genetic heritage, and carrying an Epipen, the patient undergoes a program of being artificially stung, with increasing dosage until the body becomes desensitized.

"So," Carolyn continues, "if he flinches at each new rejection, why not set him a target of getting a number of rejections in a set period of time? It'll be tough on him initially, but you know the research: having a target set by someone else reduces the personal pain of each individual confrontation. He can say, 'It's not my fault anymore, someone told me to do it.' Have a think about it."

Carolyn's suggestion is certainly worth considering for my next session with Marcel in six days time. We pack and lock our files away, turn down the lights, and emerge onto M Street to walk the four blocks to our weekly toast.

"Hello, Marcel. I'm pleased to see you." (I had decided the risk of such a personal greeting, of putting a weight on his shoulders to meet my expectations of being "pleased," were outweighed by the need to seem friendly, given what I was thinking of doing.)

He sits, hesitates, grips his folder, and stares.

"D'you know it's many years since anybody, any woman, greeted me like that?" he replies, in a deadened way.

"And what has happened this last week—have you been writing, have things improved?"

He takes a slip of paper from his folder, and I am surprised and quietly excited. I have never asked directly, but I am sure this is where he keeps his poetry. I have long hoped he would start sharing some with me. And here it is, how wonderful.

But it is a letter of two sentences from *Measure - a Review of Formal Poetry*. The first gives sincere thanks for submitting poems (how many is left blank), and the second states that, unfortunately, the editors must decline this time. There is a typed name at the bottom of the page, unsigned.

"I know how important poetry is to you," I tell him, "and I'm glad you're continuing to write and submit your work. But I understand it's hard to break through, and even Sylvia Plath (I had seen the film) had many rejections and periods of self-doubt."

"And all those doubts were gassed to silence—true?"

I know he will not say anything more until I speak again.

"I'd very much like to see your poems, Marcel. Could you bring a selection next time?" I ask, with an earnestness that surprises me. He meets the question with a stare and silence. "How was the rest of your week—have you had any of those 'small but significant successes' we talked about last month?"

"I met a woman at the Arboretum...caught her dog that wandered off, and she agreed to meet next day at Dupont Circle...waited for an hour, and then I left."

As he speaks the only sign of emotion is in his hands, which are clasped so hard his knuckles are white like bones. There is a worrying sense of peaceful determination in him today, and I decide not to wait any longer, that now is the time.

"Marcel, I think we should do two things; actually, that you should do two things. I want to explain these, answer any questions, and then I'd like you to agree. If you don't, I'd like to change our schedule to one session per month—that way, we may have more things to talk about."

This gets his attention. I know he sees a threat in the loss of a rug to cry on. Of course, there is also the risk he will see this as another rejection. I intervene quickly.

"I'd *like* us to continue meeting every week, but I really want us to start making progress. First of all, I'd like you to start journaling—you know we talked about it some time ago. I'd like you to keep the journal in your folder and write about your days, your nights, and your thoughts. And I'd like us to go through it each week. Do you agree?"

He hesitates before replying. "I do agree, but I will not keep any journal in this file, just poetry."

"That's fine, provided you keep a journal and bring it in. I also want you to go on thirty dates in the next two months. That's one every other day and it'll be hard. But I want to make it harder. I want you to try to get rejected."

He is clearly stunned. His fists uncurl. He grasps the arms of his chair, and simply shakes his head for a long time.

"I do not understand. Why would you want to put me through such certain agony?"

"I want you to do this, Marcel, and I'm going to explain why. It's a desensitizing technique that's often used as a way of reducing emotional pain. And remember, it's *my* idea, and what happens on those dates is *my* responsibility. If you have rejections they won't be *your* fault. Will you try?"

"But how am I to get so many dates?"

It is now my turn to hand a sheet of paper across to him—a website printout for a dating agency that I found online. I explain that, after receiving and vetting his profile, they will make all the arrangements. I suggest meeting the women for lunch initially so there is a time limit and less stress on both sides.

He says he'll think about it, but from the way his eyes move from side to side I'm sure he'll try. We agree to meet the following week.

I am never a pretty sight at the start of a week. Today, I woke earlier than usual, tiptoed out of bed, and wandered around the house until I thought Raymond would be waking. In my most seductive way, I put on the red bra and pants he bought me several years ago for Valentine's Day and busied myself sorting washing on the other side of the bedroom door, that I left ajar. I would be the first thing Raymond saw when he opened his morning eyes—it seems a long time since we last made love.

There is only so much parading one can do in the half-light of a corridor, and so after several minutes I walked downstairs and into the kitchen. I made some coffee, hoping that the smell of Italian roast would arouse Italian thoughts in my sleeping partner. Instead, beyond the bubbles and gurgles of the machine, I heard the shower start to run, and I knew the morning was over before it had begun, that it was bathrobe time.

He appeared fully dressed, kissed me good-morning on the forehead, and sat at our central kitchen island almost an ocean away. Peering into the box, I had already noticed that his muesli would last one more day. I had also noticed that he hadn't noticed me, or the amorous flush on my face.

"So what's your day like today?" I asked him, hoping he would ask the same.

In between the crunch of raw oats, I received the day's agenda that centered on preparing two clients for testimony to a Senate subcommittee on Wednesday. "They're fully briefed, they know the kind of questions that are going to be asked, who'll ask them, and why. They just need to sound sincere, to know what they're talking about."

"Well, I hope they learn their lines," I told him, patting his hand.

When I arrived at the gym, two young men, muscled up in shorts too tight, were embroiled in an argument, with words like, "I saw you looking at him!" Moving through rows of weights and machines, it seemed as though everyone in the room was paying one huge penance, with thoughts no deeper than the sorry lives on TV screens. My close friend, Dawn, was already working out, ears plugged in, turning the pages of a gossip magazine, almost salivating.

I stepped onto the adjacent treadmill and joined her in our half-hour walk to nowhere, eventually settling into her list of fallen stars, of who is wooing whom and who is being sued. In between, I learned that she had lost two pounds in the last week, that her hormone levels had stabilized, and that the new whitening toothpaste seemed to be doing better than bicarbonate of soda. Predictably, gossip and trivia exhausted, she turned to her work.

"And so I said to her, 'I'm not prepared to take that from him,' and do you know what she said? That 'he's not that bad, not all the time anyway. He just needs to get used to being the boss,' whatever that means."

Forceful, determined Dawn, she who knows what's good for everyone else, she who *would never take it*, and never has. Which is ironic, though I've never told her so, given her job as a senior adviser at the World Bank, an institution founded on giving advice and expecting all to heed it, to *take it*.

There were times at Georgetown when Dawn and I would talk of the injustices of the world deep into the night. I loved her passion, the way she wrestled inside with the tensions between social needs and economic reality. In return, she would often laugh when I tried to analyze world leaders, or when I talked of governments and societies in psychological terms—paranoid, narcissistic, obsessive-compulsive, dependent. But our conversations were almost always external, abstractions, and about about third parties, far from the personal—even then, she never asked about me.

We still talk of meaningful things, and I like to think that when she reverts to the banal and trivial it's a sign of her comfort with me, that this is something she could never do at the Bank. Yes, I would like to think this.

Today, as with many mornings, I found myself drawn into her womb of nothingness, dancing in her shallows, desensitized to all the bouncing pelvises and sleek young bodies around us.

Later, as I showered, dried myself, and reverted to my usual white underwear and therapist clothes, time drifted away with her soothing chatter so that, by the time we emerged, we were both late and she was in a sudden hurry.

"Vera, are you going past K and 17th? Could you drop me off? I've got a meeting and can't be late."

One would think she would have known that descending south of M Street is like dropping into a rush-hour abyss, where cars are snarled in lines of anger.

"Of course, Dawn, no problem at all."

Being late for a therapy session is inexcusable, certainly something I do not allow my patients. Being late for someone like Adam—whose youth was dominated by a mother unable to share her love beyond a bottle, who now lives his life trying to control everything around him, reacting to the hint of a slight as though it were a knife in his heart—is beyond irresponsibility. He sat in silence for most of our fifty minutes, hearing but not hearing my apologies and statements regarding "next steps," leaving with the sound of dragging feet.

With Julie it was different but the same. She started talking before she sat down, and continued as though she were speaking a diary, of her daily chores, of the cravings and the succor of food, and how she had to sleep with every light on in her apartment. So many missed chances to intervene, so many times I had wanted to say a truth, to stop her in her tracks. But I couldn't recall the notes I should have reread from our last session. I failed her today, and she knew it.

It is late morning, Wednesday. I am sitting at a table at *Smith & Wollensky* on 19th, waiting for Christine to breeze in, all flared skirt and looks to shock…waiting, fingers turning the glass's stem.

"Darling, so, so sorry I'm late. And look at you! Yes, sauvignon blanc, please. Hmm…cute." All men are cute to Christine, and Christine is cute to all men.

She has changed since Dawn first introduced us at Georgetown—that was about a month before they stopped talking to each other. Her hair is still long and flowing, her skin peachy-pink and glowing, but she no longer talks or cares about the problems of the world, only her own. And who would have thought that a driven, independent girl, one who would stand up and denounce the rule of men, who placed her money on the table at the start of every date, would marry into comfort and, after giving her husband—twenty-years her senior—two sons through his third marriage, would now spend her days whiling away the time before her next affair, which appeared imminent?

"So, what am I to do, Vera?" she asks in a theatrical voice. "David will be in London next week and the boys are full-time in school. And along comes Richard in his pressed tennis shorts. What's a girl to do?"

Of course, she is not seeking advice, just sharing in that way she has with friends.

"Is that the Richard who joined us at the Kennedy Center last month?" I know it must be true.

I know because small sparks flew off her when he pulled out her chair. I know because he glanced at her whenever David turned to talk to Raymond, or greeted some long lost friend in passing, or studied the wine list for the second most expensive bottle.

For the next hour we sit and talk. I listen to her plans for the following week.

"It all depends how the first day goes with Richard," she says.

I learn about her new underwear—that she assures me, with a smile, are teeth resistant—of the latest achievements of her two sons, of plans for remodeling the kitchen, and how surprisingly good the sauvignon blanc is. "Yes, I'll have another...." How busy, how terribly busy she is.

I am so caught up in the whirlwind of her life that I find myself answering "Yes, of course," when she asks if I can pick up the boys up from school next Monday. As we leave the restaurant, her stare fixed over my shoulder at some eyes that have been following her, she asks how I am, and I am no longer sure.

"Hello, Marcel, how are you today?"

It is 2:00 pm precisely, and he has followed me in, set his folder down, and taken up his pose of rigid fright. He manages to tell me he is fine, but his eyes dart across the room as though searching for some unseen threat, and I am immediately alert to my words. I decide to ease him into this session.

"Before we start…I took your advice and checked out the websites," I say to him with a smile. "Quite amazing what you can buy online, so thank you."

Marcel buys everything online—the few groceries he needs, books, music, and, of course, his clothes. Today, for example, he is wearing gray gabardine pants that are new. I know because the folded creases from the packaging divide his legs above the knees, and he has forgotten to remove a sales tag just above the right pocket. He originally told me buying online was just a matter of convenience. But after I probed, he admitted that he hated shops. "It seems that clerks are trained to make you speak," he said, as though even this level of interaction was terrifying.

"Anyway, we'd better start. If I remember rightly, you and I agreed two things last week." He nods. "So let's start with the dating—what happened, and how do you feel about it?"

"I called the dating agency then registered on-line. Some questions made me think about myself for hours. They called me back, to clarify some points, or so they said."

I learn that Marcel completed a multilevel questionnaire as honestly as anyone who is desperate to impress would do. He declined to say he was an accountant and described himself, instead, as working in the financial industry. I discover he likes music with a strong and steady beat, with no real preference for genre or form, just that the volume has to be distractingly loud. He apparently loves people, fine dining, and the outdoors but, in answer to my question, admits he omitted any mention of fly-fishing. His tastes in women are wide, only that he prefers "sincerity above all forms or looks." He paid by credit card.

"Did you manage to schedule any dates this week, Marcel?" To my surprise, I hear that he has had two lunchtime liaisons, both cut short in states of indignation and humiliation.

"You told me to make sure that they rejected me, and so I tried my best. The first one left before the waiter brought her soup, the second after two bites of her steak."

28

Marcel had more than risen to the challenge of being rejected. He'd met the first young lady, whose name he couldn't recall, two days previously outside a restaurant on L Street. She seemed bemused when they walked to the next block and entered a dingy, British look-alike pub. He ordered himself a beer, forgot to ask if she wanted a drink, and then demanded her phone number and home address. He says she didn't seem to have even the energy to insult him, just put on her coat and walked away. Marcel tells this an interrupted series of flat statements, but there is a new element. It is the faintest sense of achievement—he is like a cat bringing a mouse to my doorstep, a sullied, bloody prize.

My face is as professionally expressionless as I can make it when he recounts the second date, earlier in the day at a restaurant eerily close to where I had sat with Christine. Marcel had arrived ten minutes late to find an "unappealing" woman in her late twenties, around his own age, seated at a table booked by the agency. He introduced himself without apology, then sat down, and proceeded to tell her about the latest financial report he was working on, line-by-line. He remembers her interrupting politely to ask about some intricacy of balance-sheet analysis. He says he admired, "the way she tried to be polite before her smile began to wither to a pout." As the steaks were brought, he took both pieces of bread from the basket and asked her to put her credit card on the table, "in case we find we're running out of time." She opened her eyes, placed her napkin by her glass of water, rose, and walked away, whispering something unsavory to the waiter.

I know I should ask how he feels but I find myself laughing, something I can't recall doing with a patient so sensitive to ridicule. But what he has described are two events of such appalling impoliteness. At first he seems genuinely taken aback, but between the tears glazing my eyes I see him smiling for what I imagine is the first time in many months.

"Marcel, I think you may have tried a little too hard to be rejected. Any one of these things you did or said would have been enough. " The remnants of the smile are still with him.

Once we are back in our patient-therapist pattern, I lead him through my observations, no longer a series of questions but listed points for him to consider. I then take a more serious turn.

"When I said I wanted you to try to be rejected, Marcel, I meant within your value system and self. It was my mistake for not explaining this, but it's important that you behave in ways that demonstrate who you really are. I don't believe you're impolite or insensitive to the feelings of others so, from now on, try to stay within the framework of your true personality."

I am concerned that he will interpret this as criticism. So I add, with genuine amusement, "What you did was wonderful, just a bit over the top," and he smiles once more. "As important, Marcel, make sure not to do or say anything that would look bad in any report your date might make to the agency. Dating agencies will stop working with people they feel are behaving disrespectfully. If a young lady rejects the real you, so be it. But don't allow yourself to be rejected for who you're not," and again I laugh.

He says he will continue to try. But he also admits he is yet to use his journal, adding, "It's difficult to find the time to write my thoughts within a paragraph of prose." He does promise, however, that he will start writing in the coming week.

Before leaving, he opens his folder and a copy of *The Atlantic* falls to the floor. "They always publish something interesting, but what I like is searching for the poem," he says, slipping the magazine back into the folder. He extracts a single sheet of paper.

"I wrote this sonnet after we had talked about my girlfriend, Susan—just a draft." He hands it to me.

After the door closes, I read the labored words and clichés, until the jolting last line:

"I know she did not read it in a book."

Dusk has passed into night, and I am sitting next to the window, Raymond's empty glass awaiting his return from drinks with his clients. To one side of me is a half-finished Martini, on the other is Marcel's poem. I have spent the last two hours on my laptop reading summaries of a sonnet's possible forms. I already knew about the fourteen lines, but have learnt that there are three traditional forms: Shakespearian, Petrarchan and Miltonian. I have also learned that sonnets usually contain a "volta," or a turn in the thought or argument, either after the eighth line or, in a Shakespearean sonnet, before the last two lines.

I'm undressed and ready for bed, swaddled in my towel bathrobe. At the last site I visited, I read two sonnets by Milton, and a wonderful modern sonnet by a British poet, Carol Ann Duffy, that addresses Shakespeare's choice to bequeath the "second best bed" to his wife, Anne Hathaway. Instead of indicating that Shakespeare no longer loved her, the poem speculates that this bed was their love nest, the one in which they held each other—the "best bed" was kept for guests.

I can recognize the type of sonnet Marcel wrote from the way the lines rhyme—"look" with "book," and "wife" with "knife." To my untrained ear it seems too regular, too forced, a series of flat statements with no turn, except for the final stark line. But it was a gift, the first mouse left on my doorstep.

I hear the rumbled whine of the garage door closing, the rear kitchen door opening, and a briefcase dropped beside the hat stand. I hear the beat of his steps towards the living room, and the ice cubes dropped into his scotch. I want to arrange the sounds in lines, waiting for Raymond to turn towards me. Instead, as he moves a table lamp, imperceptibly, I get up and ask him how his day has been. He answers that it went well, that everyone said their lines correctly in their testimonies to the Senate subcommittee, and I find myself tightening my robe, bracing for the day's news and a monologue of triumphs, told in a very non-poetic way.

It is the end of the second week of April, a Friday. I am in the basement cafe of *Politics & Prose Bookstore* on Connecticut Avenue, with two skimmed lattes separating me from Dawn who is wearing her best power-pant suit. Outside, the trees have blown into blossom, and the streets are full of warning signs about the expected weekend congestion from cherry-tourists. It is a beautiful day—mild and sunny, with a soft breeze sweeping up from the Potomac—and we are still sweating from our early morning workout.

Groups of lonely people are seated around large tables. They come here for company, even though they never lift their eyes from their smartphones. Perhaps this is how they communicate with each other, sending messages to newfound friends across a few feet of table.

"And do you know, Sheryl took my note and sent it on without asking me. It was only a draft and she knew it," Dawn continues. "So I told her—this was not the way to work together."

"It must be frustrating," is the only way I can think to reply, and to my surprise a question comes to mind.

"Dawn, do you know a good source where I can read about climate change? Raymond's doing work on this and, although he's told me various things, I'd like to get some background. Does the Bank have any info?"

Dawn works in the African regional group. I know because she is always telling me how cheap the latest piece of jewelry was that she brought back from her travels, how she spent an age negotiating for it. She replies that the Bank has a lot of information, but a friend of hers who works in one of the environmental groups was talking about a recent report from the International Monetary Fund.

"If I know him and the IMF, it's probably heavy going, but they're usually objective and present all sides of a story. I'll send you the link," which she did later in the day.

My first patient is not until eleven and so, after Dawn leaves, I stay awhile on the ground floor, and find myself drawn into a room with a large poetry section on one wall. I find several books by Carol Ann Duffy, including *The Devil's Wife* that contains the wonderful sonnet I had read online. There are whole sections on poets that remind me of my days in high school.

I have always believed that books find you, that in some strange way they make themselves felt, pleading to be picked up. And so I decide to play a game I used to play in our school library—I run my fingernail across the volumes, row by row, waiting for the nail to stop. I find an old receipt in my purse and write down titles, eight fingernail stops in total. Here are the first four titles:

Baptism of Desire, by Louise Erdrich
Rivers and Mountains, by John Ashberry
After We Lost Our Way, by David Mura
Waiting for the Past, by Les Murray

I laugh at the first, but as I stare down the list a pattern emerges. The words "lost," "way," and "past" begin to ring in my head, and a chill rises into my shoulders. Ten minutes later, I decide to leave when, in a section on introductions to poetry, I notice a volume titled *To Read a Poem, Second Edition,* and I immediately decide to buy it. The author is Donald Hall, "ex-Poet Laureate of the United States."

It is almost 5:00 pm, and John, Carolyn and I are reaching the end of our weekly review. As usual, John pretends his mind is elsewhere—though we all know this is his way of listening—and I have started summarizing my own patients to Carolyn. Despite her habitual gray jacket and trousers, she looks regal in her armchair, green tea in one hand and the other conducting our small trio with her eraser-tipped pencil. I have tucked Julie away with her cookie-jar secrets, and we have just discussed my new patient, Charles. His urgent problems need to be addressed before the situation worsens. *Ozio's* has just opened.

"And then there is Marcel."

I leave the five words hanging. Carolyn puts her pencil to her mouth while John shifts in his chair.

"The bad news is there's no journal yet, but I'm pretty sure he'll do so soon. But he did register with the dating agency, and managed to arrange two lunchtime dates before we met this week."

I go on to describe both of his liaisons, and how I had reacted. By the time I stop, we are all laughing.

"My God, how unbelievably atrocious—those poor women," Carolyn says, putting her cup down for safety. "I mean, he couldn't have done any worse, could he?"

"Of course he could," John says, still laughing. "He could have really tried to be nice and still got the big brush-off."

"And how did he respond to *your* reaction?" Carolyn asks, returning to her usual tone and voice. "Did he take offence at your amusement?"

"That's the interesting thing. He smiled, for the first time. Oh, and one other thing: he gave me a poem, a sonnet."

"And…?" John asks.

"Well, it's fourteen lines and heavily rhymed, but it just seems so labored. It does have an interesting last line but, apart from that, it's pretty impersonal."

"But he did give you a poem," Carolyn says, "and it does seem that the unusual intervention had an effect—he smiled after all."

"Yes," adds John, using his thoughtful voice. "But I've been thinking about this Paradoxical Intervention. I took a class in philosophy once, and one thing stuck with me. There's always been a huge debate around paradoxes, but most agree they combine elements of surprise and truth. Your news about Marcel seems positive, surprising in some ways. I hope you find a way to get to the truth of this man."

We are past the time when we would normally be walking three abreast down M Street to our weekly cocktails, but Carolyn wants to continue the discussion.

"There's one thing in you haven't commented on. In the last couple of months you've given us a number of facts about Marcel—his background, his anxieties. I remember you mentioning his precious hi-fi system, but not what kind of music he liked. 'Strong and heavy beat,' you said—surprising for such a shy person."

It is indeed surprising, and in it must be a truth.

❖ ❖ ❖

The weekend is ending, and I've decided to write about our house. We bought it with a loan from Raymond's father and have lived here for twelve years. I confess that, until we paid the money back, the house didn't really feel like my own.

I've tried to make the house comfortable, lived in, despite Raymond's obsession with order. My only failure is the dining room, which we hardly use. It's like a mausoleum—I can still smell Raymond's mother's too-sweet jasmine perfume when she descended to help us arrange the antique table and chairs, the porcelain table lamps, and the side tables draped in doilies.

We're on a small side street in Chevy Chase. I loved the house as soon as I saw the large kitchen. This is where we eat most mornings, sometimes together, like today. We also have a large living room where I read most evenings, in one of two matching leather armchairs close to the window. Raymond's chair faces a large drinks cabinet that has become a sort of shrine, and in the center of the room is an L-shaped sofa we use when watching TV. Our stereo system is on the final wall, flanked by a four-shelf cabinet of CDs.

If the door is open you can look into our office, with its shared columns of bookshelves and, to each side, our desks. Mine is always cluttered, with assorted notes and reminders pasted on a computer screen smudged by fingerprints. Raymond's desk is pristine, and always locked. I know because, if I am alone, I regularly test it. I'm not sure why I do this, and each time I'm ashamed—perhaps it's a reflection of my work, unlocking people's secrets.

If Raymond is working on papers, he stacks them on the left side of his desk, furthest from me. He displays photographs of his parents, a golf reunion, and the two of us at Georgetown. Our wedding photograph sits on my desk.

We have three bedrooms, two of which are rarely used. Raymond has commandeered one as a spillover to our shared closet. This is where he keeps his suits and ties, darks to the right. Just after moving in we decided to install an extra bathroom that is now my own. In the first few months I would close the door, spray my mother's perfume on my neck, and sit there for a while before showering it off. Even now, I often sit on my footstool, listening to the sound of falling water before eventually showering.

The one disadvantage with the house is that we only have a small rear garden—I try not to use the word "yard." But we do have a slatted deck where, in the spring and fall, we sit in reclining, rattan chairs.

Earlier today, after reading the Sunday papers, we walked around the neighborhood to see the cherry blossoms. The trees were in full bloom, with hardly any of the white petals yet fallen. Some were so heavily laden that their branches touched the ground.

Yesterday morning, I printed out the entire IMF report that Dawn had suggested. In the afternoon, while Raymond sat in our home office on a teleconference, I spent two hours skimming through its one hundred and sixty pages. After harrowing sections on the latest predictions of climate change, I reached "Regulatory Mechanisms" that compares the imposition of a tax on released carbon with a model where emissions are traded.

From what I understood, in a "cap-and-trade" system governments give companies reduction targets. If a company does better than those targets, it earns credits that have a monetary value; if a company cannot meet those targets, it can buy credits from those that have. Cap-and-trade avoids the emotive word "tax," but is less effective and more complex. It also tends to reward the worst polluters—Chinese companies, for example, would receive a huge percentage of credits. It was all very depressing.

And so, on this quiet and lazy day, while Raymond studies the Books and Arts section of *The Economist*, I open Donald Hall's *To Read a Poem* and it is as though some nerve has been touched with the faintest breath. After a rhythmic and humble preface called "To the Student," I reach Chapter 1, "Good Poems," and I think how simple this is, no argument, that these are good poems.

I read it almost every day and always will, staying mesmerized by the choice of words, at how Hall describes the first poem in his book like a love affair. The poem, "Stopping by Woods on a Snowy Evening," by Robert Frost, is arranged in four verses (or what Hall calls "stanzas"), and was composed in

1923. It is intoxicating—many must have read it with the same emotions. This perfect poem now greets me most mornings.

I love the way Hall walks me through a close reading, or "explication," peeling back the layers of form, rhythm, and meaning so that I am left in wonder that Frost could have compressed so much into sixteen lines. I confess I reacted physically to Frost's description of "downy flake(s)" of snow, as though they were feathers taking their time to fall. On this third reading of Hall's first eight pages, I realize this is what I also do—peel back the layers to let my patients look inside themselves.

As the light dims across the garden, I have just read the William Carlos Williams poem, "Red Wheelbarrow." I can see it in the dirt, and can hear the sound of chickens when night comes all too soon.

At midnight, on March 1st, I had emailed José Andrés' *minibar* to make a reservation. I had been to his previous restaurant, *Café Atlantico*, many times. At one stage, when *Ozio's* cigar smoke was particularly insufferable, John, Carolyn and I would hold our Friday cocktails at *Atlantico* so John could sing the praises of its collection of rare rums. But I had never managed to eat at José Andrés' *minibar*, let alone *José's table*, one of the most sought-after experiences in DC. For some unknown reason, I was successful.

Of course, Raymond thought he and I would be tasting cocktails at the adjacent *barmini* when I gave him his birthday cufflinks earlier today, but here we are taking the last two seats at *José's table*. Raymond is pleased, and therefore I am pleased.

We chat about his day, start the multi-course marathon, and are quickly caught up in small conversations cascading across the counter—how artistically each dish is arranged, that the wine pairing fits the palette, that this reminds the woman to my right of a recent visit to Venice and the tastes of *Harry's Bar*. After ten small courses the conversation with strangers dies away, and Raymond and I turn back towards each other.

"I needed this, Vera, I really did," he tells me. "Sometimes you get so caught up the importance of work that you forget about yourself—so thank you, darling," and he leans across and kisses my hand. "It's so tense in the office and, to be honest, I can't see it getting any better."

"What's the tension about—is Cyril not behaving?"

"You don't know what a pain he can be," Raymond says, closing his eyes and shaking his head. "He just loves to control things, but in our business it's difficult, especially when you're dealing with politicians. So he takes it out on us—plans, briefings, plans—and then we have to put up with his views and opinions.

"Today, we were all having coffee and he went off on the death penalty. Sure, I can see a case for some terrorists, but he thinks *all* murderers should be executed."

"Oh, my God—even if they're mentally ill? Or if there's doubt, or…?"

"When he's on one of his rants, Vera, there's no point arguing. But the worst thing is that everyone started nodding, even me, for Christ's sake."

I decide to shift the subject—onto something different, but at least still aligned with his work. "I could see how stressed you've been lately. If you don't want to talk about the office it's fine with me, but I'd love to understand what your work on climate change is all about."

He seems pleasantly surprised, and starts telling me how the world sees this threat. His thoughts come tumbling out. I interrupt to ask small questions and, as a chef places two delicate plates of candied strawberries before us, we have an animated conversation around carbon taxes and cap-and-trade.

Fast forward to now. It is dark and quiet in our bedroom, and we have just made love. Raymond, gallant Raymond, is drifting away, and I am still glowing with the last leg trembles. I am thinking about the evening, even about several of my patients, and I have an irrational desire to speak with Donald Hall. I know I will not sleep for hours for, between my racing thoughts, the last two lines of Robert Frost's poem keep whispering to me:

And miles to go before I sleep
And miles to go before I sleep.

Early in his book, *To Read a Poem,* in a chapter called "Images," Donald Hall provides this startling thought—"When we read great poetry, something changes in us that stays changed." Sitting in the small coffee shop of the *Mayflower Hotel,* waiting for Christine to arrive this windy Tuesday, I have to stop myself from wanting to challenge Mr. Hall, to add that, sometimes, great poetry is more an awakening than a source of change. Memories that I allow to surface have been swirling, and this morning, when I should have been pounding my flesh in the gym, I sat in my car and read his second Chapter, "Poems Are Made Of Words." I have also finished Chapter 3 while waiting for Christine.

Images: Christine walking towards the hotel, never breaking step, knowing she is late, knowing I will wait; Raymond pacing the corridors somewhere on the Hill, scrubbed clean and shaven; and somewhere, in this busy city, Marcel plucking up courage to walk to another rendezvous with a woman.

I would love to read great poetry. I would love to change. I would like to think of my patients as though they were my own self, so that I could step into their shoes and minds to understand their torment, to be a better source of help. I would like to be filled with passion, for my work, my husband, to feel a constant tingle in my hands as though I were touching skin. Perhaps it will happen, for in this last half hour Donald Hall has given me "A Blessing," a poem by James Wright. As Christine walks into view, I am still savoring the poem's last three lines, that I will know change has reached me when—

> *Suddenly I realize*
> *That if I stepped out of my body I would break*
> *Into Blossom*

"Late again, late again—so sorry, Vera."

A waiter appears. Christine orders a cappuccino and a refill for me and, for once, does not add "cute" as he leaves our table.

"Oh, and before I forget, thanks again for picking up the boys last week. They just *love* you, you know!"

Did her sons sense where their mother was when they were with me? Or only later, when she came breezing into the house drenched in perfume, her hair just that little bit too perfect and brushed?

"I'm just sorry I couldn't stay for a chat," I force myself to reply.

I am dearly hoping we move on, but I know a week is a long time for Christine to keep bottled up. I learn that Richard packs a bigger stroke in those tennis shorts than she ever dreamed, that he takes control, and that she still tingles down below from his mouthwash. They saw each other every day until David arrived back late on Friday, and had parted like two lovers in a great tragedy. Of course, she had visited him only yesterday, love-all and then a quick set around his bedroom before her hair appointment.

"I think I'll tire of him," she says, absently, "but at the moment it's all lips and teeth, and I can't get enough of it."

I want to tell her there is no song in her voice. I want to say that her inner beauty seeped away a long time ago. But I only nod, with the occasional question, as though I really did want her to elaborate more. What are you looking for, Christine? What am I looking for?

"So here's the thing. Richard's got an invitation to a wine tasting in McLean early Thursday evening and would love me to come. David's going to be at a guys-only dinner at his club for most of the evening, and I've got a baby sitter lined up. But he'll wonder where I am so...well, is it all right if I say I'm going to the wine tasting with you?"

This is different from simply picking up her sons from school. What Christine is saying is that if David were ever to ask me about the wine tasting, I should lie and say I was with her. I ought to say no, but I've always been a soft touch with her. I say it is fine, knowing that the likelihood of David asking me this question is low.

I am tempted to read Christine the short poem "Nantucket," by William Carlos Williams, tucked into Chapter 3, with its enigmatic last two lines:

a key is lying—And the
immaculate white bed

but, of course, I don't.

In retrospect I shouldn't have read that particular poem, at least not today. It is late Wednesday morning, and I am at the PNC Bank at Dupont Circle, waiting for part of Julie's life to be reassembled. She had called earlier in a total panic. It took me several minutes to discover she'd lost her new checkbook, and could no longer remember whether she had a credit card. It was as though her small ship of normalcy had suddenly broken its hawsers and was drifting away.

I have been at the bank for two hours, spilling way past the fifty minutes scheduled. While Julie has been completing paperwork, on the lost card and its replacement, I have been reading Chapter 4 of *To Read a Poem*, "Figures of Speech, Especially Metaphors." I have learned that the poet Gregory Orr likens himself to "thick grass," and Theodore Roethke sees orchids as "adder-mouthed." But the reason I shouldn't have been reading is because the chapter contains one of Shakespeare's great sonnets, "Shall I compare thee to a summer's day?" This poem is so packed with metaphor that it is impossible not to feel the intensity of the love Shakespeare describes; it is more precious to his lady than any ring or flower. I have climbed and stood at the pinnacle of poetry, and later I will meet Marcel.

As we leave the bank, I wonder how Julie might change if someone were to write a love poem to her, something she could keep inside her ample bosom. But no one has or likely will. Only twenty-nine years old, she leans on her cane, rocking from side to side towards the bus stop.

Shakespeare's sonnet is still with me as I make my way down New Hampshire to the practice on M Street. I have two hours before Marcel arrives, and I find myself unable to stop creating metaphors. My office is a vault full of secrets, sealed with a door of pure lead that is too heavy for one person to open. The two chairs are battle tanks, speckled with the mud of past wars. My framed watercolor is a prison cell window. And Marcel—is he not a fish swimming in an alien sea, whose anemones wave tentacles towards his curls, stinging when he touches them? Will he ever be desensitized? Is it right he suffers so much pain?

"Hello Marcel, please come in—take a seat."

He adjusts himself into his chair, moves the folder to his side, and looks straight at me. He is wearing khaki-colored trousers today, black scuffed shoes, and a crimpled linen blazer over a white shirt with a brown tie. If it weren't for the shadows under his eyes, I would have said he was a carefree soul that had woken up for spring. His hands are in their usual place and pose, clamped securely between his thighs, palms facing out, but he seems more at ease than I remember. Before I start our conversation, he opens the folder and takes out a notebook, and I catch him smiling once again.

"Is this a journal I see before me?" I ask.

He nods. The notebook is surprisingly thin, and I can't help wondering if it's a sign he's not serious about writing about his feelings and thoughts.

"May we discuss it, Marcel, because I want to know whether we should continue with the dating?"

"I've only had three dates because it took a while to process what you said last week," he replies, immediately. "But when I did I knew had to change, and always act the way I really am," and it is clear he is going to say more. "I couldn't write the way you wanted me to write and so instead I put my week in poetry. I hope this is ok—I wrote a sonnet every day, each night."

I put my thoughts about ending the dating project to the side, for I am eager for him to recite his poems, something he hasn't done with me before. Of the sonnets, three describe his failed dates in painful detail, at least to my ears. The others describe mundane events—forgetting his credit card one morning, a list of numbers that refuse to add, retrieving a package from a postal service depot, the color of his hands in moonlight. They are pretty stilted, but their cadences ease during the week, with observation replacing self-pity. Clearly, there is progress, and I ask him to reread the three about the dates.

The first was last Friday, again over lunch, with a woman who must have been an agency mistake. She was the tallest person in the small restaurant, and they had nothing in common except knowledge of Catholicism. Her large frame clearly needed feeding. She ate quickly, drank two large glasses of cabernet sauvignon, and showed no interest in the arts except for a love of the movie-actor Brad Pitt. Marcel hardly had to say a word beyond the salad course. As they were leaving she told him it might be best not see each other again, and then thanked him for listening.

On the evening that Raymond and I had dined at *minibar*, Marcel had met up with a widow in her fifties, he guessed. She, too, had talked a lot, and she, too, had little in common with Marcel except for what he wrote as, "a loneliness much deeper than the dark/ened cleft her cleavage left before it dived." I did laugh at those lines, even complimented him on the repeated sounds and rhymes. He and the lady parted without looking at each other.

And then just yesterday, he had unintentionally arrived late for lunch, and spent the first minutes apologizing to a woman who spent three of every four weeks out of town in economy-class seats and hotel rooms. Unfortunately, her early expressions of interest in literature dimmed the more they spoke so that, even though she had said she was free later that week, he didn't ask if they could meet again.

As we talk I can sense the pain he felt when his attempts to warm the space between him and the three women turned to ice. But he is no longer speaking about rejection in the same way, now using terms like "irreconcilable" and "not the man for her," as though the stings were less hurtful than before. And with the third lady, it was Marcel who made the decision not to pursue a follow-up date. With our session closing, I remember to ask a question.

"In the second sonnet you have a line, 'Each night I hear the sounds within the walls.' I'm wondering what it means."

I should have kept it for a later session. He bends forward and then, without a word, closes his journal and walks towards the door. Before leaving, he turns and simply tells me, "I think I'll keep the journal to myself. But I have written out the sonnets. Here." With that, he hands me a folded sheaf of papers.

It is indeed progress—Paradoxical Intervention is beginning to work. But I also know we have to get to a place Marcel has never shared with anyone else.

As I drive home, I realize that each new date and rejection is breaking him free of his original level of desperation. Turning into our driveway, a strange question forms—is Marcel earning rejection credits? Will there come a time when he will trade them to me?

I have decided to speak to you this morning, Mr. Hall. I hope you don't mind, but something tells me you're the kind of person who listens. I have cheated.

I admit I skimmed through your Chapter 5: "Tone, with a Note on Intentions," last night. It seemed merely a bridge to what followed, and not one of your better chapters. I also had different expectations of your Chapter 6: "Symbols and Illusions." Writing this, I do hope you take these comments as merely impressions from someone unversed in poetry (an awful pun, I'll admit) and not some transgression of our trust.

But to return to cheating: you teased me, didn't you, after Blake's poem about the sick rose, and your comments on how poets return to this flower? And so I confess that I jumped forward—one hundred and eleven pages to be precise—to Theodore Roethke's poem "The Rose" after you described it as his "great contemporary poem." I'm sorry. I couldn't resist.

You honored Roethke by including twelve of his poems, and "The Rose" is the eleventh, over two pages of magical rhythm and sound. You said his father nurtured greenhouses, and that many of Roethke's poems return to these memories of his childhood. And you hinted that, as he aged, he produced some of his best work—"The Rose" was written in the year of his death, 1963. It rolls around the mouth before this heart-stopping sequence, starting at the hundredth line:

> *Near this rose, in this grove of sun-parched, wind-warped madronas,*
> *Among the half-dead trees, I came upon the true ease of myself,*
> *As if another man appeared out of the depths of my being,*
> *And I stood outside myself …*

Are these the lines you love the most? Do they resonate in you, did they make you hunch forward with cramps the first time you read them, the way they did with me?

But I have to leave you now. I have to take a small break—only until the weekend, I promise—because you are filling up what little space I had reserved for thought. Yesterday, in a session with a patient, I almost stood outside myself.

"Amanda dropped by the office and asked if we'd like to join her and Cyril for a barbecue next Tuesday," Raymond says. "Hmm? He's got some influential people in town. But they want to wait until Monday or latest Tuesday morning because there might be rain. I said fine."

All this is said with his eyes on the TV where his beloved Red Sox are playing the Blue Jays. Well, fine indeed. I have nothing planned for next Tuesday evening, as with almost every one. "I think I'm free."

This is merely my attempt at catching his attention. But after glancing up, Raymond returns to the TV while I walk across to top up my wine.

Deep down I'll admit I am irritated—no, dismayed—that he had agreed to the barbecue before we spoke, although I'm relieved he doesn't sense this.

"How is Amanda?" I babble on. "How did she seem?"

"Vera, I'm watching," he says, though for some reason I fail to recognize this signal and keep talking.

"I read something about how China is moving far ahead of us in technology, and that they're now leaders in renewable energy, which is pretty amazing when—"

"Vera, you've had all winter to talk to me. Look, I appreciate you took the time to find out what's going on around climate change. It's incredibly complicated. But let me tell you something about good-old China. Every week, it's building a new power plant that will burn coal—every week. And yet all *The New York Times* talks about is China's damned clean technology that, half the time, they've stolen from us. That's the real story, ok?"

I find myself speechless, not because of the sharpness in his voice, but over the sheer unfairness. He turns off the TV, walks across the room, and fills his glass with scotch.

I should leave it there. But shamefully, I say, "Sorry, Raymond." I am trying to swallow, but there is too much air in my throat, with no more words to form.

❖ ❖ ❖

"So tell me again what he said when you asked about it?"

I am with Carolyn, late on Friday, later than our normal cocktail hour because John is not with us. He is at his annual long weekend with the guys, holed up in some rustic cabin and having what he calls, "shallow talk and beer." Carolyn is quizzing me over my last session with Marcel. She is trying hard to make our meeting less professional, more a conversation between friends. But even though Carolyn is one of the most empathic people I know, she seems unable to escape the clipped tones of a rear admiral's daughter.

I describe the end of the session, the way I raised the question over the sounds within walls and Marcel's parting words, "I think I'll keep the journal to myself."

"So, how did that make you feel?" she asks again, on cue.

"I felt I'd touched a nerve too early. Perhaps his strong sense of rejection over his dates with women was secondary to something bigger."

Neither of us speaks for a while, and then she says what I had also been thinking. It is Carolyn at her professional best. It is tough love.

"You lost control of the session, Vera. You've got to re-take control. Tell him you want to move to two sessions per week."

Excellent—this is what I'll do.

We talk again about Marcel's three dates. Each woman had made things easy for him by doing the talking. We agree, after reviewing my notes, that Marcel rarely asks questions, even in my sessions with him.

"Is he just not interested in other people, Carolyn, or does he resist asking questions out of fear of being rebuffed?"

"The latter," she replies, and I know she's right.

"So how can I get him to ask more questions?"

"You've been showing him for some time," Carolyn says, with a hint of humor. "If you keep asking questions, he'll get so loaded with oxytocin he may want to do the same—well, that's the theory anyway."

I recall John talking about oxytocin a few months back. The hormone had long been known to trigger feelings of well-being, but researchers had recently discovered that people who *received* more attention—love if you will—had higher levels of oxytocin.

"So when you're asking questions, if you can convey a true sense of caring, maybe he'll generate his own ability to do this with others," Carolyn concludes.

"Oh," I remember as an afterthought. "He read his sonnets, and then gave them to me."

"Well, what do you know? A present. Cherish them."

As we are leaving, a question forms that I doubt I'll ever ask. What happens when one's own well of love is drying up, like mine?

"Hello, Marcel, is everything all right?"

This is the first time he's ever called me. It is Saturday morning.

"No, nothing's wrong, and sorry to call you, but I just think we need to stop our sessions. Maybe it is best we take a break and see how things pan out, if that's all right," he replies, stiffly.

In the background someone is screaming to the heavy beat of hip-hop. I tell him that, on the contrary, I think we should start meeting twice a week in future. I am about to suggest new times when he speaks.

"You told me that I never ask for what I want. So this is what I really want."

"I'm glad you're being decisive, Marcel, but please think again. There's so much going on that I think it would help us both to touch base more frequently." And then I take a small risk. "I wouldn't suggest this if I didn't care."

But his mind seems made up.

Rain. Wet Sundays are sad Sundays, but at least Raymond and I are talking again. Please let it rain through Tuesday. Yesterday helped, particularly earlier in the day.

We decided we needed some impatiens and begonias to fill the shaded parts of our garden and so, after a late breakfast, we took my car and drove to Annapolis, to a nursery we know well.

After selecting a trunk load, and on the spur of the moment, we headed off to *Cantler's Riverside Inn* for lunch.

The outer deck facing the small creek was filled with people dressed for summer, but wise enough to bring jackets as protection against the wind. We did our duty—a shared barrel of crabs, and chilled beers to wash it all down. We spent much of the time talking about friends lost and those still close to us, some of whom we jokingly wished were lost.

We spent the evening in our armchairs in the living room. I was immersed in a new Louise Penney novel, luxuriating in being re-acquainted with Inspector Gamache, and Raymond was reading Stephen Kinzer's, *The Brothers*. I could see from the way he kept turning away from the book to look at the ceiling that he was agitated.

"I'm not sure I can read any more of this," he suddenly said, throwing the book, and then following it towards the drinks cabinet. "What those Dulles brothers did was a disgrace. No morals, no values—no wonder we're hated in many countries."

Today, Raymond seems relaxed, his old self, wiggling the toes of his loafers as he reads the business section of *The Washington Post*. Tonight, he will do his wok magic with fresh vegetables, while I grill salmon.

Donald Hall's *To Read a Poem* is on my lap. Earlier, I cheated again by flicking through pages until I reached the section on Emily Dickinson. She wrote largely to herself, often in strange ways, and she wore her hair in a tight bun reflecting emotions tied up within her. Yet her poetry is an avalanche of feelings. Her poem, "I cannot live with You," is achingly tragic, and tragically familiar. It reminds me of several patients.

Marcel—was he still booking dates, counting the failures? His call yesterday left me with my own sense of failure, but I now feel that I am the one abandoned.

"The sounds within the walls"…what does Marcel mean?

I open Donald Hall's book to Chapter 7: "The Sound of Poems."

How beautifully you introduce this chapter, Mr. Hall. Even though the first pleasure is no surprise—the rhythm of "words in motion"—I was dancing in my chair by the time I finished the first six lines of Milton's "Paradise Lost." I was not aware of the way a small pause, or caesura, can hold the breath, as though one were on the edge of a cliff.

And then the second pleasure you describe, the "adjacent sounds rubbing together, vowels held and savored, consonants clicking together." I love the way you dissect the line "down their carved names the rain-drop ploughs," listing eight repeated sounds of Hardy's vowels and consonants. And Gerard Manley Hopkins is simply blissful.

Finally, I enjoyed your description of enjambment, "when the sense runs over the end of a line" so that each line "retains its identity." To me, this creates a sense of ambiguity, or surprise. My personal favorite, but not used in Chapter 7, is the William Carlos Williams poem, "Nantucket," that you quote on page 25. Williams could have written, "On the glass tray a glass pitcher, the tumbler toned down, by which a key is lying - And the immaculate white bed," but he didn't:

> *On the glass tray*
>
> *a glass pitcher, the tumbler*
> *toned down, by which*
>
> *a key is lying—And the*
> *immaculate white bed*

How wonderful! To me, Mr. Hall, enjambment is a point of paradox, a pivot of surprise behind which lies a truth. Do you like this description? I'm sure my colleague John would.

It is Tuesday. The traitorous sun has broken through the clouds, and tonight we will go to a barbeque.

I'm still exhausted from yesterday, especially from a harrowing session with my newest patient, Charles. He had been talking about his fat-cat clients, of how they treated him as a legal gravedigger for their sordid deals when he stopped, and in a faint whisper said, "They never tell."

We therapists are attuned to this moment. We know that, when the voice drops a tone and the face turns half away, words seep out of the darkest cave. I asked who "they" were.

Afterward, I walked into John's office and told him what I'd heard. He listened in silence before crossing the room to touch my arm. In increasing detail Charles had told me of distant nephews, of boys in parks petted behind trees, of blood on small pants that he kept in a trunk in a garden shed, of rows of videos ready to roll, and a recent visit to Amsterdam. All of them would never tell, and some, he confessed, would never speak again.

I called the police, and spent most of the afternoon answering questions from two detectives and a lady police officer. They told me they would pick him up that night. I spent the evening trying not to imagine what they would find at his house, the screams of his wife, and the stares of his teenage daughters. For once, I was glad Raymond didn't ask about my day.

Christine called earlier this morning suggesting we meet for lunch before calling back to cancel. So I have time on my hands to write up some of my notes when my smartphone rings.

"Hello, Marcel."

"I wanted to apologize. I've thought a lot about the words you said and that you cared, so can we meet tomorrow, please? I think we have a lot to talk about."

My thoughts race before I say, "There's no reason to apologize, Marcel. Let's meet tomorrow as planned. Can we make this a two-hour session?"

He agrees. Increasing his visits to twice per week is left to simmer.

Who arranges valet parking and installs a black-tied waiter to accept each guest at the front door, for what is no more than a barbecue? The Brocks.

The invitation said "casual attire," but thankfully we swayed towards the formal side of casual. This was Raymond's idea. He has chosen gray flannel trousers, a simple white shirt and a brown sports jacket. As for me, I'm layered in three silk blouses over pants, although the colors seem dull beside Amanda Brock's shortened evening dress and diamonds, and I almost curtsy as Cyril holds out his hand.

"Good to see you, Vera...Raymond," Cyril says stiffly, in his graveled CEO voice. Dressed in cavalry-twill trousers, a blue blazer, and a shirt with a paisley cravat, he doesn't look particularly primed for prime steaks and spattered fat from a grill. "Drinks are over there. When you get settled, let me introduce you to George," he half-whispers to Raymond. Braving waves of perfume, my husband is kissing the second of Amanda's powdered cheeks.

An emerald green, lookalike lawn drapes the huge, half-covered deck. Small clumps of people separate themselves at safe distances. Raymond and I collect our drinks—white wine and a scotch—and join the closest island of talk. I do not know these people, though I have met them many times.

As smoke wafts across us, and the air is filled with sizzles, Cyril reappears and takes Raymond aside. "George has yet to agree, so this visit is a chance to let him see who we are. He knows the issues from his Senate days." As they move away, I detach myself from the group and follow.

"George, let me introduce Raymond, one of our rising stars and...this is Vera, his wife."

Ex-senator George Willis, grey-haired, fit, and tanned, comes up to us and fills the silence with his southern drawl.

"I'm very pleased to meet you both."

Cyril leaves to supervise the grilling of steaks and a few potential clients. George asks as much as he tells. He is retired with his "bride," and sits on a few boards, a few advisories—"wherever I can help." He seems pleased that Raymond and I met at Georgetown where he lectures on corporate governance now and then. This lets Raymond move into the rehearsed story of his career.

George asks what I do, and seems intrigued that I am a practicing psychologist, adding, with a chuckle, that they could do with my help on the Hill. I ask him how often he visits DC, and where he lives.

"Outside Santa Fe, in New Mexico ma'am—beyond the reach of artists and tourists, where I can see the blood run down the Sangre de Cristo Mountains each night."

I am surprised by the poetry of his description. He notices.

"Did I say something wrong, Vera?"

"Oh no, not at all. It's just that your description was so right."

"Vera was brought up in New Mexico," Raymond adds. Now it is George who looks surprised.

"Where?" he asks, "And how did you end up in DC?"

I explain that I had won a national merit scholarship to Georgetown, "a shock to everyone." Before I am forced to disclose more, I decide to plead the need to powder my nose, and excuse myself.

I find the first of two ground-floor restrooms occupied, and I decide to wait. In less than a minute the door opens, and Amanda Brock walks out, still adjusting a diamond brooch.

"There, it's all yours," she says. "How do you like the wine? Do try the red if you get the chance. I hear Christine and you are connoisseurs."

The police called earlier today saying they'd arrested Charles. I was preparing a coffee before my two-hour session with Marcel and took the call in the office kitchen. They'd found a large number of photographs and videos featuring "someone strongly resembling Mr Wilson." Could I stop by the station for some further questions, they asked. I promised to do so after an appointment I couldn't break.

Now I am sitting in my office, willing the cramping in my stomach to subside. I am trying to recall all the patients I have seen over the years and wondering—one by one—whether there were things I could have missed, some signs that something truly awful was happening in their lives. It is like turning an album of photographs, and they are all smiling.

It is four minutes after two when Marcel knocks on my door. "Come in!" I shout.

"It's good to see you, Marcel," I say, meaning it.

For once, I had lost track of time. But any chance he could have been hurt by me calling him in late seems to have been dispelled by my welcome.

"And it is good to see you, Doctor Lewis." The last syllable is almost a whisper.

"Please tell me, how was your mood this last week?"

Squirming, he says only that it has been variable.

"Have you managed to start the journal?" He nods, and begins to take his journal from the folder, his hand visibly shaking.

"I read your sonnets several times. They're Shakespearean I think, because they all end in couplets"

Again, there is that smile and hesitation.

"They are indeed. I can't believe you read about the sonnet form but, then again, you said you cared. It is the simplest form—I find Petrarchan sonnets difficult."

I learned about this type of sonnet too. The first eight lines of a Petrarchan sonnet use only two end-rhymes, repeated four times, and finding unique or unusual sounds is a known technical challenge. But I am excited that we are talking of poetry so early in our session.

"This past week, Marcel—have you written any more sonnets?"

Five it turns out—two last week, two over the weekend, and one yesterday. The first four describe his dates, and he is keen to read them to me.

As before, they seem stunted, like a series of statements in which each line is a sentence, no subtlety of rhyme, no experiments with enjambment. They describe events quite well—where they met, what the woman looked like, what she said and, in almost every case, when it was clear that things were going awry, around the ninth line; things fall apart in the two final lines. I ask him to read them a second time, and then suggest we go over each of the dates.

He speaks methodically, stopping to think each time I ask a question—standards like, "How did you feel at that moment?" and, "What made you think she was feeling that way?" He appears to be less emotionally distressed upon reaching the point of rejection, and the final couplets of his sonnets are less distraught than before, almost like a light shrug.

The first three lunch dates differed from the previous week because the three women were quieter. The onus had therefore been on him, and he had filled the vacuum by talking incessantly about his work, or the food and wine, before "dying verbally before their eyes."

It is the fourth date that is of real interest. I can sense from the way he had read the sonnet that something different had happened. They had met for evening drinks at *Bistrot du Coin*, north of Dupont Circle. She had entered just ahead of him and, when Marcel heard her mentioning his name to the doorman, he had walked up and helped her with her coat. Like me, she drank gin Martinis, and he had ordered the same. She laughed when he told her he also wore contact lenses.

She had recently arrived from Portland, Maine, and was working as a statistician at a small think tank. But her main love was literature, especially nineteenth century classics. She stopped him at one point to say she loved the precise manner in which he spoke. He managed to make her smile by reciting a sonnet he had written some years back. Things turned against him after he ordered a second Martini. He spilled part on the bar counter, tried to wipe it away with his coat sleeve, and then asked for her phone number before gulping down another mouthful. She wasn't rude, but she made it clear she had to leave.

Overall, his behavior was encouraging, and I tell him so. I am also proud of him, but I decide it's too early to say this. Not only did he make more progress than before, and was clearly more at ease, but he had discovered a lot about this young woman in a short period of time.

"So what did you learn from this, Marcel? Can you see how powerful it is when *you* ask the questions? I do this with you all the time. That's how I try to bring things out, so we can both see them clearly. In the outside world, when someone questions you about yourself, how does it make you feel?"

He thinks awhile and then replies. "That they are interested—that they care."

We have taken a huge step forward, so I say "You wrote a fifth sonnet just yesterday. May I hear it?"

He reads it several times and, no matter how hard he tries, he cannot stultify its flow. There is no rhyming couplet at the end, and the turn is gradual, beginning at the ninth line. Even the subject is different from his normal self-confessing poetry. He had written it the night before in the library after reading a small book about Victorian mores in England, how what appeared on the surface was not what went on in the private lives of the elite, clad in their full-clasped dresses and tightened collars. It is a simple, descriptive sonnet that releases itself in the last five lines so that the message is deliciously ambiguous. It leads to a final line—"The prim act out their whims in wayward ways."

"What beautiful alliteration and internal rhyme, Marcel."

I am looking at him clenching his journal. His jaws tighten as though chewing my words. He splutters that he has written something else, copied it from an essay in the past. He flicks back several pages, and starts to read. After several words he stops, and repeats himself. I am certain he is going to close down on me, but he turns his head and whispers.

"I cannot do it. Will you read it for me? There is a fence of words I cannot climb."

I take the open journal from him. Here is what he wrote:

Young Johnny's father, Ben, is a bear of a man with hands as large as his heart, a heart which is pretty sound despite the endless cigarettes he smokes each time he takes the road from Pittsburgh. Today, we approach each curve too fast, three of us cramped into the front-bench seat of his pickup truck. We are driving northeast in the early hours of a Thursday before the weekend traffic madness, the city fumes drifting behind us as we roll through hills of light and mist, stopping at State College for a coffee before the final push into Coburn.

Ever since Johnny and I first begged to join him, Ben has parked at the sharp bend of Ridge Hollow, and run across to look down into the rumbling depths of Penns Creek, like today. As always, I find myself being drawn to the beauty of its flow, and the tumbling rhythm of water on stone. And each time is like the first.

It was three years ago, when I was twelve years old. I had never fished in my life, let alone held the balanced weight of a fly rod in my hand. I was given a shorter rod, with a reel full of nylon line and, on the end, a silver spoon which flashed each time I was able to cast it out and draw it through the river. I stood by the side of one of the deeper pools, perched on a rock for all the trout to see, throwing the spoon with a deep splash towards wherever I thought a frightened fish may have rushed in panic. By mid-morning I had neither caught nor seen a single trout, so I walked upstream to find Johnny and Ben.

Johnny was sitting on a rock. For the next hour we watched Ben wade upstream through the river. All the while, in a continuous way, he would lift the rod as the line snaked towards him in the current then, with a flick over his shoulder or a roll to the side, he would shoot the fly ahead of him. I watched him catch three small brown trout, and scrambled down to see the first lying in his wetted hand, all greens and gold with pink spots across its taut body, and perfect, perfect fins.

As we walk back to the truck, we break into chatter, climbing aboard to make our way towards Cherry Run, the only stretch of stream open to the public.

I am now experienced, and have borrowed one of Ben's rods, an eight-foot 3-weight with a floating line. Before the long walk down to the river, we each tackle up, and I notice how delicately Ben wraps his huge fingers around the smallest fly, tying it to nylon finer than a human hair. He is going to use a Parachute-Adams he tells us, just a single dry fly at the end of nine feet of leader. Johnny and I will be using leaded nymphs until the full sun hits the water, or we catch sight of the first hatch blowing off.

Lift, flick, cast, lift, flick, cast…the repeated action is almost hypnotizing. I am wading towards a large boulder that last year yielded two trout. Johnny is downstream in a favorite stretch, and Ben has wandered ahead. I see a swirl beside the boils rising up from the sunken stone. On the next cast I lower the rod to let the nymph sink, then notice the floating line stop and move to the left, tightening and running before I feel the fish. I know it is large for it dives deep, and nearly manages to swim around the rock before I coax it into the current. But it is many minutes before I see it, and by then I am wet with spray from the fly line and my own sweat.

You do not want to hear about the fight, and I do not want to tell you. Instead, I want to tell you this—that as the sun touches the pool for the first time, and a cloud of steel-gray duns begins to lift from the river, I hold the trout in both my hands in wonder. It is sixteen inches of life that will soon forgive me, but for now lies on its side gracing my eyes. The only sound I hear is the fast beat of blood in my ears.

You will never see this. You will never be here with me to feel the breeze in your hair, or lie down safely in a place where rhythms can dance you to sleep. I am writing this for you. I am writing so you know there is a place where time stops, where the only walls are those of canyon stone, where you can bring your piano music and the water will play it. These are only words, but the place is real. I have touched it, breathed it, and it is almost as beautiful as you.

I cannot look up because I know tears will cloud my eyes. I am trying to put to memory what I have read, so different than anything I could have expected and, much more than yesterday's sonnet, written in a voice he seems to have lost.

"I'm guessing that was an elegy to your mother, wasn't it? I can understand why it was so difficult for you to read it to me."

"I wrote it in the weeks before she died, and left it by her bed—I know she read it. But one day I'll find a time and place to read it all to her, for her alone," he replies, and I know he is talking about her grave that he has visited only once.

I have an open goal, a clear path into him. But for some inexplicable reason I back away, and ask the most inane question.

"You once told me you'd given up fly-fishing—why is that?"

He looks up, and shakes his head slowly, as though even he is disappointed by my question.

"I only hear the sounds of moving stones, and not the happy chatter of the stream." Again, he speaks of sounds.

"I think maybe we should revisit our plan to meet twice per week. Say Mondays and Fridays, starting next week?" To my relief he nods. "You know Marcel, your prose is truly beautiful. Do you ever have time these days to take a break from poetry?"

"I write the way my body lets me think, and it prefers to keep a steady beat," he replies and it is as though a dimmed light has been turned up.

This morning came the call from Christine as I was loading my tote bag into the car. She was virtually climbing into her phone. It took me awhile to realize she was referring to a lunch she'd attended yesterday.

"What the hell did you tell her? Tell me, what the hell—" Christine shouted.

"Calm down, calm down. I can't understand what you're saying. Told whom?"

It was a charity lunch at her tennis club, ladies-only. Amanda Brock had walked past and stopped to talk. Amanda had mentioned the barbecue the evening before, and that she had spent some time with me.

"It wasn't what she said, it was the way she said it!" Christine half-screamed. '" You two must have lots of fun at your wine tastings,' she whispered, and I didn't know where to turn. How the hell did she know about last Thursday if you didn't tell her?"

I tried to reassure Christine I had said nothing about a wine tasting to Amanda, even though she'd said the same kind of thing to me. I'd also wondered whether it was a reference to last Thursday.

"But going to that wine tasting was just a story—I was with Richard," Christine continued, as if I didn't know.

I told her I was certain I'd given no sign that anything was amiss, and the call ended with her slightly calmer.

Then there was my visit with the police, easier than expected. It was mainly to double-check the sequence of events that Charles had revealed to me. My statement didn't match what they were piecing together. I explained this was not surprising since his words had literally tumbled out during our session. Thankfully, they didn't share what else they had discovered.

And then, finally, this afternoon, Raymond had phoned shouting, "Fuck, fuck, fuck!" It seems that George Willis had cut his two-day visit short, and had decided not to come on board as an adviser to the firm.

"Cyril didn't take it well—laid into all of us, including me," he continued, and I knew my husband had just stepped into a bar. "Won't be too late," he ended.

Ah, but you will, I thought. You will.

So that is why I came to bed early tonight, Mr Hall, why I brought along a large glass of chilled Chablis. I have been reading for several hours, and Raymond is back. I can hear Dolly Parton at full volume downstairs.

I have just been reading about prose poems, but I want to talk to you about Chapter 8: "Meter and Rhyme." You are so right—meter is quite separate from rhythm! I love your description of meter as "number counting." As you say, it's only in combination with rhythm, and with rhyme, that poetry obtains the "pleasing sound" we demand. I like how you explain meter as a count of relative stresses and that, in an iambic foot, the second stress of two is stronger, as in neGLECT and deSTROY. Which brings me to iambic pentameter, with its five stresses and the example you used:

the UniVERsiTY of MIchiGAN

After such an awful day, at least I've some fun in the last hour, Mr Hall. I've been under the covers, trying to remember lines of iambic pentameter from my past. I think the earliest was at junior high. Our teacher would make us stand in a circle, and we would recite plays. It was Shakespeare's *The Merchant of Venice,* and I was Portia:

the QUAliTY of MERcy IS not STRAINED

I did think up a more recent example:

i WANT to SPEND my LIFEtime LOVing YOU

I should say that I am not a *Mask of Zorro* fan, Mr Hall, but I did like the soundtrack.

My patient Marcel's poetry is generally bad. Except for his most recent sonnet, it has no rhythm and is merely lines of five-stressed feet so regular you want to shake them loose. But I now see what Marcel is doing. He is punching out his regular lines of iambic pentameter so that they match the beat of music in his head. This beat seems to drive his life. It's as though he wants to drown out all other sound. I suspect that's because the labored beat provides Marcel with comfort and protection.

Mr. Hall, before I dim my light to feign sleep, I want to go back to the example you used to introduce iambic pentameter:

Bang BANG Bang BANG Bang BANG Bang BANG Bang BANG

If you listen carefully, you'll hear Raymond rummaging in the drinks cabinet. He's banging around so that the walls seem like drums. He's there with Dolly Parton, who is pleading to Jolene, once again. She's begging of her not to take her man.

she's BEGging OF her NOT to TAKE her MAN

Yesterday was a mixed day and, for Raymond, a hangover day. I left him early, sprawled between the sheets, paid my dues at the gym, and had a quick coffee with Dawn at *Politics and Prose*. Before I left, I again browsed the poetry section until I discovered David Lehman's book, *Great American Prose Poems*, and decided to buy it. As I pulled it down from the shelf, I caught sight of another book. The title on its red spine was so shocking that I almost left without paying for Mr. Lehman's book.

When I got back to the house around ten, Raymond had yet to leave for work and was arguing with the hall mirror and his tie. He had that waxed sheen of nausea.

We spoke a little about the evening before, rushed past each other, and got into our cars at the same time. By the time I found my keys, Raymond had reversed out of the garage but was waiting for me on our short drive.

"I forgot, it's garbage day," he said through his open window. "Can you put the trash out before you go? I've just washed my hands."

I saw four patients. Linda was new. Her real problem was too much time and money to worry about the two children she claimed had attention-deficit disorders, probably because of her own lack of attention to them. Linda was like a clone of the friend who had referred her to me—all smiles and thinned legs.

Next, I talked by phone to Robin, the CEO of a company in Baltimore, and someone I've never met. He and I have made considerable progress dealing with five months of arrogance, the drudge of his work, the hollowness of his life, and the harrowed state of his marriage. And then there was Julie.

She had called early to say she didn't think she would be able to make our session, but something in her voice concerned me. We ended up meeting for coffee at noon, at *Le Pain Quotidien* near Dupont Circle where I watched her squeeze through the doors already out of breath.

"I woke up today realizing every time I walk into your office I feel overwhelmed by a wave of failure. I just couldn't face it," she heaved, "So I settled down with my cat and called in sick. Then I decided to call you."

"I'm glad you did," I said, before adding my standard question. "So how are you feeling?"

She told me her self-loathing had deepened. I tried to get her to talk about this, and mentioned her mother several times, but her only response was to shake her head. We spent the last ten minutes going over her finances, small as they were, before I watched her return to the bus stop.

Walking along New Hampshire back to my office, I caught sight of a familiar figure stepping uncertainly across the road and entering *Firefly*. Marcel was not carrying his folder, nor was he was wearing his habitual brown tie—just an open shirt inside a sports jacket. Intrigued, I stopped behind a tree. A young woman with long fair hair took her seat at a small table near the window. Marcel joined her. I could see him asking questions, and listening to her explanations as her hands created shapes in the air.

Later, in the afternoon, after my fourth and last patient, I decided to write up my notes at home. After dropping into Trader Joe's for groceries, I beat the rush hour traffic, and was reading the introduction to Lehman's book when Raymond arrived.

Unusually quiet, he didn't bother to change before pouring us drinks and slumping down into his armchair.

"Sorry about last night, Vera," he eventually said. "It was just a shit day."

I learned that ex-Senator George Willis had spent the day listening to briefings of the firm's projects. During the afternoon coffee break, he had whispered something to Cyril, and the two had retired to Cyril's office for over an hour.

"When Cyril came back he was incandescent. George had decided not to join as an adviser—something about 'not the kind of project I want to get involved in,' whatever that means. Cyril said we'd 'fucked up,' and stormed out. So some of us went for a drink—should never have driven home."

The way Raymond rolled his eyes made me think he was more upset at having failed Cyril than anything else.

"Do you know what George Willis objected to?" I asked. "He seemed such a reasonable guy."

"I'm not sure," Raymond replied, loosening his tie, "but he kept asking about our belief systems and values. Anyway, today it got worse. Cyril called each of us into his office. He told me I'd screwed up at the barbecue and that…that I needed to tell you there were times when you should leave me alone with business contacts."

I waited for Raymond to express outrage, but all he did was get up and walk into the office. Since he wasn't going to share any more, I made pasta. We ate largely in silence.

As I lay in bed, waiting for Raymond's breathing to deepen, I thought about the days ahead and found only one bright light, my next session with Marcel after the weekend. The sight of him earlier made me realize that his life was slowly opening up at a time when mine was retreating into days and nights of boredom and distance.

"You said what?" John asks, incredulously. "He leaves you an opening and you ask about fishing? You could have asked more about his mother. Or why he'd written what he wrote."

He is right. But this is the first occasion when I sense my professional integrity being questioned.

Carolyn breaks the silence.

"John's right, Vera. And the way his story suddenly turns towards his mother is unexpected. Did he write something that made you personally uncomfortable?"

I sense a sharp pain beneath my ribs. The air leaves my chest so quickly that I feel as though I am falling. I try to bring myself back into the room, focusing on the faint smear of lipstick on Carolyn's teacup, and the rasp of my boots as I rub one ankle against the other.

John leans back and spreads his legs, as though this will somehow break the tension.

"We've all had times when a patient says something that triggers something in us, Vera," he says, as though answering Carolyn's question. "It may be only a split second, but it's enough to throw us off."

I steal a deep breath, and try to convince myself that what I am feeling is natural, that I have disappointed Carolyn and John.

But I know what is really being said, that Marcel touched something in me, and that this stopped me in my tracks.

"So tell us again what he said at the end of the session," John asks, more softly.

I look down at my notes and read Marcel's voice back to them. This time I concentrate less on the words than on the rhythm and, with a rush of recognition, I realize he spoke in meter, two lines of iambic pentameter so clear I'm amazed I hadn't seen it before:

> *i WRITE the WAY my BOdy LETS me THINK*
> *and IT preFERS to KEEP a STEAdy BEAT.*

I feel a lightness rising, and a strange sense of joy over this wondrous discovery. I want to shout "Oh, my god!" and laugh out loud. Instead, I suggest we go through my remaining patients, one-by-one, step-by-step.

We spend some time on Julie, and on the events surrounding Charles' arrest, but my mind is elsewhere, longing to read through my session notes, longing to search for Marcel's words uttered in meter. As we walk on M Street, still talking of Charles, my ears are filled with a pulse, and it is racing:

> *bumBUMP bumBUMP bumBUMP bumBUMP bumBUMP*

"Unknown." This time the call is on my smartphone, with that same long silence and a low howl of wind. There is no threatening breath, just the sense of a hand gripping tightly around a phone.

Someone who didn't want to be identified has been calling for some time. These blocked calls to our home commenced several months ago, and it was weeks before I thought they were more than misdials. Then, one evening, Raymond answered and remarked how often no one was on the end of the line. "Odd," I remember saying. "Happens to me as well, but the call stays open, like there's someone there."

So I had begun to pay more attention. I would sometimes stay silent. After a long ten seconds, the call would end. If I opened with a greeting, the caller would remain with me for as long as I talked.

The blocked calls to my smartphone started a month ago. For some reason I thought the caller to be a woman. She has called at all times of the day, though never early morning, nor very late at night.

Today's call arrives as I am walking across the parking lot to meet Christine at her favorite downtown spa. I see the message "Unknown" and place the phone to my ear.

"Hello." I stop in a slice of sunlight.

There is that sound of wind, faint and low, and a lengthening silence.

"So how are you today?" I decide to say. "It's several days since you called. What I told you then is true, you know. It's safe for you to speak if you want to.

"I can't stay long this time. What do you want to say? If it's too difficult, just text me." I wait several seconds before she hangs up.

Christine is sitting in her chair when I arrive, toes splayed out to dry from her pedicure, her hands soaking in a bowl.

"Sorry about the other day," she says as greeting.

She shares her tasks for the day. These chores center on the children's sports, and an evening with her husband David's "wrinkly" friends, "Old men drinking young wines and wives."

I sit next to her, lift my hands like a pianist, and allow them to be dipped into the welcoming oil. It is a soothing ritual. With Christine's monologue as background, I find myself on the edge of sleep as she talks of David's friends.

"Last time, we spent much of the evening discussing right-wing politics, for God's sake. That was after playing that stupid game where someone asks a question, and you go around the table answering it. If they'd asked 'Who's the best lover you've ever had?' it could have been fun. But 'What are people reading now?' or some question over an obscure foreign movie—give me a break."

I would be thrilled by such a conversation. If the discussion turned to reading, I would introduce the group to Donald Hall, or some of the prose poems I read in David Lehman's book last night. I would tell them of Fran Carlen's "Anal Nap," written with only the vowel "a," and perhaps we could discuss Gertrude Stein's "A Dog:"

A little monkey goes like a donkey that means to say that means to say that more sighs last goes …

After thirty minutes of one-way conversation, as the last coat is painted in synchrony on our right pinkies, I ask her about Richard. I hope this will re-open a conversation over Amanda Brock and last Thursday's wine tasting lie. But Christine simply lowers her eyes, in that "Oh, didn't you know?" sort of way. "It got boring, Vera. I told you it would, just sex and nothing in between."

As we leave the spa, and air-kiss hug our goodbyes, I'm reminded of something Marcel said about his taste in women, that he prefers:

sinCERiTY abOVE all FORMS or LOOKS"

"I still don't understand why you need to go. You're tired, and it's such short notice." We were at *Blacksalt* restaurant on MacArthur Boulevard.

I had forgone my usual white underwear, and had dressed for the evening—a matching set of pink bra and panties, topped by a calf-length beige skirt, two silk blouses—white and chocolate brown—and a chiffon wrap to fight the air conditioning. I knew it would be a heavy drinking evening when Raymond suggested taking a cab.

After being seated, we both ordered cocktails before the menu was brought—a Martini, and a Laphroaigh single-malt scotch "with a little ice." This oiled our conversation and, for once, we talked freely of friends and the latest news. We also had glasses of Prosecco with our appetizers, and were half way into a bottle of Californian sauvignon blanc when Raymond broke the news of his London trip. The flight was tomorrow, Sunday, and he would be back "Thursday, possibly Friday." In a sudden avalanche of disclosure he explained that the conference was about carbon regulation, and that it was important.

"The Europeans have a lot of experience, mainly through disappointments," he said, with an oddly gleeful look.

He clearly saw it as an honor to be chosen, but he did show some guilt. His excuse for springing the news so late was that Cyril had only asked him to go the day before.

"If it's important, you should be there," I said. "We'll need to cancel lunch tomorrow so I can help you pack."

After sharing dessert and paying the check my head was spinning. I found myself clinging to Raymond as we waited for the cab. After that it was a silent ride home, the pre-sex ritual of mouthwash and then, as a special surprise, a bottle of lubricant waiting on my pillow—how lovely.

Come join me, please, Mr. Hall. We can watch the garden together as it shades to emerald at dusk.

It's probably one of the last evenings free from the muggy heat of summer and its mosquitoes. For some reason, they seem to prefer my ankles to the brilliant white of Raymond's. He's on his way to London, and I am sitting here with your book by my side, staring in disbelief at the notes from my sessions with Marcel.

Is this also how you think? Do you wander around your tiny office or library counting the beat of your steps? I can't imagine you do. The lines you write don't merely bounce—they flow and dance. And I'm sure your spoken words echo and sing over dinner, captivating your poet friends.

That is not the case with my patient, Marcel. He speaks *always* in solid, iambic pentameter and, even when he answers with more than a single line, it is always the same—bang BANG bang BANG bang BANG bang BANG bang BANG:

each NIGHT i HEAR the SOUNDS withIN the WALLS

You don't believe me, Mr. Hall?

i KNOW she DID not READ it IN a BOOK

And sometimes there are two lines:

> *i ONly HEAR the SOUND of MOving STONES*
> *and NOT the HAppy CHAtter OF the STREAM*

or—

> *it's DIFFiCULT to FIND a TIME to WRITE*
> *my THOUGHTS withIN a PAraGRAPH of PROSE*

What discipline! I have just found a longer statement that I think you'll like. This was in reply to a comment I'd made about his sonnets:

> *they ARE indEED. i CAN'T beLIEVE you READ*
> *aBOUT the SOnnet FORM but, THEN aGAIN,*
> *you SAID you CARED. it IS the SIMplest FORM—*
> *i FIND PetRARCHan SOnnets DIFFiCULT.*

Why is he speaking this way, Mr. Hall? What is its purpose? I can't begin to imagine how hard it must be.

In our last therapy session, Marcel shared some prose he had written just before his mother's death—it was so lyrically wonderful. Having read David Lehman's book on prose poems, prompted by your description of the form (thank you, thank you), I think Marcel's prose may be an example. It even has a "turn" in its last section, when he suddenly addresses his mother. Is there such a thing as a prose-sonnet, Mr. Hall?

I have probably taken up enough of your time for one evening. I will be seeing Marcel tomorrow and, thanks to you, it will be in a new light. I can now understand why he couldn't read his prose-sonnet to me. The following two lines say it all:

> *i CAnnot READ it. CAN you READ it FOR*
> *me? THERE'S a FENCE of WORDS i CAnnot CLIMB.*

It was just a sticker attached to some files—I wasn't prying. I had been rummaging around our home office, trying to find notes on my new, anorexic patient. As I looked behind a stack of Raymond's papers, a small yellow square floated off and settled onto the carpet. I bent down to pick it up.

It was his writing, of course—I recognized the tight, upright loops from his left hand. He had underlined several words in red, and his pen had ripped part of the paper while writing, "get him!"

Raymond is fastidious in never leaving notes behind in meetings. He always reminds younger staff to write emails, "as though you wouldn't mind seeing them on the front page of *The Washington Post*." So this sticker was private, written to himself. That made the anger more disturbing.

When I placed the note back onto his stack, I noticed the article beneath was also covered in red scrawls. Raymond had scribbled, "FUCK" across the title, *Why carbon caps need to be retroactive*. The title seemed innocent enough. But something in this article had clearly angered him.

It is Monday, one minute to nine o'clock as I open my door to find Marcel in the corridor. His arms are crossed over his folder, and he is sitting with brown tie, beige shirt, and scuffed shoes, seemingly unaware that a difficult hour awaits him. It is the first of our new, bi-weekly sessions.

"Good morning, Dr Lewis, how are you?"
he asks, as he enters my office and saunters to his chair.

"I'm well Marcel—lovely of you to ask."

As he moves his folder to one side I can see brown crumbs stuck to the bottom of his shirt. This must be from his morning visit to Starbucks, part of a daily ritual he had once described: a bran muffin for breakfast ("I need a dose of fiber every day"); a take-out salad for lunch; and in the evening, after visiting the library, some protein to end the day.

Upon asking, I learn that his mood has varied this past week, and I wait as he takes the journal from his folder. He may be expecting me to ask about his week's liaisons. But I have already planned something different.

"I've thought about your piece of writing from last week, Marcel. It's like a prose poem. The way it turns towards your mother in the last section is like much of your writing now—a prose-sonnet I would call it. What about us starting today with you reading it to me? Okay?"

He cannot hide his surprise, or his fear, so I add a softener to the blow. "Only the first few lines, just to hear the sound."

He opens the journal, starts to read, and then falters. He tries several times, but always stops immediately after "Young Johnny's father Ben is..." Because I see the panic rising, I intervene in my most modulated tones.

"It is indeed like a fence of words, Marcel—you phrased it well. One day soon you'll be able to jump over it. I could help you now, of course. I could get you to follow me, word for word, until the iambic meter breaks down," and I smile to put him at ease.

"You see, Marcel, I've been trying to learn more about your poetry. I know you write in strict iambic meter, but you also speak this way—very unusual. I suspect this started after your mother died and, if I'm right, perhaps we can find out why."

He is watching me closely, gripping the folder once more, but I am not going to be deflected.

"If we were to read your opening words together, this is what we would say:
    young JOHnny's FAther BEN is a BEAR...
"That "a" really messes up the iambic meter, doesn't it? I can well imagine it's a fence for you."

This is Marcel's moment, and it is a long minute that lapses before he replies.

    "I'd like to find a way to make this work,"
he whispers.

Scooting my chair towards him, I place my hand on his arm. "Then that's what we'll do, Marcel, and we'll do it together."

He then tells me he has had two dates in the last few days, describing one lunch as "most terrible," though it seems more a case of two people not just suited to bond. But he has something else to tell say.

> *"I met a woman Thursday whom I liked.*
> *She is an artist—works by day to pay*
> *her way. And when she speaks she waves her arms,*
> *as though she's drawing pictures in the air."*

This must be the woman he was with at Firefly. I feel a wave of guilt passing over me for spying behind the tree. He tells me her name is Melissa and that they exchanged phone numbers. Though planning to call her, he had lost the small slip of paper. He is angry with himself, but adds philosophically,

> *"Perhaps God thought it would have never worked."*

We both laugh at this.

Preparing to leave, he speaks several lines of verse to thank me once again for caring and that I have tried to learn more about poetry. I say I have a present for him, and pass across another copy of Donald Hall's *To Read a Poem* I had bought over the weekend. In return, he gives me two sonnets copied from his journal. While he is flicking through Hall's book, I glance at a sonnet called "Today at Firefly," and there, in the middle of a line, is the smallest breakdown of the iambic meter. It is like a double step in a dance:

She WAVED her ARMS, PAINting the AIR with WORDS

It was my suggestion to go to meet Dawn at *Firefly*. The tables near the window—where I had seen Marcel—were taken, but we found two stools at the bar, and ordered salads and glasses of wine. After catching up on gossip, she told me about her recent trip to Rwanda. The Bank was completing an external review of public sector efficiency and, in the course of presenting interim findings, had uncovered important new sources of information. As a result, she had extended her stay for a couple of days.

I had heard her stories of chaotic airports and corruption in many African countries, but not so much in Rwanda. She returned there frequently, and had taken on an increasing role in her team's activities. She was the main point of contact with local contractor staff, and often went out into the rural areas.

"The people are so determined to help the country get back on its feet," she said. "Can you imagine us having to cope with all the atrocities these people have seen and experienced? We'd still be basket cases."

It was getting close to the hour, and she needed to be back at a workshop. She had prepared for it over the weekend, and her presentation would be mid-afternoon—comparing Rwanda's health metrics with those of other African countries. But she had a favor to ask for a Rwandan colleague who was working with the government to replace the poor's cooking stoves.

"Because they burn wood and even dung in their huts, most of the women and children have terrible respiratory problems. Modern stoves emit less soot, and they also cut emissions of carbon dioxide by a huge amount. My colleague's a really good guy, a friend really."

A smile told me this was more than a friendship.

"So I was wondering whether Daniel could be brought to the US for a while," she continued. "The Bank prefers locals like Daniel to stay in the field at home. But then I thought you said Raymond was working on climate change."

Dawn and I have known each other a long time. Of course I would have loved to help, but I didn't want to raise her expectations. This was why my guarded reply came out so clumsily.

"I don't know, Dawn. His company is in the lobbying business. There's also the issue of getting a visa, often difficult."

"But couldn't Raymond's company sponsor him? What better way to show how committed it is than to bring in someone who's so knowledgeable about terrible pollution from outmoded cooking stoves."

I promised I'd ask Raymond, again trying my best to play down the chances. As we left, couples were still at tables, some sitting upright as though being interviewed. None were painting circles in the air.

I was walking towards M Street when a lovely thought came to mind, so I turned around to walk north. Because my next patient wasn't until four, there was enough time to visit the Philips Collection.

I have always loved the Philips, with its lunchtime concerts and special exhibits, but it was the permanent collection that drew me in. Some of the paintings were like old friends.

Having climbed the stairs to the first floor, I stood for a long time facing *Luncheon of the Boating Party*. Renoir had included, among his friends, his future wife, and I remember the first time I saw it, startled by the light, by the way the figures seemed so at ease in their gaiety. Raymond also loves the painting, not for its light, form, and balance, but because it reminds him of our early years, surrounded by friends on weekends.

Turning the corner into the north wing, I stopped in my tracks. There before me were two paintings by Georgia O'Keeffe that had remained in the gallery following a major exhibition of her work. One was of a wall of her house in Abiquiu, all flat ochers except for a shadowed door. But it was the other painting that caught my breath.

Called *Above the Clouds*, it is a large work painted from the perspective of someone looking down through pastel blue sky. Her clouds were like tufts of cotton wool. The way they receded to the horizon gave a feeling of the curvature of the earth, of its smallness and intensity. I had seen it many times in magazines and photographs, but I had never felt this sense of wanting to step into the canvas and fly above the clouds.

Walking down the stairs, I almost overlooked a painting by Edward Hopper. It took me a moment to realize that he had also painted the lighthouse and small house on the cover of *To Read a Poem*. What good taste you have, Mr. Hall!

"Hello," I say

It is later, in the evening, and a sudden thunderstorm is rolling by. Raymond had called earlier from London to confirm he would be returning on Thursday, but here is a call from "Unknown." Silently, I thank her for waiting until I was settled, notes written up and glass by my side, just finishing Donald Hall's selection of poems by Adrienne Rich.

"Oh, it's you again, how nice of you to call," I continue.

On the phone I think I can hear the wind above the rumble from the storm outside. Hoping to coax her to speak, I tell her about my afternoon at the Phillips. There is no response. I walk into the kitchen and describe it to her, asking if she also has an espresso machine. There is still no response.

I finally return my chair. Reopening *To Read a Poem*, I decide to read some Adrienne Rich poems to her. I start with "Aunt Jennifer's Tigers," and "A Marriage in the Sixties," before ending with "Women," a shorter poem. Here, Rich describes seeing her sisters as though for the first time, her nervous first sister, the second who has a broken heart, and then:

> *My third sister is gazing*
> *at a dark-red crust spreading westward far out on the sea.*
> *Her stockings are torn but she is beautiful.*

And the phone goes dead.

I have some terrible news—my patient, Julie, died today in the early hours.

She failed to turn up for our session at ten, and I waited until noon before calling her number. A male voice answered and asked who I was. When I said I was her therapist, he requested my address, saying he would visit me sometime between 3:00 and 4:00 with a colleague.

Julie's neighbors, a married couple who shared the third floor, were concerned with the open door to her apartment. After ringing Julie's bell and calling out her name several times over an hour, they had alerted the police around eight this morning.

All the lights were on. The police first found a cat waiting beside an empty dish in the kitchen meowing for food. Julie was lying across her bed. She had taken an overdose, and had left no message or letter.

In my office, a female officer asked most of the questions, while the male I'd talked to on the phone took notes. Several times I had to stop her and say that I couldn't give further information because it was confidential. But I did give my overall assessment of Julie. She didn't seem at risk, I said, although she was clearly depressed.

They confided that early findings suggested she had taken a cocktail of long-expired painkillers and sleeping pills. Normally, this would not have caused death, but she had "other complications"—which they refused to explain—making her hemorrhage. It might be suicide, but it could have been an accident, a cry for help. "People leave the doors open when they want to be saved," she added.

The police had contacted an aunt in Los Angeles through a letter that lay on the floor, and were still trying to locate Julie's mother. The male officer added, before leaving, that, "Her office thought she'd left the city. The strange thing is she'd apparently left all the windows open, even through the storm last night. Most of her things were blown around the room."

Later, Raymond called. I broke down when I told him one of my patients had died. When he heard me crying he said he'd step outside from a cocktail party, reminding me that it was the first patient I'd lost, that I'd been fortunate up to now. At the end of the call he explained he couldn't come home tomorrow after all, but would definitely fly out Friday.

And so here I am at home, trying to see through the haze of Martinis and a sickening glass of white wine. Donald Hall's book lies open where I left it last night. I feel unable to speak, even with him. It is as though he has receded.

They are all receding. Christine sounded shocked but was "tied up" today. Dawn was lost in her Rwandan world; she'd responded simply, "Oh dear." John retreated into his office; maybe Julie had brought back memories of his own clients' deaths. Only Carolyn was there for me, for once in listening mode, her face mirroring my sadness. We downed a late afternoon drink before she had to rush to join her husband. She also called later.

"Take care of yourself tonight, Vera. Try to sleep," she said.

I am trying. Sleep will come later.

I saw only two patients today, Thursday. Both wore the blank faces of blank people. In between, Carolyn dropped by to make sure I was all right, but John was nowhere to be seen. Everyone else was silent, except for a text message from Dawn saying simply, "Thinking of you."

The police called to say they wouldn't need to contact me further, that they had closed the case. They were kind enough to give me the number of Julie's aunt, and we had a difficult conversation. She seemed angry, and kept saying this wasn't her job, that she wasn't Julie's mother. But she did promise she'd contact me once the funeral was arranged, that it would be soon, possibly next week. After that, I cancelled the weekly call to my Baltimore CEO, pushed other sessions to Friday, and left the office around one to nurse myself at home.

The rain started as soon as I stepped outside, and I changed my mind, deciding on impulse to drive to Meridian Park, tucked between 15th and 16th streets. I had read that the summer fountains had just started up. That's where I am now in my long black raincoat, sitting huddled on a bench under an umbrella, watching torrential rain as it spatters the path and pounds the pool's surface to gray foam.

After checking me out, two furtive men have disappeared behind bushes to do a small deal in drugs, I suppose. Part of me gives thanks that I have been noticed. Not today, but on most days, the park is filled with wives with strollers and small, impatient dogs. On weekends, friends play ball on the upper terrace. Sometimes, on a mild evening, and each Sunday starting in the late afternoon, bongo players converge to drum until the light dies.

The sound of the cascade pools drowns out the noise of traffic. I am watching rain as I always did as a girl, trying to trace a single drop out of the sky before it chooses where to land. I used to think that clouds meandered across the sky, waiting for the right time to cry. In New Mexico, you can see storm clouds for miles, stalking across the plains, trailing tendrils of virga like jellyfish.

Julie—could I have known? Was there some sign I should have picked up? They say it could have been just a cry for help. It must have been Julie who had been phoning me these last months, but for what purpose, and why had she never spoken? The last time she called, with her windows open and the wind blowing through her apartment, I had droned on about my day, my kitchen, and my damned espresso machine. And then I had recited Adrienne Rich's poems, ending with "Women" and that mysterious final line, "Her stockings are torn but she is beautiful." What had I been thinking? The park has no answers. Even the birds have become silent in the rain.

Suddenly, the raindrops begin to slow to single fat spats, and small patches of blue sky break through. Two joggers run past me, up the winding steps parallel to the falls. Birds begin their chatter, squirrels hop out ever hopeful, and sunlight arcs across the trees. As the rush hour traffic begins its hum beyond the park, a lone drummer starts to play, single notes as long as heart beats.

Bang   Bang   Bang   Bang   Bang

Perhaps there was no cellphone coverage in the park, I thought as I drove home. Or perhaps Raymond had left a message for me at the practice, because the message-waiting light when I reached home was dead.

Counting out the hours, I know it is late evening in London. He is staying at the Marriott, on the south bank of the Thames. I remember passing it on our way to the London Eye a few years back when we took a rare overseas vacation. I was terrified when we rose up over the city in one of the glass pods.

Where are you tonight, Raymond? Have you packed your bags and sorted out your business cards, laid your travel clothes across a chair, and squeezed the last gob of toothpaste onto your vibrating brush?

Me? Oh I'm fine. What's that in my hand? It's a Waterford lead crystal glass, my love, a wedding present, filled with the last of your twelve year-old Highland Park. I'm so sorry, dear. It's almost finished.

"I'm glad you're enjoying Mr. Hall's book, Marcel. We'll have to find some time to talk about it, but—"
   "I like the way he takes apart their words
   and opens up the layers. It's as though,
   they wrapped their thoughts for all of us to find
   in subtle rhymes and ambiguity,"
he interjects.

We are in the welcoming phase of our Friday morning session. We have already spoken of Marcel's dates—he has confessed to arranging only one for the week—later this afternoon—and even though, through this lapse, he "could run the risk of falling far behind," there is a sense of ease in his words, in the way he slowly writhes into the chair, enlarging his mold.
   "I'm ready once again to face the wrath,"
he says of his forthcoming date, raising his right fist high in mock defiance.

"Lovely, Marcel. Have you had any further thoughts about Monday's conversation?"
   "The only thing I realized was how
   you'd done so much to understand the way
   I write and, as you said, the way I speak.

But after that I pushed the thought away,"
he replies.

I had already decided to pace this session better, to build up gradually.

"I want to understand what motivates your writing. You've said you spend most evenings at the public library. Do you read only poetry, or do you have other interests?"

"It's mainly poetry—I'm half way through
the letter G. But in between I like
to read great science fiction—not the junk,
but classics: Heinlein, Asimov, Le Guin."

I ask him, why science fiction? He admits it lets him escape both past and present. I want to tell him that it is the same for me with mystery novels.

"I have an idea next time you're in the library," I decide to say instead. "It's something I did when I was young. In the poetry section, run your finger across the rows of books until it stops. Pick that title to read. I was always amazed, as though it was the book that was finding *me*."

His brown eyes have opened wider—perhaps he is as surprised as me that I've shared something from my past.

"So, let's start with your journal. Have you written any more sonnets and, if so, what are they about?"

"You're thinking that because I've had no dates
so far this week I must have written sonn-
nets that reveal much more about myself
than all the ones I've shown to you before."

I decide to start peeling. "Something like that, Marcel. But before we look at the journal, I have a question. What were you thinking when you wrote that beautiful prose piece about the river? What was going through your mind?"

He places his journal to the side, uncrosses his legs, and thinks for a while. He seems to be weighing up the risks of saying too little or too much.

"I wanted to describe the way it felt,
the way the river lived within itself,
the rush and peace, the way the mind can dwell
upon a rock with no one there to scream."

"And who would be screaming, Marcel?"

"It's just a world of fantasy, that's all,"

he says, as though this were an ending statement. But I am not going to let him off the hook.

"In the middle of this fantasy, you suddenly turn to your mother." I wait, but it's clear he's not going to speak.

"You said you didn't want to tell her about fighting the fish, which seemed to be speaking to you when you held it. What was it trying to say, Marcel?"

"I never try to listen to a fish,"
he replies sarcastically, writhing now.

"The only sound you hear is the blood in your ears. It's that beating sound again, and the only walls are those of the canyon. So we are back to sounds within walls, Marcel—aren't we?"

He glowers at me.

"Not long after your mother died, this flowing prose of yours stopped. You started writing in iambic meter and speaking the same way. Why are you doing this, Marcel? Does it protect you? Does it keep memories inside? Why can't you open up now?"

That last phrase does it. His eyes widen, he jumps up, opens his arms, and starts to shout.

"Why can't I open up? That's what I've heard
for all my life—why can't I open up?
And now you say the same to me, and there
I was believing that you really cared!"

He walks past me, hesitates, opens the door. "I told you it would be difficult," I say to his back. "Hope to see you Monday." He is gone, clutching the journal to his chest.

"So Julie's funeral's on Tuesday—that's quick. Her mother won't be there?"

It's just Carolyn and me, Friday afternoon. John is with a new patient. Several minutes ago my muted smartphone blinked with a message from Raymond that he had landed. Carolyn has wrapped up her summary of her patients, my few comments already typed into the yellow spreadsheet column reserved for our weekly debriefs. I have started my own summary.

"Julie's aunt wasn't sure she could find her mother. Even the San Diego police haven't been able to trace her."

"Such a tragedy, Vera. I hope you don't think there was anything more you could have done. You helped her enormously."

I still have Julie's spare checkbook in my purse. I have promised to sit with the aunt to help her close out any affairs.

"What have you been doing for yourself the last couple of days? It must have been hard with Raymond away," she continues.

"Oh, this and that. I dropped into Meridian Park yesterday on the way home. I just needed a break, Carolyn, and it was so pleasant sitting there in the rain. And then to take my mind off things I read some prose poems in the evening. This morning, I had an important session with Marcel."

"Vera, before we start talking about Marcel, I'd like to raise a concern. John and I are worried over how involved you're getting with Marcel. Is there something more going on?"

"Don't worry—I'm totally aware of the transference risk. I know I'm spending a lot time trying to understand him through poetry, but it's something I've always loved. So no, nothing's going on.

I begin to talk through Monday's session. She seems fascinated to learn about the role of beat and meter in Marcel's life—in his writing, the way he speaks, even his choice of music. She agrees it must serve a purpose, that it may have been triggered by his mother's death. She suggests I check out the concept of entrainment, and I make a note. I also tell her about Marcel's positive date with Melissa, and that he later lost her phone number.

"Intentionally, I suspect. Though he may not realize it. He's just not ready," Carolyn says, emphatically.

I turn to my second session of the week with Marcel earlier in the day. We agree that my call for him to "open up" awakened something that he then directed at me. Carolyn urges me to be alert at the next session, on Monday.

"Remember, it's when they give a reply that's at odds with what you're discussing—that's the sign," she says. This is an area of professional specialism for Carolyn—she has lectured on this many times, as she is now doing with me. "It could be a huge leap, Vera, but sometimes it's the smallest tangential shift, often with a change in tone, voice, or even posture. It just needs to be 'not right' for the moment, if you know what I mean."

We postpone Friday drinks. Raymond will be home soon, and Carolyn has a pre-performance dinner at the Kennedy Center with her husband and two friends. As we are leaving, she turns and grips my arm.

"Vera, whenever you want to talk about the effect patients are having on you, I'm always here. By the way, did you know that Carl Jung once wrote an essay on art and poetry?"

As she opens the door, a fire-truck screams by, lights flashing. I cup my hands to my ears.

"Hi! Are you home?"

I find Raymond in the bedroom, shirts and pants separated into one pile, underwear and socks to another.

"Hello, darling," he says, squeezing out a slug of hand sanitizer. "Long trip, but the worst was those awful buses, and now I have another reason to hate the name Dulles."

I go over, kiss him on his lowered head, and bend down to pick up a pile of laundry.

"So how was the week? Come downstairs and tell me how it went."

I pour a wine for myself, and a glass of Springbank scotch for Raymond. He still has that musty airline smell clinging to him, and his clothes are ruffled from "an hour's sleep" on the cross-Atlantic flight.

"I'm really glad I went. Lots of senior contacts, and some great stories about carbon trading fuckups," he replies. "In London, the important people are 'Sir this' or 'Dame that.' They're all sudden experts in climate change and carbon, without any real solutions."

We eat a light salad—he ate his fill on the flight. By 8:30 he is starting to droop. I sit on the bed while he brushes his teeth, and then tell him I will stay up awhile. As he ties his pajama bottoms, and pulls the sheets back, he finally asks me how my week has been.

"Challenging." I'm surprised by my understatement.

"Glad you've been able to take it in your stride," he says, sleepily.

I settle in the living room and decide to pamper myself with Puchini's *Turandot*, turning down the volume. *To Read a Poem* is by my side, but I will not open it tonight. I have enough emotions swirling inside and, even if I had wanted to talk with Mr. Hall, I have nothing to say. But I imagine Marcel is already in conversation with him, studying Chapter 7. Perhaps, like me, he is occasionally running ahead to the later sections. What would he do if he reached Dylan Thomas' "Fern Hill," with its magical cadences? He certainly couldn't read it out loud.

My smartphone rings twice, and I rush to answer. "Unknown" is calling. I place the phone to my ear, hand shaking, and again there is the low wind behind the silence. "Who *is* this?" I find myself shouting. "It can't be you, it can't be—don't ever call me again, ever!"

"What do you mean, you have to go out?" Raymond asked the next morning when I told him I was leaving to meet Carolyn for coffee. "I've been away all week. I want you here."

He'd been up an hour, jet-lagged and still unshaven. After too many drinks last night, and regrets over ending the call, I had phoned Carolyn, admitting I needed to talk.

"Something's come up, Raymond. Don't worry. I'll be back for lunch. Perhaps we can do something this—"

"Afternoon, or evening, or whatever time suits." He swiveled around to face his laptop.

I parked in a side-street and walked into *Kramer's* by the front entrance, squeezed my way past the browsers, and found my way into the rear cafe to wait for Carolyn. She arrived within minutes and spoke before sitting down saying, "So what's up?" I took a breath and closed my eyes.

"Something happened last night—something strange and awful."

I told her about the phone calls I'd been receiving from "Unknown," when they started, and how they shifted from our landline to my smartphone. I said I was certain it was a woman, even though she never spoke, and that there was always wind blowing in the background.

"I got one of these calls just before Julie died. To keep the conversation going, I read the last lines of a poem that was...well...disturbing. It was about a girl with torn stockings who was beautiful. I wanted to imply that, no matter how desperate we are, there's always beauty in us.

"When the police said Julie had all her windows open, I was certain it had been her calling. I felt terrible about reading the poem. You see, it wasn't just the loss of her dying—I felt I'd caused it. You always told me that, for some, suicide, was a last chance to regain dignity, but—"

"If she'd wanted to talk, she would have," Carolyn interrupted.

"But here's the thing. I was wrong. It wasn't Julie calling. Last night, after Raymond went to bed, I got the same blocked call, with the same wind in the background."

She pushed back her short hair. "So what did you say?"

"I know this sounds crazy, but I thought it was Julie again. I was in a panic, and I got...well...angry, and told whoever it was never to call again."

By now I was shaking. Carolyn waited a few seconds and then said, "Well it wasn't her, Vera. Have you contacted the police?"

I told her I'd had enough of police these last weeks. Besides, whoever was calling had a reason. Carolyn had a thought.

"Do you think it's Marcel?

Taken aback, I answered, "No. Why would you think that?"

"Vera, I told you yesterday I'm worried about you, and you explained what's behind your sudden interest in poetry. But I just wonder what Marcel makes of it. Maybe he senses more than a therapist trying to understand a patient. Maybe he's becoming infatuated with the first person to show real care for him.

"I don't think it's Marcel," I found myself replying, with more certainty than I felt. "At the moment, he's too fragile to even think of—"

"Don't be so sure, but if it's not Marcel, it's someone," she said, with some finality. "And on Marcel, I've been thinking about this issue of opening up. Vera, you've set him the task of de-sensitizing. But it's really about him loosening shackles and being himself, and he's doing well. There's something about what's happening to him that...that...is resonating with you."

And as much as I didn't want to admit it, she was right.

"Listen to me," Carolyn said, dabbing her lips with a handkerchief. "You keep talking of trying to understand Marcel. What you're really doing is trying to understand yourself. We've known each other over ten years, but I can't recall you ever sharing something personal with me. Am I right? Who are your friends, what do you feel, what do you really think about? What are your memories, the ones that matter? I'm partly to blame because I don't ask. I'll give you an example.

"I love the way you dress, the colors, the way you combine so many layers. But I've long wondered whether this was your way of covering up."

"But that's so crap, so full of crap, so full of—" I started pushing croissant crumbs towards my lap.

"Here's the thing, my darling" Carolyn said, placing her hand next to my cup. "You've reached a nexus. These phone calls may mean nothing, but Marcel does mean something—he is a mirror to you. Even more, listen to what *you* say, what *you* do, and ask yourself why."

I thanked her for being so frank, but she wasn't finished.

"I'm worried because you seem to be struggling. You see we often get drawn into what our patients are feeling. We know we have to back off, to be objective—we're trained to do this. But sometimes we see things in our patients that touch something within us."

"Like what?" I asked.

"It's clear you care for Marcel, and you've told me that he's awakened a love of poetry in you. But there's a risk you could see aspects of him, or the things he's struggling with, that are touching places *you* don't want to go. You have to face them, Vera. If you don't, you're letting your patient down, the practice, and yourself."

I suppressed the urge to shout into her face, "I don't need this!" But I knew that she was being sincere.

"So what do I do?"

Carolyn stroked an invisible ripple from the tablecloth. "You have to be alert to anything a patient says or does that sets something off inside you. Recognize it, write it down, but don't let it stop you working for that patient. Maybe we should meet more regularly. Not as therapy. Let me be your mentor. I have a slot most Wednesdays at two."

I hesitated only for a moment.

"All right, Carolyn. Thank you!"

It was almost eleven before we left the table, sidled past the literary conversations at the bar, and made our way to the door. As we reached the hassled guy at the register, I found myself confronting a figure with tousled brown hair, holding a book aloft.

"Marcel, how lovely to see you. This is Carolyn."

> *"It's very good to see you. Sorry that*
> *I left so quickly yesterday. I'm pleased*
> *to meet you, Carolyn. I am a friend*
> *of Doctor Lewis. She's been helping me."*

Carolyn shook his hand, and I glanced his book—*Collected Poems, 1934-1953*, by Dylan Thomas.

It is a beautiful Sunday, with light wind and that faint truffle scent of humidity before summer's heat. Raymond and I are once again sitting on the deck of *Cantler's Riverside Inn* overlooking the creek. Several boats have broken its calm on their way out to Chesapeake Bay. Two beers sit in a bucket of ice, and our laps and hands are covered in crab flesh, sweet and sticky.

Raymond, close to being relaxed, sits rearranging the broken shells of crabs into small piles. I decide to bring up Dawn's Rwandan friend, Daniel, but Raymond cuts me off.

"No, I don't think it's a good idea to bring him here. He should stay in Rwanda where he'll do the most good."

I crack a crab claw with a wooden mallet, harder than is probably necessary. As I wipe a strand of hair from my eyes with the back of my hand, I feel my pulse rising. There is a chance to make a difference for Daniel, and so I try again.

"I promised Dawn I'd mention it. She thought it could be an interesting angle for what you're doing—having someone with experience of the front-line."

Raymond puts down his mallet, wipes his mouth, folds the paper tissue twice onto a growing pile, and stares at me.

"Rwanda is not in the front line, Vera. The United States is, plus China, and India. Countries like Rwanda can do whatever they want, but it's what we do that matters. The last thing we want is for some do-gooder with no experience of the politics involved to go sounding off."

An adjacent table erupts in laughter, a large group of friends out for an afternoon of fun and gentle ribbing.

I decide to drop Dawn's idea. We are arms deep in crabs and broken shells and I don't want to break anything else. I decide to change the subject. Perhaps I should talk about that day, with Christine, on this very deck, the way David bounced up the steps from his small launch, his hair matted with salt. We could laugh at the look in Christine's eyes as he walked past, and how he found an excuse to later join our table. But I don't.

"No problem—I'll tell her. You haven't told me much about the London conference. What did you learn, and what were the fuckups? Oops, excuse me on a Sunday."

"It's complicated, but here's the gist. Too many carbon credits were issued and so their value dropped. But the regulators weren't ready either. So a lot of companies, and some countries, cheated. The lesson is Europe jumped too fast, without thinking about it, just too damned fast."

"But isn't there some kind of urgency in all this? From what I've read, we need to act quickly. Some say it may even be too late. All those melting glaciers and—"

He picks up his mallet and slams it down on a claw. The sound rides over conversations, and several people turn to look at us.

"Look, it's not that simple," he says, in his office voice. "The consensus is the climate's changing, and we may be the cause. But you've got to think about the private sector's point of view. Companies—and nothing happens without them—have to be incentivized to do things. Getting that right is what we're all striving towards. If it takes a lifetime, so be it."

"Is that what you believe? That we have all the time in the world and the most important thing is to protect industry?"

He takes his bottle from the bucket, swigs down the remaining beer, and tells me with finality, "It's not what I think. It's what industry thinks. Check please."

I stare at my feet.

That evening, Raymond told me he just wanted to sleep. Still awake, beyond the time when the clock still moved, I listened to the ceiling fan blades as they beat their way around the room. Exhausted, I slid out of the sheets and found my bathrobe on the floor. Closing the door, I stepped downstairs and into the kitchen, poured myself yet another wine, and settled down to read several poems from Donald Hall's book.

It may have been the accumulation of wine, or the discord at lunch, but I found myself unable to focus on a single line. Even Frost's "Stopping by Woods on a Snowy Evening" failed to keep me interested. Eventually, I went back to bed, although the night seemed longer than a week.

When I awoke at six-fifteen, I dressed for the gym, but packed my day clothes in my large tote bag. It took some time to find my second boot, but by then Raymond had opened his eyes. I left with a cheerful cheerio.

I had no intention of working out. I wanted to be alone at the practice, something I had never done before. I drove directly downtown, and reached a still-locked building just after seven o'clock. I changed clothes quickly, and settled down to closely read my notes from each of the sessions with Marcel. Today's meeting would be very difficult since I now had two people to monitor—Marcel, and myself.

Two minutes to nine…."Hello, Marcel, please come in."

He carries no folder today. In the morning's heat he has draped his jacket over his shoulder, held by a finger.

"What a surprise to see you Saturday," I say, as he settles into his usual pose of a wary prisoner.

"I was surprised as well to see you both,
but then I guess you gossip on weekends,"
he replies, without a hint of humor.

So he did recognize Carolyn. I decide not to react.

"Yes, funny bumping into each other like that. I couldn't help noticing the book of poems by Dylan Thomas. It reminded me to ask you something."

"And what is that—what question do you have?"
Marcel replies, in his iambic pentameter.

"I wonder how you can read Dylan Thomas' poetry. The meter is so irregular in places. I didn't know you could read anything that wasn't in strict meter."

He slowly uncurls from his moment of tension. His hunched shoulders unfold, his arms uncross, and his legs begin to straighten. I can now see two holes, one in each sole of his shoes.

"When I am reading words I never say
them to myself. They stay inside my brain."

"That's wonderful. You've managed to find a way over your fence of words. Have you written anything over the weekend? I see you didn't bring your journal."

He tells me he hasn't written any more long entries, though he had been motivated on several occasions. I ask him when and why, and his replies seem evasive. I decide not ask again. I want to see if the silence will prompt him to say something, perhaps something unexpected, one of those "tangential" comments that Carolyn mentioned. But he merely stares, moving his head slightly from side to side, until I relent with a small cough.

We talk about his date last Friday that, he is proud to say, lasted almost ninety minutes. He knew because, for the last half an hour, he had looked at his watch repeatedly. The young woman, far from being irritated, was moved to even longer responses to his questions. At the end of the lunch, she insisted on splitting the check, writing her phone number on the customer receipt. He later tossed it into a trash bin.

We are halfway through our session when I ask how he felt at the end of our last meeting and since. I let him steam in silence for a few seconds.

"But you came back this morning, didn't you? Do you come here for comfort, Marcel, or for punishment?"

He tenses his arms, as though he is going to rise from his chair. I press on.

"If you keep returning, you must be getting something from our sessions. Or perhaps something you'd *like* to get out of them, even if you don't know what. Like I said last week, it may be your chance to open up, to—"

And then it comes, this small aside:

"I bet ya open up furrill yerself."

His sudden reversion to a Pittsburgh accent is surprising. Does he mean that I am also reserved, that I too need to open up, or is it perhaps the opposite? He says it quietly, almost slyly, with a leer I haven't seen before. It is deeply disconcerting, but I have to maintain the momentum.

"That's a strange phrase, Marcel. But this isn't about me, it's about you."

He looks startled, almost stricken, and then his demeanor changes. His hands curl into small fists, and the muscles on his jawline tighten. He is like a bottle about to explode.

"It's not about you, it's about her. You
are just like him — he never asked, just pushed!"

Just one half inch Marcel, just one half inch and you'll be there…

Sweat moistens his top lip, and the color in his face starts to drain. He almost seems translucent. The final turn of the screw…

"What did you hear, Marcel? Tell me what you heard in the walls? Tell me about the sounds, tell me about—"

And then he is there, head jerking and body heaving, speaking slowly in his normal monotone until the words tumble out, as though he were possessed.

> *"She never screamed. She never made a noise*
> *before she died. She never made a noise,*
> *even when she had to open up…*
> *she never made a sound. She opened when*

he opened.

> *"Walls are made to hide the sounds, but the walls*
> *let the sound seep through before she died.*
> *"She never made a sound. I never heard*

her screams in the walls after she died.

"After she died, the walls would scream. The walls screamed before the light went out…and then it was just thumping, thumping sounds, and I thought I could hear her sobbing, even when I cupped

> *my hands to my ears, thumping sobs and screams.*
> *The screams, so many screams, so many screams."*

Words and tears are now pouring out of him, and he is thumping his fist down on his knee with each stress of his voice. It is hard not to concentrate on the fist, to watch the way its steady rhythm has changed into a tumbling set of punches, moving in and out of a regular beat, faster and faster.

> *"Then you, you tell me I must open up,*
> *you fucking tell me I must open up…*
> *when all the time that's what he did. Each night*
> *he came home drunk, opened her up, and fucked*

her against the walls.

"I remember hoping it was her head he was bashing against the wall, because that way she'd fall unconscious. In the morning, no one would say anything. She would just be there, shuffling around the kitchen in her slippers, trying not to look at me. I tried not to look at her but, most of all, I

> *avoided him when he came down the stairs.*

"If...
            I didn't catch his eye I didn't have
to say anything. It was just fucking cowardice, wasn't it? I could've asked, all innocent like, 'What was all that noise last night?' But I didn't even say that, didn't even have the guts to ask that.

            "So here he is one morning, ranting on
            about some thing, saying that I should get
out more, get a job, play with the guys in the street, put on some muscle. I'm reading and she's washing up, and he says, 'That's the trouble with you, just like your mother—you need to open up more.' I want to get up and hit him, but I just sit there, and the pictures start flashing. He's forcing himself on her, forcing himself in, and she's lying there, and
            her legs are opened wider than her eyes.

"Each night, if he'd hadn't had his fill of that whore he later brought into the house, he'd stagger home, stumble up the stairs and fall into the bedroom. He'd pull the sheets back without the decency of even taking off his clothes, and open her legs with one arm while
            pulling out that pig-iron dick of his.
            She never said a word, and when he ent-
            ered her and slammed the bed to the wall
            she never screamed...she never screamed even
when he bruised her deep inside.

"And good old me, her doting son who worshipped the ground she shuffled over, who led her to her piano bench where she could heal and forget, who read her...who read her stories, who read her poetry, who wrote about beautiful places for her, who would have done anything for her, who would do anything to have her back, this son did nothing. This spineless, shitless shit. And the way he looked at me at the funeral, like I was a wad of trash, worthless.

"When I first heard them,
            that very night, they wouldn't go away.
            I couldn't stop the screams and so I drowned
            them out with anything that had a beat
            to cover up her voice until she tired.

"She wouldn't take the pain killers. The last time he raped her was in her final week. Her cervix must've been the size of a grapefruit.

"She died when I was at school. She'd told me not to be late for class, but he was pissed, said, 'Just typical, books before your mother, never around when she needs you.' That really cut me up. That was before I went in and saw her lying there, all grey, even her lips. That's when I saw my essay by the bed, what you called a prose poem. It was crumpled, as though she'd squeezed it in a fist. There were smudge marks around some words that made me think she'd traced them with her fingers. But it was the writing at the bottom that I mostly noticed. She'd written in pencil, each letter at a different angle, shaky and uncertain, except for her words, 'I'd like to go there one day.'

"I went to live with my friend, Johnny. His father, Ben, would always ask me if I wanted to go fishing with him. But I couldn't go back to that place, not without her—it would have been another betrayal, you see. I also knew I wouldn't be able to control the river sounds, the way they would bubble up and around any beat I tried to keep. I knew that if I lost control of the beats I'd be ambushed by the voices, that she'd have screamed for help from the canyon walls.

"So I kept turning Ben down. I guess he thought I'd just turned off fishing, like it was a fad I'd dropped. It wasn't the fishing. It was Penns Creek.

"In all those years I never really wanted to touch my girlfriend, Susan. If she opened her legs, I'd feel sick. I know she thought I was just shy, at least at first. It used to drive her crazy, and she would do all kinds of things to get me going...you know, things.

"*I know she didn't read it in a book.*

I know she did not read it in a book."

The only sounds now are deep breaths from a young man damaged beyond anything I could have imagined. He seems to have lost weight in the last twenty minutes, and his eyes have sunk deeper into sockets hidden behind wet curls of hair.

Before I can say anything he suddenly comes alive, transformed into a man of purpose, bristling and busy. He looks at his watch. I do the same. He raises himself up, brushes invisible crumbs off his trousers, and runs his other hand and fingers through his hair.

> *"It's almost ten! I've overstayed my time.*
> *Forgive me, but I've got to go to work."*

Avoiding my eyes, he is gone. I walk quickly around the room, trying to recall every detail so that I can write accurate notes. Looking down on M Street, I watch Marcel actually running. I'm still hyperventilating.

I saw two patients later in the morning before a catch-up lunch with Dawn. I didn't have the heart to tell her about Raymond's reaction to her suggestion, and I invented some excuse over not having had time. But my mind was elsewhere.

Carolyn dropped by in the afternoon as I was writing up my notes to ask about my session with Marcel. She was in a hurry after a call from a patient's mother and was jamming papers into her briefcase as she spoke. I told her it had gone well, "as expected," and that I had to capture everything that was said. But my pulse was still racing.

On the way home, I drove along an avenue of elms, repeatedly passing through their shadows into fleeting bands of sunlight. I remember thinking this is what it is like—the sudden flash of a memory rising up, the urge to rush forward to drown it out, searching for the glimmer of light, to be someone else.

When I got to the house, I fixed a quick dinner for Raymond. I watched him tease apart a tuna salad with a fork as I asked about his day, reciting the latest news from NPR, talking, and talking. After he disappeared into our office, I decided to take my wine outside. I felt the need to sit down and try to think. That is when I began to write in a blue-lined notebook that someone had given me several years ago.

What you have been reading, what you will read, is my journal. The first two words I wrote were *MARCEL MALONE*, as though I needed to reassure myself I would write only about him. This is why my earliest entry, but not the first I wrote, was of a session with him, our ninth, when he lay curled up on the floor of my office. I remember how tentative and stilted my initial words sounded, how impersonal, unsympathetic, and wooden were my thoughts and observations. Perhaps they're still like this.

Over time, I have gone back and added details, from my notes and, as you will see, from Marcel's own journal. But I have never changed the words I entered that Monday night. I have kept them as much for what they don't say, as though, even in the first opening of my personal iris, I was still blind to what was inside. This is what I wrote:

My name is Vera Lewis. Twelve years ago I married my husband, Raymond. When we first met I was inwardly shy but outwardly gregarious, and it seemed that everything he or others said would make me laugh.

I have never taken his name—Watson seems so full of questions. I regret to say this has been my only act of defiance to his parents. As for Raymond, he defied his father twice—in marrying me, and in his choice of career.

Here is what I am like. Some say I'm pretty, though I'm too short to be beautiful. I often wear my hair long on weekends but braid it during the week. I like the ritual of braiding my hair without a mirror—it allows me to sense my mother's hands for a few minutes at the start of a working day. I dislike asking questions, even though that is my job as a psychotherapist. I have only lost one patient. Tomorrow is her funeral, and I will wear layers of black.

Like my two colleagues, Carolyn and John, I am childless. I have never tried or not tried to get pregnant. I guess I should be grateful because I wouldn't want a son. Besides, Raymond has never wanted a child—"too much mess and clutter," he once said. His mother regularly hints to Raymond that she would like a grandchild. She never does this with me. In fact, she rarely addresses me directly.

Tonight the tiger mosquitoes are out—those small ones you can't see. I hear them around my ears. If I'm being truthful, and I know I should be, I would say that I could never have imagined ending up in Washington, DC, or any other city for that matter. When I was young, my horizons were mountains. The day I left home for college it surprised everyone and, even though I was determined never to return, I know that my past held me by a tenuous thread for several years. I think that's now broken.

I have two close girlfriends, Dawn and Christine, both of whom I met at Georgetown University. I feel they use me, but I am used to this. Like me, they have changed over the years. Dawn is now twice the size of the studious girl I first met, despite her regular workouts. She has grown in other ways, though. She owns a house in Columbia Heights and holds a senior position at the World Bank. She is still insecure. Christine, by contrast, has shrunk physically and mentally, but I still love her.

I never remember my dreams, although Raymond told me once I mutter in my sleep. I'm not sure I know him any more. When he is the person I first met there is a sense of calm within me, but I see this version of him rarely. Instead, these days he seems to be full of frustration and impatience. I suspect he regrets marrying me.

Sometimes, I don't like who I have become, but then I have chosen to become that person. I used to care about everything and everyone. This is now rare, at least on the surface. Perhaps the problem is my work. Perhaps.

I have started reading poetry again. It captures my mind and gives my life some sense of rhythm. In my early teens, it seemed as though poetry surrounded me— I loved listening to it spoken aloud.

I enjoy natural places and wind, although I am terrified of heights. Someone has recently been calling me from a place with wind. I hope the voice belongs to someone alive.

I normally don't allow myself to be sensitive, but lately things have started bearing down on me. There are things that seem to put me off balance, though only for a moment. Criticism is one, but I guess that's not unusual. Another is…how should I describe it? I dearly love my time alone, but I also feel alone—not physically, but inside. My colleague, Carolyn, thinks I should open up more. I have to protect myself.

I work out, not every day, but several times a week. I eat little and often, although I am probably drinking too much. When I met Raymond I never drank alcohol.

Several of my patients do not really need therapy—they are at various crossroads in their lives, whether they know it or not. Others have more serious problems. Marcel is one. I am very fond of him, and he is making progress. He…he unbalances me.

I need to talk to someone. I have many secrets.

Did Julie want cremation? Her aunt thought so, although there had been no will, nor any sign of her mother's whereabouts. The aunt was a nightmare, with that small dog tucked under her arm, yapping like a purse snapping open and shut.

Several friends and family—another aunt, and three cousins—attended. Like Julie, they were all heavyweights, squeezed in three to an aisle with no space between, like one large heaving shape with three heads. They dabbed their eyes constantly, sniffling and coughing whenever a small gap of silence emerged. And, after the memorial service ended, when the minister had spoken his solemn words, except the ones that mattered—that here was a woman ignored by all, that she had not lived a life—we walked out into the heat.

Her aunt was polite but impersonal. Like many survivors of suicides, her irritation suggested everyone else was to blame for her niece's death, including me. To the cousins—all women—I had merely said I was "a friend," but most knew I had been Julie's therapist and acted out their quiet suspicions.

As we drifted apart, what small conversations there had been had slowly died away. By the time I slammed my Golf's door shut and watched her friends and family drive away, there appeared to be nothing left of Julie.

Afterward, I felt the need to talk, but both Dawn and Christine were busy. Carolyn was always back-to-back with patients on Tuesdays, so I would have wait until the next afternoon to speak with her—just as well given my hangover the next morning.

I started drinking as soon as I got to the house—vodka over ice, no smell. Raymond arrived home around 7:00 and by then I was just happy. I started bouncing around and babbling nonstop to him until he told me, frankly, to stop. It must have taken him no more than seconds to realize I was quite drunk.

We ate in silence, a chicken salad with anchovies, washed down with a dry Sancerre. I kept waiting for him to ask about the funeral. I wanted to talk about it, and I even tried to start a conversation before choking on the first or second word. As I opened a new bottle, thankfully a screw cap, he said, "Don't you think you've had enough?"

I was confused at first. I thought, ridiculously, that he was empathizing with what I had been going through these last days, and that perhaps he understood.

"I'm going to the garage for a while," he announced, probably just to get away. "I forgot to clean the trowels."

He was gone less than ten minutes before I heard the door to the garage open and close. There was the sound of running water and then silence. After a few moments, the latch of the cupboard below the sink gave a small click and water started flowing again. The latch clicked once more. This probably meant he had returned his kitchen nailbrush to its plastic container.

I was pouring vodka into my wine glass when he walked into the living room. I was in that dream state, between numbness and the edges of thoughts. I wanted to dance, with the walls of the room, even the shelves of CDs.

"Vera, you've had enough. Put the glass down," he said, continuing into the office. I followed him.

I watched him unlock his desk while his laptop started up. I saw him separate papers and notes from his briefcase before setting them onto a small pile of documents in a side-drawer. I bit my lower lip and, as my breathing slowed, I found anger rising in my throat.

"What does 'had enough' mean to you Raymond?" I had no idea what I meant by this. "I haven't 'had enough' in years."

"Meaning?" he replied with a sigh.

"Meaning, I haven't had enough attention for years. It might be OK for you to just come home and say hello as you wait for me to ask about your day, then sit in the living room or hide away in our office—night after night—until you decide whether you want to fuck. But one day it'd be good if you just wanted to hold me, said you loved me."

I am someone whose memory is not affected by alcohol. I've awoken many times so parched you'd figure the first thing I'd think of was water. Instead, every detail would return and, as each word formed itself, it would become harder and harder to swallow. Did I really say that?

As you can imagine, a hangover dominated my early morning. Raymond left me in my mildew-smelling sheets without even kissing my cheek. When I eventually rolled to the edge of the bed, and lifted myself into my bathroom, my head was a ringing gong.

Thankfully, my first appointment was a phone session. I had been treating Gordon off and on for some time. Nothing had really changed. He still claimed to be racked with remorse over his long-term affair. As always, I asked about his feelings of guilt. He gave the same answer—what a good mother his wife was—and I would have replied if I hadn't been swilling down another two ibuprofen. And so Gordon started filling the silence. As he spoke he left so many hints and asides and openings. He even repeated a small slip and, with only minutes left, my brain suddenly cleared, and I mumbled, "So it's your mother then?" As the session ended he was crying inconsolably. "She stayed with him no matter, just for us...out of loyalty to us...and I'm letting her down, like I always did."

Finally, it is afternoon—two fifteen to be precise, and Carolyn and I are into our first mentoring session. "So Marcel's 'opening up' was sexual," Carolyn says. "His dad raped his mom, and he needs to drown out the sounds. How interesting."

We had started our meeting by talking about Julie's funeral. I told her how depressing the whole thing was, that no one seemed to have known Julie or even cared. She told me I looked pale, and asked if anything was wrong.

"After the service I went home and had a bit too much to drink, I'm afraid. Pretty bad really...and I didn't behave well with Raymond."

She resisted the temptation to ask the obvious question—I think she understood—and suggested we talk about Marcel instead. "How was he on Monday?"

She listens closely to my description of the session with him, right down to his running away. As I flick through my notes I catch Carolyn's familiar scent. Perhaps it is the same antiseptic soap our headmistress used, the way she ruled the classroom on days our teacher fell sick, dropping rare words of praise like raindrops in a drought.

In a break in my narrative, Carolyn compliments me in how I waited and listened to Marcel, and how I let his emotions pour out without interruption.

"We both know he's likely to miss the next session," she continues. "But tell me how you felt."

"I was pleased, of course. He finally opened up and—"

"Yes, those two words again—opening up," she interrupts. "So I'll ask again. How did *you* feel in the session? What does 'opening up' mean to *you*?"

Even though we have couched these meetings as mentoring, this one feels like a therapist-to-patient session, like the role-playing I had to endure at Georgetown.

"Well, when he first reacted to it—"

"Vera, I don't want to hear what Marcel thought. This is about you."

"I know, but…well…it sounded innocent at first, but it's clear he—"

Carolyn stops me with a finger in the air. "Again."

"In the context of what we're discussing, Marcel's 'opening up' is, as you pointed out, sexual and—"

She shoots up her hand. "Vera, I want to know what opening up means to *you*—not to anyone else! Don't start until you're ready."

I feel my pulse quickening and the heat in my face. I want to flee, but I wait for my mind to clear before starting.

"My first thought was…that…that I knew Marcel meant it sexually. His face and the tone of his voice told me that. But I kept thinking about when he said it before. Then, he was talking about me opening up my self."

"And what does that mean, Vera?"

"To me…opening up means revealing part of myself," I whisper. "It means wanting to reach out. It means sharing, being honest, it means—"

"So what stops you from opening up?" she asks.

Sometimes the simplest word is the most difficult to say. It can hide behind a smile of gritted teeth.

"Trust."

We both shuffle in our chairs, looking in opposite directions before resuming eye contact.

"So what does this tell you about yourself? Don't answer now—let's talk about it next time. Also, keep asking why opening up is so hard for you. Maybe what you've learnt about Marcel can help. With him, is it merely a metaphor for rape, or is there something else? When he gave you his poems, was he testing whether he could *trust* you? Think about these things, Vera. Why not start your own journaling?"

"That's a good idea." I'm not sure why but I decide not to reveal that I had already started a journal. "I could ask myself questions by looking at Marcel. Perhaps I could go back through my notes, look for times when I felt something over what he said or did. You told me I needed to distance myself from him while at the same time getting closer."

She seems to want to close, folding up her spiral-bound notebook, and closing her tablet. I take my chance quickly—it's a thought that has started to surface for several days.

"I've been thinking of something else to help me with Marcel. It plays into what we've been talking about," I say.

"And what is that?"

"I'm thinking...well, only thinking...of signing up with a dating agency myself—see what it's really like."

"Go on," she encourages me, all attention now.

"I'd do it anonymously, using a different name—not Vera, of course. Most agencies require lots of personal information so I'd have to choose one that's discrete."

"You've thought about this a lot, then," Carolyn says. "What's the reason?"

"Two really. The idea started as field research, to understand what Marcel has to face on blind dates. But then I started thinking...maybe talking with someone I don't know, someone I will never see again, will give me the space to open up."

She half-laughs and then turns more serious.

"It might indeed, Vera. And what about Raymond? Is this a reaction against him in any way? It might be better to face up to that first."

"No, that's not it, Carolyn—things are fine with us," I lie. "But I don't think I'll tell him. He wouldn't understand, but I know you do."

"I'm not sure this a good idea," she says, her frown deepening. "Too secretive for my taste. But if you're going to go ahead with it, be careful."

I arrived home in time for a power nap. When Raymond arrived, I was up and as fresh as a wilted flower. I had busied myself for half an hour folding a pile of tangled wraps that had accumulated in the corner of my closet, pairing up my boots and shoes, and bagging long-overdue skirts and blouses for the dry cleaners. I was already settled in the living room when I heard him padding up the stairs to get changed.

Laurie Lisle's *Portrait of an Artist: A Biography of Georgia O'Keeffe* was spread across my lap, open to a photograph of the artist by her husband, Alfred Stieglitz. This was one of a series he took in their early years in New York. I bought the book years ago, and I truly loved the images of her hands with their long, sensuous fingers. This photograph his was of her face, with those flawless lips that rose to a wry smile.

Raymond walked through the living room without a word. He had changed into shorts and a polo shirt, and carried his laptop in one hand. When he didn't emerge, I decided to join him in our office

"Sorry about last night, darling," I said. "I don't know what came over me."

He sat for a while with his hands resting on the keys. Without turning to face me, he said in a resigned tone, "That's all right, Vera, you had to vent, I guess."

"No, it's not all right. I just had a really bad day…and it sort of got out of hand—should never have been like that when you got home."

Later, we largely ate in silence. When I'd washed and dried the dishes, I walked back into our office and found him leafing through his stack of papers. The bin at the side of my desk was almost overflowing and I bent down to push the trash deeper.

"When you were in London, I was clearing up in here and that yellow sticker fell off. I couldn't help noticing the red pen. What does 'Get him' mean? You sounded pretty annoyed. Is everything all right at work?"

His chair creaked as he swiveled around to face me.

"No, everything's *not* all right. I also had a rough day yesterday and today was no better. It's fucking hard working for someone like Cyril, and the last thing I need is for some academic to stir things up. Harvard used to be pro-business, but this piece of shit," he said, poking the stack of paper, "is shit! Then I come home and find my wife drunk out of her mind with not a single word of sense, like everyone else I seem to meet."

"I did say I was sorry. It's just—"

"Listen Vera, I'm really trying to understand what's going on with you. I know I'm not the easiest guy to live with, maybe, but what's going on? Why are you drinking so much? What's this sudden interest in poetry? Where have you gone for Christ's sake?

"Last night you told me I'm not giving you everything you need. Well, let me tell you—I'm not getting enough, either. You're never there for me. You probably use up all your emotions on those patients of yours. If you think all I give you is the odd fuck, well that's all I know I can get. And if I didn't make the first move, you never would. The only interest you show in me is nosing around in my papers."

Even though I was hurt by his words, I forced myself to respond to him lovingly by closing the space between. I touched his forehead, his hair, brushed flecks of dandruff off his shoulders. I knew I had upset him deeply the night before for no real reason—he was a target for my sadness, for the confused fury of drink.

And so I told him about Julie's funeral, that some of my patients were difficult and very fragile. My interest in poetry was research for one of them.

After he disappeared into the bedroom I thought to read some poetry, but it seemed indulgent. I returned instead to Georgia O'Keeffe, drifting through her discovery of Stieglitz' affair, his death, and her move to New Mexico. I loved reading about Abiquiu where she painted her great landscapes and the shadows falling across the walls of her adobe house.

Long ago, I visited that house, wandered through her garden with its watered ridges and riffles, its crooked flagstone paths, and defiant fruit trees. Afterward, we drove up to Ghost Ranch and walked to the very place where she would have looked across the red and ocher hills towards the flat-topped Pedernal, waiting for the light to change. It was dusk when our school party stumbled down.

For the last hour I have been surfing O'Keeffe's name, reading blogs and small critiques, pulling up images to watch her face age until it seemed just lines and creases around youthful lips. I also found a haiku, by Elizabeth Searle Lamb:

> O'Keeffe's 'Black Cross'
> the wind blows and blows
> in the high desert

Rumors were that O'Keeffe became bitter as she got older, and certainly her crow pose, hunched forward and staring through lowered lids, fit the part. I once heard that as she gained fame people would turn up to her adobe house, thumping on the door to be let in, climbing the garden walls—and she would simply close them out.

Her house was her space. She could paint it, share its form and shadows, but inside it was hers. A number of her friends described her as "funny," "energized," and "irreverent," and, if you look, you can see that in her eyes...and in her lips. She dressed in layers of black.

On this wet Thursday, Raymond seemed to have pushed the previous evening to the back of his mind, even bringing me coffee in bed. After he left, I did everything I could online to avoid landing on the dating agency's site. I read *The New York Times* headlines, checked the NPR website for latest news, and scanned the weather forecasts on at least five sites. All warned of thunderstorms during a hot and humid weekend. I even looked at the website of *Strand Bookstore*, and ordered a book—William Higginson's *The Haiku Handbook*—before reaching the dating site and its online registration form.

I started off by being myself. But after several aborted entries, I logged off to set up a new email account, using my middle name—Rayne4321@hotmail.com—then started the registration once again. The first boxes were straightforward, but increasingly the questions seemed strange, ambiguous, and intrusively personal. It was then that I decided to frame the personality as my opposite:

Name:	Rayne Lewis
M/F:	Female
Ht/Wt:	5'3", 108 lbs
Photo:	No
Physical Description:	Dark brown hair and eyes, slim
Occupation:	Event Planner
Favorite Color:	Purple
Favorite Book:	Atlas Shrugged
Favorite Person:	Genghis Khan
Likes:	Cities with buzz, confrontation, rock climbing
Dislikes:	Literary conversations, museums, large dogs

I discovered that Rayne preferred men who were in their forties, jazz clubs to opera, and high-end shopping in yet-to-be-discovered designer stores. Large restaurants bored her, and she sought "cozy, long meals" with good wine and "an attentive partner" who always took the check and, even if he weren't interested, had the courtesy to ask for her phone number.

Rayne found dependent people "sad," hated "tree-huggers," and believed in the free market and the pursuit of wealth. The best part of her job was making people happy and working with dynamic teams of driven professionals. Oh, and despite her gregarious nature, she preferred to first get to know people casually—lunches would be ideal.

By nine-thirty, Rayne was complete. I poured another coffee before hitting the Save button. I took my shower, and spent a longer time than usual brushing my teeth before putting on my work clothes. As I was about to leave for the practice, my smartphone bleeped. On the screen I saw the name Marcel Malone and, intrigued, opened up the text:

> I have to cancel.
> My boss has called a meeting.
> Don't be cross with me.

He was ducking our Friday session, just as Carolyn had predicted. My first impulse was to call him, the second to text a simple "OK." But standing in the half-lit garage, I remembered something I'd learned in high school, and tapped out a reply:

> I never get cross.
> See you tomorrow—let's talk
> about your haiku.

And that was it. Though my heart felt sure he would come, he didn't.

It is Sunday evening, late, and ten days have elapsed since I was able to write. As I look back, the many things that happened were like a series of blows. I'm sure this turbulent time will prove to have been a turning point in many ways but, living through those days, some hours were so eternal that my life seemed to stop.

Marcel did not turn up for our Friday meeting, and he didn't text or phone the following week. My denial was so strong that I waited in my office the full hour for each of the three missed sessions, working on patient notes, thinking he would arrive, breathless and apologetic, his folder full of offerings.

I later learned from him that he had left our last session annoyed with me, spending the weekend intensifying this anger. Over the next days it shifted towards his mother, Isabella. Why had she accepted the abuse, he repeatedly asked himself. The result was that Marcel was left with scars, and with sounds that now haunted him. But at first I served as her surrogate, a blatant instance of transference.

Towards the end of that first weekend, Marcel later told me he had forced himself to arrange a couple of dates for the following week in what we joked was our first separation.

On Tuesday, he met an older lady from Bethesda who seemed fascinated by his wit and invited him to a dinner party that weekend. When he declined, it seemed to spur her interest even more, and she had called him several times, to no avail. Here is what shocked me. He said that if he'd known I wasn't in DC that second weekend, he would have accepted her invitation, perhaps even the sex that was clearly on offer. He needed to know I was absent before he could cross that physical bridge.

Marcel laughed when describing a second liaison, amazed to discover that his date was an intern at his accounting firm who had lied about her age. They had gossiped their way through lunch, meeting later for drinks. Jean was intrigued to learn that his passion was poetry, remarking that she could hear the cadence in the way he spoke. They agreed there was no major attraction between them, but from that point on they started to meet each morning at the coffee machine where they split a bran muffin he had saved.

The strangest tale he told was of Thursday night in Virginia where he had gone to listen to two visiting poets. He'd put his name on the list for the open-mic reading that followed, and had recited from memory a sonnet he'd written several years ago. The few mistakes he made had broken up the wooden iambic pentameter of the original so that the poem, in his words, "seemed to dance." Several people approached him afterwards with compliments that sounded sincere.

And then on the second Friday, when he should have been with me, he was walking into work and literally bumped into Melissa. She seemed more embarrassed than he so that, even though his speech descended into heavy meter, it was nothing compared with her mumblings. Later, they dropped into a Costa coffee shop, and she apologized for not being in touch, as promised—she had been away. All the time, she used her left hand to tuck a strand of hair behind her ear. He managed to tease out her phone number again, lying that he'd lost the contacts in his phone.

As for me, over those two weekends and intervening week I felt as though I was suspended, waiting for something that I refused to acknowledge. I wrote nothing in my journal. Even Donald Hall's book rested on my bedside table like a phone that doesn't ring.

Dawn and I spoke twice, once last Sunday when she suggested we meet, and then early Monday when she called back to say she was too busy. Christine continued to keep her distance, though I had no doubt she was out hunting for some new beau, that I would soon receive a call for cover-ups or nanny services.

I saw Carolyn on the Wednesday. I resisted the urge to say I was trying to open up but there seemed no one to open up to. Instead, I talked about Marcel, that he had now missed two sessions. It may have been my tone of voice because she suddenly asked if I missed him, and I had to admit I did. We then danced around warnings over attachment. She insisted that Marcel had to find his own space. She avoided raising again my dating proposal of the week before, and it was left to me, in the final minutes of our session, to announce that I'd put the idea on hold for the time being, which was true. My online application was merely saved, and I had pushed all thought of dating to the back of my mind.

I had several heart-stopping moments when my smartphone rang and the word "Unknown" appeared on the screen. Two calls were from market-research companies, interested in my views, which I gave quite strongly. One was from my new patient, Brenda, urgently seeking an appointment the next day. I can laugh now, but even I was surprised when I told her, firmly, never to call me again from a phone where the caller's ID was blocked. "I need to know who's calling. Always remember that." Click.

I'm happy to report that Raymond and I made love (sex, actually) last Sunday after reading the papers. It seemed so detached, so anonymous in its lubricant-rich movements. I jumped out of bed to wash up immediately afterwards to find my pulse quickened by the warm water. I reentered the bedroom with a smile, holding out a handful of paper tissues with the relief of having satisfied us for a while.

This provided a perfect platform for Raymond to tell me we could not take our vacation at the start of the summer recess of Congress. Instead, Cyril and Amanda had decided to go to their summerhouse in The Hamptons, and Raymond had been chosen to act as CEO, to hold the ship during what Cyril described as critical times. "So darling," Raymond said quietly, "why don't we run up to Boston this coming weekend? My parents would love to see us."

What my husband meant was how much his mother loved to see her baby boy. Even though she never touched him, she could fawn over him and pad his bones with summer puddings, puff up his bed pillow each evening, and fold his boxer shorts and socks into neat piles. If she did address me, there would always be a barb lurking. Raymond's mother once said she thought I'd done so well, considering where I came from. Nowadays, she is less direct. Silence to a question from me is her new favorite. Or if I'm able to stop Raymond and his father talking over me to express an opinion during dinner, she often mutters, "Whatever," as though this is the last word.

We flew to Boston. We returned this evening. I survived.

I forgot to write about Tuesday afternoon. When I returned home after three back-to-back sessions, I found a small, boxed envelope from *Strand Bookstore* on the porch. Tucked inside was my copy of *The Haiku Handbook* by William Higginson and Penny Harter, 25th Anniversary Edition. I am sure *Politics & Prose* would have stocked it, but I hadn't wanted to face the red-spined devil again, at least not yet.

Like many schoolchildren, in many classrooms, I had been taught that haiku comprised seventeen syllables arranged in three lines of five, seven, and five syllables. I remember the time our English teacher set us the task of composing five such haiku as homework—"Think of each as a short story," she said.

Donald Hall's *To Read a Poem*, on page 91, also says that haiku have seventeen syllables, but he elaborates to explain that they comprise "two images, of which the second is a surprise, a leap from the first." *The Haiku Handbook*, or *Thaikubook* as I now call it, agrees only with the latter.

In what would be a surprise to many, Higginson and Harter point out that in Japanese a syllable or *onji* is much shorter than in English, and that seventeen syllables is simply too long, more than a breath, more than a moment. You can see this in English translations of Japanese masters, as in this famous haiku by Matsuo Bashō from 1686,

> old pond…
> a frog leaps in
> water's sound

I find it hard to explain how a haiku works, how the poet uses words to evoke a taste, or image, or time of year. What I can say is that I am no longer sure if my slow week opened me to haiku, or whether haiku slowed my week. It is a source of wonder to see a haiku in its true light, stripped of all but that *moment*.

I read *Thaikubook* twice last week. In a mysterious way, it helped me survive the weekend in Boston. Raymond's mother's doily-covered armchairs brought to mind frosted trees waiting for spring and birds; the remains of Sunday lunch recalled a picnic spoiled by rain; and the room we slept in—preserved as an altar to a young son—became a shrine beside the road on some sharp bend in the high desert. In an odd way, I saw Raymond's parents as a physical haiku, two people separated by an emotional cut, dividing two temperaments. He was large and blustery, full of bigoted advice; she was thinned and quiet, with a seemingly endless ability to dote on her son.

We landed at Reagan airport earlier this evening. After circling the city twice, the plane made its usual mad dash up the Potomac before dropping onto the runway. I enabled my smartphone and saw a message of eleven syllables:

> I've been away
> but now I'm back—
> tomorrow?

I wanted to applaud the sparseness of the message but shout this was not a *moment*, that there weren't two concrete images juxtaposed. Instead, I sent a simple *OK*.

I almost hit the Submit button to the dating agency as soon as I walked into our office this morning. I was still fired up and angry over the behavior of Raymond's parents, and if I had been dreaming it would have been about what I should have said, what I should have done. But at the last second I exited the site—I knew I wasn't ready.

My hair braided tighter than usual, I drove to the practice and found Marcel already waiting in the corridor, a plastic cup of water in his hand, crumbs on his pants. Sarah had started her vacation, and the eyes of the temporary receptionist told me he was there before I saw him. I tasked him to wait a moment, unlocked the door, settled in my files, and reopened the door to let him in.

So here I am, watching him calmly sit back in the same old chair as though finding his mold once again. There is something different about him today—many things. He has combed out those unruly curls into a set of brown waves. He has also cut his nails. If I hadn't used the last of a tangerine shower gel an hour before, I could swear he was wearing cologne. Oh, and there's no brown tie tightening the collar of his shirt.

"Good morning, Marcel. How has your week been?"

At first, he speaks in that regular five-beat rhythm that I now find so soothing, before his voice rolls forward in an excited rush, growing into a tumble of words. His eyes seem to glow and glaze as his meter softens.

In a syncopated cascade, I hear stories about lunchtime dates and coffee machine conversations, of how he feels liberated and that "time just rushes by." He is particularly excited when he tells me about the poetry night in Virginia. He is melodic, and I notice how much he gesticulates with his hands and eyebrows as he describes his new world. It is lovely, wonderful, and it is not right.

Twenty minutes into the session he has read two new sonnets from his journal when he stops to steal a sip of water. I take Carolyn's lead, quickly raising my arm and pointing my finger to the ceiling. He seems confused as he looks over the rim of his plastic cup.

"I'd like to go back to our last session," I say. "You shared a lot of things we'll talk about, but tell me why you left so suddenly."

He has had ten days to prepare. But as his body hunches forward, he clasps his hands together and stares at the rug. This is not the first question he expected, it seems.

"I don't believe I left abruptly. We'd
already used our scheduled hour in full."

I let his words hang themselves for a while. He starts fidgeting in his seat.

"I assume you didn't come back here after missing three sessions just to tell me how your week has gone. Why did you run, what were your feelings?"

Outside, I can hear the usual Monday traffic snarl its way along M Street, the honk of horns, and the occasional squeal of a tire. I am in no hurry.

"You made me angry!" he suddenly shouts, and looks away towards the window.

"Any why was that? Something I said?"

"You made me open up!" We are finally where I want us to be.

"Let's talk about that, Marcel. You've used that phrase several times and—"

"Why don't *you* open up?" he breaks in, still angry.

"You've already asked me that, Marcel. Like I said, this is about you, not me."

"You never open up—just sit there closed.
I want to know what makes you so unique,"

he says, turning back to face me.

"All these sessions are about you."

"So show me that you care…" His voice trails off, not softly, but with an edge of accusation.

I know I should plow on until his barriers break down once again. But his obvious agitation, the way he keeps tightening his hands into fists as he rocks back and forth, makes me change tack—I need to slow the pace.

"You know, Marcel, when we started working together I listened more to what you said than what you didn't say. But when you started sharing your writing with me I began to read about poetry, and it's made me appreciate many things you tell me. It's also opened up some memories and thoughts for me."

"Like what?"

"Like how much I used to love hearing poetry, for example. But here's another: because great poems hide their meaning deep below the surface, we have to dig through layers of metaphor and allegory to reach them, at least that's what I think. And so you and I need to start to listen more to what you *don't* say, Marcel, those things below the surface."

I let this sink in before continuing.

"One more example. Just yesterday, I read a fascinating essay by Carl Jung," I continue. I open my notebook and find the page. "Here it is. It's called 'On the Relation of Analytical Psychology to Poetry.' Would you like to hear about it?"

Still rocking, he nods.

"Jung talks about the creative arts, and poetry in particular. In his view, there are two basic types of poem: introverted, coming from a poet's wish for a particular result, almost mechanical; and extroverted, when something or someone else seems to seize the pen. He calls this something the 'autonomous complex,' when the psyche splits and is unleashed." I have Marcel's full attention now.

"I think what's happening to you now is that you're accessing something you've buried for some time. That's why I was so pleased to hear about the praise you got for your sonnet at the open-mic last Thursday. The way you spoke from the heart made the poem dance. Isn't that what opening up really means, sharing things honestly in a new light?"

With his wide-eyed, open-mouthed stare, he is trying to give the appearance that what I am saying is incomprehensible. It is a poor façade, but he cannot hide that he has calmed. Focusing on slowing him down, I continue.

"I want to talk about something else. Do you remember me texting you the other day saying I'd like to talk about the haiku you sent?"

His frown eases and the edges of his mouth seem to soften. "I know about the haiku form," he says melodically. "But I didn't realize I'd sent seventeen syllables until your reply."

"I tried to text back the same, Marcel. But what we wrote weren't haiku, even though they had seventeen syllables. For the past week I've been reading about haiku—believe me, I'm no expert. But almost all haiku written in English today have *less than* seventeen syllables and they contain two contrasting images. Haiku are supposed to capture *moments*, times when the poet stops to thinks about the very instant.

"You're probably wondering why I'm telling you all this. It's because I'd like you to slow down, Marcel, and think about your own *aha* moments. Also, because I want you to realize that I'm taking the time to learn about these things…because I care about you."

As the morning light slants through half-opened blinds, I walk towards my desk and return with my copy of Higginson and Harter's *The Haiku Handbook*. "I'd like you to keep this for a while, even if you don't read it."

He takes it in hands that are shaking.

"So why did you really run, Marcel?"

> *"I ran at first because I was embarr-*
assed, but I later realized that the real reas-
> *on was the fear of what I'd said to you,*
> *of what I heard and what he did to Mom.*

"They didn't seem like my own words, Doctor Lewis. I feared that if I believed them the voices would return and I'd be punished again. So I ran back to my accounting work where the voices couldn't reach me. But all those things I said were true weren't they? The banging, the screams…"

He shifts his legs, and I feel certain he is going to stand, give his excuses, and leave. But he sits there, gripping the book with both hands.

I lean forward and almost whisper to him, "I'm glad you came today. From now on we're going to be open with each other. I want you to slow down and become willing to share other secrets—will you do that? In return, I'm willing to open up my time for you. Text me how you feel whenever an *aha* moment occurs. You may think it's something small, but share it with me. And promise me you'll use less than seventeen syllables, in three lines." In that moment he looks up and smiles.

I am inserting this for you, Mr. Hall. This was the day where I went back and started to edit, not delete but add. It was when I stopped smiling, at Carolyn, at John, even at my husband. That was two months ago, the day that Marcel started to open up. Looking back, I wonder how I failed to notice my speech slowing as the nights shortened, as summer tightened its grip on the city. While the heat built outside, inside I grew cold. Though I continued to write in my journal, increasingly to you, I feared doing so because of the secrets I held. Only now, late August, have I felt strong enough to fill in the gaps in the days and weeks following that Monday, in the third week of May…

It is ten minutes past five, and I am nursing a Martini at a downtown bar waiting for Dawn, but thinking so hard of the morning's session with Marcel that I fail to notice when she arrives until a chair scrapes nearby.

"Sorry I'm late," Dawn announces. "And thanks for agreeing to meet at such short notice."

I nod, say "Hi, Dawn."

She orders a Manhattan with a glass of iced water and then settles herself opposite me. She has new blond streaks in her light brown hair, and the neck of her suit is darkened with sweat from her five-block walk from H Street.

I want to tell her it's not all right she is late. I want to ask whether she ever lies awake at night worrying about me, or smiles when she thinks of me with patients, or wonders why, when I'm nervous, I slide each hand into the opposite sleeve. I want to open up and share my own worries with her, get them in the open, but I can't find the words. As I look across at her, I see a quizzical look pass across her face.

"Are you all right, is anything wrong?" she asks.

My first words sound strange, familiar, metered like Marcel's.

"My name is Vera—can't you say my name?"

Have I suddenly become my patient? The thought is terrifying. I bend down, pretending to look for something in my tote bag, emerging with a paper tissue. I try to compose myself.

"Listen Dawn, I've had a really bad day. Seeing patient after patient can wear you down. Don't pay any attention to what I say or how I say it, OK?"

This seems to satisfy her, for she starts in about how she spent the weekend alone, working up a document about a new set of African transport metrics that no one had yet bothered to read. I see that once again she's given in to her obsession of over-plucking her already thin eyebrows, and her untouched, caked lipstick makes her mouth look tired. She asks my advice on some office question before answering it. This gives me time to re-gather myself. I order a wine to her second Manhattan as she pitches the question she really came here to ask.

"Have you spoken to Raymond? Did he like my idea of bringing Daniel from Rwanda? Did he think clean cooking stoves would help his company's work on climate change?"

Once again, I want to open up to her. I would love to tell her the truth, that Raymond seems not to like anything at the moment, that the only time he's been animated was when his mother cooed over him during the weekend, or when he phoned this morning to announce we'd be hosting a dinner party in two weeks, on a Friday, "to give us the whole weekend to clear up." Instead, I find myself spinning a lie. "He loved the idea, theoretically, but said his company has no money to turn it from dream to reality."

She offers arguments she's already made, but she can tell by the way I fidget with my glass that the case is closed. I know she's upset, and I'm ashamed of myself. My head stays down, even when she gets up and leaves. And in that moment, feelings of being used wash away my guilt.

"Everything OK?" asks Raymond.

I have just settled in the living room after throwing my coat against the wall and rushing upstairs to brush my teeth. I decided on the drive home there would be no pretending tonight, that I would be open. I wanted first to talk about Raymond's mother, and then explain why passive aggression has such a negative effect on me.

Raymond finds me slumped into my armchair, first glass of pinot grigio in hand. "You look overwrought," he says. "Excited about the dinner party, though, I guess."

"Yes, great idea—no problem at all."

"Most of the senior guys are coming—thought it would be nice to show Cyril he's leaving things in safe hands when he goes on vacation."

To Read a Poem is lying close by, but I have no desire to open it. I look across at Raymond standing in the doorway to our office and say, again, "No problem at all."

In a miraculous way, this seems true, the chance to spend a quiet evening staring across a dining table at a mask behind a facade. Soon I'll have to raise myself to toss another salad, and after dinner force down ten pages of my novel before sliding into bed…where I will wait for the rhythms of poetry to carry me into sleep. The following words come silently:

> *"It would be good to have some company.*
> *We wash the same two dishes every night."*

There is still no text from Marcel. All day I have waited for my smartphone's telltale chirp. I've told myself it's irrational to expect one so soon, it will come when it comes. But no text has arrived.

This morning was familiar, reassuring in some ways.

I awoke early and wandered into Raymond's and my office to read my notes for the day. Linda was my first scheduled patient, but I was looking forward to lunch with Robin, my CEO from Baltimore, who had a business meeting in DC and asked if we could meet. I would finally see him in person.

Humidity fogged the office window promising another sticky day. I finished reading my notes, stuffed them into my tote bag, and opened my web browser. After scanning the headlines on NPR.org, I went to *The Washington Post's* site, saw the same headlines, and clicked on the Arts section. *Blues Alley* in Georgetown was hosting "Guitar Week."

Raymond appeared around seven thirty and stood flat-footed in his bathrobe to ask, "What's wrong?" I stared at him awhile, caught in two minds: touched that he should question me using such assonance, but thinking how dreadful to start the day with spondees, like two sharp slaps in the face with no rhythmic foreplay.

> *"There's nothing wrong, it's just I had a lot*
> *to drink last night—today's a better day,"*

I answered. Raymond merely shrugged, not even noticing that I was speaking in meter. He shuffled into the kitchen in an ugly, syncopated way.

This was how I saw and heard him through breakfast, the clatter of his plate in the sink, in the way he rearranged jars in the fridge and struggled into his suit, and in the errant rumble of the garage doors. The whole time I kept tapping my fingers, even nodding back twice when he said "Goodbye."

After waiting for the rush-hour traffic to clear, I drove to the practice. Linda was sitting quietly on the chair in the corridor, waiting for me. I knew the quiet would be temporary. As soon as we walked into my office the world revolved around her.

Searching for any hint of rhythm in her voice, I gave thanks that my role for fifty minutes was merely to say "hmm" and "oh."

Linda told me she'd acted on my advice. She'd spent more time with her children, and they had become less excited and aggressive. Her youngest had even crawled into bed with her, on the side where her husband used to sleep. She was so pleased with the progress that she thought we could meet less frequently, perhaps once per month. She left in a breeze of hair and skirt.

After filing my notes, I tightened my braids and walked into the heat to hail a cab, crossing the city to 9th Street and emerging onto the small square beside *Zaytinya* restaurant. Robin had suggested *Zaytinya* after asking if I liked Mediterranean food. He was waiting at the bar, a larger version of his company photo but as tanned as any CEO should be. We must have looked like a besotted couple, smiling at each other for such a long time.

He suggested still water and chose a Greek white wine from Santorini. After fussing over the menu, he ordered a cascade of small dishes. "We're not in any hurry are we," he stated, rather than asked.

He was dressed elegantly in a light beige suit, brown shoes, and a powder-blue shirt open at the neck. He got down to business fast.

"It's so great to finally meet you in person, Doctor Lewis. I feel I've known you for years, even though it's only been by phone. It's also wonderful to be able tell you this will probably be the last time we meet, professionally at least."

He clinked his glass against mine.

"When my friend, Andrew, told me about you and what you'd achieved with him, I never thought it would be possible with me. I knew things weren't right, but it was something that came with the job. And the way we started—you asking all those questions and setting me tasks—I can tell you, that threw me a bit. Been a long time since I'd been set tasks to do!"

The fuss the waiter made over the first plates he brought released me from replying. We split the self-assembled mezze between us.

"So it's my treat today, to say thank you. Sure, I hate my job—there's only so much fun you can have in a packaging company. But I've just agreed to a time frame with the Board to implement our succession plan. After I step down, who knows what's next?

"That's incredible news, Robin," I replied, scooping hommus onto my pita bread. "Congratulations."

"But that's not all, Doctor Lewis. Last weekend, Samantha and I had that long chat you said should have happened years ago. I told her I didn't love her any more, but that I'd always take care of her. She teared up and asked if there was someone else; I could truthfully say no. Then the most amazing thing happened. She kissed my hand—can you believe that? She said she'd wanted to move down to Sarasota, close to the girls. You helped me do this. You gave me the courage to see what needed to be done—and now it's now up to me."

Here was yet another patient I had helped confront and begin to overcome those personal sores that drained the soul of the essence of life. But rather than feeling joy, my voice froze, and I could feel panic rising. I looked at the sea of couples, tablemates leaning towards each other in that let's-get-to-know-each-other-better kind of way. I forced myself to breathe, and a sense of sadness came over me. It was envy.

"Oh, Robin, I'm so glad to hear this," I forced myself to say, "that you took control. You remember how much we talked about accountability? This is only the start you know, and—"

He raised his hand, and I instinctively cowered.

"And I'm taking the next steps alone."

It seemed as though the whole restaurant heard this. I saw eyes everywhere. The level of noise dropped, and my panic returned. But wasn't this what all therapists desired—a patient who takes his life back into his own hands? And then I knew that something worse than envy had crept inside me.

Now, it is late afternoon. Robin's file is in my hand, waiting to swallow the notes I've been writing of our lunch together. I have also been struggling for some time to make sense of my emotions and reactions.

When Robin raised his hand, the feeling was fear, if only for a moment. The sense of envy was more troubling: was it a reaction to the intimacy of the surrounding couples, or Robin's decisiveness to act? But what has concerned me most was what I felt at the end of lunch. Robin didn't need me any more. I had been dismissed, discarded. This was rejection. It was what Marcel suffered most days, and it was sickening and dark.

I think I've captured my final words to Robin as I slide the file into the cabinet's waiting slot. If he'd noticed anything strange about the cadence, he hadn't shown it.

> *"I'm proud of what you think we have achieved.*
> *I'm proud of what you've done and how you've grown,*
> *but in your future life I hope you'll feel*
> *I'm always just a call away from you."*

I will indeed be there for him, as with all my patients. I only hope that one day someone is there for me.

I am about to leave my office for the drudge drive home when my smartphone chirps, and birdsong fills the room. Here is a haiku from Marcel, thirteen syllables, mysterious.

> the head appears
> within the splayed trunk
> a bruised plum

Carolyn called early today to say she had to travel at short notice to speak at a conference in Philadelphia. The original speaker had fallen ill. Her allergies were playing up, but she felt obligated to the session chairman, an old friend from graduate school. She had been up most of the night preparing her talk on the therapist's role in involuntary commitment. She was deeply apologetic and asked how I was feeling. Had I been working on what we discussed last week? I replied,

"I'm working hard to try to open up."

She suggested we talk more on Friday, before John joined us for our weekly debrief.

With the free hour suddenly available, I decided to call Christine, just to catch up. After several rings, a swollen voice answered that sounded like Christine with toothache.

"We really need to get together again," she said. "I really miss talking to you." So apt that she used the word "to."

After an early lunch at the tennis club, she'd decided to take a nap when she got home. She told me things were increasingly difficult with David. He had taken the boys last weekend to a soccer festival to which she was not invited.

"Two free days on my own, but no grown-up boys to play with," she lamented, clearly more awake, "though things may be changing."

Raymond had earlier texted that he had a business dinner tomorrow night. Christine had said that David was working in his DC office all week, and so I asked her whether he'd mind if she and I went out for the evening.

"Not a bad idea—no need to lie this time. I could check…"

"What about doing something different?" I continued. "I've never been to *Blues Alley*, and I think I can get two tickets. The first set's at eight, and we could be home just after ten."

She paused before replying.

"Not sure I like jazz. You do know it's jazz, don't you? I've been to *Blues Alley* before, and everyone sits at tables. There's no chance to meet anyone." We both knew what she meant.

Changing the subject, she asked if I could pick up her sons from school next Monday and drop them at a friend's house.

David would be in Phoenix for two days on business and she had something on that night. I'm ashamed to say I replied, "Of course I'll pick them up—the usual time?"

I was waiting for her to thank me, but she asked in a conspiratorial tone, "And who were *you* with at lunch yesterday?"

I asked how she knew.

"My friend, Theresa, saw you at *Zaytinya*. She said you were with a very dishy guy and that the two of you seemed to be, well, pretty engrossed in conversation."

I regained my composure and told her it was a patient, and that he wanted to treat me to lunch to celebrate the end of our work together. He'd made some difficult life decisions and wanted to thank me for helping.

Christine probed again, searching for cracks, asking if things could now move beyond therapy with him. I found my rhythm and closed her off by saying,

"*He'll only call me if he needs my help.*"

She had one last question, this time blatant prying.

"So what were these life decisions?" she asked.

"He decided to quit his job, Christine. And he faced up to the fact that he didn't love his wife, that they were wasting their lives staying together."

It is Thursday evening. I didn't have the courage to go to *Blues Alley* on my own. So I am comforting myself with a bottle of chilled Chablis at home. I am luxuriating in being alone this evening after two strained nights with Raymond. Tonight, he is dining with Cyril and two congressmen at *Rasika*, in the Penn Quarter.

Two nights ago, I reached out to suggest we might meet one evening after work for a quiet drink and meal downtown. He said he was too busy this week, that sometimes he just wanted to decompress with a home-cooked dinner—that I would toss, grill or fry, of course, then watch him decompress in front of a TV screen.

I am lounging in bed in my pajamas, nodding off while holding David Lehman's book, *Great American Prose Poems*. What

I really want to do is continue reading from Eavan Boland and Edward Hirsch's *The Making of a Sonnet* that I bought at *Kramer's* earlier today. I did try for a while, but I found the iambic pentameter so strong that I couldn't focus on the words' meanings.

Suddenly, my smartphone chirps. I thumb it open to a new message from Marcel:

> her older sister
> has her mother's daughter's
> wizened eyes

To me, for some reason the text implies something big has happened to him tonight.

Having pulled the sheets over my head to drown out sounds, I can still hear my husband's shoes thudding up the stairs. He opens the bedroom door as I send a reply to Marcel from under the covers.

"Are you all right, is anything wrong?" Raymond asks.

"Hello, Marcel. Come in and take a seat,"
I say in greeting, with as much lilt as I can muster.

He sits, looks around and smiles.

"Hello, Doctor Lewis—thanks for replying last night. How has *your* week been?"

The question catches my breath. I can feel my fingers itching to move, and the more I try to steady them the more the muscles in my face begin to tighten.

"I'm very well—"

His innocent, questioning look stops me before I can finish.

I find the energy to thank him for the two haiku he sent during the week. I look at my notes and recite part of the first haiku. "'The head appears within the splayed trunk'—quite mysterious, Marcel. And you finished with 'a bruised plum.' What were you thinking when you wrote it?"

He says it was an experiment. After reading *The Haiku Handbook*, he had thought hard about seminal "moments." The image that came to mind was a photograph of childbirth. He didn't think it worked as a haiku—"You know, Doctor Lewis, I think they're right. Two images are perfect, but three crowd the scene."

I am eager to move onto the second haiku he sent the night before, but Marcel wants to talk more about *The Haiku Handbook*. He reads aloud from his journal, examples from Japanese masters he had copied there. He repeats his favorite twice:

> rippling waves
> with the wind scent
> beat together

I ask why he liked it so much.

"I know I've been obsessed with beat," he says, "but it wasn't that word, Doctor Lewis. I just love Bashō's mixture of three senses."

I am surprised by his self-awareness and suppress a smile.

"Interesting, Marcel. Can we talk about last night's haiku? What did you mean by 'has her mother's daughter's wizened eyes'?"

Her name is Maureen. He met her last night, socially, not out on a date. She gave him her number, and he wants to ask her out. He asks for my permission.

"That's an unfortunate turn of phrase, John."

This is Carolyn, using her best military voice. I am still processing my reaction to what John has said.

She and John have talked about their patients, and I have described my own sessions, including the lunch with Robin, when John quipped, "So you've lost another client."

He was only commenting that another patient had decided to move on with his life. But Carolyn immediately saw his unintended link to the death of Julie, as now does John, who apologizes.

"Yes, I see, that's something I didn't, well, I didn't mean. Sorry, Vera."

His hesitation sets me back more then his remark, and my head begins to pound. Trying to relax, I move to the week's two sessions with Marcel.

"So we know now why he ran," Carolyn says, pulling a wet handkerchief from the sleeve of her jacket. "And I like the way you answered his desire for 'caring' and 'opening up' by suggesting texting."

"It was just an idea to get him to slow down, to think and write in the moment. I've leant him a book on haiku, and he told me his writing had started to change."

I recite the two haiku Marcel sent me.

"I'm a couple of weeks behind in all this," John interjects. "Is there anger behind the first haiku he sent you, the one about the plum? Is he angry with his mother, I wonder?"

"Initially, he directed his anger at me, but I knew it was a deflection. He did say his mother was at fault, though, for not objecting to the abuse and for leaving him.

"On the haiku, no. We talked about it twice, and I pushed him hard on the first line, the head appearing. He eventually admitted the splayed trunk was his mother, and he was the bruised plum emerging at birth."

"Could the plum have been his father?" John asks.

I am saved from thinking and answering by Carolyn who is eager for more information.

"Maybe, John. But tell us more about Marcel. How did he seem to you?"

As a chastised John leans back in his chair, I try to capture an image of this new Marcel. He was more relaxed and confident, even in the way he dressed. He started the session by asking me a question, how *my* week had been. I also tell them he was more melodic in the way he spoke. He only reverted to meter twice."

"Can you give an example?" John asks.

"When I re-opened the issue of the sounds he'd heard at night, and how his mother looked in the mornings."

"What was the other time?"

"When he asked for my permission to ask someone out."

"He did what?" says Carolyn, leaning forward.

I try to compose my thoughts.

"Yes, I was surprised. Do you remember me mentioning Jean, the intern at his office he had that coincidental date with?" Carolyn dabs her nose and nods. John looks confused. "She and Marcel were leaving the office together when her sister arrived. Jean said they were going for a drink and invited Marcel to join. He and the sister, Maureen, really hit it off and exchanged numbers."

"And that was the second haiku he texted you?" asks John.

"He said he wanted to capture the moment when he looked into eyes that were so like Jean's, just six years older."

"And he really asked for your permission?" Carolyn adds. "That's definitely placing trust in someone else—quite amazing."

As the meeting closes and we prepare for our drinks at *Ozio's*, I tell Carolyn and John, as a postscript, that Marcel and I have decided we can revert to meeting once per week, on Mondays. I also say that Marcel will be away next week for an audit in Chicago.

With a wry look in her eye, Carolyn quietly replies, "What *will* you do with yourself?"

It is the first Sunday of June. This year's unseasonably early heat and humidity has now abated, and I am alone on our rear deck with Eavan Boland and Edward Hirsch's *Making of a Sonnet*

in hand. I am willing the minutes to slow before Raymond returns from a round of golf with a client.

I'm sure you know many of these poems, Mr. Hall. You include several in your book, *To Read a Poem*, most written in iambic pentameter. Others in Boland and Hirsch's book are very irregular with shortened lines. I find these difficult to read because I am like a moth to the five-beat line. Sonnets from the First World War by Wilfred Owen, Siegfried Sassoon, and Rupert Brooke are particularly beautiful. Here are notes on others that I love:

Coleridge: "Work without Hope draws nectar in a sieve, / and Hope without an object cannot live." (What you would call an opening inversion in the first line.)

Emily Dickinson's double-sonnet: "The Prodigal" (Uses pigs as a metaphor.)

Robert Graves: "In Her Praise" (Another open inversion, this time in the final line.)

Hart Crane, wonderful Hart Crane: "To Emily Dickinson" (Painful to read. So lyrically tender.)

James Wright: "My Grandmother's Ghost" (First and last lines in perfect iambic pentameter.)

Longfellow: "Night" (Argues that night protects us from the "molestations" of daylight. Those of my patients who can sleep would agree with this.)

Dylan Thomas: "When all my five and country senses see" (Musical but, I'm ashamed to say, totally unintelligible to me. Ninth line (volta) mentions a lynx…

…though where I come from we call them bobcats, and we kill them on sight.)

It is over a week since Marcel left for his audit in Chicago. The days have been so empty—I have very little to write.

I did collect Christine's sons as promised on Monday, drank too much wine most nights, spent an hour avoiding Carolyn's questions on Wednesday—successfully, I believe—and had one session with a new patient who decided not to continue after our first hour together, which hurt. All I remember most is how frenzied I felt before and during Friday's dinner party.

We had hosted four couples before, and there was no shortage of place settings or glasses. Amanda and Cyril would arrive last, after Raymond's peers and their wives, but still with plenty of time for me to socialize before filling the vol-au-vents with shrimp. But I was anxious, and so was Raymond.

Before: the usual argument with Raymond over whether I could sit at head-of-table close to the kitchen, which I lost; days of simmering pots and, on Thursday, failed pastries rescued by an urgent drive to *Patisserie Poupon* in Georgetown (no one would know the lemon meringue tart was bought); Raymond's need to choose my shoes, settling on blue—I think he approved how I looked; the musty smell when I first opened up the dining room—almost forgetting to gather up the "spring-flower" potpourri sachés before the first couple arrived; my last minute panic over the cutlery (did the knives face in or out?).

The guests: the smell of hair spray before the oh-so-formal air-kissing of cheeks (what *was* her name?); the customary ladies' tour of the house, the polite comments—"Lovely the way you've framed that shadow from the window," "I just *adore* separate bathrooms;" Cyril's wife, Amanda—her regal arrival, even wives rising to stand; Raymond pouring Cyril a glass of Prosecco, hiding the label.

Dinner: the initial ritual of shallow talk to one's right and then one's left; inviting Cyril to carve the meat so he could claim the center of attention; orchestrated conversations, the asserted tones of male voices; an occasional attempt of someone's wife to be heard.

I remember little else except for one moment. While I was hunched over the sink re-washing the forks for dessert, Amanda appeared with her water glass and sang to the rhythm in my head, so perfectly iambic:

"D'you need some help? Is everything all right?"
she asked, and both of us seemed to know.

And now, late Sunday afternoon, after a weekend clearing up dishes and misunderstandings with Raymond, I am immersed in the sound of sonnets. I know Marcel is back from his week in the windy city, for here, on my smartphone, is a haiku that must have been written when he was staying in Chicago, playful and poignantly sad:

5-star hotel
every smile
paid for

He has added a small P.S., breaking our rule of less than seventeen syllables. "Can we meet at ten instead of nine?" After checking that I could reschedule another patient, I text him back, "OK."

I imagine he returned on the late flight on Friday. Perhaps he has spent the weekend with Maureen—I may hear tomorrow when we meet. But for now, the book of sonnets is closed. The sun still hovers high in the sky as I open the patio doors to enter the house. Raymond's metallic gray BMW is turning into the driveway, and I make a decision. I quickly walk into the office and log onto the agency's site. As the garage door begins its angry rumble, I access my account, pull up my saved registration form, and hit the Submit button. And this I say to you, Marcel:

I didn't even ask for your consent.

"Hello, darling, it's me," Raymond says behind me, and I jump.

When I woke up this Monday morning I knew I was Rayne, my middle name, the name I gave to the dating agency. I decided that I was going to be her, and it was going to be through her that I would open up. I felt a sense of abandon and lightness of step as I walked out of the bathroom in a mist of cologne. Raymond, who fails to smell or see many things, immediately noticed that my hair was down—no braids—and asked me what was going on, "Someone special today?"

I've always found it difficult telling a complete lie on the spur of the moment. And so I started by speaking of an old patient that had suffered from years of being tied to her infant cot with rope. It was then easy to glide into the present, saying I was seeing this patient today. She was making progress I explained, despite deep trauma, but I knew she reacted badly to my braids.

I listened to NPR as I drove down Connecticut Avenue towards the practice. The program featured the Argentinian composer, Osvaldo Golijov, and as soon as I heard his music I turned into a side street in Kalorama and parked. The combination of wailing voice and staccato rhythm from his short opera *Ainadamar* almost took my breath away. I heard mention of the word "poet" and turned up the sound.

Golijov's opera focuses on the last days of the Spanish poet, Federico Garcia Lorca, who was murdered by the fascists at the start of the Spanish Civil War. Little was said about Lorca, but as the music returned someone recited lines from one of his poems. The program ended with an orchestral sequence, a series of sharp hard raps, like the shots in a firing squad. I decided to find examples of Lorca's poetry.

It had begun to rain, and as I waited to pull into the traffic I realized I had been crying—opera does this to me. I scrabbled around with my right hand, finding the lipstick on the passenger seat and slipping it into the tote bag in front. Rayne was now gone, and Vera was back.

When I reached the practice, twenty minutes remained before my first session. The first thing I did was lock myself in the ladies washroom. I had no makeup remover and it took forever to wash the foundation and rouge off my cheeks. Leaving the mascara, I tied my hair in a single long braid, wrapping and wrapping the tail in a rubber band as though it would never again escape.

In my office, I rummaged at the back of an old filing cabinet until I found two silk wraps I had stored as a contingency for some unknown, unimaginable emergency. I draped them around the shoulders of the simple, long-sleeved dress Rayne had chosen to wear. After pouring myself a coffee, I returned to my office and checked my emails—mainly weekend thank you notes, and messages from my patients—before opening Rayne's hotmail account. A single message rested in her Inbox. It was from the dating agency. The email requested Rayne to schedule an interview.

"Hello Marcel, and how are you today?"

I'll admit a clichéd welcome, but all I could do in the circumstance.

Beneath a sports jacket I'd never seen before, he was wearing a cream-colored shirt with a mandarin collar that was open halfway down his chest. A tight knot at the side of his throat held a blue bandana. He couldn't have looked more bohemian, except for the hair. The curls and waves were gone, making his close-cropped head seem improbably small and his face rounder.

I asked about his week in Chicago and discovered he had only returned that morning. He had landed an hour earlier and had left his luggage at his office before rushing the few blocks to see me. The week's work had been, "tedious beyond belief," he said.

He and Maureen had gone out to dinner before he left for the audit. Near the end of his week in Chicago he decided to invite her to visit him, and they had stayed together over the weekend. The highlight had been a visit to *The Green Mill's* Sunday night poetry slam. As he spoke of it, he clicked his thumbs, waving his arms in the air. "So much passion," he said. "So many ideas to later talk about."

"Sounds wonderful," I responded. "By the way, I heard that Robert Frost called poetry a conversation in the room next door, muffled through a wall." I had found this quote online, but my not-so-subtle link to "sounds within walls" seemed quite lost on this version of Marcel.

He seemed unable to talk of anything but Maureen. She had whisked him through the shops on Michigan Avenue to "get a new look," and followed this up by suggesting the haircut — "to open up the face." They had visited the library at the Poetry Foundation, and yesterday had walked several miles north along the lakeshore before taxiing back to the hotel, "to make love in the afternoon."

This was not the Marcel I knew. I should have been pleased with his joy and ebullience. But he seemed to have left himself behind, together with his missing file and journal. Not once did he ask a question, or how I was.

As we approached the hour, I tried to bring the conversation back to therapist and patient. I outlined what I thought we should talk about when we met in one week's time.

"I loved your hotel haiku, Marcel, but I think we need to talk again about that swollen plum."

I was shocked to see no response, not even the flicker of an eye so I added,

> "And maybe tell me why you asked
> for my consent to see Maureen again."

I can still see the look he gave me, the nonchalant way he replied. "You misunderstood me, Doctor Lewis. I didn't need permission for that. I only wanted to suspend my target of thirty dates."

I was blushing with embarrassment long after he had left my office.

It was a relief that Carolyn was unavailable on Wednesday, the day I visited the dating agency for my personal interview, hair unbraided and brushed across a face I didn't recognize—all make-up and pre-drinks smiles; they told me the name Rayne sounded "catchy."

A young woman with long fingernails asked most of the questions read from a tablet. Her colleague, also blond-haired with a crimson dress and matching lips and shoes, spent most of the hour studying each wall of the room from her chair. But she was the one who asked the question I'd prepared for, "Are you looking for a partner or something else?"

I told them I had an open mind since I hadn't dated in a long time. As they looked at each other with knowing looks, I recited what I'd rehearsed, a version of their own marketing blurb. "But there has to be a match out there, someone I can love and will truly love me." Long nails clicked the tablet, and I looked across at two sets of smiles, and perfect teeth.

Later, Raymond called to say he would, "probably catch a cocktail with the guys, if that's OK," which it was. Christine was not answering calls. When I emailed Dawn I got an out-of-office reply saying only that she would be away "for a while." I spent a long evening with Henning Mankell and his Inpector Wallander, shivering in a Swedish sea breeze, driving a Volvo.

Thursday was a bigger bust—seven sessions, two unplanned, followed by a half-drunk evening weeding the garden with Raymond. He was in bed asleep by the time I finished treating the mosquito bites on my legs.

But happily, Friday was a quieter day. Carolyn and John were away for long weekends, and I had not yet filled the 9:00am slot vacated by Marcel's move to once per week, on Mondays. I worked out at the gym for over an hour, showered twice, and reached the practice at eleven—just suntanned Sarah and me.

With time on my hands, I decided to follow up on Carolyn's mention of entrainment. I found several references to a book, *Why do people sing? Music in human evolution*, by Joseph Jordania, and ordered a copy on strandbooks.com.

I did receive snail mail during the week—two thank-you letters for the dinner-party, one from Amanda Brock. "Let me know if you'd like to get together some time," she wrote in a strangely irregular scrawl.

Of late, I have mainly been writing in my journal on Sundays, but tonight I write with the weekend ahead of me for I wish to get the following down on paper before I forget.

I feel trapped in a net of my own making. There was a time when I was a happy and caring person, but I think I have changed, certainly more than Raymond. I don't know who I am any more.

Several times this week I tried to escape the person I have become. Most mornings, I have emerged to face the day with my hair down before resorting by lunchtime to braids. Today, I stared at an email, believing I could be someone else, for a moment. It was from the dating agency—a short thank you for signing up, followed by three email addresses highlighted in blue. I saved it in my Archive file.

Over the last months I have rediscovered my love of poetry, but the joy is shallow—I cannot run the risk of hearing such beauty through his voice, the way he used to recite poems to me. I long for his voice, but as I try to remember it fades away like my dreams. It is as if poetry were teaching me a lesson in the beauty of what is lost, of what cannot be achieved, a desire that cannot and should not be satisfied. Someone else has said all this.

Born in 1898 and executed in 1936, Lorca was obsessed with the notion of lost possibilities, of unfulfilled longings. In his later years, he wrote of the power and necessity of "Duende," not the "theological demon of doubt" but something that "burns the blood like powdered glass"—the passion of the soul, the knowledge of death. He believed great art was possible only with Duende.

Oh my beautiful, gay Prince, did you foresee your own death when you wrote your famous "Lament," or was it truly an elegy for your bullfighter friend, Ignacio Sánchez Mejías? This evening I read your "Lament" once again, recited the sonnets you returned to in your last years.

I bought your *Selected Verse* on Tuesday, braving sight of a book I fear, a book with a red spine. But it was only on the following night that I could rest my head on your shoulder and read the poems in their glorious entirety.

Is this what my patient, Marcel, needs—to pull death closer to himself, to feel it like a shadow on his words? Is this what makes a poet? Is this what I need Federico, are you my metaphor?

I am here with another full glass of Chablis, waiting for the sound of a garage door. Duende is so close it tastes like a rusted key, but for now there is only Golijov's music soaring out of the stereo. The CD I bought today tells me the one-act opera's title, *Ainadamar*, translates *Fountain of Tears*—how perfect.

❖ ❖ ❖

Now I'll share my weekend…

It wasn't because I wore my hair down—I do that both days on most weekends—but I felt caught between two personas. Raymond remarked several times that I seemed different. Certainly that was my intent.

In those hours when Rayne surfaced I became aware of the faintest sound or smell, with a new source of energy, uncontrollable at times. The dining room now feels less austere with the table angled away from the walls. Even though Raymond rarely responded in the way I would have wished, I wonder whether he sensed that I had opened up, just a little, that I was showing parts of myself he had not seen before.

I tried to avoid immersing myself in work or reading in order to become a better wife, a better listener for my husband. I surprised him by booking a dinner last night at *Redwood Restaurant and Bar* in Bethesda, insisting that we take a cab so that we could enjoy a cocktail before a bottle of wine, a red Zinfandel, spicy.

And this morning, after I had done that thing he liked, I bullied him into joining me at the gym, never once commenting on how spindly his legs had become. But for most of the time my weekend activities as Rayne seemed so false, like one long masquerade party. I could hardly wait for the quiet of Sunday evening when I, Vera, could once again indulge myself with Lorca.

These last two days were truly days of *lost possibilities*. Reading Christopher Maurer's introduction to Lorca's *Selected Verse* earlier this evening, a phrase is working its way into my bones. Lorca believed that, "Desire is never fully defined, only gestured at, and therefore unable ever to be satisfied."

Is this why I am usually so closed? Is it a form of defense to temper the despair of unreciprocated love, a protective shield against what I am truly searching for? And does this mean for my patients, too, that no matter how hard I try to peel back layers to reveal their innermost desires, they are doomed forever to be unfulfilled?

This may be the true paradox of therapy. But as I prepare for the weekly review of my notes I am tempted to believe the opposite: I *can* surface my patients' desires, and the key lies in establishing an aura of honesty, love, and trust before confronting them with their pasts and their demons. I'll start again with Marcel tomorrow, Monday, at our new time of two o'clock, and I intend to lean heavily on Lorca. But there will be no mention of Duend*e*, and on no account will I leave a copy of Lorca's *Selected Verse* with him—some of the poems are painful, even to me, and the thought of any damage done to Julie through reading Adrienne Rich's poem "Women" still haunts me.

Raymond is busying himself for bed, lining up his clothes for tomorrow, and I am about to turn off my reading lamp when my smartphone rings. The screen says "Unknown," and my heart skips a beat as I wait for the sound of wind. "Oh, it's you!" I find myself blurting, before listening to the familiar voice. "I'd love to," I reply. "Tuesday at five in the Mayflower is perfect," or as Lorca would have said,

"At five in the afternoon."

It is Monday and eight days since my last entry. Once again I have been unable to compose a single sentence in my journal, though my patient notes are up to date. But now, sitting in my office approaching two o'clock, I am driven by anger.

Last Thursday, sitting again on my bench in Meridian Park where I'd gone to recover from a telephone call, I tapped a simple text to Marcel, three short lines, twelve syllables. I had hoped to trigger a response-in-kind, but no haiku reply came—probably just as well in the circumstances.

But now I shall write about a week in which I've learned a lot more about poetic technique. I have discovered trochees, dactyls, pyrrhics, iambs, and monosyllabic feet. I can add trimeter, tetrameter, and hexameter to pentameter, and sonnets are no longer my default form—I can now recognize ballads, sestinas, villanelles, triolets, and terze rime. All this is thanks to my new little book, *The Poem's Heartbeat* by Alfred Corn, that Marcel gave me earlier in the week.

Despite my new knowledge, I now think of each page of Corn's book as a form of penance, a kind of masochistic sating of the intellectual soul. But for such a short book *The Poem's Heartbeat* is remarkably complete. At least, this is what thought until I searched online yesterday for "verse forms." What I found there accounts for a small slice of my anger. I will try to explain later, if I have time.

How was the week? Troubling, tiring and, at times, terrifying—which is, as Mr. Corn would say, alliteration.

Last Monday, June 11

Carolyn looked into my office when she saw the door ajar. I had just let my hair down and was eating from a take-out salad bowl while reading through the notes of my last meeting with Marcel.

"Don't you look nice," she said, giving every impression of sincerity. "Make-up suits you—and I love the simple dress! Sorry to have missed you last week. Everything ok?"

The dress was indeed simple—a long-sleeved, cream smock dotted with small violets. My sandals almost matched.

I answered, "Yes, everything's fine," which was a lie, though the morning had been busy and refreshingly shallow.

First had been an in-person introductory meeting with a new, prospective patient. Jason was yet another referral from Andrew. Unlike Robin, he was not a CEO, though certainly aspiring to be one, tanned, soft side parting, gray suit. Jason's behavior also fit the mold perfectly. He was totally caught up in his work and himself and, after asking me three times to confirm my hourly rate, we agreed to start with phone sessions on a weekly basis, "Just to iron out a few things," he said.

Jason had been followed by Adam, poor, rejected, Adam who, once again, rejected every suggestion I put to him. I then had a telephone session with long-divorced Peter who confirmed that, despite our last "serious conversation," he hadn't changed. He continued to lounge around all day longing for his ex-wife to return, bruises healed. They all seemed like foreplay for the real event of the day, at two o'clock, my meeting with Marcel.

It had come to me earlier on the drive into the practice, and I was sure this was the right thing to do. I had been struggling with how to deal with Marcel's predictably strong reaction to the challenge I would give him. He would almost certainly retreat into fear, and in my own state I was unsure whether I would have the strength to reach in and draw him out. So I decided I would allow Rayne to join me, to linger in the background, and to appear when called, and only when called.

Two o'clock: "You look nice"—three emphatic spondees.

Once again there is neither folder nor journal, although he is clutching a book.

Neither praising nor condemning how I look, he says, "I don't believe I've seen you wearing make-up before, but you did have your hair down the other Saturday when I saw you at *Kramer's.*"

He slumps into the chair and stretches his legs, crossing them casually at the ankles. He is wearing orange socks that clash with a mouthwash-blue, open-necked shirt, and he has several days of designer stubble on his cheek, so chic.

"Well, that's a lovely thing to say, Marcel.
So tell me everything about your week."
As I speak, I see his index finger tapping the book ten times. I look away, and he hesitates a moment, then he's off and running.

"I can't tell you how good things are, Doctor Lewis. I feel sort of free for the first time in ages.

"Wherever I go, and whomever I meet, there's something new. Just like Maureen—she seems new everyday. I keep seeing a different part of her, and she knows so many people and interesting places. It's like discovering DC all over again."

I find myself staring at his face, his hands, trying to picture him as he was. Hardly stopping for breath, he recounts each day, each evening, each night and morning, detailing how Maureen helped rearrange his bedroom to mirror her own. He ticks off dinners, walks, and drinks, and seems proud announcing he spent part of Saturday bagging up his old clothes.

Marcel has yet to describe Maureen, but an image starts to form. I picture her with blond hair, cut short so that it styles itself as it dries. She is constantly on the move, but she is physically out-of-shape for a woman in her late twenties. She diets between relationships. This is when she buys her blouses, skirts, and belts that—by the time she wears them—are unflattering for her square frame. She covers up her narcissism by being overly attentive, motherly, on the edge of being bossy—she is searching for the perfect man she can create and mold. Rayne doesn't like her.

Marcel continues to talk me through his week, but not once does he speak of how his true self feels. After fifteen minutes of waving his arms and high-pitched laughter, he starts to run out of steam, and I am able to intervene.

"So many moments, Marcel, but no time to text?" To me, I sound petulant.

He first opens his hands and raises his eyebrows before replying, "It's hard to stop and focus when there are that many moments, one after the other."

"So have you written anything this week?"
I continue, wishing I had kept the meter flat. "You haven't brought your journal."

He tells me he has taken a break from writing.

"No, I don't have the time right now. But if I do get back into poetry I think it'll be free verse and perhaps poems better suited to slams."

This gives me the opportunity to tell him I have been reading the poetry of Federico Garcia Lorca, largely free verse,

"though he returned to sonnets late in life,"

I add. Marcel stops me immediately.

"Yes, but then he was obsessed by Duend*e* wasn't he?"

This is not a path I wish to follow and, apparently, neither does he. He steers the conversation elsewhere, a first.

"Doctor Lewis, you seem to be drawn to metrical lines so I thought you'd like this book on prosody—it's called *The Poem's Heartbeat* by Alfred Corn. I used it as a reference when I started writing. When I see you next I'll return *The Haiku Handbook*. I'm almost finished with it."

"Well, thank you! What a lovely gift. Speaking of haiku, I'd like to talk about the one—"

"I'm glad you liked it," he interjects. "I thought it was funny the way the hotel staff smiled when they passed, that this was what one really paid for."

It is my turn to correct a simple misunderstanding.

"No—I want to talk about the one with the plum in the tree."

As he breathes out, his shoulders drop and his head begins to nod, as though he were saying "right, right, right...." I wait for the first drops of sweat to appear on his upper lip, for his flushed face to drain to a gray sheen. Instead, his new stubble gives him a menacing look as he replies.

"I *told* you. I was inspired by a photo of someone giving birth and then, as I edited it, I thought about my own birth."

"Why do you think that is, Marcel?"

I am listening hard for him to regress to meter. But he inhales, sighs, and explains his long interest in photography.

"You've never mentioned photography before." I say. "Is there something else important to you about that haiku?"

At first he stays composed, repeating the long exhale, nodding slowly. But then his slim shoulders hunch up to his ears, slumping back to reveal a flushed neck and chest. I am certain words will pour out of his mouth if I can just wait long enough. They do, indeed.

"Her legs were wide apart and she just op-
ened up and there was the head! Not like you, Doctor Lewis—
no, you've never opened up like that and you never will."

It's not what I expected—it is like a punch in my stomach. I
need to hold onto something, anything. And then I am falling,
falling, and with nothing to stop me. The air seems to have left
the room, and it's all I can do to breathe.

Someone is calling as I fall, a repeated scream that grows
louder with each heave of my chest. But suddenly she is there,
Rayne who thrives in confrontation, able to throw back her hair
and shout; a female with passion who hates large dogs, whose
bark is deadlier than any bite Marcel could give.

"How dare you speak to me in that manner!" Rayne shouts.
"These sessions are about *you*, not about *me*, and I'm not going to
let you use the safety of this room to abuse me. This is the
second or third time you've drawn me into *your* issue of opening
up. You've alluded to sex. Now, you're suggesting I'll never
have children. This is totally unacceptable, I'm outraged, and I
demand an apology."

He seems genuinely stunned, but not as much as I am. After
a long pause he leans over his thighs and I can barely hear his
words. "I'm sorry, Doctor Lewis, please forgive me."

I can feel Rayne sliding back to the shadows, alert and ready.

"We can deal with that later, Marcel. But we have to talk
about this haiku, particularly in the context of our session a
couple of weeks back. I'm wondering if this plum is a different
metaphor for you, the head of a penis, your father's, the splayed
trunk your mother, split open and violated."

His reaction is immediate, and predictable.

"He raped her every night before she died."

Wide open himself now, he starts crying. I have to be careful.
I have to give him time and space, but not so much as to lose this
opportunity.

"I've read about Lorca's fascination with Duende, the
passion of a soul," I say, opening my notebook. "But do you
know that he also said, 'Mystery is where language can only
point at, and never adequately name, what we desire, what we
want'?

"Your haiku surfaces an image that surprises and frightens
you. Rape is something you don't want to think about and I can

understand that, Marcel. But let's focus on Lorca's 'desire'—do you *desire* closure on this? If you do, you'll have to face the nightly rapes."

He closes his eyes and his head begins to roll in a slow figure-of-eight.

> *"But why? It's bad enough remembering*
> *the sounds, without having to see her—"*

"Marcel, look at me. A couple of weeks ago you asked whether what you remembered was true. Do you remember that? As well as the sounds you heard, are you trying to drown out doubt?"

He stares at me. His demeanor has become that of a child, with the saddened eyes of someone truly lost.

> *"I don't know any more. I cannot think,"*

he says quietly, closing his eyes once more.

Admittedly, introducing doubt is a risk. But I have to help him look beyond the wall of his bedroom. It is clear that I have touched something that is having a strong effect.

"Marcel, we all find ways to cover up horrors, things we never want to see or hear again. You've done this ever since your mother died. You've also built yourself extra protection through sounds, beat, and the rhythm of poetry, anything to drown the groans and screams of your mother.

"People suppress memories in different ways. Some invent stories. Some resort to little tricks to stop them remembering, or use alcohol to deaden thoughts. You, for example, have created a completely new persona, someone hip who doesn't need to think, who can leave behind the real you and live a shallow life that isn't real. Everyone has used one of these at some point.

"You have to get back, Marcel. You have to get back to the person you were a few weeks ago—what you were then was *you*. That's the Marcel that has to do the work necessary to get closure. If what you think you heard in those terrible days before your mother died are true, then let's deal with this truth. But there's a possibility you imagined what you heard, or that the sounds were not what they appeared to be. If that's so you have nothing to drown out, and much to learn.

"Remember, you can contact me any time. But, when we meet next week, I'd like to meet the real Marcel again."

Head still bowed, he whispers that he will do what I have asked. Summer rain streaks down the window as he rises. He turns before reaching the door.

"Is that what he really said?" he asks.

"Who's that, Marcel?"

"Did Robert Frost really say that poetry was like a conversation muffled through a wall?"

After Marcel left, I spent more than an hour writing, trying to capture everything that was said. I had to stop several times, reminding myself these were patient notes, that my own feelings had no place in them. Even when finished, I couldn't let go of the word "doubt"—it was like an echo, pulsing behind a growing headache.

I searched for Carolyn, but she had left the practice only minutes before. Driving home through early rush hour traffic, I bailed out of Connecticut and switched to Wisconsin Avenue, ending up alone in *Clydes*, drinking. I still reached home before Raymond. After draining the last dregs of Sunday night's sauvignon blanc, a particularly nasty number, I settled myself to start the book Marcel had given me, *The Poem's Heartbeat*, only to fall asleep in the chair. Before bed, I washed up Raymond's plate and cutlery.

Last Tuesday, June 12

Hangover most of this morning…

Therapy highlight or lowlight was Linda: children had regressed; ADD transferred to her; ill at ease, as was she.

It was five o'clock in the afternoon, and at first I failed to see him. I had to fight my way through the crowd before reaching the bar.

The Mayflower Hotel foyer was choked with conference delegates still spilling out the State Ballroom. Most stood in clusters, trying to read each other's plastic nametags, while a few introverts hovered near the bell stand, pretending to wait for a friend or the concierge.

I found him sitting at the far end of the Edgar Bar, head bowed over a drink. It seemed longer than the three months since we last met at the Kennedy Center, and he had aged. Gone was the brushed-back hair, the lightly creased face, and pressed flannels—the person who looked up as I approached looked like one, long crumpled shirt. His eyes were dull and reddened, and his chin grayed with stubble.

Christine's husband, David, snapped his fingers, knowing to order me a Martini, dry-up-with-a-twist, exactly how I felt as I slid onto the stool he had covered with his jacket.

"You remembered," I said. "How are things going?"

"I'm fine, just fine—don't you think I look fine?"

Against my better judgment, I asked why he wanted to see me so urgently. I flinch even now as I remember how he raised his hand and slammed it onto the bar. Heads turned towards us before the bar chatter continued.

"I'm away for three days in Atlanta on a business trip, at least that's what Christine thinks. I hired a car and checked in here Sunday evening—have followed her since yesterday morning. Do you know—I'm sure you do—that she was already fucking a guy twenty minutes after dropping the boys off at school yesterday? She threw her torn pants into a trash bin next to a restaurant where she met some other guy for lunch. And then again this morning—"

"Oh, I'm so sorry."

"You're sorry?" he hissed. "You, her best friend, one of *our* best friends, you're sorry? For what—that you've helped her do all this, colluded in her lies? If you're sorry for me, forget it, because I'll get over it, but she won't.

"You asked why I wanted to see you so urgently. Well, here it is—I wanted to look into your eyes and say you disgust me. I wanted you to be the first to know I'll be seeking divorce immediately and it will be very, very ugly. I'd decided this even before the last two days, ever since that wine tasting evening— the night she said she was with you."

Alarm bells were ringing in my head—should I respond as a friend or a therapist, and where was Rayne, where was she?

"Have you told Christine yet?" was all I could force myself to say.

As he gathered up his jacket and signed off the bar chit, he pushed his lips towards my ear and whispered, "You disgust me."

Last Wednesday, June 13

No call from Christine.

Coincidentally, unhappy marriages and infidelity dominated my morning sessions—tried to remain detached, professional.

Met with Carolyn. I didn't mention the meeting with David. Answered most questions, avoided some, survived.

Read most of the evening. Two Martinis.

Last Thursday, June 14

There are still no calls from Christine. Perhaps David is having second thoughts, or maybe he is immersed in discussions with his attorney. This is what I was thinking when an unexpected call arrived—an oddly familiar 202 number.

She introduced herself as one of the police officers I had met the day of Julie's death, calling now to thank me for my cooperation. She wanted me to know that the case was recorded as "accidental death." Yes, they had finally made contact with the mother, "who seemed totally detached and uninterested." I told her this is often the case with bereavement, a withdrawal into a protective shell, though I thought otherwise.

Then she said there were a couple of things she wanted to share.

"Your patient had bruising on her forehead, self-inflicted, we believe—there were faint imprints of her textured wallpaper. And we found a scrap of paper under her pillow. The writing wasn't hers. It seemed to be a short poem of three lines: *pawnshop   the musty smell   of sorrow*. It didn't seem important until her neighbor told us that Julie had an occasional visitor, a thin young man with curly hair. I thought you'd like to know that she did have had some form of private life."

Which is how I ended up at my bench in Meridian Park half an hour later. Had Julie and Marcel been in a relationship? I originally thought to call him but was too angry—why hadn't he mentioned it to me? Or was it platonic? Did the pawnshop haiku refer to a shared experience—was he helping her to raise money? I had so many questions, and I think I texted Marcel as a way of stopping for a while.

As I sat looking out at the deserted playground, darker thoughts started to surface. Had Marcel forced Julie to take those pills? Why had he changed his appearance, was Maureen real or

150

merely a construct? Who was Marcel, really? If I didn't know the answers to these questions, what legitimacy did I have as a therapist?

Eventually, I called his cellphone. A voice began, "You have reached…" before inviting me to leave a message. Trying not to sound frantic, I said I had a list of things we needed to talk about before next Monday, and they couldn't wait. I asked him to call me back, but he didn't.

That night I hardly spoke to Raymond. I mixed a Martini before and after dinner, but I didn't read. The sense of falling had returned. I knew that only Rayne could rescue me, that I needed her now, not in the shadows but in my daily life.

I found myself in the office staring again at the email from the dating agency, asking Rayne for her advice. She said she would prefer her dates to center on lunch, at a cozy restaurant she knew that was very discrete. I thanked her and said I would contact the three names the agency had sent, just as soon as I sorted out some things, possibly next week. As soon as I was able, I promised.

Last Friday, Saturday and yesterday morning, June 15—17

The three days following the police call were predictable in many ways, culminating in Raymond bringing the Sunday papers to bed, a sure sign that he had sex in mind. I found this predictability a relief because it gave me time to plan for Rayne's increasing presence.

After speaking with Rayne on Thursday night, I allowed her to emerge in a checkout argument at CVS where I'd stopped to buy eye drops. Christine called later in the morning, irate and full of tears. "I told you not to say anything to *anyone* about the wine tasting, and yet you did!" It was Rayne who replied that she, Christine, was the only person who deserved to be blamed, and it was Rayne whose thumb ended the call.

But by Friday afternoon, Rayne had tired of dragging me along, and I needed to resurface for the weekly debrief with Carolyn and John. Second to speak, I summarized the week, avoiding any mention of the police call the day before. We discussed all the patients I had seen, but focused once again on my session with Marcel at the beginning of the week. All agreed I had made a necessary intervention, and John was pleased to hear that his hunch over the symbolism of Marcel's "plum" had been correct. I added that, although not obvious at first, Marcel's new persona was his own way of avoiding thinking about the days before his mother died.

For one small moment, my guard went down. It was when John asked about doubt, and why I'd chosen to introduce it to Marcel. As I answered him, I felt my voice sharpening before I could regain control.

"Sounds like you're analyzing me again," I said, closing my notebook. As I stared at him, his blue eyes blinked back slowly, just like a cat, comfortable, in no danger. "Seriously, John, it just seemed the right thing to do at the time."

Thankfully, Carolyn rescued me by moving onto her own summary, or so I thought. As we were leaving, John leant forward and whispered, "When you're ready, we need to talk."

And then yesterday evening, June 17…

By Wednesday, I had vowed to stop reading Alfred Corn's *The Poem's Heartbeat*, even though it was a present from Marcel. It is undoubtedly an informative book and, for aspiring poets, clearly invaluable. But I found it soporific. Plus, it disheartened me to see that much of poetry's magic could be reduced to terms and techniques. The book did encourage me to start an online search of verse-forms. This how I discovered the Rubáiyát last night, a Persian form made famous by Edward Fitzgerald in "The Rubáiyát of Omar Khayyam," a poem that, remarkably, I had overlooked in Donald Hall's, *To Read a Poem*.

I have already told you I am angry. Let me explain one reason. Here is a letter I wrote immediately to Donald Hall that, one day, I intend to send.

Dear Mr. Hall,

The reason I have not spoken to you of late is that I have withdrawn from many forms of communication. For this, I apologize. I have even lapsed in my study of your book, *To Read a Poem*, although I have returned most mornings to Robert Frost's "Stopping by Woods on a Snowy Evening." This is the principal reason for this letter.

How could you?

I can forgive the cursory treatment you give the haiku form on page 91, squeezed between the Limerick and the Sonnet. I can also forgive you for not mentioning Federico Garcia Lorca. But I can't forgive what you left out when writing about Robert Frost's poem. As the first poem you discuss in your book, you knew your readers would study your explication intently. Some, like me, will have memorized each line of the poem against each paragraph of your analysis.

So, tell me why, in almost eight pages devoted to this poem, you omitted to mention it was a Rubáiyát (see page 233)? Was this intentional? I am both shocked and disappointed. I feel let down and, as strange as this may seem, patronized, even rejected.

It may take me quite some time to come to terms with this betrayal.

I should have added a footnote, long perhaps but necessary. I can, of course, still do this, but in my mind the letter has been sent, and the damage done. I should have said I love you, Mr. Hall. I love the fact that you have opened up, that you have laid bare what drives you, the passions within you, and those ecstatic moments when you read and write great poetry. Your wonderful book is a gift, the distilled essence of you and all your beautiful poets. I should have said these things and trusted in you, Mr Hall.

Today, Monday, June 18

Here are the main reasons I am angry:

Earlier today, at 1:30pm, I received a text from Marcel saying he was unable to attend our 2:00pm session as planned because he'd decided to take two week's vacation. The message was so impersonal, seemingly final.

I had expected a reaction following our session last week and the challenge I laid before him, but not this. I was insulted and outraged that he felt he could tell me so late, lacking the decency to call. Taking two weeks vacation was not an easy thing to do—he would have needed approval from his company, either by Friday or certainly over the weekend. The longer I thought the more I simmered. Then came the feelings of rejection.

I started recording my thoughts and feelings in my journal at two o'clock, as though I wanted Marcel in the room as I wrote. I left the office at three and drove home to Chevy Chase. Working from the house during a weekday was unfamiliar, and so I decided to continue writing in my journal, catching up on the last week, day-by-day.

When I reached Thursday, my anger shifted. Marcel hadn't replied to my text, nor to the voicemail I had left. I resurfaced my questions about his relationship with Julie, dismissing whether he was involved in her death as a wacky idea. But when I focused on what the police officer had told me, I wanted answers, and now I was denied them for two more weeks.

Raymond arrived home at six-thirty, and I still had my hair down. We had an almost pleasant chat and a surprisingly good stir-fried chicken before settling down to read and, in my case, continue with my journal.

These last two hours, Patsy Cline has allowed me to write facts, details, and quotes from sessions and the long weekend. I have left plenty of personal gaps for Billie Holiday to fill, emotional spaces, the kind she'd understand. She is singing now, raspy and mournful, giving voice to my new sense of anger, the anger of fear.

I could lose Marcel. I am concerned that his false persona will grow and take over. Once this happens I will not be able to get him back. Having placed him at a crossroads of doubt, I have been replaced by a woman who wants to mold him further from his true self.

Placing my journal in my tote bag, I walk into our office. I remind myself that one should not do things in a state of anger. This is why I pull back at the last minute, releasing those three blue email addresses of prospective dates back to Archive.

Raymond smiles as I return to the living room. I surprise myself by smiling back, walking across to his chair and kissing him on both eyes, watching the way his face softens and his arms relax and gently shiver below his shoulders. From now on, Rayne will be allowed out to play more often, but only during the evenings, at home with my beloved.

"My God, this is wicked. What a great idea!" Raymond exclaims, wiping his fingers. He drops a Lysol wet-wipe into a wicker bin before reaching for another chip to plunge into the jalapeno hummus I bought earlier in the day. It was my idea.

I called him at his office late morning, and I could tell he was surprised. "Any chance you can get home early?" I asked. "Perhaps we can watch the game together."

I figured that he would be so immersed in the game that we wouldn't have to talk. And so far I've been right.

Rayne welcomed him home with a tall glass of single malt scotch from a new bottle of 12-year old Highland Park, two ice cubes, and a red cocktail umbrella. Tammy Winette was singing country western on the stereo, and a print out of the team sheet and stats from the official website rested on his side of the sofa— this Raymond studied in silence until the game started.

My hair is down, my lips glazed with a pink moisturizing balm. I am wearing pajamas that Raymond bought me several years ago—light green flannel with cowboys lurking among cacti. Raymond is wearing khaki chinos and a red baseball shirt his mother bought him. We are watching the Red Sox play the Yankees at Fenway Park.

"Jesus, shit, what's wrong with you!"

A player called a pinch hitter has again failed to connect, and Raymond is jumping out of his cushion.

"Why's he called a pinch hitter?" I ask.

Raymond tries to explain but it's lost on me.

"I love you," he says then. "Welcome back." He can't be talking about Rayne, who's laughing at him.

At the end of the eighth innings, with the score at three-three, I go to the kitchen to cut more carrots and re-fill the chip basket and hummus bowl. As I lift the last red carrot shaving from the floor, I hear a roar.

"Vera, come back, quick!" Raymond shouts.

The Yankees have struck out, and the Red Sox are at bat. The pinch hitter is on the plate. Three batters are already out on bases. Raymond says they're fully loaded.

"He's going to fuck it up, I know it," he says, but the pinch hitter waits and the pitch is bad.

Then, on the very next ball…

"What a bunt, oh my God, what a bunt!"

As the ball bobs and bobbles towards the pitcher, the batter on the third base starts his run, and runs and runs and scurries home. The crowd roars again, louder than before, like a great open throat. The TV camera swings around the crowd, delirious, hysterical, and Raymond does a small dance around the living room. The Red Sox, it seems, have won.

As Raymond gulps down his scotch I ask him, "What's a bunt?"

He sits down on the sofa and leans across, lifting two fingers of my hand onto his arm.

"It's what he did, Vera, and I never thought he would. Did you see it? In the last second, he slipped one hand up the bat and blocked the pitch, placed the ball just out of reach so his third-base man could get home."

"But why's it called a bunt?"

"No idea. But it's one of the great things about baseball, placing the needs of the team first. That's why it's sometimes called a 'sacrifice bunt,' so noble."

Rayne pretends to understand but, deep down, Vera knows. She knows all about sacrifice.

The next day, Wednesday, I told Carolyn about Dawn. I hadn't intended to bring her up, but after Dawn and my conversation over drinks, I felt troubled. I regretted being so angry with her, and I called her office at the Bank at the end of the week. Her assistant told me that Dawn had called in sick and then, the same day, had called again to say she was taking a leave of absence. I'd tried her cellphone several times with no success, not even a voicemail prompt. I was now worried and decided to share this with Carolyn.

"I also got angry with my other friend, Christine. I'm just feeling angry, Carolyn."

I told her how I could never say "no" to Christine and about David's confronting me the previous week. Carolyn listened closely, shifting papers across her desk as I talked through Christine's history of infidelities and my role in covering for her.

"So her husband just called out of the blue?" she asked.

"Yes, a week ago last Sunday—gave me quite a shock. He's obviously blocked the ID on his phone because my smartphone showed it was from 'Unknown'."

"He must have been suspicious for some time to have made so many 'Unknown' calls to you," she replied. "I wonder why he never spoke before? He's right, you know. Christine's behavior has been terrible. Personally, I blame her for roping you in but— and Vera, I have to say this—too bad you couldn't find the courage to tell her no. You're going to have to tell Raymond, too. It'd be awful if he found out from someone else."

In her usual blunt way, I knew she was right. And I had to tell Raymond, but when and how?

As we were ending, she returned to my news about Marcel. Carolyn said she was glad Marcel was taking some time for himself. I would have agreed were it not for the text I received two days later:

> child lock:
> still trapped inside
> my father

Where had Marcel gone? What was he doing?

As I walked aimlessly around my office I noticed a snail-mailed letter in my in-tray. I recognized the writing immediately: Marcel.

Tuesday, June 19

Dear Doctor Lewis,

This is a small note of apology. After our last talk I spent a long time thinking about what you said and about the efforts you have made with me. By the end of last weekend—well, yesterday morning really—I had made up my mind to face up to some of these things but, as I write this, I have still not left DC. The reason I cancelled our appointment is I was determined to leave for

Pittsburgh yesterday afternoon, but things got in the way.

I'm cleared at work and now ready to go. After rearranging the apartment tonight, I will take an early train tomorrow.

I will text you if anything happens to keep me here. Once again, I'm sorry to have let you down.

Yours,
Marcel

"She's such a nosey skid sometimes. Caught me at the bubbla yesterday, with that puss on her face."

Raymond has always put on a Boston accent to amuse me. I used to love the way it squeezed out the up-scale northeastern dialect his "Mum" drummed into him. Why, she'd turn in her kitchen grave if she heard him. So would the subject of his ire, Amanda Brock.

He has spoken like this since returning from his tennis match this afternoon with "da guys," but I think by my expression he has finally taken the hint that I am finding the accent tiresome.

It is Saturday evening, after dinner, and we are reading and chatting to the homey sounds of Patsy Cline. I have already told him jokingly that he has one more CD of country music before it is my turn to play some jazz. In a fit of false pique, he has replied "OK, but not that Joe Pass stuff."

Not surprisingly, I find myself again liking this banter and teasing—something we used to do a lot, a long time ago.

"Amanda's often in the office," he says, back in his normal voice. "Most people try to avoid her, but she found me. Kept asking me how you were."

"She's probably just making sure you're not overworking. You're going to be left in charge in a few weeks with Cyril gone."

"I guess you're right," he murmurs, putting down his copy of *Foreign Affairs*. "It's going to be pretty stressful while they're away—I'm going to be loaded with work. So let's make a pact. Let's not talk about our work a while. Evenings like this are so much more relaxing than shallow talk around problems in the office. What do you say?"

Vera wants to tell him that her work is not shallow, and that most days her patients' crises are larger than anything Raymond can imagine on L Street. But she allows herself to be guided by Rayne, positively at first, even playful.

"Not a bad idea, but I have one condition," Rayne says, "and one offer. First, you have to promise that we'll start to plan to get away as soon as they're back. I'm thinking of some place where there's something for you, like country western music, and something for me."

"Uh-huh, and ...?"

"In return, I promise not talk about poetry anymore. I think I've been reading too much anyway."

"Good! I accept the condition, and I accept the offer!"

I want to kill Rayne but I can't find her. I feel a sense of loss, but on the surface all looks well, the room full of smiles. Patsy is singing her last song, longing for sweet dreams because he doesn't love her anymore.

Out of nowhere, I ask Raymond a question that had never occurred to me.

"When did you first get interested in country music? It's not a favorite of your parents, and Boston's hardly the wild west."

"Oh, I don't know," he replies, with a laugh. "I like the heroic aspect, even though it's usually the girl that's jilted. But here's a little secret that I haven't told anyone. In my teens we had a cleaner—from Oklahoma, I think—who used to tune into a country station. I'd be in my bedroom listening to her humming the music...lovely woman."

"Lovely woman?"

He smiles and turns his palms upwards. "What can I say? It just happened one day and went on for a couple of months. She was my first."

Rayne emerges from behind the drinks cabinet. She finds Raymond's "little secret" fascinating and wild. "And what happened—how did it end?"

Clipping Patsy Cline back into her CD case, he answers almost off hand. "One day she just dried up on me."

❖ ❖ ❖

old Beatles tapes
dad says I'm not the man
he used to be

Marcel's text arrived on my smartphone two days later, on the Monday, just as I was ending a difficult session with a new patient, Emma.

I learned later that Marcel had checked into a small hotel on the south side of Pittsburgh, wandering the streets of his old neighborhood for two days. He passed by his childhood house several times, but no one seemed to be home. He admits now that this is what he wanted to believe, that he wasn't ready to confront his father.

On the second day, he brushed past two men that he recognized as classmates in high school, but they failed to notice him. He took the bus downtown each night and ate at the same steak house before finding a tavern to pass the time until eleven o'clock, his self-imposed deadline for returning to the hotel and sleep.

It was only on the Saturday that he found the courage to climb the three steps to the front door of the house. It was raining and his face was streaked with water. There was a light behind the doorbell, but he wrapped hard on the cast-iron knocker and stood back.

His stepmother, Margaret, had aged but was still recognizable. To Marcel, it seemed as though time had stopped. There was a small gasp before she said, "My God, it's you," in a hoarse whisper. Forgetting to invite Marcel in, Margaret turned and shouted down the dim corridor, "Frank, Frank, come quick!"

When Marcel's first haiku arrived, I had a suspicion he had gone back to his home in Pittsburgh, that he was indeed still locked inside his father. But it was the second Beatles haiku that told me they had met. It would be a week before I learned how they had sat in silence in the kitchen before making small talk, minutes of polite catching up, the furtive stares at each other's faces, the stumbling words.

160

His father wore the same blue dungarees and lumberjack shirt that Marcel remembered from his childhood, and the house still smelled of reheated Irish stew. Margaret had quickly excused herself, "to run some errands," and the latch in the front door soon clicked.

I was initially surprised to learn that Marcel fired the first salvo. To the man opposite, with the thin, gray hair, he hissed three words, "You total shit."

"You can't say that to me," his father retorted, leaning back, hooking his thumbs into the straps of his dungarees. "You of all people have no right to say that."

Marcel told me that this reply had broken the seal on the voices inside him. An avalanche of insults and accusations had followed. At one stage, he pushed his chair back to stand so he could look down on his father. As he spoke of his years of pain, his father sat with his head bowed and arms now crossed. Marcel circled before homing in on those tragic weeks leading up to his mother's death.

"How could you have treated her that way? How have you been able to live with yourself all these years, and with that whore?"

That last word was the one that made his father look up. Marcel waited for the right hand to be raised, but it fell to the table. He looked into his father's face, expecting to see that old anger. Instead, his father whispered, "Is that all?"

Marcel slammed the door behind him.

As he walked away, the rain was still heavy, the clouds dark. But he could still make out the face of Margaret, cowering behind a black umbrella at the corner of the street.

All that week I wondered about Marcel. He was in my mind constantly. This must have been so with Rayne, for she took pleasure in pointing out something I had missed—if Marcel had gone to meet his father, he would be alone, without Maureen.

At first I was concerned and worried about him. I became more relaxed as the week wore on, convinced that whatever was happening to him was necessary, a form of healing. I believed that Marcel would return a different person, perhaps someone he used to be.

As for me, my life continued with days of patients, notes and patients. I did find time to scan through Joseph Jordania's, *Why do people sing?* that I'd ordered online. It arrived on the Tuesday, and one section on entrainment particularly caught my eye and brought clarity and excitement.

With Marcel gone, I found my approach to my patients changing, not always in a good way. I lacked energy and became predictable, repeatedly using my metronomic,

"And how exactly did that make you feel?"

I was content to just sit back and listen, to count out the minutes until the hand approached ten to the hour.

I did manage to get through my meeting with Carolyn on the Wednesday, but I had to draw on Rayne's lightness to reassure her that I was opening up, particularly at home.

The evenings were a different story. Raymond began to love Rayne. She was bubbly and full of the latest news, though she never spoke about my work or patients as my husband and I had agreed.

When Raymond retired to our office Rayne would follow him, talking all the while, making him the center of attention. He puffed out his chest and spread his feet as he walked, and as he sat. The more Rayne fawned and stroked, the lower Raymond's voice became. Yes, he loved her—ebullient, idolizing Rayne.

When Carolyn, John, and braided, serious Vera met for our weekly debrief on the Friday, we spent most of the time talking about one of John's clients who had threatened legal action.

He had made a claim that John had caused him emotional and physical harm. But if this "client" had stayed with the medications John had prescribed, his psychosis would have been better controlled. He had chosen not to.

In the end, we all agreed that the relationship should be terminated. John seemed satisfied, but he wasn't his old self, and he made no comments to help solve the problems that Carolyn later shared.

During my turn I merely said that Marcel was in Pittsburgh, and I knew nothing more. But I did bring up my new patient, Emma.

"She's been cutting herself for some time—first, small cuts up the arm out of sight. Lately she's shifted to a box cutter. They're far more visible. Her father, who noticed them, confronted her. He booked the appointment. He even brought her, waiting outside in the corridor while she and I talked. Now she's started cutting in other areas, mainly in her groin."

John suddenly became animated.

"Did she talk about her father at all? Or more importantly, did she not talk about him—change the subject?"

We knew that, while some people cut because they hate themselves, most are driven by the experience of abuse. Bullying is a common trigger for some girls, but most of the cases Carolyn and John had shared were sexual abuse, usually by a close relative.

Contrary to what many laypeople think, cutting is rarely a cry for help or attention. Instead, it results from the need to inflict physical pain as a distraction from a deeper pain. It would likely be many sessions before Emma and I reached this level of disclosure, but I needed some advice now.

I told John that Emma hadn't mentioned her father, and she didn't react when I asked about her parents.

"So do you think she is being, or has been, abused by the father?" John asked. "How was he when you walked out of your office?"

"He looked worried, kept shifting his stare from Emma to me."

"Try to get her to trust you. Ask her questions about her childhood, what games she played."

Sitting in *Ozio's* one hour later, two empty Martini glasses and a wine flute before us, things had loosened up considerably, and John was down to the last two inches of his cigar. I had even forgotten that in two and a half days I would see Marcel when I heard my phone buzz:

> evening calm
> a trout glides through a bay
> of spent caddis nymphs

Well! It looked like Marcel had gone fishing.

❖ ❖ ❖

Had Christine called during my working week I might have answered. But Rayne had not forgiven Christine's false accusation that I had talked to others about the wine tasting evening, even implying that I may have said that she and I hadn't been together. More importantly, Rayne blamed her for forcing the unfortunate conversation with Raymond that was going to take place this very evening, Sunday. Christine called twice, late morning.

Raymond and I spent the afternoon in the garden, scrubbing down our small Webber grill, and weeding our new begonia flowerbeds. Before drinks, and on the spur of the moment, we decided to drive to Meridian Park to hear the bongos. I'm pleased to say I managed to get him to dance a little, a sort of hunched waddle before the mosquitoes forced us into retreat to his BMW.

As he started the car, I teased him to think beyond our deck or living room, to choose somewhere nice for cocktails. This is how we ended up at *Proof*, in Chinatown, one of his after-work haunts.

Even on a Sunday, the bar was full and buzzy. We sat on stools and played our old Georgetown game, guessing someone's job, inventing his or her personality. At one stage, Raymond suggested we try to imagine each person's deepest secret. He admitted I'd won when I unfrocked a large young woman as a cross-dressing senator wearing a fat suit, adding that his Negroni was spiked with a lobbyist's blood. Raymond was graceful in defeat, but claimed psychologists had an unfair advantage.

It is in a lighthearted mood that we fall into our chairs at home. Raymond is filling my glass with Chablis when I am reminded of our game at *Proof* and his mention of deepest secrets. I suddenly remember the calls from Christine. Had David decided to go public on her affairs? Was she trying to warn me he was planning to call Raymond? I can't wait any longer.

"Raymond? I have something I need to tell you."

"A joke?" he asks and laughs. "Or what first got you interested in opera."

"No, about Christine and David. They're probably going to divorce."

"What?"

I tell him about Christine's affairs. His eyes widen when I mention names—men we have met, even sat beside at dinner. He walks to the drinks cabinet to top up his scotch before sinking back into his chair. He asks how I know all this.

I take a deep breath, put down my wine glass, and admit that I often picked up her children after school when she was in some liaison. I confess that though I hated it, she always seemed to have a way of coaxing me to accept. The worst time was when she asked me to pretend I had accompanied her to a wine tasting.

"What the hell came over you?" he asks. His voice has taken on a lower tone, one of patronizing gravitas. "Well, I'm glad you finally told me."

I can see my husband is furious. Suddenly, his forehead wrinkles. "Why are you so sure they're divorcing? Did Christine tell you?"

There is a growing pulse in my ears, a rising dryness in the throat. I reach behind my neck for my hair, twisting and twisting as though I were about to start braiding.

"Because David confronted me last Tuesday."

I tell about David calling me, asking me to join him at the *Mayflower Hotel* bar. He had wasted no time announcing he knew all about Christine's infidelities—had even witnessed some—and knew that I had covered for her many times, including the wine tasting evening. He told me he was going to file for divorce and had engaged an attorney. He wanted to meet to say that I disgusted him.

"You stupid, stupid bitch!" Raymond shouts, making my shoulders jerk. "You do know that you're going to be quoted in the divorce proceedings, don't you? Dragged through the mud together with that skank, Christine. You may even be called to testify. Oh, my God, what are my parents going to say? Stupid bitch!"

I am about to say how sorry I am, when he finds a new source of anger.

"And fucking hell. Cyril is going to find out about it, if he doesn't know already. He and David are members of the same club. Fucking, fucking hell!"

As he storms up the stairs, I decide this is the real Raymond: not my sometimes fun-loving, sports-obsessed partner, nor even the imperious and demanding husband, but someone quite different—someone who puts his reputation ahead of anything and anyone. Raymond's mentioning of Cyril tells me something else: this is how Amanda Brock knew about the wine tasting— she knew Christine and I did not attend and were not together that evening; Amanda Brock knew this only days after that fateful Thursday, and so did her husband, Cyril.

I stay in the kitchen, washing glasses, drying them, and washing them again, recalling the few times Raymond and I have seriously argued. He will wake early tomorrow, making his exit before he is forced to speak or even look at me. As I set the breakfast table and make ready for bed, my smartphone rings. It is a call from "Unknown."

"Hello?" is all I can say before I hear the sound of wind, and the faintest sense of someone breathing.

My two-week delayed session with Marcel is scheduled for two o'clock, but first I have my morning patients: a recent, introductory referral, before a more difficult session at eleven with Emma.

She is more composed than the week before. Gone is the nervous picking of the scabs on her arms, the flicker of her eyes towards the door on the other side of which her father waits, the wary look whenever I ask about her family life. She is even dressed differently, with a smart long-sleeved blouse, pressed slacks, and pink ballet flats. Her spider tattoo still peaks up from behind her collar, and the single pin still skewers her left eyebrow, but she carries the whole session off with a smile.

And that smile is the problem. It never wavers, no matter how many questions I ask. Today, Emma had arrived protected by a veneer of preppy chic. She seemed to have taken her father in—"She's so much better, Doctor Lewis," he said, before settling into the chair outside. I had seen this so many times. Once more, I was looking at a false persona, a construction to stifle doubt or questions, even in oneself.

The standard therapeutic response to someone who has suffered trauma is to use an early session to gain trust and encourage openness. I ask about her friends, what music she likes, what is her favorite time of year. I even use John's suggestion, asking what games she used to play, whether she has kept her dolls or childhood books—she hasn't. To each answer, I give a little bit of myself, like, "I often feel the same."

When our fifty minutes end we have made no obvious progress, but she does agree to meet the following week, though she cancelled the appointment on Thursday.

It was in all other respects a fairly routine Monday morning. But the calamity of last night, including Raymond's shouting and his stomping of stairs, hung around me like a sour cloud, and I knew I had to clear my mind before Marcel arrived.

This is why I am sitting on a bench at Dupont Circle, rereading a section of Jordania's book? Some young women are lounging on the grass, sunbathing in the midday sun. I am cool and content. What slight breeze there is ripples between my three layers of silk, and I can feel my arms prickling.

A group of tourists is gathered around the central fountain and, on the northeast side, chess games abound. People amble on the circled path. One fails to move beyond the bench so I look up, and see Marcel.

"Good morning, or is it afternoon, Doctor Lewis?" he says. "We're seeing each other soon, so perhaps you'd like to continue your quiet time."

"No, not at all, please, take a seat—I've finished my reading. My goodness, you look very well. Appears you've caught the sun."

He looks almost plumped up if one can use that phrase on such a slight frame. He is clean-shaven, smartly dressed, and there is a whiter band of skin near his hairline above a reddened face. He tells me he has spent the last half hour at *Kramer's*— "Just browsing."

He settles down one space away from me. "We don't need to talk about the plum anymore, Doctor Lewis", he says calmly.

He catches me off balance before I think to say, "Perhaps you'd better tell me everything."

"When I got to Pittsburgh I checked into a small hotel on the south side and sort of wandered around the streets of my old neighborhood for two days..."

Listening, I don't utter a word until fifteen minutes later when he takes a small break in his story.

"How did Margaret find you?"

After storming out of his father's house, Marcel had chosen to walk back to the hotel but stopped for breath at a small cafe. Over a long coffee he had decided to return to the house to rant some more. But as he was about to climb the steps, he turned away. Which is when Margaret had seen him, had slipped out of the house, and followed him to the hotel.

She arrived at his door in the early evening. Marcel was listening to music and initially didn't hear her. She banged harder. He thought perhaps the maid had arrived for turndown service. Instead, Margaret stood there in a gray raincoat, arms crossed. She walked into the room and sat on the near side of the bed. "Tell me exactly what you said," she demanded. Marcel complied, adding additional accusations.

Later, much later, they walked to a small Italian restaurant. They had to wait for the first Saturday seating to clear before they could get a table. Margaret, whom he learned was trained as a grief counselor, had dissolved each of his points, dispelling so many demons.

"Terminal illness is a time of personal grief, Marcel," I say. "So, Margaret was working with your mother?" He nods and continues.

Margaret had come to the house most mornings in the last months of his mother's life, arriving at nine and often staying into the afternoon. After failing to get Isabella to take pain killers, Margaret had spent hours just holding her hand. Marcel's father, Frank, would sometimes return early from work, or even slip away for an hour at lunchtime. Seeing how distraught he was becoming, Margaret recommended he join a cancer support group.

That's where he was three evenings a week. Isabella would sit or walk in pain until Frank returned to the house, when her bravery would leave her and she'd fall apart, often into his arms. Late at night, the pain became so overwhelming that she would bang her head against the wall. These were the sounds within the walls that Marcel heard.

By the time Marcel arrived at the house the next morning he felt clear at last of the misunderstandings that had terrorized him for years. Earlier, over breakfast, Margaret had gone over her conversation with Marcel the night before with Frank.

Now, sitting across the kitchen table, Frank challenged Marcel. Why had he left his mother on the day she died—didn't he realize she was close to the end? And how could Marcel have behaved so rudely at the funeral when he walked away from the family and stood under a tree, and in the days following when he just moved out? It was inexplicable and inexcusable. From that day, Frank had decided to disown Marcel and, even if he had wanted to return, the door to the house was closed.

Marcel told me that, over time, Margaret had slowly worked on Frank, easing his bitterness, allowing him to wonder more and more often what had become of Marcel. Frank had heard from Marcel's friend, Johnny, only that Marcel had graduated from some college, but he hadn't asked or been told where.

In the months following Isabella's death, Frank had crumpled emotionally, and at one stage had taken two week's sick leave, the first of his working life. Thanks to Margaret's occasional visits and the cancer support group, Frank started climbing back into the world. It was almost two years before he and Margaret became romantically involved.

Marcel stayed into the evening all that Sunday. Much more was said and explained, and the more they talked the more their voices calmed. As Marcel was leaving, standing below the porch light above the steps, Frank said that he was proud of what Marcel had achieved, and especially proud that he had the courage to return home.

Frank offered to take the Monday off work but Marcel told him that he needed a day to himself. He went to the sculpture court of the Carnegie Museum of Art for most of Monday and filled almost half of a new journal, a journal I would never see. That evening, and every evening for the rest of the week, he walked from his hotel to his old home and sat at a table with his father while Margaret cooked, keeping a close ear on their conversations.

On the Tuesday evening, Frank asked Marcel if he was happy with his life. With a shiver of anger, Marcel spoke about his increasing withdrawal. When Margaret left the kitchen, he even talked of his problems with women, how he feared making love, how his first real girlfriend, Susan, had left him. Margaret returned as he was describing the work he and I had been doing together, of the target of thirty dates with women I had set him and why. Frank and Margaret laughed at that. Most of all, he talked of the need to suppress memories by burying them in sound and meter.

Sitting with me on a bench at Dupont Circle, Marcel takes a small breath so I tell him about the book that is in my lap.

"A colleague, my friend Carolyn, recommended I look it up. What you've been doing is called entrainment—internalizing rhythmic sound."

"You're quite amazing, Doctor Lewis. I can't think of anyone else who'd insert something like that." We both laugh.

"Thank you, Marcel, but it's key to what you told your father and Margaret. The author of this book believes entrainment allows a person to stay balanced when threatened or attacked.

Think of soldiers marching into battle to the sound of drums—they don't sense fear, they don't feel pain. That's what you've been doing. But I'm interrupting—"

He talks more about his father's question, whether Marcel was happy with his life. He could only whisper the answer, "I'm wasting it." He had expected his father to ask him why, but the reply was phrased differently.

"So my father asked what I *really* want to do. He told me to follow my heart—whatever I decided was good with him. I said I'd think about it. I still am.

"The next day, I decided to get in touch with my friend, Johnny. I hardly recognized him. He's got two kids now but said he'd take Friday off so we could go fishing."

It is almost one o'clock and the story of Marcel's last two weeks is almost complete. He took the train back to DC the evening before and, in answer to my question, admits that he hasn't contacted Maureen.

"She called a few times the first week I was away. I think she's guessed by now I don't want to continue, but I think I ought to tell her to her face that she's not right for me—maybe for the man she met, or the one she was trying to turn me into, but not for the person I am now. I owe her that."

As we walk down New Hampshire, before he breaks away to get to his office, he says, "Thanks for listening, Doctor Lewis. I guess there's no longer a need for us to meet at two."

I touch his forearm and he stops.

"Oh, no Marcel, there is a need. We have to talk of Julie." He gives me the strangest look.

"So, Julie—tell me, and take your time."

We are sitting in my office. He still has the same strange look on his face—it reminds me of a prairie dog on guard, eyes too large and mouth pursed into a pout. After passing across my copy of *The Haiku Handbook* with "many thanks," he replies:

"What can I say? She had a big heart. She was always good to me and—"

"How did you get to know each other? I've seen the haiku you gave her. Had you been to her apartment?"

He turns his head to the side then stops suddenly. His eyes widen even more, and he smiles.

"Oh, you're talking about Julie, your patient."

"Of course that's who I'm talking about—my ex-patient, Julie."

I sound irritated, and I am. Evasiveness and a smile is not what I need when talking of someone I cared for. He places his palms on his face and draws them slowly down, as though washing. The smile is gone.

"No one told me, or I would have gone to the funeral," he says. "I dropped by her apartment the day after. The guy on the first floor said she'd died."

"I repeat, how did you get to know her?"

"Look, Doctor Lewis, you don't know this—how would you? But your patient Julie reminded me of Johnny's mom in lots of ways. Her name was also Julie."

Now it is my turn to be confused, at least for a moment.

"Julie—that's Johnny's mother—watched out for me after Mom died. She was a lovely woman, but often depressed. She made up for it by eating. She was hugely overweight, which made her even more depressed. She even walked like your Julie—you know, swaying, stopping for breath, no cane though. I think it was only Johnny that kept Ben and her together. Then she died. It was a heart attack, very sad. But you want to hear about your Julie."

"Do you want to talk about Johnny's mother first?"

"No, Doctor Lewis, it was so long ago. I remember seeing your Julie leaving your office about four months back. And then a couple of months ago I bumped into her at the Starbucks on Connecticut juggling a coffee, a plate of muffins, and a large bag. So I helped her to a table and joined her. My God, she was shy until I told her I also was seeing you.

"She asked if I could help her later in the day. She wanted to go to a pawnshop on 14th but was afraid. So I left work early and waited for her at *Crown Pawnbrokers*. Well, to be honest, I waited next-door—less seedy looking.

"She was only a few minutes late. I thought she wanted to browse, perhaps buy something. But she had half a houseful of things in a large bag—old teapots, candlesticks, a cool Sony Walkman, that kind of thing.

"The shop's got a glass corridor entrance, for security, I guess. She almost got stuck before we reached the door. The owner bought most things, and she seemed pleased—told me she was having difficulty with money."

This "difficulty" was because I was helping her manage her bank account, but he wasn't to know.

I try to calm an emotion I sense rising from my waist into my chest. Respect for someone is something I haven't felt for a very long time.

"On our second visit to the pawnshop there was a new guy behind the counter. He didn't want to buy anything, and so she was faced with lugging the bag home. It was pretty heavy so I went outside and caught a cab—her place is not far from mine.

"She invited me in for tea and to meet her cat, apologizing for the disorder. I lied and said it was tidier than my own apartment, said I couldn't bear to be alone there. 'Just come around when you want—I'm here every night,' she said.

"And that's all there was really. There was no physical intimacy if that's what you're thinking, though I did write her that haiku. It slowed down when I started doing that online dating, Doctor Lewis. I think I dropped by three or four times."

I tell him what he did was wonderful. With this mystery resolved, a thought occurs to me.

"I know this may sound odd, but have you been phoning me late at night?"

He is immediately defensive, saying he would never do this after I asked him to text. Soon, he relaxes and admits he has enjoyed the challenge of texting less than seventeen syllables.

"So after all that's happened in the last two weeks, are you still in need of heavy beats? I'll admit I can hardly hear a trace compared to how you used to speak."

"No, the sounds are gone, but in a strange way I miss them. By the way, how did you like *The Poem's Heartbeat*? I thought you'd appreciate the chapters on meter."

I remember the harsh words I had written in my journal about the book. They now reek of ungratefulness, adding to the emotion I already feel. I weigh my reply carefully, but I cannot make the words dance.

> *"It's heavy work—I had to scan the lat*
> *er chapters, but I learned a lot. My life's*
> *been pretty stressful lately, I'm afraid.*
> *I promise I'll reread them when I can."*

He may have noticed that I used the word "life" instead of "work," but he is too busy tapping his fingers on the arm of the chair.

"That's good, Doctor Lewis. Right now I need to think about what I really want to do and make some decisions. Would it be possible to meet later this week, perhaps Friday for lunch?"

I think that is a splendid thought, Marcel.

Just text me when you've chosen where to meet.

Though my words refuse to dance, as I speak I can feel their rhythm. It's called entrainment, and it helps to bury pain.

I knew it would take some time for Raymond to forgive me for supporting Christine. But four long evenings have elapsed and there is little sign of a thaw.

True, he hasn't created much opportunity for this, leaving early for work and later finding a combination of cocktails and a working dinner, and, last night, a lecture on US energy policy to attend. But Rayne keeps reminding me that Raymond was also in the wrong, and I must admit she's been a constant source of fun, if not wickedness at times.

On Tuesday, for example, Rayne and I were alone all evening. At one point, she picked up Donald Hall's, *To Read a Poem*, despite my promise not to read poetry. She danced around the room slapping the book on side tables and chairs to the beat of an old Crusaders album, *Southern Comfort*. I laughed and told Rayne to stop, but she was happy, spinning, and spilling her drink—thankfully, gin doesn't stain.

On Wednesday, Carolyn relieved the tedium of my day of back-to-back patients and notes. When we met, she seemed genuinely thrilled by my news of Marcel, remarking that she could see the effect it had on me too, that I was "lighter," and to my eyes so was she. But Carolyn did say it was early days and, at first, I thought she was referring to me.

Speaking of Marcel, he texted a particularly enigmatic haiku the next day:

> trying to recall
> from the Sent file

what I said

So yes, Carolyn, I too am thrilled by Marcel's news. Was it my imagination or did I see a pinkish hue in your standard starched, white shirt this morning, and was that you making coffee without your jacket?

I confess, I would love to share Marcel's story with some of my patients, or perhaps with Raymond, Amanda, Christine, Cyril, and Dawn—with anyone who wishes to know the smell of fear and what courage looks like. You never know, perhaps they might even see me in a different light through the prism of my work. But these are early days. Though Marcel believes he's exorcised his demons, this is just the first stage of his recovery. Soon, he will likely hit a wall. Perhaps he has already done so.

Tonight, Thursday, Raymond and I are at home. He has just informed me he has business in New York early next week and wants to visit his parents in Boston for the weekend. I am not invited, which is a shame because I suspect they would like Rayne, at least some parts of her. Now Raymond can scurry home to his "Mum" and tell her what a bad girl I've been, and on Sunday he'll don his best golf clothes and play a round with his father, both dropping names at every stroke.

I believe Raymond thinks being alone in DC will be good for me, a time when I can "reflect on things." Indeed, he has just spent the last minutes before brushing his teeth mapping out my whole weekend, step by step, lash by lash—I must shift the dining table back, tidy my side of the office, and one drink per night is my limit.

Dear Raymond, here is something wicked for you, inspired by Rayne and written by Vera, an exercise is simple enjambment:

> *Don't tell me what I need to do. Don't tell*
> *me what I need to do. Don't tell me what*
> *I need to do. Don't tell me what I need*
> *to do. Don't tell me what I need to do.*

Rayne or Vera, Vera or Rayne—what is it to be today? I settle on Vera, allowing me to withdraw into myself as I watch Raymond refold the shirts I had folded. My pulse slows as he packs, unpacks, and then packs again. I can even be the quiet, little wife as he says goodbye before driving off in his polished BMW, his coat hung from the hook above the rear passenger door. He can leave his car in the office parking lot before flying to Boston this evening, but to me he is already gone.

The real reason for choosing Vera today is my forthcoming lunch with Marcel. After reading and rereading his last haiku, I have been apprehensive over what happened to him during the week. Unleashing Rayne on him would be unwise. He is still my patient, despite us having lunch together.

He, however, has already broken protocol. His text to me last night was not a haiku, a mere four words and five syllables— *Tabbard Inn at noon.*

Which is where I found him, sitting at a small table set back in a corner, wearing a simple white shirt and smart-casual jeans. He got up as I approached and offered me the chair facing out, "So you can people-watch if things get dull." I thanked him, with a complicit smile.

After a waiter filled our water glasses, neither of us knew what to say until he suddenly asked, "Why do you wear so many layers, Doctor Lewis?"

I replied that perhaps it was because I have so much to hide. My joke was enough to break the ice.

Was it work or was it social? It was neither really, yet both. He was certainly relaxed. He asked many questions—what my husband did, where I lived, what were my tastes in music? I marveled at how at ease he seemed while, like a good therapist, watching his every move.

After we ordered main-course salads, it was time for me to ask a leading question.

> *"How has your week been? Have you had the time*
> *to think some more about your trip back home?"*

Again he smiled as he tapped his middle index finger on the table. He stopped and took a deep breath.

"Yes, I've had plenty of time to think. As you may have guessed from the haiku I sent you, I quit my job on Wednesday. Did it by email and then regretted it—I tried to recall it but it had already been opened. Call it divine intervention.

"Wednesday was also my last day at work. Even though I have to give a month's notice, I've been working on some confidential stuff lately. My boss said it was probably best if I just left straight away."

"My God!" was all I could say.

"And yes, I've had further thoughts about Pittsburgh. On the train back to DC I was so happy that Dad, Margaret, and I had reconciled. But there was also regret over lost time. Thankfully, joy exceeds regret, and I think that's how I was when you and I met on Monday.

"But since then, in fact since Wednesday, I've started to feel guilt. I can't take back the years, but I do need to make amends somehow. Don't get me wrong, Doctor Lewis, I was expecting this to happen. You see, while you've been delving into poetry, I've been reading up on therapy, particularly how to deal with trauma.

"I've learned there's an early phase when all seems resolved. But it's just the beginning, like where I am now. All I know is I had to quit my job and search for the life of passion that Dad begged me to do."

"My goodness Marcel, you never cease to amaze me. Yes, you *will* confront some obstacles, and you'll overcome them. And this feeling of guilt is very common."

"This guy, Jonathan Shay, says some people suffer moral injury after trauma," he continued, "and that makes a lot of sense to me. Wrongly accusing my dad of raping my mom was pretty terrible, but the way I behaved after the funeral was worse. He was suffering more than me. My guilt *is* a kind of injury—to myself, but also to Dad, Margaret and anyone else who's had to suffer me."

"Of course you're not finished," I said, reaching out to touch his arm. "It will take some time for this injury to heal. What are you planning to do?"

The waiter placed two Cobb salads on the table. I ordered a white wine. Marcel declined.

"I'm not sure," he said, "but I'm leaving DC. First stop will be back to Pittsburgh to spend some time with Dad and Margaret. He's buying a new mattress for the bed in my old room and a cabinet for my hi-fi equipment. After Pittsburgh, who knows?"

"When are you planning to leave?"

"Tomorrow, in the afternoon. I've given notice on the apartment, and I'll be putting my furniture in storage later today. There isn't very much. I'm sending the hi-fi stuff."

It seemed too early for me to lose him, a selfish thought but I felt it deeply—I still feel it. Someone else will now see him emerge and grow into the man he should be. Others will be able to hear him speak lyrically.

"Will you write?"

"Always," he replied. "I told you that I'd moved on from poetry, but that's not true. I've been playing around with free verse, as though I've started to fear meter for what it was doing to me. Anyway, I'm sure I'll try sonnets again sometime. Yes, I'll always write."

"What I meant was will you write to *me*?"

It was his turn to be caught off balance, and he muffled a laugh into his napkin. "

"Oh, Doctor Lewis, forgive me! How unbelievably narcissistic that was. Of course I will."

I invited him to ask me questions about our sessions together. He had many, picking up on the subtlest techniques I'd used. I confided that our working together hadn't been a one-way process. Through him I had rediscovered poetry.

"I thought you might appreciate borrowing this—the enigmatic journal," he said. "I started a new one on the way to Pittsburgh. This was the one I brought to most of our sessions, the one you kept asking to see. Here it is."

He placed it in my hand and gave it a slight pat as though saying goodbye.

"I'll cherish reading it," I said, solemnly. "And now we have more than a promise of writing—we have an implicit agreement to meet again so I can return it to you."

"Good. And Doctor Lewis, I think you'll learn a lot from its pages. I didn't write much, but there are some things I should have told you. And one last thing—I won't need to go on any more of those dates. Someone else will have to take up the slack," he said with his most crooked smile.

Yes, perhaps. But at least I now had his permission.

Marcel texted me the next day, and it was this, together with his slim journal, that prompted two decisions. The haiku was so seemingly heartfelt that it brought a few tears:

> Thesaurus search:
> so few words
> for goodbye

The first decision was capture the last months more completely. This is why I spent all day Sunday and the last two evenings writing in my new journal, a thick, leather-bound volume I bought many years ago at college. On its cover are the words "MARCEL MALONE," a safeguard in the unlikely event Raymond searches in my tote bag. And if my husband is in the room as I write, he will merely see me recording notes on a patient.

I am pleased to say the new journal is now up to date. Transcribing from my blue notebook, I expanded some early notes but did not cut—there are things that I said about Raymond and my feelings for him, for example, that I would not say now. The only part that is truly new is my account of my lunch with Marcel last Friday. I have tried to sound unemotional, but that's not how I felt—watching Marcel walk away was almost unbearable.

It seems remarkable that I had only twelve formal sessions with Marcel following the day when he lay curled up on my rug. For some time I wondered whether I should even write of my sessions with him, whether this was a breach of confidentiality between therapist and patient. I also struggled with what to do with the writings in the journal he gave me. I will seek his permission before ever sharing them.

It is now late Tuesday evening. Raymond returns from New York tomorrow. From now on I shall try to maintain the discipline of writing—I no longer wish to rely on my memory and the distortions it will weave. But before I sleep I want to reread Marcel's journal because it surprised me so much.

He has written nothing about his dates with women except within the safety of sonnets. He mentions Julie only twice and Maureen not at all. Many pages are blank; others contain only a word or phrase. There are two other features that are unusual: except for the last weeks, he avoids writing about his own feelings; indeed, most of the entries focus on our sessions together, addressed to me.

Since I have promised to return Marcel's journal to him, I decided to copy his entries into my own journal so I have them forever. I also inserted my own notes and comments. Marcel's entries start on April 4th, shortly after I suggested he start journaling. The final entry is June 17th, the weekend before he first went to Pittsburgh:

Wednesday April 4
This is the journal of Marcel Malone.

> On the next page is a single word:

Registered

> This would have been with the dating agency.

Wednesday April 11
She laughed at me—it wasn't painful. She
believes it's better if I am myself.

> Two blank pages precede seven sonnets on consecutive days. There are no edits or corrections. I suspect they have been copied from a poetry notebook.

Wednesday April 18
She homed in like a laser on the words,
"Each night I hear the sounds within the walls."

I think I'll keep this journal to myself.

Two sonnets follow.

Saturday April 21
She says she cares. She says she cares. She cares.

> Two sonnets follow the next day. The Monday
> entry is the fly-fishing essay, transcribed in a firm
> hand. There is another sonnet on the Tuesday.

Wednesday April 25
She's reading a lot of poetry. She thinks my writing's beautiful; I
saw her tears. I must ask questions more.

The prim act out their whims in wayward ways.

Thursday April 26
Met Melissa. Lost her number.

Monday April 30
She gave me a book by Donald Hall. Bought it just for me.

Wednesday May 2
I think she listens to my every word.

Friday May 4
And there was I believing that she cared,
but it's a trick to make me open up.

Saturday May 5
She had her hair down. I like it that way. Spoke to her at
Kramer's.

He lists eight poetry books. He must have played the "fingernail game" at the public library the day after I suggested it.

His first four choices are in a block:

The Beautiful Librarians, by Sean O'Brien
A Martian Sends a Postcard Home, by Craig Raine
Another Life, by Derek Walcott
Shall We Gather At The River, by James Wright

The first three titles are iambic, the last one trochaic. The titles seem innocent, unemotional, unlike the remaining four his fingernail found:

My Heart Is Broken, by Mavis Gallant
The Death Notebooks, by Anne Sexton
Dread, Beat and Blood, by Linton Kwesi Johnson
Far Cry, by Norman MacCaig

Monday May 7
OH GOD
OH GOD
OH GOD
OH GOD
OH GOD

This is the day of our first breakthrough where his metered speech broke down, and he revealed so much about the sounds he heard in his parents' bedroom.

At the end of the session he ran away from the practice.

Two blank pages, then…

No voices

Tuesday May 8
> This entry fills a page. It covers more than a
> week, possibly ending around May 16th:

She made me say those things. She set me up.
I trusted her. She's so obsessed with me
opening up and then look at what happens. But she's closed herself—I know, and I

bet it's not only with me. She totally deserved what I said. Oh,
Christ, I'm breaking up. I lost control. I lost control of the beat.
Still no voices. No way I'm going back to her.

I've got to erase these thoughts inside my head, blank out the
images, or...

No voices.

Still pissed. Can't believe what I said, but what's worse is that I
could think such things. And there was I blaming Dad, but Mom
was as much to blame. She didn't have to put up with it. She
could have said something.

Maybe Dr. Lewis thinks she was doing the right thing. But she
doesn't know the risks of opening up. Tonight, I thought I heard
someone. I turned the sound down low and there it was.

Feel a mess, felt a mess—she didn't seem to notice. Smarten up,
but isn't that what Dad used to say?

Still no voices.

Give it one more try with her.

Wednesday, May 9. Just heard. The funeral was yesterday.

Poor Julie's death's a lesson to us all.

> Two sonnets follow, then a blank page.

Thursday May 17
I lost my way and a sonnet danced tonight.

Friday May 18
Had coffee with Melissa. Said I'd get in touch with her. I like the way she tucks a strand of hair behind her ear.

Dylan Thomas. Now as I was young and easy...

Monday May 21
Need to read an essay by Carl Jung.
Need to become more extroverted.
Need to read *The Haiku Handbook* then return it.
I am allowed to text her if I use less than 17 syllables.

Wednesday May 24
> Marcel has listed six haiku. I recognize two by Bashō, and there are two more with the letter "B" to the side. One is circled—it speaks of rippling waves and the scent of wind beating together. The letter "I" is next to the remaining two— these, I know, are by another famous Japanese poet, Issa.

Thursday May 25
> What looks like two sentences have been written but they are scratched out using a different colored pen.

Friday May 26
What is it with her? It was just a plum.

Never noticed before. Perhaps it hadn't happened before. Think she saw me tapping my fingers:

"Hello, Marcel - come in and take a seat," she said as I walked in.

No date

A single word in the center of a new page:

Chicago

Monday June 4
She wanted to talk about that plum again. Handled it well—ignored it. Should have asked more questions...dropping my guard.

Didn't comment on my hair, but I don't think she approved. There was a flicker in her eyes when I talked of making love. Is it this attachment thing?

So, it's Robert Frost now. I used to love his work, but he is so controlled.

Sounds within the walls...

Does she think that speaking this way gets her closer to me—is something happening to her?

"Hello, Marcel ... and how are you today?" was her welcome today.

"And maybe you can tell me why you asked
for my consent to see Maureen again?"

Another lovely couplet.

Perhaps it's because she wants to show me how boring metered speech can sound. It's too late Dr. Lewis. I'm opening up, giving breath to the extrovert, whoever he is.

Three blank pages follow, the last of which has a round coffee cup stain. The next page is therefore a shock—tiny script in pencil, almost illegible in places.

Monday June 11
Session didn't end well. It was just too much. So let's talk about you, Dr. Lewis.

"Well, thank you. How are you today, Marcel?"

You were strange today, like a different person. But you couldn't help falling back on that five-beat line. When I said you looked nice, you replied,

"Well, that's a lovely thing to say, Marcel.
So tell me everything about your week."

And then the way you asked about my writing, stressing the word "anything," as though you were upset:

"So have you written *anything* this week?
You haven't brought your journal once again."

You even shouted at me, though I deserved it. Once again I apologize.

You say I've created a new persona, but who are you to preach? Aren't you doing the same? Yes, I liked the way you looked today, even the makeup. But please don't touch your eyes—my mother also never plucked her eyebrows, just left them natural and perfect, like a pair of raven's wings.

Anyway, wasn't it you who said I needed to be more extrovert, at least in my poetry? That's all I'm trying to do. Now you want me to go back, to "get inside" myself. I could do exactly that. I could regress, and then try to deal with the past. But unlike you, I can't just braid my hair and wipe away my makeup. The "me" that I am now is stronger—this other person you were today should know this.

But despite the lipstick and the long-sleeved dress, I thought I saw something you are hiding; perhaps "struggling with" is a better phrase. I sensed it when you mentioned Duende, and when you talked of Lorca—he who eschewed strict metrics,

"though he returned to sonnets late in life," you added.

I loved your response when I gave you Alfred Corn's book, *The Poem's Heartbeat*:

"Well, thank you! What a lovely gift, Marcel."

So perfectly metrical!

But then you had to bring up that plum again. And here's some more of your iambic pentameter, Dr. Lewis:

"Oh, no—I want to talk about the one
in which a plum was nested in a tree."

"That's strange, Marcel. It must have had a strong
effect on you—why d'you think that is?"

There are voices. I can hear them, on the edge of the guitar solo.

Wednesday June 13
Did I really question whether what I heard was real?
Can you really hear conversations muffled through a wall?
What did I hear? What did I really hear?
So who am I?
Really, so who am I?

Thursday June 14
Thank you for the text, Dr. Lewis. I really like this haiku:

two dealers
in the park opposite
empty swings

When did you write it? Why did you send it?
Two concrete images, dealers and swings, with the middle line as a pivot—it could go either way, with the first or the last line. And how interesting, the ambiguity of "empty." One could read it as an adjective or a verb.

When you were talking of Lorca, you said that my plum haiku could have been pointing at something I didn't want to face. Is it the same with this haiku of yours? Is it the dealers, or the empty swings, Dr. Lewis?

Friday June 15
A haiku captures a moment—that's what *The Haiku Handbook* says. And you spoke about moments a few weeks ago, didn't you? That was when I asked you if everything I'd described surrounding my mother's death was really true.

If I think back, what *were* the moments in that house? If I were to write haiku about the weeks before Mom died, what concrete images would I use? Would they have to be images, or could I use sounds, or even smells?

I hate this apartment, and I hate who I am becoming.

> A page has been torn out. The very next page looks as though it has been written in a hurry.

Saturday June 16
I made a list of images, sounds, and smells. Tried to match them with moments—most seem to fade into fog. The only ones that don't are sounds.

Those thumping sounds—when did they start? I can't remember them when Mom was well.

Why would he rape her while she was dying? Was it an outlet for Dad's own anger? But he didn't seem angry, even with me—just disappointed.

Was I angry she was dying, that she was going to leave me? Was I angry with her, or did I choose to pour anger onto someone else, even myself?

I hope Dad was bashing Mom's head against the wall—that way she might have passed out and not have to suffer any more pain.

Mom didn't scream—why? Why be silent if Dad kept abusing her? Why not whisper something to me in the mornings?

I'm sure he staggered home drunk. But I can't remember seeing him when he got home—am I blocking this out? Did I ever smell alcohol on him? Were his eyes bloodshot in the mornings? I avoided looking at him, so I don't know.

My essay about Penns Creek on her bedside table was crumpled—why? Her hands were always clean, so who smudged the paper? Why did she write, "I'd like to go there one day" when she knew she was dying?

I told Dr. Lewis her cervix was as big as a grapefruit—how would I know that? The cancer had spread, and she had tumors everywhere. I even saw one under her armpit. What is the plum in my haiku? What is it trying to tell me?

And then the last entry…

Sunday June 17
I'm frightened, Dr Lewis. I'm frightened of doubts and of the truth, of going back to the person I was. Perhaps the thumping sounds will come back. They're with me now.

I'm frightened of seeing you tomorrow, that you will raise new doubts. But most of all I'm frightened that you'll ask more questions, and I will tell you what I'm going to do.

Do you remember telling me about myths, the myths we create to bury our concerns? I'm going to create a myth. I am going to tell myself that *you* want me to find out if my father raped my mother, that *you* want me to go to find the truth, no matter what it is, because you care. If anything goes wrong it will be *your* fault, Dr. Lewis. Forgive me. It's the only way.

I'm also creating a myth for you. In my crazy head I'm going to convince myself that going back to confront my past will show you that it can be done. This is my gift to you. I care about you, too, Dr. Lewis, very much.

After I read Marcel's journal last Friday evening I was so overwhelmed that I skipped dinner and just drank. When I dragged myself into the bedroom, anger had grown that Marcel had not shared the concerns in his journal in our sessions together. I wish I'd known how constant his terror was over the voices returning.

I always knew he was pleased whenever I offered praise, but he remembered what I said word-for-word. And the last four poetry book titles his fingernail had found at the public library—"My Heart Is Broken," "The Death Notebooks," "Dread, Beat and Blood," and "Far Cry"—would have been so revealing if he had shared them with me.

My anger had mellowed by Saturday afternoon when his *Thesaurus* haiku arrived on my smartphone—there are, indeed, so few words for goodbye. By then, I was already filled with awe over his honesty and bravery.

Rayne surfaced after I reread Marcel's comments on the different person he had seen in me. She and I spent an hour rearranging the CDs in our stereo cabinet. My small opera collection now uncomfortably runs from Albinoni on the left to Wagner on the right. Rayne convinced me this was merely to contrast with Raymond's vintage country western CDs. They are no longer perfect—all we did was return the recently played stack at random slots on his three shelves.

I spent the evening thinking whether what Marcel considered to be insights about me were true. That was why I started reworking my own journal. I even wrote a haiku in reply to Marcel's, although I didn't send it:

> first day
> trying to breathe
> without you

Tonight, Tuesday, four days since he left, I am still trying to breathe easily. I wish he were here so I could reaffirm that his first myth was indeed true, because I did want him to confront and resolve his memories with all my heart. And yes, I would have been there for him if anything had gone wrong. As for his second myth, that by returning to face his past he was setting an example for me—it was a gift, but it was only a myth.

Before I end tonight, before I clear the debris around my chair—chip crumbs, unread newspapers, Martini picks—I need to write one more thing. I'm going ahead with online dating, following Marcel's lead. This was my second decision on Sunday and surprisingly easy to make. After dragging the agency's email from my Archive, I clicked on the first blue address. The reply came back within an hour. I meet him tomorrow, at noon, at Rayne's chosen restaurant.

To many people, *Bistro Lepic* is off the beaten track, and at lunchtime it is discrete, a two-mile trek for those of us who work downtown in the M and L Street corridors.

I had decided to take a taxi rather than my disheveled Golf, and asked the driver to drop me half way up Wisconsin Avenue. I needed time to shop. At a boutique I found a gaudy purple blouse to match my beige trouser suit. I changed into it before visiting a lingerie store, staring at rows of flimsy thongs before buying a new sports bra.

Walking up the hill, I rehearsed my opening words. I wanted to be lively, all arms and laughs, with the quiet confidence from "working with creative people to tight deadlines." I planned not to ask questions, just talk about myself in that vacuous way I had heard most Fridays at *Ozio's*. But two blocks away my steps slowed, and a cold trickle of sweat dropped to my lower back. By the time I arrived I was shaking.

He was sitting with his back to me. A comb-over almost hid a bald patch. When he rose to greet me, in a brown, checkered suit, dark blue shirt and tie, and black shoes, I saw that we were the same height.

This was his first time at *Lepic*—"Great choice," he said, in a thick New York accent. He confided, with a smile, that lunchtime liaisons were a regular feature of his life, and no doubt, I thought, his waistline. As much as I tried, I couldn't get my hands to leave my lap.

I settled for my usual salad, this time a Chicken Caesar, and joined him in a glass of merlot from a bottle he insisted stay on the table "to breathe." He claimed he worked for a retail distributor of office equipment, spending several days a month in DC. He was yet to book into his hotel that he told me, winking, was "pretty close."

As the minutes dragged on, I began to wonder what had made the agency pair us up. As far as I could see, Rayne had nothing in common with this middle-aged man, but I was wrong.

"I couldn't help noticing that your favorite book, like mine, is *Atlas Shrugged*," he said. I was so astonished that he'd finally expressed interest in me that I took an extra sip of coffee. He continued.

"I made both my sons read it before they were twelve. I just love how Ayn Rand urges us to pursue personal wealth and happiness, reaffirming that liberty is an inalienable right. Hell of a shame more people don't think like that. We'd be a better country if they did. And why should anyone be allowed to take my hard-earned money to give to those who refuse to work?"

The check was on the table, and he had just offered to pay when I felt anger rising once again. It was triggered by a sense of humiliation. I'd planned this as a way of trying to understand what Marcel had to confront. But Marcel had left. Why was I subjecting myself to this expected prelude to a romp in some hotel room? I was debasing Rayne!

I would probably have left politely if he hadn't added, "Let's get rid of all federal spending, and kick those liberal clowns out of Congress."

As he was holding down the check, I noticed a circle of pale, waxy skin at the base of his left ring finger. Draining the last of my wine, I shoved my chair back and stood.

"I guess you'd scrap the Federal Reserve, the CIA, the Air Force, the Navy, and the Army—perhaps you think each State should have its own. And what about the National Institutes of Health? You know, the place that does the medical research drug companies feed off. So Dennis, when your heart attack comes, or when your wife brings back some stomach bug from Cancun, plan to pay for it from your own bank account, right?"

And with that, Rayne stomped off, and so did I.

Carolyn was surprised to see me back so early. I had cancelled our weekly session, but she had a few minutes so I joined her in her office. She and her husband had been away for another long weekend—Charleston, this time. Her face had caught the sun and, from what I could see of her bare ankles, so had the rest of her body. Sitting down, I complimented her on her amber studs, the way they matched her butterscotch linen suit. Both were new, she told me.

I gave her the news about Marcel. She wanted to hear everything—how had he seemed, what did he say? I talked her through Friday's lunch, not mentioning his journal. I told her he realized he was just beginning his real journey, and he had promised to write.

"I'm going to miss him, Carolyn. To be honest, working with him I've learned a lot about myself and the way I approach patients. There are so many questions I didn't have time to ask him."

"Like what?" she replied, tilting her head in her therapist way.

"Like what did it really feel like going on those dates? He talked a lot about rejection, but did he ever feel humiliated, or angry?"

Carolyn nodded. "What else?"

"Why was he so certain his mother was being raped by his father? When I placed doubt in his mind, it was as though he was waiting for it—what signs of doubt had he seen but buried? And finally, how hard was it for him to decide to return to Pittsburgh to confront his father?"

Again, the small tilt of the head, but Carolyn had her own news. A young woman had been to the practice late this morning looking for me. She hadn't given her name. From Carolyn's description of her spider tattoo it had to have been Emma—I reminded Carolyn that Emma was the patient who cut herself and had cancelled our third session together.

To Carolyn's eyes Emma didn't look well and seemed to have been sleeping rough—broken fingernails, torn shirt, cracked lips. I told Carolyn that I only had her father's phone number. We agreed that, for the time being, I shouldn't contact him. Carolyn tried to offer Emma a coffee but she seemed in a rush. After hesitating, Carolyn added that she left behind blood spots on the carpet.

A strange and strained atmosphere pervades each room of the house like dust before rain. You could call it an uneasy peace. It has been like this for several days.

Raymond was already unpacked from his trip to Boston and New York when I got home on Wednesday. He was standing in front of the stereo cabinet, a country western CD in each hand. He turned his upper body and head as I walked in.

I felt uncomfortable in my combination of beige business suit, purple blouse and braided hair, but he didn't seem to notice. He just said "Hello" in return to my "Hi" before disappearing into his office.

By the time he emerged I had dinner ready and was on my second glass of wine. We sat without speaking while he played with his food, carefully separating chicken from chickpeas, pasta from peppers. He did eat, eventually.

Later, as I was getting ready for bed, he came to the door of my bathroom. I'm not used to removing makeup. With my eyes streaming, I didn't see him at first—I only heard his voice.

"So, do you want to hear about the trip?"

"I thought you might have phoned," Rayne decided to reply. "But you probably had no time."

He either ignored the jibe or didn't recognize it as such.

"Had a good time in Boston. Mum and Father are fine, although she had a little scare a week ago—small lump on her neck. Seems it was a cyst, benign. I didn't tell them anything about David and Christine's probable divorce."

Why would he? Raymond's parents had only met them once.

"But I did raise the subject with Cyril on Monday evening. He already knew, had been speaking with David—so like Cyril not to say anything. Anyway, he said he was pretty disappointed when David told him you'd covered up for Christine. Then he said the strangest thing."

"Uh-huh, and what was that?"

Raymond was leaning against the doorjamb, appearing to pick some blemish from the paint.

"He said at least you were discrete, something he values a lot. I had to agree with him, although I'm still pretty pissed, Vera. But I did tell him that discretion ran in my family and was also very important to me. I think he appreciated that."

As for Raymond and me, discretion has ruled every night since. We have kept to our promises—he will not talk about work, and I will not read poetry, at least not in his sight. If I'm honest, I haven't wanted to, anyway. As each evening has passed, it has been fashion magazines for Rayne, pajamas and TV for me. Even my work has seemed dull, but I am beginning to see some of my patients in a softer light—after all, divorce, physical abuse, and the loss of child custody drag their own chains of grief. I would have shared this at our Friday debrief, but Carolyn had to cancel and John was not available.

"He's having problems of his own at the moment," was all Carolyn said.

Marcel still has not texted me. Should I worry, should I be hurt? He'll write when he writes, I repeat to myself, and he's in good hands with Margaret, if indeed he is in Pittsburgh.

But on this first day of a new week, I am more than hurt. I am devastated.

Emma's father called this morning, as I was about to start a session. I heard Sarah, our receptionist say "Emma you said?"

I was expecting to hear Emma's voice when I picked up the phone. Instead, it was a deeper voice, controlled but with a waver at its edges.

The police had found her dead on Saturday. Her father was calling to let me know. She had started staying out at night over the last week. He and Emma's mother thought she might have met someone.

She came home for an hour last Thursday to pick up some food—energy bars, mainly—before rushing away without speaking to her mother. Emma was found in Chinatown, hunched in an alley with her wrists cut. Foul play wasn't suspected.

I could only say I was sorry, also Carolyn's words when I told her the news. We knew Emma was at risk, yet we hadn't acted. The fear of alerting her father last Thursday, someone over whom I had voiced my concerns, had outweighed our professional judgment.

The purple blouse is hanging in the closet. The high-heeled shoes are already in their box, and I am working on second Martini. My only hope is that Rayne stays with me tonight—but then she doesn't like dependent people. All I need is company, someone's voice to drown out the sounds of flesh being cut, the soft gasp, and the crumpled slump.

I need some company, Mr. Hall.

"Anthony, but just call me Tony."

I had half expected the agency to contact me and cancel the lunch. I had dutifully submitted a post-date report that was generally complimentary, before closing with the phrase, "There was no match," but I had no idea what Dennis had written.

Thanks to the agency, here I am, Wednesday, sitting opposite Tony at a table for two at the rear of *Bistro Lepic*. The same waiter who served my first date has seated us, but thankfully he gives no hint of recognition—so discrete.

At first appearance, Tony looks to be a better match. He is tall, for one thing. I'm guessing he is in his early forties. At the end of his long, denim-covered legs, he is wearing sneakers—black, with white laces and a matching mid sole rim—and no socks. With the sleeves of his white shirt rolled up, his tanned forearms match his ankles and his face. Were it not for his blond hair, he could be mistaken for an Arab—thick eyebrows, high cheekbones, and a beautiful curved nose.

"And you...Rayne's such an unusual name."

I say my parents wanted a boy so they could name him after Ray Charles. "They were huge fans of his, which probably explains why his crooning leaves me cold."

Tony tells me he is a creative director at a small advertising agency—"boutique," he calls it. This explains why he is dressed so casually, he says. His confidence encourages me to open up. I wave my arms as I tell him of my work in event planning: "Organizing those razzmatazz parties that companies hold to get their employees fired up. I love trying to frame the whole event around the values of—"

"Yeah, those values," he interrupts. "I branched out a few years ago into crisis management. Companies talk values, but when the proverbial hits the fan it's every man for himself."

"Don't I know it," I say, though I have no idea what I mean.

"Sounds like we both love our work," Tony says. "What most turns me on is creating subliminal messages within TV commercials. Never ceases to amaze me how gullible people can be—it's almost as though you can change their self-will, like pulling the strings on puppets. Talking of puppets, what's your favorite cocktail?"

It's more than a segue—it's a jolt, but for some reason I laugh. "Gin Martinis, very dry with a—"

"That's the problem with DC. They always shake their Martinis. Should be stirred, always. I'm a vodka man. Let's talk about music. Who's your favorite jazz musician?"

And so it goes on. He asks a question, and before I can answer he interrupts and shifts onto a new subject.

"Joe Pass."

"But he's so limp—chords and old classics. I reckon his brain was totally fried by all that alcohol. Talking of alcohol, twist or olive? Oh yeah, if you like jazz guitar why didn't you mention Al di Meola or Allan Holdsworth? Those guys rock."

All I can do is nod.

As the waiter takes the last course of the *pris fixe* away, Tony suggests we split the check. He neglects to ask for my phone number.

"Nice meeting you, Rayne, but, sorry, there's not much chemistry on my side," he says, sliding his wallet into his back pocket.

Walking down Wisconsin, looking for a cab, I try to pass off the whole lunch as just one of those things. What little of Rayne that's left listens as Vera explains that Tony has Attention Deficit Disorder. Rayne would have liked to tell him this, and she rehearses the words in her head. Vera would like to believe that it wasn't about her, that it wasn't personal. But both know that it was, and both know they were rejected.

One more date to go, Marcel. One more, and I'll have lunched with three strangers, just like you used to.

Carolyn looked very tired. She was on suicide watch with one of her patients and the woman's friend had called three times during the night. At our scheduled meeting she said wanted to discuss Marcel, which I knew would be an entry into me. But first Carolyn said we needed to agree that if the police called she would tell them straight away that my ex-patient, Emma, had visited the practice a few days before she died.

"The police are probably trying to piece together her last days. And they would have seen her self-inflicted cuts, talked to the father." I didn't need to say so, but I told Carolyn that I totally agreed.

"Anyway, back to Marcel," she said. "We were talking about him the other day, and what you learned or experienced working with him."

"Yes. At one stage it seemed hopeless, but then…you know, looking back, it was a hell of a risk to take, wasn't it?"

"But it worked, Vera. He went on those dates and, over time, built up some resistance to rejection. If things went wrong it was never his fault because it was *your* idea—*you* had insisted he did it."

"That's how it worked out, but it could have played out differently."

"In what way?" Carolyn asked.

I know I hesitated before replying.

"Suppose he wasn't able to think that way. Suppose he went into those dates with no protection against rejection—it would have been terrifying. But he was lucky. He met women who did most of the talking. They gave him time to build a shell and come out slowly. But I just wonder how much he suffered in those first weeks."

"No more than the women he dated," Carolyn said, on cue. "Sorry Vera, that's pretty heartless of me."

I told her it was OK, but she interrupted and apologized once more. Running her finger around her shirt collar, she agreed it must have been difficult for Marcel, that he had indeed been very brave. I had not seen this softer side of Carolyn in a long while. Breathing in, she continued.

"Anyway, how are *you* doing? I must say I like the new look—pretty flats, pressed slacks, and such a lovely flowered blouse. You look so much younger with your hair down."

I thanked her, and said I was absolutely fine. I described an idyllic life at home, and said Raymond also liked the new look. I had become so used to lying like this that I almost believed it.

"He dropped in to see his parents in Boston the other weekend. He had some early-week business in New York and got to spend some quality time with his boss—came back refreshed and energized."

"Well that's great." Making moves to end our meeting, she asked, "Do *you* ever go home to New Mexico? I've never heard you speak of it so I was just wondering."

I ran my hands through my hair and put on my best Vera smile.

"I haven't been back home for many years.
There's nothing to go back to I'm afraid."

The tension is still there, but at least for another reason. It is now just a week before Congress goes into recess and, when that last Friday in July arrives, Cyril and Amanda Brock will leave for their two-week vacation. Raymond will then be steering the ship. For the last two nights he has been reviewing his upcoming tasks, printing out pages of "must do's" by the hour. But it has given me some time for myself.

On Wednesday night, for example, I thought about how I had treated Dawn, and Rayne had treated Christine. Over the years, both have increasingly used me. If I had some small crisis, they were rarely there for me. When my patient Julie died, they were nowhere to be seen. But that was no reason for me to behave the same. Even though I blamed Raymond for rejecting Dawn's idea for her Rwandan friend, I had been insensitive and no source of support. Rayne had been particularly harsh with Christine at a time when she really needed someone. I wondered whether they were both feeling rejected and abandoned.

Last night, I spent over an hour online searching for a place where Raymond and I could have our own two weeks away. Oregon seemed the leading candidate, I told him. We could cruise through the pinot noirs of the Willamette Valley, and he had the choice of attending several country music festivals. Yee-haw!

Now, on a Friday lunchtime bathed in sunshine, I open the door to *Bistro Lepic* at five minutes past noon for my third and final date. My favorite waiter saunters up, smiles, and turns for me to follow. As he leads me across the room my heart stops. Sitting alone in a corner reading a menu is a man I know well. It is too late to turn back, even though he is yet to see me. I pray he doesn't look up.

I still haven't fully recovered, and I must say our Friday afternoon debrief meeting was pretty bizarre. Thankfully, we focused mostly on Carolyn's patients because, as she told me again beforehand, "John is having problems of his own," and my review was dull without Marcel.

As for *Ozio's*, for once we managed to secure one of the shaded outside tables. Again, John's cigar helped pass the time—he could lean back and appear relaxed, while Carolyn and I played games avoiding the smoke, silently watching beaten-down pedestrians stream past. It was a long way from the events of earlier in the day…

As the waiter pulls out the chair for me, John jumps to his feet, his eyes wide with bewilderment.

"So you're Rayne4321!" he says, trying to regain his composure by smoothing back his graying hair. "Oh, my God, who would have thought?"

It's likewise a shock for me. I am also confused, not least by how quickly Rayne fades away, and how reluctant Vera is to take her place. John is wearing tapered slacks I've never seen him in before, and a shirt that is open almost to his sternum, three buttonholes down. As I pull the cuffs of my blouse down over my wrists, John's face fades and is replaced by a red tunnel with pulsating walls.

The silence is sudden. Rayne has disappeared into the tunnel but, with profound gratitude, I see her running back. I try to remind myself that John is a colleague and a friend, someone who respects me, who knows part of who I really am. Vera hears this and stops Rayne's return, bringing a sense of peacefulness… that perhaps this may be the beginning, the time to stop all the hiding, to start to open up.

"And you must be jheartless@gmail.com," I find myself saying, in a voice of unexpected lightness.

"My God, Vera, tell me what's going on. By the way, you look so…so different. I'm not sure I would have recognized you on the street, though I definitely would have noticed you!"

Behind his words I feel a playfulness that I have long missed, kind and comforting. I return his smile and decide to confide in him.

I explain about signing up for three dates with an agency while treating Marcel, and that this was to be the third. He listens closely and is not distracted when a waiter asks if we want drinks. I stop and order us a bottle of white Châteauneuf-du-Pape, expensive, but we are worth it.

"I wanted to understand what blind dating was like for Marcel. Of course, it's not the same. He was struggling with rejection and, well—"

"I understand," John says, quietly. "Anne left me a couple of months back and it's been pretty difficult. She was sleeping with a younger guy, a child psychologist, actually. I knew about it for some time."

"Oh, I'm so sorry to hear that. I've wondered where you've been recently."

He explains that he decided first to see a counselor twice a week. He'd also hung out with a friend who was going through his own problems—both parents had died recently in the same week. Golf took up a few days, mainly afternoons, but what John dreaded most were evenings alone. He'd rejoined his old bridge club and played twice a week. The online dating was his own idea, trying to regain his self-esteem.

"Has it worked?"

"Not really. It's pretty difficult keeping a happy face, and sometimes something sends me off. Earlier this week, I almost lost it when my date said her name was Ann—nice lady, but that was it, game over. But overall it's been good. I haven't met anyone who lights a fire, but my mo-jo still seems to work. And talking of Marcel, I've only had two outright rejections."

"You'll be a catch to a lot of women, John."

"Not so far. What's been your experience?"

I summarize the two dates I've had and his eyes roll. I tell him I've made the decision to stop, that I've learned enough. "Jheartless was to be my last date and, lucky me, that's you!" We clink our glasses.

I had forgotten what good company John could be. On a couple of occasions during the hour he becomes melancholic, and I ask him what's wrong. He admits he misses Anne. But he also feels *he* should have been the one to have walked out, possibly years ago. He is angry that he didn't "stick it to her." I remind him that anger is a good sign, an early part of healing. Over coffee, he turns the subject back to me.

"So who is Rayne?"

"Oh, my middle name—I thought it would be safer."

"No, I mean who are *you*?" he asks. He waves his left hand in front of me. "Carolyn and I have been worried about you. Recently, she said you were doing great. But you look so different."

"Well, I decided to change the way I looked. I've still got my boots and the long silk shifts. But I've bought several pairs of shoes and a few dresses like this. I seem to have a lot of purple in my wardrobe. Carolyn thought I wore all those layers to cover up something inside me that I was ashamed of. And so here I am, shameless! Anyway, Raymond likes the new look and that's the most important thing."

My words sound leaden; my smile fades a little too quickly. I hope though, I've fooled John.

"How *are* things at home?" he asks, innocently.

Pauses are so powerful. Despite all the years I had studied and practiced, I feel the tension in the silence. Looking down, I say, as softly as I can, "Things are not good, John. I don't know what's happening, but things aren't good."

"Do you want to talk about it? And before you answer, Vera, let me tell you something. I used to think that showing vulnerability was a sign of weakness, but it's actually a sign of strength, liberating. I tell my clients that we all deserve to be vulnerable at some point. I've shown mine. Do you want to share what's going on?"

I find myself unwilling any longer to resist. I say that I'm uncertain who I am. I am drinking too much, and I don't know why. I also tell him I cannot recognize the man I married.

"This Rayne thing started as someone I could use in dating. It was innocent, just a ruse, although I must admit I liked her better."

"What do you mean by that?" John asks.

Gazing across the restaurant, I cross my hands and run my fingers into the cuffs of my sleeves as I search for the right words to surface, honest, vulnerable.

"I don't like who I've become. You've known me for over ten years, John, ever since I was a grad student. I used to be proud of the way I treated my patients, how much I cared about them. But now, apart from a few exceptions, I don't respect my patients, and I certainly don't respect myself for feeling this way. As a therapist, I'm projecting a lie. Working with Marcel really brought this out because he did make me care, at least for him.

"Rayne is erratic and shallow, but she projects confidence and a sense of purpose. Raymond adores her. If I try to be Vera, all I get from him is sullen silence, or that I'm closed down, that I'm not there for him."

Anyone but John, perhaps even Carolyn, would have mixed sympathy with soft denial. "Oh, I'm so sorry," Dawn would have said, and I can hear Christine reassuring me, "But I like you—what's there not to like?" John responds gently and professionally in the way I used to work with my patients.

"Has Rayne become more than what you call a ruse? Do you feel she is another persona, another side of you?"

"I don't know, John. But I'm frightened. Marcel kept using the word 'frightened'. He also started to develop a different persona, until I pulled him back."

"Vera, everyone's different, but I recognize a lot of what you're saying. Do you think there may be something else going on? Has Marcel awakened something beyond the need to be caring?"

"You mean, have I fallen in love with him? No, nothing like that."

"Then what *has* he surfaced?"

I know that if I answer this question it would be more than slowly opening up. I tell him, simply, "I don't know," searching for something else to say.

I decide to start to talk about the strange phone calls backed by wind I've been receiving at night, as though someone were calling to me.

"You remember my patient, Julie. I was convinced she was the caller. After she died the calls started up again. I got a similar call from a man, a friend's husband. I even asked Marcel if he'd been calling at night, and he denied it. It's a mystery."

He knows, of course, that I have avoided his question, but he allows it to pass.

"It could be anyone, Vera. One of those marketing groups, perhaps. I wouldn't worry about it. But it's interesting you said it might be someone calling *to* you. If you ever need to talk just let me know."

We both agree it has been a wonderful two hours. We also agree not to tell Carolyn about the lunch and our online dating activities.

"I did share with her I was thinking of dating to learn more about Marcel," I confide, as we are splitting the check. "But I said later I'd changed my mind, which is partially true. There's no longer any need with Marcel gone."

May I make a suggestion?" John says, rather than asks. "Drop Rayne. She's not real. Be yourself. And if Raymond doesn't like the real you, if he rejects Vera, blame it on me. It'll be my responsibility."

I still haven't fully recovered.

Dear Mr. Hall,

Let me say up front that I apologize for the tone I used in my letter to you about Robert Frost's Rubáiyát. Actually, apologizing seems to have become part of my life.

In recent days, starting last weekend, my husband Raymond and I have argued. He seems to have taken every opportunity to get angry with me. I have repeatedly apologized. It's true that I have withdrawn the sexier side of me that he so much enjoyed. I've withdrawn her because I just don't feel sexy with him.

I can understand when he says I've once again become more closed. When I have tried to re-approach him, or touch him, he has brushed me off. I don't feel rejected—I half expected his reaction. Besides, it wasn't my decision to take away this other side of me; a friend suggested it, because it wasn't the real me.

Raymond doesn't like to hear me talk about poetry, my love of which is why I am writing to you. I promised him that I would not read poetry, at least not in front of him. This is why your book *To Read a Poem* has been so important to me—I can read *about* poetry. After reading the appendix, "Writing About Poems," I want to share some similarities and differences with my own work as a therapist.

What you call explication, which you so brilliantly use in Chapter 1, bears many resemblances with how we therapists help peel back the layers and pasts of our patients. Your statement that, when one explicates a literary work, "you unfold its layers...showing its construction as if you were spreading it out on the table," applies directly to the human condition, it seems to me. I'm trying to do this with myself, with little success so far. I have a small issue with your subsection on "Analysis," however.

You write that analysis (of writing) "discovers part within part" and that you "use summary or paraphrase to establish the whole of which you analyze a part." It's not the same with therapy. In fact, it's quite different.

Therapists do try to peel back the layers of their patients. But the important difference is this: we do this to *analyze the whole* of what's inside a patient, not parts of the patient's core. There's one other important difference. Analysis of a person is not an end in its own right. It is only complete when this analysis leads to action, usually through a change in behaviors.

I realize that one can hardly expect a poem to change its own behavior but, like you, I believe poems change the perspective, and even behaviors, of the reader—they certainly have with me.

Again, I want to say how much your *To Read a Poem* has helped me get through long periods of silence and anxiety over the last few evenings.

"Happy birthday!"
"My goodness, how kind of you. What is it?"
"Open it up and you'll see."

Earlier in the day I had awoken to a coffee by the side of the bed. After writing to Mr. Hall the night before, I had poured a final large gin on ice without thinking. I was paying the price. Whatever moisture I had in my body had leaked into my pillow and sheets. My left arm was numb, my eyelids flaps of sandpaper. Raymond, by contrast, was already dressed and about to leave for work. He did return to the bedroom and, when he saw I was awake, said "Happy birthday, darling." Then he was gone.

I tried to focus on his three words through a pink fog. I concluded the final iamb was not necessary. The first two trochees were sufficient to create a sense of joy. And by ending with "darling," he had broken any sense of sincerity. It was a throw away "darling," a relic.

When I finally reached the practice, still suffering from dehydration and an ache at the base of my skull, Carolyn suggested skipping our Wednesday meeting and taking a late lunch at *M Street Bar and Grill*. She also had a present for me.

"It's heavy," I said, as I teased back the green and white wrapping. "How lovely, it's a book."

It was indeed heavy. Simon Ortiz's *Woven Stone* comprises three hundred and sixty five pages. After clinking our glasses of Prosecco, I opened the book at random.

"Poetry! That's so thoughtful of you, Carolyn."

"You've talked about poetry so often that I asked some of my friends for recommendations. But when you and I touched on New Mexico the other day, I thought I'd check out well-known poets in the state. That's how I came across Simon Ortiz. He's still alive you know."

I didn't know, but a memory floated back.

"I thought I recognized the name. He used to visit schools in the area, but I don't think I ever met him. I do remember someone reciting some of his poems from memory. They were so passionate. Others were almost like prayers. I guess for some of us he was a bit of a role model."

"I'm so pleased you like it. How lovely you know of him," she said, with obvious pleasure. "I always admire people who can recite from memory, something I can't do. Can you remember who it was?"

"Oh, just someone I knew. Just someone."

❖ ❖ ❖

That evening, Raymond and I met for dinner at *Mon Ami Gabi*, a French bistro in Bethesda that he knew I liked for its huge Martinis. Raymond had come straight from his office. I had stopped at the house, changing into a long, peached-colored dress with matching wrap, and replacing the rubber band on my braid with a green bow.

We reached the car park opposite the restaurant at the same time. I avoided kissing by struggling to put on my earrings, a pair of turquoise drops I haven't worn in years.

Our table in the large, rear room wasn't ready, so first drinks were at the bar—my Martini, and an Old Fashioned for Raymond. The bartender was chatty and we spoke to each other through him.

For the first time in a long while, I couldn't finish my drink and left it on the bar. I told myself I was feeling the effects of lunch with Carolyn, that alcohol was probably still in my system from the night before. The truth was I didn't want it.

I was already tipsy before starting the bottle of Côte-Rôtie that Raymond insisted on ordering. Whenever I spoke, I called Raymond "darling," with a heavy stress on the first syllable. The first time was when he handed me my birthday present. In a non-recyclable plastic bag was a hardback copy of *Spectacular Wineries of Oregon*—"How thoughtful, darling." I've never opened it.

By the time we were ready to leave I was quite drunk. I did manage to open my car, placed my plastic-bagged present on the passenger seat, and then just sat. Raymond appeared at the car window and suggested we leave my Golf overnight, a wise decision. I felt a sense of unease during the two-mile drive to our house—I had left Simon Ortiz alone overnight, in my car.

There is something else: at dinner, Raymond broke his promise by twice talking of work. It allowed me to tell him that I missed reading poetry. I would likely start again. He couldn't really argue. As T.S. Eliot would have said, it was, I should say, satisfactory.

It is now Thursday morning and my head is finally clearing. My first patient arrives at 11:00. Shortly, I will take a taxi ride to collect my car. But before I leave, I will cherish one last scent of the gladioli that Raymond also gave me last night. They are so fresh, so alive, and they are purple.

I didn't know Simon Ortiz was from Acoma Pueblo, Mr. Hall—did you? Then again, I didn't really know Simon Ortiz until yesterday. There's a whole *Wikipedia* entry on him. One section describes the "cultural dissonance" he felt during his time in Santa Fe—where he learned to speak and write English—something that featured in his earliest writing.

My 7th or 8th grade class once visited Acoma Pueblo. It was one of many cultural trips we made. We stopped below the mesa and were loaded into a bus for the winding drive to the pueblo. Even then, there was no electricity or running water, and ladders were still used to access the upper levels of many of the adobe houses. There was this sense of being a tourist, but I think all of us felt the deep spirituality of the place.

When I first heard Simon Oritz's poems recited, what I remember most was the passion behind his words. He wrote about the preciousness of nature, and his pride in being Native American. Yes, I remember that so well.

Was there a reason you didn't include him in your book, *To Read a Poem*? I ask this purely out of curiosity. It must have been difficult deciding which poems to include. But I believe there may have been another reason, Mr. Hall—one Ortiz poem in isolation wouldn't work, would it? You only get the full effects of his writing when reading a sequence, one punch after the other.

Tonight I have reached page 46 of *Woven Stone*. Simon Ortiz writes mainly free verse. In some poems I found it impossible to detect meter or rhythm. In a strange way, this seems to liberate the subject matter, and I confess I have not missed the beat of metricality. He rarely uses internal rhyme. The poetry is raw, emotional, and is heightened by the use of repeated alliteration, like forcing in a nail.

Reading poem after poem, I get an overwhelming sense of outrage over the desecration of the environment and society. Each poem is a plea for his people to return to their roots. And then, when least expected, I encounter lines of descriptive beauty that almost stop my heart.

I've had to stop reading it, Mr. Hall. Raymond will arrive home soon after hosting a dinner for DC representatives of several companies. I'm sure he'd hate to have to wade through a forest floor of wet tissues to get to the drinks cabinet. My eyes were red and puffy when I used our guest washroom about an hour ago. I have to look presentable.

Let me say one final thing. What I find amazing about Simon Ortiz's poetry is that English is his second language. His first language is Keresan, and he is a native speaker, unlike me.

The Brocks have started their two-week vacation in The Hamptons. Today is Raymond's first day in charge. As I write tonight, he is decompressing alone in front of the TV with a second scotch in hand. I have just finished rereading a poem from Simon Ortiz's *Woven Stone*, having devoured all 365 pages over the weekend.

Raymond spent most of yesterday in his downtown office, but tonight I have had no qualms over reading in the same room as him. I am also cradling a glass of sparkling water after leaving my chilled Chablis half finished. It was something that John said to me earlier in the day.

He had come into the office kitchen where I was refilling my coffee cup after a difficult session.

"Hi," he said, "and a belated Happy Birthday! Carolyn told me you two celebrated a little. Let me say it's nice to see Vera back—she looks like the girl I used to know, created by nature and not the makeup counter at Macys."

"I'll take that as a compliment. Looks like you've caught the sun."

He had more than caught the sun. His nose was the color of a red chile, blistered and shiny. He closed the door and walked back to where I was standing at the sink.

"I spent the weekend camping, alone in case you were going to ask," he said, with a wink. "Lying all night in a sleeping bag with sunburn gives you time to think. Like you, I think I'll give the dating a break awhile."

"Probably a wise move. How are things at home?"

He confided that he had decided to file for divorce, and felt a sense of relief until last night. He had told Anne he'd be away for the weekend and said she could drop by to pick up more of her things. When he returned he discovered she'd gutted the place. "Even took the Art Deco cocktail cabinet, and that was mine!"

"A sad time." I told him Raymond would sympathize.

"You know," he said, "what Anne did has turned out to be cathartic. All that stuff, all those memories taken away, like that." He snapped his fingers.

"John, can I ask you something? At lunch you said being vulnerable could be liberating. How?"

"You remembered! Seems odd for a psychiatrist to be explaining this to a psychologist, but, well...most people don't want to expose their weaknesses to others. It shows how vulnerable they are, true?"

"Some of us have many weaknesses."

"It takes inner strength to reveal our weaknesses to others, Vera. But here's the thing—if those revelations allow you to ask questions you wouldn't normally ask, or even ask for help, it changes our perception from 'I can't do that because if I do...' to 'I can do this because there's nothing left to hide'. By the way, showing vulnerability is not only for how you interact with others. You can do it with yourself. Try it – it's liberating."

Earlier this evening I took John's advice. We had just finished dinner, and Raymond was easing the cork out of a bottle of Springbank.

"Do you drink because you like it?" I asked, "Or is it because it stops you thinking?"

"Because I like it."

"I used to drink to loosen up, but I'm drinking too much," I said, surprised by my confident tone. "Some mornings, I can't believe I had the strength to get into bed. I'm wondering why I do it, what I don't want to think about? I'm going to cut down."

Swirling the ice cubes, Raymond says, "I drink because I enjoy it. I don't know about you, but I've said a couple of times that I thought you'd had enough."

Now, with Raymond watching news re-runs on CNN, I am in my own leather-chaired world, reading Simon Ortiz again. The poems in *Woven Stone* became part of my life over the weekend, and I have returned to one in particular many times.

"For those brothers and sisters in Gallup" appears on page 88. The title already reveals it's set in the western part of New Mexico, a desperately poor area that includes the edge of the large Navajo reservation.

The poem is harrowing.

Mr. Ortiz uses the image of a stray dog as a metaphor for all the down-and-outs who lie beside the road or cower in the shadows of underpasses.

212

He is that twisted shadow
under the bridge: he is
that broken root.

The poem moves from the objective to the personal halfway through. I can almost smell the alcohol on these people.

O my god, I know what is my name:
she stumbled like a stuffed dummy
against me, looked into my mouth
with her opaque remorseful eyes
and asked me for a drink.

I have witnessed this so many times in the high desert. I can see her rotted teeth and the caked vomit in her hair. I can smell the stink oozing out of the cracks in her skin. She was once a woman, but now only her eyes writhe in a seductive dance. She's way past vulnerability.

Yet in his magical last verse, Mr. Ortiz holds out a hand of forgiveness veined with hope. It's a benediction for her and others like her. It's a call for her and others to return to their roots, that they can regain their pride.

Be kind, sister, be kind;
it shall come cleansing again.
It shall rain and your eyes
will shine and look so deeply
into me into me into me into me.

Raymond has no idea of the emotions and memories from New Mexico that are swirling within me. They are like dirt slurried to mud after rain that by morning has dried to a crust. In the fading light of a summer evening, I can see the fallen and those yet to fall, stumbling on legs soaked with urine. I can hear the coughs and moans sicked up in the depths of the night. One of the fallen becomes a broken root, crumpled in the shadow of a cottonwood as a hearse drives away. There is blood in the dust, more blood drips around my feet. Dust to dust the wind whispers.

This is why I have retreated into myself, why I have decided to go to the bookstore, *Politics & Prose*, to buy a red-spined book I've avoided for months. This is how I know who's been phoning me in a wind late at night.

Today, Tuesday, the Vice President's security service decided to return him to his residence on Observatory Circle via Connecticut Avenue. It has happened many times. The fear of endless roadblocks is why I changed my own route home through Rock Creek Park. Unfortunately, most of northwest DC had the same idea.

When I reached Tilden Avenue, I pulled off into a small parking area that leads down to the Western Ridge Trail. I decided to kill time until the traffic eased up by walking north to the second stretch of riffled water.

With the water level so low, I could see every can and plastic bag trapped in the mud. At one point, I thought a shadow moved behind a sunken tree trunk, but it was just a play of light. I tried to remind myself that the adjacent woodlands were full of wildlife—deer, raccoons, even coyotes had been seen. But today, staring into the clear and toxic water, I felt a deep sadness sweep over me and decided to cut the walk short.

As I returned to the car, lines from a number of Simon Ortiz's poems surfaced, and I found outrage starting to replace the sadness. I drove back onto Beach Drive, up Broad Branch, and then onto Brandywine to rejoin Connecticut Avenue safely north of any traffic. By the time I reached *Politics & Prose* I was incandescent.

I felt nothing but rage as I entered the bookshop. I turned left and, without a second thought, pulled down the slim book with the red spine. Scanning the shelves a final time, I saw Donald Hall's new book, *Essays After Eighty*. On the cover was an aged, sad face, with an unkempt beard that fell below his name. I bought both books.

I still haven't opened Robert Bly's book, *Leaping Poetry*, with its red cover and spine. But I *did* force myself to read the synopsis on the back cover. At first, I was confused. Then relieved. Now, all I feel about the synopsis is amusement.

How many weeks or even months have I lived in fear of this little book? I only saw its title on the spine of the book, but its first word held such terror that every time I visited the bookshop I prayed it had been bought. Now, it is late in the evening. I promise to start reading it tomorrow, but I need to write one more thing before I sleep.

Contrary to what I feared, *Leaping Poetry* is not a collection of poems on suicide. Instead, as the synopsis says, *it is Robert Bly's testament to the singular importance of the <u>artistic</u> leap that bridges the gap between conscious and unconscious thought in any great work of art."* The underlining is my own.

"I've hardly seen Raymond. He's in charge for a couple of weeks, likely to be entertaining clients most evenings."

"If you get lonely, just call," Carolyn said. "Things are OK otherwise?" I could have answered in many ways.

I could have said that *we* were OK. After a week touching Raymond with only a smile as response, I woke him yesterday morning with a need for just plain sex. I think he was as surprised as me. Of course, this was just one moment in a difficult period, but we did seem more at ease afterward.

I could have also said that *I* was OK. I had phoned Christine earlier on a sudden impulse. I wanted to reach out to her, ask if she needed anything. Instead, she started in on me, complaining that I hadn't answered her calls. I stopped her mid-rant and told her she had caused me pain and embarrassment by making me complicit in her adultery. I also demanded she not contest any of David's allegations to make sure I wouldn't be called as a witness. Rayne would have been proud.

Yes, I was OK, which was more or less true. I was OK when I didn't think for too long. I was OK when I could read poetry and write in my journal. But the sense of peace and longing to open up that I had felt at lunch with John had ebbed away. With Rayne subdued, there was no one to lift me up.

"Things are fine," I replied.

"And how is Raymond doing?"

"He's just overworked. His boss is a control freak, wants daily reports. Raymond's been up late the last two nights writing them."

"I couldn't help noticing yesterday you've gone back to no make-up. I remember you saying how much Raymond liked the new look, so I wondered—"

"I kept getting mascara in my eyes," I said, offhand. "The only thing Raymond's missing is me drinking with him."

"You've stopped drinking? Something wrong?"

"I haven't had a drink since Friday, and I'm not sure I will for awhile. It's because of a poem in Simon Ortiz's book."

"Tell me about it," she said.

So I described Mr Ortiz's poetry, quoting a line from his Gallup poem, "she stumbled like a stuffed dummy." I repeated the line to myself and something seemed to shift inside. I started to talk about my own past. Yes, I had seen many alcoholics destroy their lives and those of others in New Mexico.

"I remember you saying you didn't drink when you met Raymond, what, sixteen years ago? If you felt so negatively about alcohol, why did you start? To be honest, Vera, I thought you've been drinking too much for some time."

"Maybe I wanted to see if I could take it. Peer pressure, I guess."

Holding my coffee mug in two hands, I thought back to John's advice two days ago, to become vulnerable, to open up. I started slowly.

I told her of the joys of growing up in New Mexico, the lilac light at dawn, the way the cottonwoods blazed yellow in the fall. Sounds were something I remembered well, especially the whistle of wind in the vigas before a summer storm, the way the dirt cracked and crackled as you walked to school after the first hard frost. I missed licking the grease of frybread from my fingers, my tongue tingling from green chile, the metallic tang of piñon nuts we gathered in our skirts. We would stand beneath a laden tree and shake a branch—just once, to leave the tree with enough seeds for nature.

I didn't talk about other memories, though I could feel them eager to surface. Because I became so upset by the end of the hour, she wanted to continue as soon as we could. We settled on Sunday if, as I expected, Raymond drove downtown to his office. As Carolyn shuffled her notes for her next patient, I stared at the floor, at my brown suede boots, the sheen of my black skirt across my knees. I uncrossed my hands, undid the buttons on the cuffs of my outer blouse, and rolled the sleeves a few inches up each arm.

"Carolyn," I said quietly, "I used to cut myself."

❖ ❖ ❖

Robert Bly begins *Leaping Poetry*, first published in 1972, by writing that, "A great work of art has at its center a floating leap," and that, "The real joy of poetry is to experience this leaping inside a poem." I am half way through, and I am excited—the poetry is astonishing.

In the anthology that Mr. Bly has assembled, most poems involve huge leaps of the imagination—some so large that, without his comments, I'm not sure I would understand them. They are free verse *in extremis*, I would say. To use John's word, they are "liberated" beyond anything I have ever read.

Lorca features strongly, as do a number of other Spanish and Latin American poets. Many are gathered into a chapter entitled "Wild Emotions" that includes a wonderful introduction centering on Duende. I loved Bly's statement that, "The magical quality of a poem consists in its being always possessed by the duende so that whoever beholds it is baptized with dark water"—a wonderful thought. But my real excitement was when I saw Bly applying neuroscience to poetry!

In his chapter "The Three Brains," Mr. Bly references a theory proposed by neurologist Paul MacLean. I remember studying Dr. MacLean, and I think I still have his book somewhere, *The Triune Brain in Evolution*, quite controversial at the time. Dr. MacLean believed that there are three parts to the human brain: the reptile brain, a limbic system (Bly calls this the "mammal" brain) and, uniquely to humans, a recent addition embedded in the neocortex; Bly calls this the "new" brain. Each plays its separate role: the reptile brain is all about survival; the mammal brain deals with emotion and motivation; the new brain evolved as language developed, and centers on abstraction and perception.

Mr. Bly believes the reptile brain is incapable of creating poems. He thinks the mammal brain can, and he cites Chaucer as a poet who does this. But he feels that the greatest leaps of imagination occur when thoughts cross from the mammal brain to the new brain.

After reading Mr. Bly's words, I was reminded of a poem by Theodore Roethke I had read in Eavan Boland and Edward Hirsch's *The Making of a Sonnet*.

"For an Amorous Lady" begins on page 217, a quite lovely, almost cheeky letter to his "dearest." From what I've read of Roethke, I'm sure, like him, his dearest would have had an active new brain. But Roethke decided to highlight two other features of his dearest when describing their pursuit of the "amorous arts:"

> *You are, in truth, one in a million,*
> *At once mammalian and reptilian.*

No hint of amorous stirrings as Raymond scribbles comments on a stack of briefing notes. I'm afraid his reptile brain is on overload. As Dr. MacLean writes, quoted by Mr. Bly, the reptile brain is characterized by "aggression, dominance, territoriality, and ritual displays." Soon my husband will stop working—the Red Sox are playing tonight and his red shirt is already on.

We had finished our main dinner of the week, and I was rinsing the dishes. It is one of our rituals when I cook several courses—I rinse, and Raymond stacks the plates in the dishwasher, large ones to the rear, side plates to the front.

"I'm going to the office tomorrow afternoon," he said.

"No problem. Carolyn and I wanted to get together. I'll give her a call."

"Uh-huh. Work stuff for you also?" He poured himself a second scotch, having chugged the first.

I told him Carolyn and I needed to sort out some issues with the practice, but we also wanted to catch up. "Things have been pretty busy, and I've hardly seen her these last weeks."

Later, as I was reading a brochure from the Kennedy Center on the new opera season, Raymond turned down the volume on the stereo.

"When you and Carolyn get together socially, what do you talk about?"

"She likes opera. By the way, have you seen the new—"

"Do you talk about *me*?" he interrupted.

I said, of course we sometimes talked about other people. "We don't talk about you specifically."

"What the hell does that mean—*specifically*?"

Knowing this could spiral down, I searched for words to soothe. "I've told her about some of the restaurants you've found for us. She was pretty impressed when I said you were in charge while Cyril was on vacation."

"OK, let's try a different tack. Do you ever talk about *you*, does she do any off-the-cuff analysis?"

"Why would she want to do that?"

"Ask her where you've gone, ask her why that person you were a couple of weeks back has disappeared. Have a drink, for Christ's sake. Let your hair down. Then tell Carolyn that I want the old you back. I expect to see that Vera when I get home tomorrow."

I was still staring into space when he raised the volume on the stereo. Loretta Lynn was pleading,

Don't come home a drinkin' (with lovin' on your mind).

'Tell me about the cutting," Carolyn says.

It is two o'clock, Sunday afternoon, and she and I are sitting on stools in my kitchen. A large pot of chamomile tea sits between us, and steam is rising from two bone china cups with matching saucers. It is the first time I have seen Carolyn with no make up.

"I started just before Mom died—Leukemia's such a terrible disease. It happened so quickly, and she was in agony all the time at the end—wasn't able to say goodbye, or even tell me who she wanted me to be.

"The cutting was only for three or four months. Before you ask, there was no sexual abuse. I think I was trying to mask my emotional pain with physical."

"Is that really why you cover up—the long-sleeved blouses?" Carolyn asks.

"Long-sleeves, perhaps, even though I've hardly got any scars left. The layering is different. It's one of the few things I keep—we always dressed like that, even in summer."

"Tell me more about your mother."

"It can't have been easy for her, living the way we did. Even though our house was outside the pueblo, we had pretty strong tribal traditions. Dad insisted on that. A lot of his family still lived around the main plaza, and then there were all the gatherings. Mom was always an outsider.

"Mom kept the house pretty tidy in her Anglo way, but the yard was always strewn with scrap and beat-up cars. We used to play in them all the time. She won one small battle, though. When I was five or six she hired a few guys to build a small portal. They used some of the vigas from a derelict house down the way, and it was pretty simple, just an open frame. But the deck was beautiful. She'd found some French terra-cotta tiles in Santa Fe, laid them out in a checkerboard pattern. I used to sit outside with her some evenings if Dad had wandered off.

"She and Dad met at what used to be called the Fiesta Indian Market, in Santa Fe. Mom was training to be a ceramist at the time, and she'd stopped by the stall of Dad's aunt—her pots were pretty famous, still are. Dad was hanging out with a friend, and he and Mom got talking. Mom said he was a perfect gentleman while courting, even in the first years of the marriage. Then he started drinking.

"He began to beat her up every couple of weeks. I used to feel sick every time he raised his hand. At her funeral, Dad was so drunk we left him under a cottonwood at home—he was still asleep when we got back. My Aunt Rayne moved in and took care of me until I won the scholarship to Georgetown. I've never gone back."

Carolyn slowly rubs her upper arms as I talk about my childhood, the festivals, and the rituals. Her eyes never waver from my face.

"Unlike most of my friends, I loved junior and high school. Most days would start with someone reciting a poem, and one Christmas I was given Eliot's 'Journey of the Magi' to read to the class. I can still recite it from memory."

Suddenly, Carolyn stops listening. "You had a lot in common with Marcel. Your mothers died when you were about the same age. You both love poetry. Before he left for Pittsburgh, you even started to talk like him."

"Marcel did reawaken my love of poetry. But besides both of us losing our mothers when we were young, I don't think there are other parallels. He's carried terrible memories with him and sought to drown them out, and—"

She is quick to interrupt. "And you've carried your own memories and found your own way of burying them."

Large spats of rain are darkening the deck outside, and the kitchen windows are turning to mirrors. I pour more tea, and we sit quietly until Carolyn breaks the silence.

"I still don't understand why you started drinking. Alcohol was a source of evil for you, so it's kind of strange. On Friday, you mentioned you started drinking to prove you could take it, or words like that."

"Like I said, there was a lot of peer pressure in college," I tell her, then I stop. In the safety of my own kitchen, there seems little point in maintaining her confusion. I take a deep breath.

"Alcoholism's a problem in many native families. Drug addiction may be hereditary. Mom was Anglo and, even though she would drink tequila some weekends, she could go months without it. I suppose I wanted to see if I could drink without it taking over my life, though I've not missed it since I stopped last week."

"But you were drinking pretty heavily. I've got a different thought on this, Vera, and it may be another parallel with Marcel. Could it have been your own form of Paradoxical Intervention? What I'm saying is that, if alcohol brought back such bad memories, were you subconsciously immunizing those memories through drinking?"

I find my mind beginning to spin.

"If you're right, maybe that's why the memories are coming back now. Stopping drinking has opened the flood gates and—"

"No Vera! I doubt that's what's happening," she quickly interjects. "From what you've told me, I think reading Simon Ortiz's poems had a lot to do with it, but I also think you learnt something else from Marcel. After you helped him bring his memories to light he was able to confront them. He's given you a lesson."

We are interrupted by the grinding sound of a garage door opening.

"How much does Raymond know about all this?" she asks quietly, standing to leave.

"He knows I'm part Native American, of course—that was a big act of defiance to his father. He also knows how my mother died, but not much else. I told him there was a big bust up before I left. He used to ask occasionally, but then he stopped, thank goodness."

Raymond walks into the kitchen. "Hello, Raymond," Carolyn says. "We were just talking about you."

That was five hours ago. After glaring at me during and after dinner, Raymond went to bed, claiming he needed an early night. It has allowed me to finally open Donald Hall's book, *Essays after Eighty*. I have now read most of his essays. I feel the need to talk to him about some.

This is a wonderful book, Mr. Hall, although I was so sad to learn you no longer write poetry. "New poems no longer come to me … prose endures," you say. I have just one small complaint. In the listing of your previous books, I am mystified why you omitted *To Read a Poem*, a book that has been my bedside companion these last months.

Having read some of your essays, I can well appreciate that some emerged only after sixty drafts, and all required more than thirty. They are quite perfect.

Do you still go by the name of Donnie, the name your mother called you? I was pleased to read that Willa Cather was one of your mother's favorite authors. When I left New Mexico, *Death Comes To The Archbishop* was one of the few things I brought with me. I was reminded that Ms. Cather wrote about Acoma Pueblo.

And you are a Red Sox fan! You share this, and only this, with my husband, Raymond. On coincidences, I was amazed to discover you were the first to publish Robert Bly's work when you were poetry editor of the *Paris Review*.

I so enjoyed "Essay After Eighty." The writing is spare and concise while still ensuring that "Rhythm and cadence...carry the reader on a pleasurable journey." And your statement that "Poems are image-bursts from brain-depths" is something I will never forget, nor the admonition that one should never begin a paragraph with "I." I assume you mean in essays—surely, not in one's journal.

My favorite essay has to be "Out the Window," your experience of sitting, day after day, looking out of a window, reflecting that this was what also occupied your mother in the last ten years of her life. No wonder it received so many accolades.

When his wife, Eurydice, died, Orpheus descended into the underworld to rescue her. Armed only with his lyre and a beautiful voice, he so charmed Hades and Persephone that they allowed him to take his wife back to earth. Their only condition was that Orpheus should walk in front of Eurydice and not look back until they reached the upper world. When Orpheus emerged from the underworld he turned around prematurely. He had failed to realize that the condition was that *both* should reach the upper world before he looked back. Eurydice then vanished for a second time, and was lost to him forever.

Marcel's letter arrived earlier today, Monday, in the afternoon post. I knew it was from him the moment I saw the precise writing on the envelope. I had no chance to read it until reaching home.

August 1st

Dear Dr Lewis,

I hope you are well. I'm sorry it has taken almost a month to write. I also apologize for not texting, but to be honest I've moved away from haiku…well almost, but more on this below. I'm in Pittsburgh.

The good news is that I've found some form of peace. It's taken many hours of talking, and at times it's felt like entering a cave—so much darkness. But we're getting there, and for me some of the guilt is starting to seep away. Dad has been feeling much the same. You would be proud of me, Dr. Lewis—I've asked lots of questions, and I've listened! So many misunderstandings unsnarled, so much time to make up.

I can't do anything about the wasted time, but I can do something about the hurt. I wrote to my ex-girlfriend, Susan, the other day—just a short letter to the last address I had. I told her I'd got over some of my hang-ups without talking about our, sorry, my, sexual problems directly. I wanted her to know that it had all been my fault, not hers. Margaret's been great. I talked a lot with her in the first week here, and I apologized.

I went with Dad to Mom's grave last week. He's kept it looking beautiful, Dr. Lewis—fresh flowers once a week. I played her some piano music by Chopin from my iPhone, and Dad and I cried a lot.

Then there was the day we spent at Penns Creek. The fishing wasn't so good—water too warm—but I loved wading the river and looking up to see Dad there. I think it was the first time he's seen nature in years! He told me he'd always wanted to go there with me and never thought it would happen.

So the only remaining hurt I know of is in me. I've not forgot you telling me I'm not cured of my problems, that I would come across obstacles. Going to Mom's grave was one, trying to re-capture key moments I'd buried is another. I wrote a haiku about one:

> open casket—
> the antiseptic taste
> of her pearls

That was last time I kissed her, on her cheek and on her neck. Her skin was colder than the pearls.

Being able to think back, to visualize memories, has also opened up thoughts on poetry. I started to read a lot of free verse but, even though I liked it, I had this nagging feeling that it was appealing to the kind of person that Maureen would have liked. Now something tells me poetry may be guiding me back to my true self.

I'm returning to formal verse, Dr. Lewis. Yesterday, I drafted a sonnet very different from those I've written in the past. You see I no longer need strict meter, so I no longer need to avoid it. I don't need wild free verse to feel liberated inside. There's comfort and beauty in form.

It seems odd to use poetry when talking about healing, but therein may be a metaphor! If anything of this makes sense to you, Dr. Lewis, I can recommend a tiny but wonderful book. It's by Glyn Maxwell, a British poet, and it's called *On Poetry*. Knowing your love of formal verse, I think you'll like it.

I'll be staying at home in Pittsburgh a few more days, and then plan to wander west. It was Dad's idea. I've bought a small truck, and my friend, Johnny, helped me fix it up.

That's all for now, Dr. Lewis. I will write. No, let me correct that—I shall write.

Yours fondly,
Marcel

Last night, I had an urge to reply immediately, but something else came up that disturbed me. It still does. I will try to get to the bottom of it tomorrow.

Today, while listening to harrowing stories from two of my patients, I found Marcel's words soothing. They even made me see those sorry souls in a different light. At other times in the day I found myself doubting what I was doing. Again his letter saved me—all I had to do was close my eyes and imagine what he was becoming, and that I had helped bring on this transformation.

After reading Robert Bly's *Leaping Poetry* again tonight, I have something to share.

Hello Marcel,

I hope you received my text saying how pleased I was to hear from you. I would love to snail-mail you this reply, but you're traveling. Never mind—I'll keep it safe in my journal until you text me back with an email address. If not, I can show it to you one day. Remember, we promised we'd meet up again.

It sounds like you're dealing with things wisely and cautiously. You *will* overcome all your obstacles with time, and your brave description of viewing your mother's coffin is one example—thank you for sharing that moment.

You're also right to consider the wider realms of addressing hurt—healing others is often a balm to one's self. It is also very common that, after bad things happen, all sides feel their own sense of guilt, so I'm not surprised your father feels the same as you. It's wonderful that you and your father have wanted to spend so much time together. You now have a bond that will never break.

I found your thoughts behind why you're moving back to formal poetry fascinating. I'm reading a lot of free verse at the moment in an anthology by Robert Bly. To use your word, I feel "liberated" reading many of the poems.

There's also serendipity in the timing of your letter. Over the weekend, I was reading a chapter in Mr Bly's book called "Surrealism, Rilke, and Listening" that discusses Rainer Maria Rilke's "Sonnets to Orpheus." You probably know that Orpheus descended into the underworld to rescue his wife—and he did so through a cave, something that you referred to in your letter.

But there's more to the story of Orpheus, Marcel—I believe it's an extended metaphor for aspects of psychotherapy. Only by entering the depths, and there confronting our fears and demons, can we reemerge into the light. It's what you and I talked about, and I'm so glad you had the courage to go back to Pittsburgh and confront your past.

Some would say there's a flaw in using Orpheus this way. They would point out that when Orpheus emerges and looks back he pays the ultimate price by losing his wife a second time. With us mere mortals, however, it's *only* by looking back that we can create a vision for the future. It is not a perfect metaphor, but I wanted to share it with you.

Safe travels, Marcel, wherever they take you. And do please write again.

Yours,
Vera Lewis (Dr.)

❖ ❖ ❖

I've not spoken about Claire who has been coming to see me for two months. Her symptoms indicate abuse as a child, probably sexual: low self-esteem, inability to maintain relationships, a feeling that she doesn't belong.

She had built strong walls around her memories, and it had taken a major intervention in our last session for her to admit that she had been "hurt" by her father. She didn't want to look back.

This morning, despite a canary yellow dress and matching hair band, she seems particularly distraught, twisting and twisting a paper tissue in her hands.

"So when was the first time your father hurt you?"

"I was about six, maybe seven. It's hard to remember exactly."

"And it continued for—?"

"A long time—two years."

"Can you remember how he would hurt you?"

"I don't *want* to remember! How many times do I have to tell you?"

"But this is what we have to do, Claire. Pain in your past is behind many of the things you've described to me—panic attacks when a man tries to touch you, those feelings that you're someone else looking at yourself. We've got to confront those memories."

"Why Doctor Lewis, why? Tell me why?"

For most of the morning I'd thought about a probable flaw in the Orpheus metaphor I'd written about yesterday in my journal. Something clearly didn't fit. Claire presented an opportunity to eliminate that flaw. So, leaning forward I told her the story of Orpheus. I then decided to alter the metaphor.

"Many people read Greek myths and draw lessons for today," I shared. "From Orpheus, it's that only by going down into the depths can we re-emerge into the light. Now, you might want to counter and say, 'Ah yes, Doctor Lewis, but he shouldn't have looked back, and neither should I.'

"Orpheus *could* have looked back, Claire, if he'd first made sure his wife had emerged too. When we go back into our pasts we meet who we were and the pain that person suffered. We lovingly bring our old self *with* us back into the present, but we leave all the pain behind. Then we can look back safely at the pain, and all that caused it."

"So what you're saying is that I have to go down there, back there, to—"

"Yes Claire," I said, "And best of all, unlike Orpheus who had no guide, I am going to be yours, easing the journey."

That was earlier today, Wednesday. Four days have passed since Carolyn and I were forced to curtail our conversation in my kitchen.

"Hi Vera, come in—no wait, let me move those papers."

I could tell by her hair's disarray that she felt flustered.

"If there's a better time, Carolyn."

"I've only got half an hour, I'm afraid," she said. "I've delayed two patients because I had to check one into the hospital."

"That's all right, I just wanted to—"

Carolyn was clearly in a rush. "Have you thought more about what I said, that you need to surface more memories if you want to confront them?"

I told her I'd been thinking a lot about what we'd talked about. In truth, I spent early Sunday evening failing to convince Raymond that Carolyn and I had *not* been talking about him. Donald Hall's *Essays after Eighty* had followed. And as for New Mexico, I had packed Simon Ortiz away, and in the last days had read only Robert Bly's *Leaping Poetry*. There was, of course, the happy letter from Marcel and the Orpheus thoughts it had surfaced, but they could wait for another day.

Instead, I replied by sharing more about my youth and the new memories that had apparently surfaced, small things, innocent, incidental—when a coyote got trapped in one of our scrap cars, hearing the trilled hum of a hummingbird for the first time, junipers shedding pollen like smoke in the wind. At one point she asked how Raymond was, that he seemed on edge when he came home on Sunday.

"Like I said, he's overworked. By the way, and not wishing to change the subject, do you know anything about PACs—you know, Political Action Committees?"

"Not much," she answered, with a perplexed look. "Why do you ask?"

"Something came up the other day, that's all."

We moved on to talk about Emma. The police hadn't called, but Carolyn felt there was one thing we should discuss.

"We didn't call her father that day she came to try see you, even though I thought she looked distressed. You and I know why—we suspected he'd been abusing her, and that was why she was cutting herself."

She seemed to be building up to say more.

"I've treated many women who cut themselves, Vera, and almost all had been or were being sexually abused. But the statistics tell a different story. Many, like you, were trying to bury a different pain. We should have remembered this, intervened, contacted her mother, even the father."

"I know what you're saying," was all I said. In fact, what Carolyn was inferring was more than *our* failings. As someone who had cut without any sexual abuse, I should have been the first to suggest contacting Emma's family.

She rose from her chair, leant across her desk, and touched my arm.

"You have to go back you know."

At first I didn't grasp her meaning. "I'm not sure I can," I replied. "What I told you of my childhood is as far back as I can go."

"No, Vera. You need to *physically* go back to New Mexico."

I knew she was right. I had known that I had to go back for some time. But I also knew there were memories worse than any I had shared with Carolyn, so I said,

"There's nothing to go back to anymore."

"You don't know that," Carolyn said, softly. "And perhaps taking some time off may not be a bad idea. John and I can manage with your patients just fine while you're away."

Our half hour was drawing to a close, and I said I'd think about it.

"I don't know how to say this," Carolyn said, running the fingers of her right hand through her hair. "There's a risk that unresolved issues from your past will negatively affect your work."

This was not only a reference to Emma. I had also backed away from Marcel when a phrase he said touched something from my own past. Carolyn had more to say.

"You've got to confront your past, Vera. Think about Marcel, how difficult it must have been for him. Look at the effect it's had."

As she started gathering together the scattered papers on her desk, I could see that she was upset. Though she turned her head away from me, she couldn't hide the glint of small tear in the corner of her eye.

"Think about it, and let's talk again soon," she said, without turning back. "One more thing. When you were telling me about your childhood you kept saying we—do you have any siblings?"

I replied as casually as I could. "I had a brother, Nick, but he's not around anymore."

It has been a work evening for both of us. When Raymond announced he had a call coming in, I used it as an excuse to carry my laptop to the privacy of the kitchen.

I now know all I need to about PACs. I have learned any company can create a "Connected PAC," and that the regulator of PACs is the Federal Election Commission. It has been dull, deadly research, but necessary.

Raymond finished his business call almost an hour ago. I heard him clicking the lock on his briefcase, walking up the stairs, and opening the door of the spare bedroom to hang his tie. By now, he will be asleep, which is just as well. I will bring up PACs tomorrow, "keep my powder dry" as he would say.

Returning my laptop to the office, my smartphone rings. The screen tells me the caller is "Unknown." I raise the phone to my ear, the familiar sound of the wind.

"Hello, Keith," I say and, after several seconds, I hear the click.

The parcel had arrived from our accountants on Monday, and I was filing last year's income and expenses away. Each section has its own place in our storage cabinet, and I had already dropped the bank statements into the hanging file. I wouldn't have paid "Donations and Gifts" any notice were it not for our CPA's handwritten note at the end of one line that read, "non-deductible."

It is mid-evening, Thursday. After washing the dishes from an unappetizing chicken quinoa salad, I am sitting in my leather armchair, waiting for Raymond. He has finally found his favorite coaster, and can now safely place his scotch on his side table. Soon, he will disappear to write his penultimate note to Cyril. I have been waiting for the opportunity all day, even though I dread the outcome.

I walk across the living room and place the single sheet of paper on Raymond's open *Foreign Affairs* magazine.

"What's this?"

"What's what?"

I point to the line that ends with our CPA's note. "Care to tell me about it? We're Democrats, for God's sake! What the hell are you doing?"

The line item for five thousand dollars reads *BrockPAC donation*. From my online research last night I know this is the maximum annual amount allowed for personal contributions to a PAC.

"It's just a donation to the company's PAC," he replies, sheepishly, and then erupts. "What the hell's it got to do with you, anyway? It's not from our joint account—it's my money!"

"Let me say it clearly. We're Democrats. You gave five thousand dollars to a PAC that Cyril has set up. I checked online with the FEC. Do you know where that money is going? It's going to hard-core Republicans, Raymond."

He tells me this is what is expected of senior executives in the firm, adding that Cyril thanked him personally. Cyril rewards loyalty. That's why Cyril asked him to take charge these last two weeks. "We can afford five thousand—*I* can afford five thousand," he emphasizes.

I place a second printed sheet in front of him.

"It's not about the amount, Raymond. This is where BrockPAC actually spends its money. Recognize any of the names?"

He pretends to study the sheet intently.

"Yeah, I recognize them, so what? Don't try giving me this better-than-thou shit. We all have to do things we don't like sometimes."

"What about your values, Raymond?"

He stares at me, and I can see a neck artery beating.

"Values? Let me tell you about values. They don't pay the bills. They don't help you keep your job. Sometimes you just have to swallow and close your eyes."

That's my cue to look away. In the silence that follows, I get up and cross the room. Raymond may be hoping I'm going to pour myself a drink. Instead, I switch on the stereo, find the CD I am looking for, and slide it into the player.

"You *disgust* me," I say and turn the volume to its highest setting. I trudge up the stairs and, closing my bathroom door, hear the first notes of Monteverdi blasting out. Raymond is about to descend into the depths of *L'Orpheo*, and I hope he never comes out.

Raymond was nowhere to be seen the next morning, and the day passed slowly. I had several sessions in the morning, one with a new referral who had compulsive symptoms and refused to sit during our fifty minutes together, even after I'd covered the chair seat with kitchen roll. But the afternoon was largely free, and I spent the time writing up my notes.

I did drop by Carolyn's office around three o'clock. I lied that I had to leave early and would miss our weekly debriefing. She said John had just called in, also to cancel. He was likely to be too late back from a house call.

She asked me if everything was all right at homre, and I talked around a number of issues I knew would satisfy her: Raymond was still stressed, I didn't miss drinking, that sort of thing. After I turned to leave, behind my back she said softly,

"So you had a brother, Nick ..."

I twisted my head around. "Yes. We were close but he's gone. I'd rather not talk about it right now," I said, and left without another word.

But this Sunday evening I find myself thinking about my brother Nick. Some memories are still too painful and I have to push them away. This is why I have decided to write about Keith, Nick's best friend. Raymond and I have hardly spoken these last two days, despite his attempts to start a conversation. He finally stomped out, saying he was going for a walk, and I have precious time alone.

The earliest I can recall of Keith was when I was around four years old. He and Nick were three years older than me, and whenever Nick's back was turned Keith would pinch me. They did everything together—Mom used to joke they would get married one day. I think the first time she said that I'd just turned seven, and I remember feeling suddenly hot. Keith had stopped bullying me by then and had grown taller than Nick.

After Mom let me go out with them beyond our yard, I was the one to do their dirty work: shin along a narrow branch for a blue jay nest; when old Mr Johnson was in the outhouse, throw stones on the tin roof. One day, when I was ten, they locked me in a car in the yard for several hours. Dad gave Nick a beating for that.

But over those years my role changed. They stopped rushing ahead and laying in ambush. Sometimes they let me walk between them. They even allowed me to see them naked one day, though I was far too young to appreciate it. What I do remember was their long hair, and how it flowed in the stream like black riverweed.

By the time I reached thirteen, I was smitten with Keith. If a day passed when he didn't visit the house, I would stop eating. That was about the time they started drinking.

This is becoming too painful to write. I'll try again later.

The Brocks came back from The Hamptons yesterday.

I wavered for several hours this morning over whether to call but finally did so. After all, Amanda had reached out to me twice, and it was just a courtesy to respond. "Yes, I'd love to get together," I told her. "Five o'clock tomorrow at your place would be fine."

Later, in my break for lunch, something that had been gnawing at me resurfaced. When I returned to the office, I booked the admission ticket online. I was about to confront fear.

Some say fear is in the mind. For me, I feel it in the legs. If I think back to summer days with Nick and Keith, I can't recall ever being afraid when climbing trees. Heights are now my deepest dread.

Construction of the Washington Monument started in 1848, on a site reserved by Pierre L'Enfant, the designer of central DC's road system. Robert Mills, the architect, died in 1855, twenty-nine years before its eventual completion. It was built in two phases. By the time the second commenced, the quarry that supplied the basal layers had closed. Despite attempts to match the original marble facing, there's a distinct change in color above a hundred and fifty feet.

As I stood in the monument's small elevator I was already shaking, and when we emerged onto the viewing platform five hundred feet up, I was terrified.

I must have looked psychotic. The guard had probably seen it all before, hardly giving me a glance. But two small children pulled at their father's shirt and pointed at me repeatedly. It took all my strength to reach the wall and then, inch by inch, to slide myself toward the north window. I closed my eyes to slow my pulse and, when I eventually looked out, the shaking had subsided.

A heat haze hung over the city, but I could still make out Meridian Park on the hill east of 16th Street. Closer by, adorned with its large Stars and Stripes, stood the White House. I felt more confident now and moved towards the east window. After waiting for the crowd to clear, I could see the Capitol Building at the far end of the Mall. There was a wonderful view of the Tidal Basin and the Potomac from the south and, at the west window, the Lincoln Memorial stood in all its glory.

Nick adored heights. He would have loved it.

I had been to the Brock's house many times for cocktail parties or the occasional barbecue. Amanda suggested we sit in her large kitchen.

For once, she'd tied her hair into a small ponytail and not a pearl was to be seen. She was simply dressed in a blue tee shirt, with white slacks that stopped halfway up her tanned calves; a pair of old, unlaced tennis shoes completed the look. She asked if I would like a glass of wine, and we settled on tea; she chose Earl Grey for herself, which matched her eyes.

Amanda said conspiratorially that we had at least two hours before Cyril returned from work at seven. She asked me if things had been difficult while Raymond was running Brock & Associates. Was I busy at work? How did I like my Lapsang Souchong? She said they'd had a relaxing two weeks at their summerhouse, and she would have stayed on but Cyril was planning to host some clients at home next week.

In this peaceful house, with its kitchen smelling of baked bread, Ella Fitzgerald was singing in another room and it would have been so easy to just sit and chatter. But, I found myself saying, "I was wondering why you suggested we should meet."

"When Cyril and I came to your dinner party a few weeks back, I could sense something was wrong. You seemed to be struggling. I wondered whether it had anything to do with knowing Christine and David might divorce because of her affairs."

"You should be a therapist," I said.

"David told us what was going on a few days after that infamous wine tasting night. He'd been watching her for some time, poor man. While we're on Christine, don't punish yourself over it. I think we all know what happens in friendships. Keeping things in confidence is often what binds us women together."

Perhaps it was the warmth of the room, the kindness in her eyes, Ella singing that it was a lovely day. In retrospect, I can hardly believe I trusted her with some of my thoughts.

"I think I've been struggling with some painful memories for some time, Amanda. Funny as it sounds, they began to surface when I was working with a patient. I've been burying them for a long time."

"If you want to talk about them, I promise they won't leave this room," and believed her.

"I think I need to deal with them myself, first. A friend of mine is urging me to make a trip back home, to New Mexico."

"If you do, don't forget George Willis—you met him at our barbecue a month or so ago. He lives near Santa Fe—wonderful man."

"The real problem, Amanda, is that Raymond and I aren't getting along. He seems to love his work more than me. I feel that I don't exist. And just last week I found out about a secret he'd been keeping."

I told her of my discovering the PAC donation. I made every effort to avoid being critical of her husband, but I wanted her to understand how important this was to me. Her reply was a revelation.

"I'm going to tell you something that will surprise you, Vera. I don't agree with Cyril's politics. But I owe a huge debt of gratitude. Being his secretary for many years, I knew his marriage wasn't going well, but I had my own problems at the time. I'd started drinking heavily and it had started to take over my life. Cyril sat me down one morning to say if I signed on to AA he wouldn't fire me.

"How many bosses would do that? He also followed up, even driving me to meetings. I haven't touched a drop since, thirteen years now. Eventually we fell in love. His divorce was ugly, as you can imagine, but I think you have to reach the bottom before you can climb out."

I sat quietly for some time. Here was another descent into the depths before returning into the light.

"My family has a history of alcoholism," I said, "although I don't seem to need AA. I've stopped drinking for a while, anyway.

"Glad to hear it! Remember—if you ever need to talk, about anything, just call. What you said about Raymond and his work, ignoring you…this project he's working on…not something I approve of, frankly."

"What about the project, Amanda?" And then she told me.

Nick was always restless indoors. Whenever he had the chance, he would escape to the hills beyond our house and I, of course, would follow.

Even in the high meadows, Nick walked as if he were on a tightrope. His steps were so silent he would often startle a resting White-Tailed Deer, or, in the forest, a Cooper's Hawk, its eyes the color of a woodpecker's torn throat. He touched everything as he walked. I remember the first time he pried open bark on a large Ponderosa Pine for me. As my nose touched the small crack, I caught the heady smell of vanilla.

We always walked back the same route. "Never disturb any more than you have to," Nick would say. Everything beyond our yard was precious to him, provided it was not man-made. We were guests of nature, he repeatedly told me.

One day, he looked up at the cobalt-blue sky and asked me if the hole would ever reach New Mexico. That was the first time I heard the word "ozone."

Today, I learned that my husband is leading a project sponsored by the coal industry. The goal is to block or delay any legislation that could hinder the use of coal. An early theme was to influence political and public opinion by questioning evidence of climate change. That has recently been modified—it is a *human* cause of climate change that must be refuted. Amanda Brock told me they had the support of key Republicans and a number of Democrats from coal-producing states.

Amanda is remarkably knowledgeable on Raymond's project—Cyril shares a lot of things with her. Cyril thinks it's only a matter of time before opinions harden against carbon-based fuels. The new lobbying push anticipates, but seeks to delay, carbon regulation.

Energy utilities are also funding the project. They have insisted that any new legislation should only apply to *new* coal-fired power plants; existing plants, no matter how dirty and inefficient, should be exempt, or "grandfathered." The project was reviewed a few weeks ago in New York. The clients are pleased with progress.

This is why, when I got home this evening, I did some research. The coal industry alone is spending millions of dollars per year lobbying for their interests. Much of this ends up in the accounts of Brock & Associates, and some has entered my own house. I also browsed some back issues of *The New Yorker*—I remembered various commentaries and articles on climate change, and I found them, read them all.

There was a time, when we first met, that I was proud of Raymond. He would speak so passionately of his desire to make change that was "a force for good." We've spent many vacations walking through woods and wading clear streams—now, I realize, only a concession to me.

I feel soiled, disrespected, and ashamed. Everything in this house is contaminated and, tonight, after visiting with Amanda, I have not been able to eat. As I write, there is the unfamiliar sound of Raymond loading the washing machine. I want to bloody his face with my nails. Instead, I intend to read poetry in Donald Hall's book until my eyes won't stay open.

As for Raymond, let him smolder, let him soak.

dwnwilliams27@gmail.com
To: Vera Lewis
From Rwanda

Dear Vera,

I'm so sorry to have left without saying goodbye. I'm writing from Kigali. This is my private email address. I'm still with the Bank, though I've taken a leave of absence. I'm lobbying for an extended transfer to Rwanda. If that doesn't come through, I'll have to look for work with an aid agency here. Wish me luck.

I'm lost in admiration for the work Daniel is doing. He's managed to get funds from a Canadian charity that I recommended, and six families now have new cooking stoves in a small village in the east of the country.

Rwanda as a whole is still struggling to recover, but there's progress every day. No one has forgotten the hundreds of thousands killed in the genocide, but all want to find some kind of reconciliation—tribal loyalties can be so damaging! I was astonished to learn that drought and disputes over water played a large role in the initial killings. I mention it because you once asked me about climate change.

You were always kind to me—listening, sending those flowers to the office, ferrying me around DC. I don't think I ever said thank you. The one time you needed me, when your patient died, I wasn't there for you. Please forgive me. I was going through a crisis of my own at the time. The last time we spoke you didn't seem your usual self. I hope things have improved for you.

I'm happier than I've ever been. It was a difficult decision to make, accompanying Daniel back to his home. Perhaps Raymond's negative feedback on my asking if his company could give Daniel a job in DC made my decision to leave easier.

I'd love to hear from you when you have time.
With kindest thoughts,
Dawn

Her email arrived as I was finishing my morning sessions, and I replied immediately. I told Dawn that all was fine, and said I would write more in a few days.

On this gorgeous Wednesday, I decided to walk to Dupont Circle with Donald Hall's *Essays after Eighty*. There were no free benches, and so I turned around and walked south on Connecticut, stopping to buy a salad box before continuing down to Farragut Square.

Melancholy began to sweep over me. Groups of down-and-outs were sprawled on the few shaded benches, some raving at sounds only they could hear. Couples and colleagues sat elsewhere, oblivious to overturned shopping carts and trails of litter from trashcans.

I have always been a person with few friends. Now I was alone, opening a see-through box of lettuce, mushrooms and chunks of tuna in the middle of a busy city. Suddenly, I realized that my self-pitying and preoccupation with Raymond were simply more ways of deflecting childhood memories. But I had made a start. Nick had surfaced, like me outraged over what Amanda Brock had divulged.

"So, how are things?" Carolyn opened in a cheery voice. "I've got time today if you have."

Hanging my tote bag behind the chair, I sat, and breathed in deeply. I had already decided I would tell her everything, well almost everything. I could hardly keep her in the dark after disclosing so much to John and, more importantly, Amanda Brock.

"Yes, plenty of time. Things aren't good, Carolyn."

"Do you want to talk about it?" she asked. For once, I did.

I spent a long time explaining how my marriage had changed for the worse. I started with small things that I had got used to: Raymond's insensitivity to me; the utter lack of appreciation for meals, clean clothes, and a full cocktail cabinet; the bouts of sudden rage. I repeated what I'd told Amanda about him loving his work more than me, that he made me feel invisible. Carolyn tapped the rubber end of her pencil when I described Raymond's reaction to my confession around Christine's affairs. And then I told her about his five thousand dollar contribution to his company's PAC.

"Why that's awful!" Carolyn exploded. "I'd have gone crazy if Clive had done something like that."

"That's not all. I've just found out that his precious project involves lobbying for the coal industry against climate change. I'm not sure what's worse—the project, or his secrecy."

Carolyn got up and walked to the window. She placed one hand against the glass, and tilted her head as though asking the street below for advice.

"How are you, inside?" she eventually said, turning and walking back to her chair.

"Disappointed...angry...disgusted...ashamed."

I told her Raymond would be out late, and I would confront him tomorrow.

We talked for several minutes about the four words I had used to describe my feelings, why I had chosen them. Carolyn's next question caught me unawares.

"So are we going to get to talk about your brother?"

I tried to be dismissive, but she pushed, waited, and pushed a little more until I knew there was no way out.

"Why don't you want to talk about him?"

"I do want to, Carolyn."

I told her I was pretty certain that the mysterious "Unknown" caller with the wind behind him was my brother's best friend, Keith."

"Why would he be bothering you?" she asked.

"I'm not sure. But it's brought back a lot of memories." I reached down for my tote bag. "I wrote about them last weekend."

I'd been keeping my journal with me constantly these last weeks—there was already too much for Raymond's prying eyes. I'm certain Carolyn noticed Marcel's name on the cover, but she made no comment. I read her the three paragraphs I had written on Sunday morning.

"But that was all about Keith," Carolyn said. "You hardly mention your brother at all."

My lunch was rising in my throat. I swallowed, tugged at an eyelash, but the feeling of nausea increased.

"OK," I eventually said. "I'll tell you."

Carolyn held up a hand. "One moment, Vera." After leaving her office, she returned, and resettled herself into her chair. "We've got another hour, more if we need it. So tell me about Nick."

Words poured out. As I stared at the carpet in Carolyn's office, I began to see faces and scenes in the coarse-grained weave, some forgotten, most painful. This is what I told her, now stripped of my ramblings, and the many times I repeated myself, as though I was circling before leaping over the next chasm.

"I loved my brother, Nick. Maybe I was besotted with Keith, but it was Nick I loved. He had these beautiful green eyes. When I was five or six I spent my whole time chasing after him.

"When I reached puberty, Nick would let me hang out with him on weekends, but most evenings he just disappeared with Keith. He was very protective of me, even with Keith. I remember him jumping in front of me when my father raised his hand to hit me—Nick must have been about fifteen. They never spoke after that. Nick would often spit in the dirt as he walked past our cottonwood. My job was to collect the empty bottles if Dad had staggered off somewhere else.

"I think Nick first grew his hair long to fit in with the pueblo boys. They had a grudge against anyone who lived outside, especially half-Anglos like us. Keith was the one who had to fight them. Even when Nick got bigger, he'd just walk away if some boy pushed or kicked him—he was gentle like that. On days when he did get angry, I would only have to touch him with my finger and he'd stop and smile. He said I had a magic touch, called it 'the touch of love.'

"Things changed when he got to sixth grade. He'd argue with teachers, refuse to do homework. He became a kind of leader to the other kids, a rebel. By the time he was thirteen he would play hooky from school at least once a week. Some of the boys said Nick had a secret girlfriend, even a part-time job, and he never denied it. But on those late afternoons when I searched for him in the hills, I'd always find him sitting alone reading a book.

244

"He knew the names of almost every bird and could track a deer for miles, even if we were in the middle of a drought. On weekends, when I went with him and Keith, he would always turn around to make sure I was there. If he climbed a small bluff, he'd reach down his hand to pull me over the last ledge. Sometimes he would leave me dangling and we would both laugh. If Nick and I were alone he'd read to me. It was always a poem he was trying to memorize.

"Mom's death hit him hard. Guilt may have intensified it because, in her final months, he was always outside. I just think he couldn't stand to see her in pain. He and Keith had started drinking a couple of years earlier. Mom told me she'd found an empty bottle of cheap bourbon a couple of times in his small backpack.

"After she died, their drinking got worse. I'd sometimes hear them staggering around the yard late at night, though by morning Nick was always asleep in his bed.

"The week after the second anniversary of Mom's death, Nick, Keith and I were sitting in the kitchen when Aunt Rayne walked in. Nick had just been fired again—this time, by Thelma at the 7-Eleven—and Keith was out of work. Aunt Rayne started laying into Nick, telling him he had to shape up or he would end up under a tree like Dad. "Your mother would be ashamed of you!" she shouted at one point. Nick just stared at her and, without a word, walked outside. Keith followed. That was the last time I saw my brother. He was eighteen years old.

"The coroner concluded it was accidental death. Keith claimed Nick had gotten staggering drunk and slipped off a high ledge, a place we'd often visited. It had a soaring view of the pueblo and the river beyond, and Nick would sometimes sit on the edge. I always suspected Keith of holding something back. Nick was buried in the same plot as Mom, next to our small adobe church.

"I haven't spoken to Keith since. I blamed him, of course. In fact, I blamed him, Dad, Aunt Rayne. In the months that followed I started cutting my forearms again.

"Aunt Rayne became more and more eccentric. She began to rant that the house was cursed. She started getting angry, mostly against me. It was never direct, always subtle: snide asides; forgetting to tell me a friend had called; throwing some of my school notes out "by mistake," those kind of things. I've had a hatred of passive aggression ever since, probably why I dislike Raymond's mother so much. Aunt Rayne's behavior did stop me cutting, but I had to endure a painful three years with her. By the time the scholarship to Georgetown came through, I couldn't wait to leave.

"In the first semester of my freshman year I got a message that Dad had died of liver failure. I didn't go back for the funeral. Aunt Rayne may be still alive, for all I know."

When I finally looked up, Carolyn stared back and simply nodded. I'd hoped to feel relief, but only felt sadness.

"What was your mother's name?" she asked.

"Clara. I'm not sure what to do now."

"I think you know. What would you have advised Marcel to do? Like I said before, you need to visit where you grew up. And soon."

That was six hours ago. It is now ten o'clock. Raymond has just texted me, saying he will likely be home near midnight. Tonight, of all nights, I have needed a distraction. I've been reading Donald Hall's, *Essays After Eighty*, and now I need to talk to someone, to write something I should have written ten days ago.

Dear Mr. Hall,
Forgive me, but when I last wrote to you I should have said something of your wife, Jane Kenyon. You mention her many times in your book, *Essays after Eighty*, and the love you had for her is evident in almost every story you tell. Yes, leukemia is a terrible disease. In the essay "House Without a Door" you describe the day of her funeral. As her body was being carried out, you shut the dog in your workroom "so that he would not see her leave." The only dog in my own house didn't need to be locked away, Mr. Hall. On my mother's funeral day he lay slumped under a cottonwood.

I always prepare meticulously for sessions with patients. I often rehearse what I will say at key moments, including contingencies. But in my private life I am one who ruminates afterwards. When I was young I would often lie awake at night, replaying what I should have said to some bully, a witty comment I could have used in an English class. But today has been different. I have prepared.

I will speak slowly and deliberately to Raymond tonight. Each sentence will be honed to its purpose. Only I will question. I will demand answers.

After cancelling my last patient of the day, I stopped to buy some bath salts and two take-home dinners at Whole Foods. I paid with cash, my own money. When I got home, I ran a bath and soaked myself for almost half an hour. I emerged smelling of vanilla.

After I'd eaten my chicken salad, and left Raymond's on the table for when he arrived, I settled myself in my chair in the living room.

It is now seven-thirty. I've been reading bookmarked sections of prose about poetry in Donald Hall's *Essays after Eighty*. Raymond has finished his meal, and is scraping the last slivers of lettuce from the market's plastic container. I suspect he'll rinse it twice and then place it in the recycling bin.

He enters the living room, rubbing sanitizer into his hands. I twist to watch him drop two ice cubes into a glass, squeeze the cork stopper out of a half-empty bottle of Highland Park, pour in the scotch, and top it up with water. He walks across the room, sits heavily, takes a gulp—fascinating me with how his Adam's apple bobs—and spreads his legs.

"Your message said you wanted to talk about something," he says. "So let's do it."

"Why not? I'd like to know more about the project you're working on."

He lifts his eyebrows. He fans his knees at me like a moth, takes another chug of scotch, and places his glass back on its coaster.

"I thought we agreed we wouldn't talk about work."

I tell him I've changed my mind. Even I can hear what's new for me—the bitter tone of sarcasm.

He shoots back quickly, asking what business it is of mine.

"Because I'm living with someone who's morally corrupt," I say, getting up from my chair.

"Oh, God, not that PAC stuff again. We've been over that. Let it go."

"We have *not* been over that. But right now I'm interested more in that damned coal industry project you're leading."

"It's just a lobbying job."

"For those coal industry moguls. Helping ensure demand for their dirty coal."

For a moment, he stares directly at me. I've rehearsed for his argument: they pay the bills, for the little holidays we take, those spur-of-the-moment dinners in Bethesda. But this is not what he says.

"Someone's got to put the counterargument to all the scaremongering. The science isn't proven. And even if climate change is happening, is it serious enough to jeopardize our economy? Think of the jobs that'd be lost. Why should *we* take these risks when other countries are only going to renege on their promises?"

He walks past me slowly, slips more ice into his glass, and empties the bottle. It's clear he thinks the conversation is over.

"It's not about fucking climate change!" I blurt out. "I don't care a shit about your views on climate change or the economy. It's about manipulating facts. It's about doing everything you can to put roadblocks in the way of anything that would harm the interests of your clients. I could argue it's about you compromising your own values, but I'm not sure what they are any more. Most of all, it's about you being deceitful, engaging in all this behind my back."

"It's none of your God-dammed business," he hits back. "Cyril thinks I'm doing a great job, and my father said he was proud of me—not like when I wanted to marry *you*."

"So now it's about me? You're blaming *me* for the reprehensible things you're doing, that it's a way to prove yourself to that bloated father of yours?"

He slams his glass to the side table, fountaining scotch out onto the wood. I know he wants to clean it up immediately, but he just sits there wringing his hands until:

"Let's make it about you, then. I'm making a difference in how we run this country. And you? Having little chats with deadbeats all day. What makes you think you can share anything useful when you can't sort out your own head? Half of your patients come to you with problems they should solve themselves." His raises his voice to a falsetto: "'I'm cheating on my husband, and I don't know why.' 'I can't seem to lose weight, and I hate myself.' 'I'm just not happy—should I change my job?' Oh, Christ. The rest of your patients have lost it totally. Even if you manage to stop any of them from offing themselves, they're going to be a drain on society for the rest of their sorry lives. So don't preach to me!"

He gets up, stomps into the office, and slams the door. I can hear the notes of a country music song as his laptop starts up. I search the living room, spotting *To Read a Poem* on top of the stereo, and return to my chair. I need to find a poem to lessen the loathing and disrespect I feel. Frantically flipping the pages, I stop at a short poem by Walter Savage Landor, written in 1849:

> *I strove with none, for none was worth my strife.*
> *Nature I loved and, next to Nature, Art;*
> *I warmed both hands before the fire of life;*
> *It stinks, and I am ready to depart.*

My eyes scan the room. Everything seems alien, part of someone else's life. I open the door to the office to confront the husband who sits at his desk, laptop lid raised.

"I'm going." The words are calm, sincere. "We both need space."

He reaches back to scratch his head.

"Where are you going?" he asks, as though this is important.

"New Mexico. Santa Fe, specifically, where I can think. To visit my home."

I slept in the spare bedroom that night and the night following. On Friday, I told Carolyn what had happened first thing, and later broke the news to John that I would be going away awhile.

My original thought was to leave my car in our garage and book the earliest cheap flight to Albuquerque. If I hired a car at the airport it would be a mere one-hour drive north to Santa Fe. I planned to be away for at least a week, perhaps two. I was so distracted that it took John to point out that we would need to make arrangements for my patients. I would need to stay in DC over the weekend so I could contact them on Monday morning.

At first John said I could stay with him, but then reneged, saying he didn't want to give Anne ammunition to counter-file, that "It wouldn't look good for a pretty lady to be seen at the house." Carolyn called her husband, Clive, immediately, and the next morning, after Raymond left for a round of golf, I packed a suitcase into my car and drove away to their house in Reston, Virginia.

Carolyn and I spent most of the weekend sitting in the conservatory, looking out over a large lawn. Prompted by her blue, lightweight jogging outfit, I stayed in my gray pajamas during the day, changing into blouses and a skirt in the evenings. Clive mostly busied himself in the garden, pulling weeds and repairing a mosquito spray system they had installed when they bought the house eleven years ago. On Sunday evening he barbecued steaks.

Carolyn repeatedly returned to two questions: Could I see myself going back to Raymond after this trip? And what did I want to achieve in New Mexico?

By Monday morning at least I knew I wanted to be gone for a month, anyway. That was when I decided I would drive to Santa Fe.

Carolyn and I divided my patients into categories of seriousness. I had been too optimistic, and it took most of the week to speak to all of them. Most agreed to move temporarily to either John or Carolyn. Those left wished to continue with me, using telephone sessions.

Raymond called several times over the weekend and once on the Monday, leaving the same short voicemail message, "Call me back." I sent him a text on Tuesday saying we both needed some space and not to call me again.

It was a painful time, with occasional waves of disloyalty and guilt washing over me.

On Wednesday morning I received a texted haiku from Marcel:

> a patch of glass
> in the lake's ripples
> where a trout rose

He signed off, "Thinking of you. M."

Imagining him fishing somewhere west of Pittsburgh, perhaps wading in a pristine lake, brought a warm smile. I replied immediately to what was a new smartphone number and gave him my private email address. We have corresponded regularly ever since.

That evening, as I waited in a parking lot in Bethesda to drive home and collect some personal things, I dumped years of debris from my car to a large trash container. Finally, Amanda Brock called to say Raymond had arrived at her and Cyril's house for the party they were staging for coal industry executives. The coast had cleared.

When I entered the house, any remnant of nostalgia was swept away by the smell of bleach. Raymond had polished the kitchen counter to a mirror. In the living room, he had stacked our magazines on three small tables, the most recent at the top of each stack.

I spent an hour carefully folding clothes into a large suitcase I found in the garage. I filled two carrier bags with books, added a number of CDs, and returned for my mother's clay pot. Turning it over I saw the familiar writing inscribed into the base—"Clara 92."

Three tasks were left before I could leave DC: meet Christine; buy Glyn Maxwell's book that Marcel had recommended; get my car serviced.

❖ ❖ ❖

Christine and I met for lunch at the *Tabbard Inn*—my choice, a small act of remembrance. She ordered a white wine and was surprised when I asked for iced tea.

"Not drinking?"

"I've stopped," I told her.

She seemed to have aged. Crescents of blue skin hung beneath her eyes, and several of her fingernails were bitten down to cracked nail polish.

"So..." was all she said, as if she didn't know how to start. She reached for her glass then withdrew her hand as though the gesture had burned her flesh. The glass remained untouched for the rest of the meal.

"I'm glad you could come, Christine. I thought we ought to talk."

"I just want to say I'm sorry, Vera. For everything, for—"

"You actually did me a favor. When Raymond found out I'd been covering up for you, he went ballistic. He showed a side of him I should have seen long before."

"Huh?"

I broke the news that I had decided to take a break from the marriage and was driving to New Mexico, to visit my hometown for maybe a month, to try to get some clarity about how I wanted to live my life.

"I'm envious," she said. "I've thought a lot about why I kept having those affairs. It wasn't because I'm some sort of nymphomaniac. I just hate myself and wanted to prove I'm still attractive to men. I feel so *trapped*."

David, she told me, was *so* successful. When they were on their honeymoon he told her she would never need to work again. She felt so grateful at the time. After the first year of the marriage, she started to feel stifled and, when the boys came along, increasingly bored. Beyond his work and his club, David had few interests, and she found herself dumbing down.

"I also want to say sorry for the way I used you," she said, at one point. "Not just in covering up for me, but all the times I asked you for favors. So let me know if there's anything I can do."

I didn't want to share any more of myself.

"Do you remember that house party in our second semester at Georgetown? Dawn was so happy. What you did was terrible, Christine. Tim was nothing to you, but she loved him. When you lured him into that bedroom, it almost destroyed her. Why did you do it?"

Christine's hand moved towards the wine glass, then pulled back.

"I've always said it was the drink," Christine said. "That's not true. You were my first real friend, Vera. I know Dawn introduced us, but she seemed to be everywhere, always around you. I was so jealous. I wanted to hurt her. It was spite."

By the end of the meal she had promised to try to reach out to Dawn. She also agreed to consider seeing a therapist. I recommended Carolyn, of course. While we were signing the checks, Christine admitted therapy could help for another reason. David was still arguing for custody of the boys, but in the latest exchange between attorneys he'd indicated a willingness to share custody, "if presented with consistent evidence of change and increased responsibility on the part of my wife." We had a good laugh at the clumsy language.

Standing on N Street, I turned to her one last time. "Don't do it for the lawyers, Christine. Do it for yourself."

She offered me a lift, but told her I wanted to walk. It was mild and not too humid, and my Volkswagon Golf was waiting for me at the garage. I'd only requested a mini-service—"oil, filter, and tires"—but they'd found two other small ailments, as they always do.

The car purred. I drove up 14th Street, cut through Rock Creek Park, took Davenport to Connecticut, and parked at the rear of *Politics and Prose*. The young cashier found the book easily. I'd ordered Glyn Maxwell's *On Poetry* earlier in the week. It was, as Marcel had said, a tiny book.

Friday evening, my last before leaving for Santa Fe, John joined Carolyn, Clive and me for dinner. He arrived around six, kissed Carolyn and I on both cheeks, and disappeared with Clive to get two cold beers from the fridge. John and Clive had known each other for almost twenty years. We watched them walk around the garden, chatting, turning to each other, and then settling down in two Adirondack chairs, facing the lawn.

Later, we ate a barbecue of burgers and marinated chicken, and sat outside talking well into the night. Carolyn asked John about his future plans. She cautioned him, with a wink, that it was probably too soon to fall in love again, but asked whether he was still using the online dating agency he'd mentioned to her weeks ago. Glancing at me and smiling, he told Carolyn no.

When I was younger, I could have completed the drive in two days—twelve hundred miles the first day, eight hundred on the second. But I was in no hurry and besides, I'd made things more difficult, with a longer route than advised on Mapquest.

The direct route would have led me south, but I was determined to avoid Nashville, indeed any town or motel where I ran the risk of hearing country music. And so I drove west, through Louisville to St. Louis before heading southwest into Oklahoma. On the second night I stayed at a quaint bed and breakfast outside Claremore, in Rogers County, and last night, in a fit of extravagance, at a four-star hotel in Amarillo. I drove slowly, took many stops. I was delaying.

"White," the first chapter of Glyn Maxwell's *On Poetry*—a collection of essays—was my companion on Saturday night. Initially, I found the combination of formality and sudden flights of fancy unsettling. "Black" followed on Sunday morning, and, since then, I have read a new chapter at the end and start of each day. When reading "Chime" last night, Mr. Maxwell's love of sound was overwhelming at times. Increasingly, as I read, I felt cleansed and awakened to life.

I woke around three this morning. It was warm in the hotel room, but I was shaking as I searched in the depths of my tote bag for the small receipt. I found it, crumpled into one of the seams, and unfolded it on the bedside table. In my handwriting was the list of eight poetry book titles my fingernail had found that April day at *Politics and Prose*, five months ago. I remembered the first four well—I had copied them into my journal: *Baptism of Desire, Rivers and Mountains, Waiting for the Past, After We Lost Our Way.* But as I worked my way down the list I realized that the titles had indeed found me, Vera. But I'd hidden the last four titles, buried them:

Gathering the Tribes, Carolyn Forché
High Windows, by Philip Larkin
Fall Higher, by Dean Young
Death of a Naturalist, by Seamus Heaney

I am no longer unsettled—I am exhilarated. *On Poetry* is a deeply philosophical work written with love. It is a lament for the loss of form in much contemporary poetry. Glyn Maxwell believes great poetry comes from the harmonization of mind and body, and that poetic forms originate in human necessities—breath, heartbeat, footstep, and posture. He dislikes free verse unless the line breaks "feel the pressure of silence" and the poem interacts with the reader "in a way that resembles a human encounter."

This morning I took a long, late breakfast in Amarillo before setting off on the remaining three hundred miles. From Clines Corners I continued on to Albuquerque before heading north on I-25. It was a longer route, but I had in mind a place to stop.

The basalt plateau just north of the Cochiti turn off is where I have been sitting for the last hour. Years ago, on high school trips south, we would always stop here on the way home. For some it was a comfort break, but for me it was the view. It is the first rest area you reach after climbing from the desert plains.

The Cerrillos Hills to the east are changing from ocher to deeper red. Cerro de la Cruz, one of many small volcanoes, is half in shadow, and the hot wind is cooling and dropping to a breeze. A few small clouds are allowing a last-gasp sunset to blaze at the southern edge of the Jemez Mountains. In minutes the Sangre de Cristos will take on their remembered lilac hue before turning through purple to black.

I am going to sit here until the desert turns itself over to night. Already I see the first flickers of light in Santa Fe, ten miles north. Soon, the city will be as startling as the Milky Way, a sky-full of stars at the base of a mountain.

White space is time. "Poets are voices upon time," and "A poet can shape time in a poem, and form is how that's done," Glyn Maxwell writes. Now I think I understand.

Mr. Maxwell believes that when a poet writes he inserts himself into time, the blank, white page. "The white is everything but me," he says. "In poems the black is someone." The black provides the human presence, for "What is a poem if it doesn't act, think, breathe like a human?" Poetry is how humans create music with words.

Meter—even pentameter, "this magnificent engine of English poetry"—serves only as the bars of this music. It allows time to pass in the background. It is the framework within which the beauty of the words can dance and sing.

This depth of understanding must be the reason Marcel urged me to read *On Poetry*. I suspect it was his way of admitting his own poems' subservience to a pounding beat. He allowed no space for rhythm, for what it takes to be truly human, in his poetry or his life. He was locked inside a clock that never moved. But time has opened up for Marcel, as it has for me. Time heals.

It's ten o'clock and I've pulled into the El Rey Inn, a small, family-run motel on the south end of Santa Fe. I am in bed, finishing "Time," the final chapter of *On Poetry*, before switching off the light. Tomorrow evening I'll try to find my own music, drive to the opera house north of town and wait in line for any ticket returns. There are only ten performances left in the season, and I plan to queue up each night. Until I strike lucky, I will do what I used to do. I will stay in the shadows of the large car park, listening as music rises into the sky.

I have now been in Santa Fe four months. Rental houses outside the city are pretty rare, but I found one within a week. I took Marcel's advice and negotiated a monthly rent, with an option to extend for three months rolling forward.

In retrospect, I was wise to take a pitched-roof house—the tar-and-gravel, flat roofs of adobes often leak. The odd-job guy that Keith recommended managed to replace the aluminum roof before the first heavy frosts, but there's still a leak above the front door. My two-bedroom, one-bath, stucco, temporary home is located between the opera house and the pueblo, and some days I drive south into Santa Fe to collect some cash. All the ATMs nearby have been vandalized.

I've visited the old house, even the pueblo, many times. Aunt Rayne had left the place in quite a state. Keith told me he spent three days boarding it up with some old plywood he found, but the pack rats got in anyway. The old windows need replacing with double-panes, and the fireplace needs rebuilding. But I've told the builder to focus on the kitchen, my old bedroom and the rear patio—the rest can wait until after I've moved in.

Keith had somehow traced my numbers online. I ran into him walking along the dirt-track verge of the road the first time I visited the old house. If it hadn't been for the way he scuffed the ground with his shoes, I wouldn't have recognized him. It looked as though his gray ponytail had drawn his face back into a permanent look of pain. His shirt was smeared with grease on both sleeves, his oversized jeans were ripped, and the knuckles of one hand were blackened nubs. I told him to get in the car.

We stopped for a coffee at the gas station in Nambé. Initially, he kept shifting from one foot to the other, looking around at anything but me. I told him to relax, that it was good to see him.

Aunt Rayne died old and bitter, according to Keith, buried in purple. In the following months, rumors swirled that the house would be demolished since no one claimed ownership. Keith got one of the elders, a friend from school, to intervene. Keith told him he was going to contact me. That's when he started trying to find me. He said he wanted to speak many times but, at the last moment, something held him back.

Today is the winter solstice, one of two days in the year when "the sun stands still." I am sitting at my window, Mr. Hall, watching nothingness and everything. Views to the south and east light up in the mornings, but sunsets elude me. I am longing for the work on my childhood home to be finished by spring. I read poetry most nights, always recalling Robert Frost's words, hoping that some sense of purpose will enter my life.

And miles to go before I sleep,
And miles to go before I sleep.

Marcel has been helpful in many other ways. In the times I've called in the evening he's always stayed on the line, listening to my thoughts and concerns. "And how did that make you feel, Doctor Lewis?" When the builder sent me a long quote, I emailed it to him. His detailed questions and suggestions, line by line, arrived the next morning.

One day, in the fall, he sent me a delightful one-line haiku of nine syllables, something my new haiku group calls a "monoku:"

sunlight through aspens no petticoat

He was very coy when I asked about the petticoat. Marcel has promised I'll meet her soon.

After leaving Pittsburgh, it turns out he continued driving west until Oregon, eventually ending up at Grants Pass on the Rogue River. There he tried his hand at becoming a fly-fishing guide but, as he wrote, "I have much to learn about steelhead, and they know too much of me already."

He is now in Yellowstone, working as snowcoach driver for so-called winter safaris. Whenever I think of him in that harsh, unforgiving place I feel an ache inside. I find myself worrying whether his small frame is sufficiently wrapped against the cold. He still sends me haiku:

freezing lake
Monet
in monochrome

But I can share something else about Marcel and me. I had helped him. I was proud of him, and proud of myself. And as I continued learning about his search for meaning in his life, thoughts of my own surfaced: of what it meant to be alive, of purpose, of what I might be. Marcel and I in a way had become soul mates.

Ex-senator George Willis has also been of enormous help. I bumped into him at a small lunch spot in the Railyard area south of downtown Santa Fe. I recognized him immediately, and introduced myself. He invited me to join him and his bride at their table.

After listening to why I was back in New Mexico, he told me he empathized with my reaction to Raymond's project. He had felt the same way. Even though he had no gripes with the coal industry, he was not happy with the underhand way Brock & Associates were working. He asked me about my plans. At the time, I wasn't sure. Since then, he and I have met and talked regularly.

It was George who helped draft the first business plan, if I can call it that. It was also George who helped me navigate the complex planning rules. My new therapy office will be an annex to the house.

DC now seems like one, long, bad dream, though I have returned there twice. The first was to address an emergency with one of my phone patients. I stayed with Carolyn and Clive, but before the week was over I longed to return to New Mexico. The second time was six weeks ago, in early November. By then my future seemed clearer, and I doubted I would be visiting again.

Carolyn, John and I survived the *Annual Meeting of Members* through giggles and coffee. John and Carolyn would buy out my interest and remain as co-owners. The price was more than fair—in fact, I protested. They responded that I was to host them once per year. John would visit for skiing, and Carolyn and Clive for Indian Market weekend in August. My meeting with Raymond was far more strained.

We met for coffee at a Starbucks on 19th Street. He was already sitting in a leather armchair reading the *Wall Street Journal*. He looked like most middle-aged men in DC—wrung-out, beneath an arrogant veneer. When I sat opposite, he waited to finish the article before putting his newspaper aside.

I asked about his parents. He asked about my car. Then he surprised me by saying there was no need for us to wait the statutory year for a divorce. If we both agreed, we could split legally after six months of living apart. Fine by me. We agreed to divide the assets fifty-fifty. He will keep the house, re-finance, and buy out my share.

As we were leaving, he told me he'd not changed the locks, and that I was free to visit the house. "Just put stickers on what you want," he said. Carolyn and I bought a pack with smiley faces and spent ten minutes that afternoon placing one, on my mother's flat top trunk.

Re-reading what I have written recently, I appear to sound melancholic, but in truth I am not. I am in a '"good place" as John would say, have been for some time. Trying to understand my wasted years with Raymond has taken many evenings of thought, often when day's light was fading to black.

I'm now clear I'd been leaving Raymond and DC for many years. Marcel, partially, was the trigger, as Carolyn once suggested. His courage in confronting his past provided a path I could follow. But what first drew me to him, what began to unlock buried memories, was poetry. As my brother Nick used to say, it is always poetry.

Marcel and I regularly email each other. We share thoughts on
formal verse, and he still sends me texts of a moment he has
observed, always less than seventeen syllables. I think when he
and I write of poetry it is to avoid the personal, though I can
always sense more beneath his words: his breath and his
heartbeat, certainly; perhaps the way he is sitting; even the echo
of his footsteps from a walk the evening before:

birdsong dies in the hush of an owl

After his foray into free verse, what he called "a necessary
aberration," he is now writing poems regularly, experimenting
with form, though always returning to the sonnet. I confided to
him recently that, even though Glyn Maxwell had joined Donald
Hall on my bedside table, I was still drawn to more experimental
work. My latest love is the discovery of the haibun form, a
combination of prose poem—something Glynn Maxwell
disparagingly calls "prose written by poets"—with one or more
haiku.

Last Tuesday morning, Marcel sent the sonnet he had first
started in Pittsburgh. He claimed that, so far, it has gone through
over thirty drafts.

MASK

Exactly like the first time I flew:
sitting beside a baby and its mother,
the voice so sickly sweet "…should the plane suffer
a drop in pressure, please ensure you should do
the same as shown by members of the crew—
Make sure your mouth and nose are fully covered,
then tighten the straps before you help another"
even if your child is turning blue.

I used to think I'd never pull the mask
to my face first, that this could finally earn
my father's touch, that while I choked and shuddered

a better life would live. Until I asked
why you had left, and you said I must learn
to love myself before I can love another.

He has submitted it with several new poems to the online poetry journal, *Autumn Sky*, but he is prepared for rejection. I am so proud of him. I already have the final eleven words of his sonnet framed above my desk. They now form a beautiful sentence that—and please forgive me, Mr. Hall—begins with "I."

That evening, I called him to say how much I liked the poem. He was about to watch *A River Runs Through It* for what he claimed was the hundredth time. I asked him why he liked the movie so much.

"It's almost spiritual, the way he describes fly-fishing, the oneness with the river." He hesitated, and then continued.

"The scenes of fly-fishing are wonderful, but that's not the real reason I love it. I guess you know that the book is semi-autobiographical—Norman Maclean wrote it in memory of his brother who was beaten to death. The real story is about not being able to help someone you love."

Yes, I always learn something.

It was almost three months ago, in early January. The morning was particularly cold when Keith arrived at the house to ask if I would take a walk with him. He had shaved and cut himself. Even though he had gained some weight of late, I suspected from his level of agitation that he was still shooting meth. I asked if he felt strong enough, but he convinced me this was something important.

I drove us beyond the pueblo into the hills along a track that ended at an arroyo, parking in a clearing strewn with cans and bottles. The few stunted junipers were coated in frost and, as we hiked up a narrow path, thickets of Ponderosa Pines creaked with the cold. Keith looked increasingly worried as we reached the top of the last switchback. But the ledge was still there, as it always will be.

Following Keith towards the edge, I could feel an ache growing in my legs. I waited for the shakes to start, but they didn't. There was no wind as we looked past the pueblo and over the Rio Grande to the Jemez Mountains. "He didn't slip," Keith said. "He jumped." I told him I had suspected it for a long time.

"That's what I wanted to tell you. I was going to tell the cops but I got worried…well, you know…that he wouldn't be buried right. You know how they are around here.

"You shoulda seen him that day, Vera. Sure, we drank a lot but he was so happy. Said he was getting ready to fly."

Today, I would have seen the signs. I would have seen the hollow, haunted look in Nick's eyes, the way he hung around the house waiting for Mom's voice to call him in before walking away into the hills.

Standing with Keith so high above the valley, I imagined it had been one of those summer days when the ground heats up and a storm begins to form. Nick and Keith would have been standing above the clouds, looking down through the first white cotton wool puffs. And I felt sure that my brother would have splayed his arms like the falcons he loved.

Keith's eyes had filled with tears. I reached up and put my arms around his boney shoulders. "It was an act of dignity, Keith, the one thing he could control."

I felt released, felt the lifting of a heavy hand. As the wind picked up, I thought I could hear James Wright whispering:

> *Suddenly I realize*
> *That if I stepped out of my body I would break*
> *Into blossom*

Nick, do you remember when you used to ask me to pat the beat with my hands as you recited poems? There were times when I would lapse into what seemed to me to be the framing of the rhythm. And you would always stop me, and then start again by exaggerating the stresses before letting the verse find its natural rhythm.

You truly loved that poem by Hart Crane, "At Melville's Tomb." You would always recite it when we were at the lookout ledge. What gave you the most pleasure was seeing me wince in anticipation at the end of the first line:

Often beneath the wave, wide from this ledge
The dice of drowned men's bones he saw bequeath
An embassy.

Crane battled alcoholism for most of his short life. Like you, Nick, he leapt to his death, but in his case from a ship.

I'm not trained to deal with drug abuse, at least not yet, but I do have experience with alcoholism. There's so much to do, yet there's so much being done.

Word of mouth is sending drinkers and addicts who want to stop to my rental house. After their first visit, if they wish to continue to see me they must abide by one simple rule—no drink or drug for twenty-four hours before they walk in. Keith has tried to fool me several times.

When the work is finished on my permanent home I'll be closer to the pueblo. With George Willis' backing, I've submitted plans for the purpose-built annex, for meetings and perhaps overnight stays. In time, I intend to work with all forms of substance abuse. Dealing with tribal culture and prejudice may be a particular challenge, but eventually I hope to share my experience with other therapists, and perhaps develop a small training institute.

George suggested I offer my services for free. For this, he helped me set up a small not-for-profit, even made the first donation. The salary it pays will be modest, supplemented by more conventional therapy work—I already have several new patients. For the nonprofit work, my vision is to move towards abstinence through the restoration of pride. Yes, it *is* a lofty goal. How I'll reach it still eludes me.

When Nick began reciting Simon Ortiz's poems I was not the only one affected. The passion infused all of us, but I am sure this was what turned Nick to writing. Keith told me that my brother would create poems or snatches of them constantly, on torn pages of newspaper, even on cigarette packets. But despite searching my childhood home, we failed to find a single poem. Keith believes that, as Nick's depression deepened, he destroyed them all.

What may be the last heavy snow of the winter fell in silence last night, and I am sitting at my window watching nothingness and everything. For several minutes, when the clouds broke near noon, I thought I saw the sun stand still, but the world outside continued. Time has hardly missed a beat. Outside the window is a blank page, and it is white.

He is curled up on the carpet, knees tucked into his chest and arms wrapped around his head. They are ten minutes into the session, and he has lain like this for most of the time, ever since he tried to tell her about his father. Of course, she could just wait him out, wait for him to unwrap and turn to her with another inane example of the way he was treated, how he was never good enough.

This would have been an image of closure to leave you with. There is Raymond in deep therapy with Carolyn, looking back to confront the father of his past, beginning a journey of healing of the mind and soul. It is not a pleasant image, and I paint it not from malice, nor from any need for retribution. It is merely a scene from my imagination—it has never happened, nor likely ever will.

Raymond continues to lobby for the coal industry. Cyril's wife, Amanda, updates me regularly. In her last email she hinted he might be dating. Amanda also sent news of Christine who, I hope, may feel able to write to me soon. After signing up for counseling, Christine was able to retain custody of her sons. It probably helped that David has less time for them now. The young woman who, the day after the divorce, became his fiancée, is teaching him fast the art of pampering her. Christine, meanwhile, has signed up for a course leading to a master's in interior design.

John writes that he's still acting like a monk. After filing for divorce on the basis of Anne's adultery, he has been religious in refusing to date. He jokes that, when he's not working, he barricades himself in the house. He cancelled a planned skiing visit to me earlier this year for fear of raising any of Anne's suspicions, though he has promised to come in a few months, possibly in March. I'm sure he'll fully emerge by next summer, bleary eyed and pale-skinned, primed for camping and the blistered joys of sunburn.

And Dawn? For months she didn't write. I began to worry when a series of emails from me brought no response. In May, she wrote that she'd returned to DC from Rwanda. She says she has no regrets, that she and Daniel had an amicable parting.

"When it came down to it, we were just too different. What held us together was more mutual admiration than love." I remember thinking that some couples stay together with less than that.

There is something magical in sunsets, like watching a painting emerge, flare to brilliance, and then fade through pastel pinks and purple to black.

By a miracle, my old home, just six miles south of the pueblo, became move-in ready in April. All but one of the scrap cars have been removed, and I now have a new portal. The vigas will take time to age, but the floor is the same. I insisted in laying out Mom's French terra-cotta tiles personally, in a simple checkerboard grid of browns, ochers, and grays. One tile is larger, triangular, and points to the west. Each evening, I sit and look beyond a gnarled cottonwood trunk towards the Jemez Mountains, waiting for the moment when the sun's rim disappears.

For several weeks I thought only about the way the sky's colors changed with time. But then I reread the chapter "To the Student" in my bible, *To Read a Poem*. In introducing his thoughts on the power of ambiguity in poetry, Donald Hall writes of scientific truth, and its relation to poetic beauty. I thought perhaps I could do the same with the science of sunsets.

In northern New Mexico's clear, high-desert air, sundown is a glorious time. Early refraction of the sun's last rays creates swathes of orange and red and then, as the sun passes the horizon, the light reflects back to the east, bathing the Sangre de Cristos in their "Blood of Christ."

But there is one rare sight that I have never seen. It was photographed for the first time in 1960 and occurs when the last tip of the sun disappears over the horizon.

If there is what's called a thermal inversion, the dense air below acts as a lens that refracts the light and, in that final moment, a flash occurs. Even though blue light is refracted the most, it is scattered beyond the line of sight, which is why the sudden flash is brilliant green.

Each night I watch and wait.

Donald Hall writes that, "As the mind becomes more sensitive and receptive to poetry, it may become more sensitive to all sorts of things." With Nick, this sensitivity increasingly turned inwards, away from the birds and mountains he loved. But with me this sensitivity has triggered an awakening, an opening to the emotional rhythms and joys of life. Donald Hall's conviction that, "When we read great poetry, something changes in us that stays changed," rings true to me, especially after studying the great poets Mr. Hall highlights: John Keats, Emily Dickinson, Richard Frost, Theodore Roethke, and Adrienne Rich.

Marcel has also changed. Even his haiku have a new crispness, wasting no words. This is one he sent to me in April:

> Yellowstone—
> in spring snow, a bison bull
> steams

❖ ❖ ❖

Marcel and Melissa stayed for two days and two wonderful nights. He has grown his hair and his curls are back. The only remaining sign of his old shyness is the way he insists on buttoning his checkered flannel shirt up to his neck. But his heavy tan and the calluses on his hands make him look more rugged, even manly, though he still walks as if testing the ground with each step. The way he placed his hands, palms outwards, between his thighs when he spoke, and the delicate manner in which he touched Melissa's cheek with his fingertips, showed that he had not lost his gentleness.

The first time Melissa called his name was a shock.

"Marcellus!" she called. "Can you pick up that last bag?"

Even now, I find myself laughing at his answer to my simple question.

"I had to change it to Marcel," he replied. "marCEL maLONE—two iambs, two rising beats. Can you imagine me trying to say marCELLus? I would never have got past that amphibrach!"

Melissa, or as Marcel is now able to say, meLISSa, is how I imagined her to be. She around my height, but she is beautiful, more than pretty, with hazel-colored eyes, and long fair hair that she repeatedly hooks behind her ears with delicate fingers. When I opened my wardrobe so she could find a wrap against the late evening chill, she chose a rough silk in orange. "It's more than enough," she told me. I don't think she will ever need to dress in layers.

Marcel had first called Melissa when he was in Oregon. They spoke regularly and, when he secured the Yellowstone job, he invited her to visit for a long weekend. She has stayed with him ever since. While Marcel ferries winter tourists around in his snowcoach, Melissa paints delicate watercolors. She gave me one as a hostess gift. The framed image of a lone bison bull standing in deep snow now hangs proudly in my small dining room above a table supporting a simple clay pot. Melissa was like a little girl when she told me that some of her paintings would be exhibited in the foyer of the Lake Yellowstone Hotel over the summer.

Marcel's "Mask" sonnet has not yet been accepted for publication. He is writing some other interesting poetry, though. Melissa and I pestered him over dinner to read some of his poems to us. You would have loved the ballad, Nick, a story of a snowshoeing trip they had made that used each new vista as a metaphor for what they were discovering about each other. The other was a villanelle about a line-dancing class where I could feel their pivots and turns in the repeated lines.

They took a week to drive down from Yellowstone. For two days, they waded the North Platte River in Colorado before crossing the border to fish the San Juan River below the Navajo Dam. "Awesome trout, tiny flies," Marcel said. On their first night here, when Marcel's eyes began to close, Melissa took his hand and led him to their room. I heard them making love just before dawn.

That morning, Marcel told me they were on a long journey. I replied to say I understood, that new relationships took time to build. He burst out laughing in his bubbly way, and called Melissa into the kitchen to relate what I'd said.

"That may be true, Doctor Lewis—sorry, Vera—but I was talking about our journey around Colorado and New Mexico!"

Later that day, while they toured Santa Fe, and I contemplated Marcel's emotional journey in the fourteen months I'd known him, I made a decision. That evening, sitting on my patio, I returned Marcel's journal to him. I had told him many times, in emails and on the phone, about my brother Nick, Mom, my father, Keith, but I had never spoken about his journal.

"Those two myths you wrote about were true, Marcel. I *did* want you to go back to Pittsburgh to confront your past. And your courage to do that *was* an example to me, a true gift. I will never be able to thank you enough."

I reached behind my chair and lifted a ring-bound file. I hadn't rehearsed what to say, but as I gave my little speech I could feel a slight tremor entering my voice.

"I've photocopied these pages from my own journal. I've omitted those where I mention patients, including my sessions with you. But you're there in so many pages where I wrote about poetry—your voice is in the ink, opening a human heart, my heart, Marcel."

From an initial look of astonishment, his features softened. "Thank you. I'll treasure it."

Transference can take many forms. In our case, Marcel's descent into the depths, his confrontation of the past, and his emergence into the light reflected onto me. But who would believe that on a cool May night mere months ago, after staring at stars, a patient could become the therapist? As we closed the screen doors and stepped inside the house, Marcel let Melissa walk on.

"I'll always be there for you," he said. "Just know this, and always remember that I care."

They left the next morning, waving from the windows of their red Chevy truck. They planned to drive south, and then west to Chaco Canyon, camping overnight before exploring the magnificent Anasazi ruins. Over a breakfast of eggs and fresh fruit, Marcel said that he and Melissa would likely leave Yellowstone for Jackson Hole at the end of the summer. His goal of working as a fishing guide was still there. He wanted to become so intimate with the South Fork of the Snake River that he would know every boulder, the unique markings of each male brown trout, the day the salmon fly hatch would start, and the rate it would move upstream.

That evening it inspired a haiku of my own that I texted to him:

after the flood
a new rock
in the quiet glide

Carolyn and Clive visited three months ago over Indian Market weekend, the successor of the event where my parents first met. It was Clive who emailed a month ahead to suggest we read poetry to each other each evening. He knew I had joined a writer's circle as well as a haiku group, and I'm sure this was his way of honoring the host. Carolyn had predictably written that Clive's idea seemed "too embarrassing by far." That was until I sent her this small quote from Donald Hall: "Reading poetry adds tools by which we observe, measure and judge people and the properties of our universe—inside and outside."

Carolyn said it was the "observing" and "judging" of people that converted her. I can imagine the familiar questioning tilt of her head as she opened the package I sent two weeks before their flight. It was small book with a white cover and two words, "On Poetry."

We had a wonderful time together, though the market was too crowded for our tastes. Clive had put on more weight and didn't seem to care. Some of this must have rubbed off on Carolyn because she had grown out her hair to a five-inch cap of steel gray that flowed into waves of her old dyed blond. She wore skirts and cotton shirts the whole weekend.

On the first evening, Carolyn and I watched Clive as he barbecued a rack of lamb on two stacks of adobe bricks next to the foundations of the new annex. As he stopped to sip his drink, a hummingbird flew in to inspect his glass of pink rosé, and he turned to us with a grin as wide as his waist.

Carolyn and I drove into the hills early the next morning before hiking up to the ledge where Nick had jumped to his death. We stood in the cool wind, and spoke a lot about our work and what drove us, what was important. Later, in the evening, the three of us sat on my small patio and read poems to each other. I had intended it as a lighthearted break, but Carolyn became animated when I spoke of White and Black, that poems were opportunities to hear voices upon Time.

On the Sunday night I shared my thought that reading poetry was like talking with someone, someone who would listen and who cared. Carolyn's eyes filled up. She spoke softly, said she and Clive wanted to spend more time together. They had talked of travel, of signing up for cooking classes, perhaps joining a gardening club, but there was something missing, a sense of purpose. She asked if I could help them put more meaning into their lives. Could she and I talk each week? Could I recommend some reading for her?

After walking into the house, I returned with the book that had lain on my bedside table for over a year. I placed Donald Hall's *To Read a Poem*—with Edward Hopper's painting "Lighthouse Hill" facing upwards—in her hands. I told her that this book had been my own guiding light, a beacon of help and support through my worst times—perhaps it could do the same for her and Clive. And it was at that moment that an idea surfaced.

At first, I saw it as an opportunity to make *my* life more meaningful. It was triggered by something Glyn Maxwell wrote in his book, *On Poetry*:

> "What evolutionary psychologists—and I—believe is that aesthetic preferences, those things we find beautiful, originate not in what renders life delightful and endurable, but in what makes life *possible*."

It was on the Wednesday, two days after Carolyn and Clive returned to DC, when we met at our usual place, a side room at the La Farge branch of the Santa Fe public library. We had a full house that evening—two poets, three short story writers, and me—sitting around a tressled table, listening to each other's recent compositions. I was usually able to pluck up the courage to read first, to "get it out of the way, before the group wakes up," I would tell myself. But on this day I held back, still uncertain whether I was ready to share this. As the conversation finished its dance around Rita's new rondeau, I unfolded a sheet of paper and read Glynn Maxwell's words.

Several "Ahs" gave their assent. Notebooks were opened, and I saw Glyn Maxwell's name being written below "On Poetry." I withdrew from a polite discussion about aesthetic preferences, vaguely hearing words like "If I could build on that…" and "I agree, but…." Suddenly, a chair scraped the floor and two hands gently slapped the table. I looked up to see a pair of eyes staring across coffee cups and notebooks. Breaking his habitual silence, Terry asked me why this sentence resonated so much.

"The beauty of making life possible," I found myself saying.

There was a moment's silence while our new member, Sonia, began sharing her thoughts on fertility symbols, of the ecstasies of conception and birth. Terry cut her off.

"Vera, tell us what *you* thought when you read those lines."

"It gave me an idea," I said, uncertainly.

After the library closed, Terry and Rita invited me to join them for drinks—"We have to talk," Terry said, with an unmistakable gleam in his eyes. We ended up at the *Pink Adobe*, taking the last three stools at the bar. I watched as the barman pulled two glasses of beer ahead of our order.

Although Terry and Rita were well-established poets, I knew little more beyond their introductions when I attended my first writer's circle meeting. Rita was a dental hygienist, but Terry simply said he was retired and was a volunteer in the city. They both wanted to know more about me. Rita asked where I had got my idea, what was the source, why it was so important to me.

Cupping a coffee in my hands, I told them of my work as a therapist, and why I had decided to establish a not-for-profit to tackle alcoholism and substance abuse. I spoke of rediscovering poetry with Donald Hall, and through working with a patient. I talked of the childhood memories that Simon Ortiz had surfaced and, yes, of you, Nick.

After being away for a number of years, I could see that many things had changed, yet many things were unchanged. There was still the stale smell of hopelessness and, for many, those early flames of pride and purpose were like the first fireflies, a faint flicker before being snuffed out.

Terry confided that poetry had saved him in the months following his wife's death from breast cancer, "eleven years and forty-nine days ago." He and Rita had met a year later at a small poetry retreat near Taos. She was detoxing after losing custody of her daughter through addiction to painkillers; they had remained friends ever since. "Strictly platonic," Rita added, with a wink.

Santa Fe is not short of wonderful poetry programs. Many, like *Poets in the Schools* and the *Spoken Word* program at the Santa Fe Indian School, are bringing poetry to a large number of children, and volunteer poets are also working with some of the homeless shelters in the city. My idea was less grand. I wanted to bring poetry into my not-for-profit work.

"I wonder whether it would help them rediscover pride, to hear the words of some of the great Native American poets—you know, N. Scott Momaday, Sherman Alexie, Joy Harjo, Simon Ortiz. It would be such a fulfilling thing to do," I remember saying. "For whom?" was Terry's humbling reply.

Two weeks later, I was sitting in the last row at an open-mic when I heard Rita read a poem about her struggles with addiction. She was going to read a second but stopped. Looking at me, she spoke with passion about the importance of poetry, that it could make life possible for those who simply have to matter, despite how desperate they were.

It started simply. After polling many who visited the annex, I organized a one-hour meeting one Saturday afternoon—twelve people came. I left the selection of poems to Rita and Terry, and they read beautifully and passionately. We have since repeated this every other week, and we now have a core of eight—six men and two women—who always attend. I shelled out and bought each a copy of Donald Hall's *To Read a Poem*, and several have started writing and sharing their own poems.

I first introduced Terry to Marcel because of their shared love of sonnets, and they now email or phone regularly. It didn't take much prodding for Marcel to agree to host two half-day workshops on formal verse, and he and Melissa will visit in June. In one call, Marcel mentioned a documentary he'd just seen, *Louder Than a Bomb*, about an inter-school poetry slam competition founded in Chicago. Terry told Marcel that Santa Fe had something similar called *Poetry out Loud*. When Rita and I met with him two days later, Terry was almost jumping out of his jeans.

"If schools can do *Poetry out Loud* among themselves, why can't we do it with groups like your not-for-profit?" he said, waving his arms.

It will take both work and time, and certainly more poets. Terry has contacted several who are interested, and I have reached out to a number of groups dealing with alcohol addiction. If the results so far with my own group are any indication, our hope is that the joys of poetry and writing will enter the lives of addicts beyond my pueblo. And who knows—perhaps we'll see poetry slams between addiction groups, not as competitions but as a way of sharing each other's words and stories, knowing there will always be someone who listens.

These are things you would have done, Nick, and I will try to take you there, whenever I can. Sometimes, when my legs tremble as I step up to the podium and pull the mic down towards my face, I see you in the last row, smiling, reaching out a hand to help me climb over my fence of words. I am getting better, and I have read my own poems often, but there is one I shall keep for you.

THIS MOMENT

And so it is, that in the last light of day, as night begins to eat its way up lilac forests in the eastern hills, the air already chilled, I take my pen and write to you as though you were still here, as though you were not still.

> autumn sunset
> waiting for the green flash
> of your eyes

I'm really looking forward to seeing you, John, although be aware that the snow has been light this winter—there's talk they'll close the ski basin early. Fingers crossed!

You said there was a lot to catch up on, and I agree. But I know I never fully addressed the questions you raised during that lunch, and so not to bog us down I thought I'd send you a summary of some notes I wrote recently in my journal. This should appeal to the academic side of you. ☺

Countertransference: The analyst's transference (often unconscious) to the patient of emotional needs and conflicts from the analyst's past experiences...(Farlex Partner Medical Dictionary, 2012).

As you probably know, Carolyn still believes it was countertransference, and I consistently deny it. My past never played a direct role in Marcel's therapy, either on the personal level or diagnostically. I can only recall one or two moments when I shared my past with him and, with few exceptions, I always kept my emotions inside. I have told her this many times.

Of course, she continues to give examples of my obsession with Marcel, and I remember you raising the same concerns. If truth be told, I admit that I looked forward enormously to our sessions together, and I did focus on him more than any other patient during our weekly debriefs. He was a fascinating case, after all—so fragile, and so lost.

I think what I really objected to was her idea that I transferred emotions from my past *to* him, *onto* him. But in the last weeks I have partially reconsidered—I shall tell her when we speak face-to-face in August. It was this definition:

Countertransference: The surfacing of a psychotherapist's own repressed feelings through identification with the emotions, experiences, or problems of a person undergoing treatment...(Stedman's Medical Dictionary, 28th edition, 2005).

Why partially, I can hear you asking? My sessions with Marcel did nothing to surface how repressed I felt, how unfulfilling my life had become. I was surrounded by shallowness—my friends, patients, marriage—and even though rays of awareness would occasionally peek through, I quickly ignored and buried them; what I *saw* in him never reflected back onto me, never unlocked thoughts of the present or the past.

I would also like to say that I recognized my own shallowness but, as you probably know, this is not true. Days and nights of boredom had transformed me into an unlikable shadow of my past, yet I was unaware of what I had become. No, Marcel *never* aroused these thoughts, or almost never.

But there was something in Marcel that unlocked my past, beyond his *emotions, experiences,* or *problems.* Even though it was one of the first things I learned about him, it approached me tentatively, as something shy and mysterious. At first, I responded cautiously, even academically, convincing myself that I was doing research on a patient, to help me better understand him. But it persisted, and as its rhythms began to wash over me it was as though I were slowly drifting back, rediscovering it all over again.

It was poetry. It is always poetry.

I wish to thank the editors of *A Hundred Gourds, bottle rockets, Frogpond, Modern Haiku, The Heron's Nest,* and *Tiny Words* for first publishing the various haiku and haibun included in this work, as well as Carolyn Lamb for permission to use the haiku, "O'Keeffe's 'black cross'," by her mother, Elizabeth Searle Lamb. The sonnet "Mask" appeared in *Autumn Sky Poetry Daily,* and I wish to thank its editor, Christine Klocek-Lim, for her comments on the poem. I would also like to single out Charles ("Charlie") Trumbull, past editor of *Modern Haiku,* who has been a friend and haiku mentor for some time. I am also deeply indebted to Simon Ortiz, the wonderful Native American poet, for allowing me to quote from, and comment on, his remarkable poem "For those brothers and sisters in Gallup" that appeared in his collection *Woven Stone* (1992). Finally, I would like to acknowledge Donald Hall—not only for being a great poet and essayist, but for being comfortable with the way the narrator, Vera, has treated his work, spoken to him, and sought his advice.

Lines from a number of other poems are quoted in the text, and I am grateful to the following poets, publishers, and copyright holders for permission to include them:

Excerpt from "Preludes" from *Windows and Stones: Selected Poems,* by Tomas Tranströmer, translated by May Swenson with Leif Sjöberg, © 1972. Reprinted by permission of the University of Pittsburgh Press.

Excerpt from "Stopping by Woods on a Snowy Evening" from *The Poetry of Robert Frost* edited by Edward Connery Lathem. Copyright © 1923,1963 by Henry Holt and Company, copyright © 1951 by Robert Frost. Used by permission of Henry Holt and Company, LLC. All rights reserved.

Excerpt from "Nantucket" by William Carlos Williams, from *The Collected Poems: Volume I, 1909-1939,* copyright © 1938 by New Directions Publishing Corp. Reprinted by permission of New Directions Publishing Corp and Carcanet Press Limited.

Excerpt from "A Blessing" by James Wright, from *The Branch Will Not Break,* copyright © 1959, 1960, 1961, 1962, 1963 by James Wright. Reprinted by permission of Wesleyan University Press.

I have long been interested in mental health, but very much as an amateur trying to understand what happened to a mother lost too soon. And so I am, and always will be, eternally grateful for the thoughts, advice, and support of Dr Layla Kassem of the Malachite Institute for Behavioral Health. Indeed, it was she who first introduced me to the concept of Paradoxical Intervention, though I wish to stress that any shortcomings in my descriptions of psychotherapy and various mental disorders are entirely my own.

In addition to Dr Kassem, a number of people made suggestions for improvement on earlier drafts, in particular Christie Hefner, and Julie Jacobsen. My editor, Michael Scofield, was meticulous, challenging, and a pleasure to work with. Susan Gardner, my publisher at *Red Mountain Press*, deserves more than thanks for having the courage to publish this book, and for her painstaking guidance and advice throughout the process.

Finally, I wish to thank my wonderful wife, Roxanne, for all the support she has given me, and for the patience to tolerate days of vagueness, weeks of self-absorption, and years of shredded paper and nerves.

Marcel Malone is set in Palatino,
a 20th century font designed by Hermann Zapf based on the
humanist typefaces of the Italian Renaissance and named for
the 16th century Italian master of calligraphy
Giambattista Palatino.